Outstanding praise for Scott Nicholson and *The Harvest*

"A very atmospheric, often creepy and definitely well-written horror novel."

Science Fiction and Fantasy Chronicle

"Nicholson has constructed a small wonder with *The Harvest,* a story with the outlines of a B-Movie narrative, but with complex, sympathetic characters and an emotionally satisfying plot. Nicholson continues to prove himself a writer to watch."

Locus

"*The Harvest* combines southern charm with the otherworld . . . enjoyable to read."

Greensboro News & Record

"Horror story devotees get a certain macabre joy from a good creepy read. Scott Nicholson knows the feeling and is adept at passing it on to his fans, first in *The Red Church* and now in *The Harvest.* If this is your genre, Nicholson's books are worth a look."

The Durham Herald-Sun

"Scott Nicholson's second book, *The Harvest,* is a well-crafted novel that seemlessly blends elements of science fiction and horror in the tradition of H.P. Lovecraft and Stephen King. *The Harvest,* a standout suspense novel worthy of your attention, is a satisfying and frightening read. Scott Nicholson has shown himself to be a refreshing voice in contemporary horror and is definitely someone to watch."

About.com

"Nicholson is an old-fashioned storyteller, through and through, and his books are an enjoyable diversion when the pressures of daily life get to be too much."

Creature-Corner.com

"Stephen King and Dean Koontz fans need to sit up and take notice of this talented author. Scott Nicholson has created a new terror that will keep you up late into the night!"

Huntress Reviews

Scott Nicholson gives us ... straight to the bone in this scary novel t... H.P. Lovecraft."

B...

"Extremely well written ...

E...

Please turn the page for outstanding pr... Nicholson's debut novel, *The Red Church!*

Praise for Scott Nicholson's debut *The Red Church*

"The Red Church can be summed up in one word—scary."
Wilson Daily Times (North Carolina)

"Spooky enough to make the hair on the back of your neck stand stiff. And you should be warned it is not a "before bedtime read." You might be up all night finishing it."
The Pilot (Southern Pines, North Carolina)

"A good story for anyone who likes a spooky, eerie tale. *The Red Church* is a scary, well-crafted horror tale of supernatural revenge and evil."
Greensboro News & Record

"Scott Nicholson writes with a mixture of H.P. Lovecraft and Clive Barker, stirred with a liberal dose of his own originality, to tell an effective and atmospheric tale."
Kevin J. Anderson, New York Times bestselling author

"Nicholson provides a satisfyingly creepy, gory, violent ride with a swift read and a delightfully disturbing end."
Carolina Mountain Living

"Much in the tradition of Stephen King and Clive Barker, Nicholson is adept at creating a kind of supernatural evil that is all-powerful. Scott Nicholson certainly pulls out all the stops in *The Red Church."*
Smoky Mountain News

"Guilty pleasures are too few these days. *The Red Church* is a healthy dose of fright served up by a very skilled writer."
Inscriptions

"The Red Church is a very impressive debut. If you're a fan of horror fiction or are looking to become one, you owe it to yourself to read this book. Let's hope it's not long before Nicholson puts out another!"
SFReader.com

"With news of Stephen King's retirement, many fans of the horror genre may be wondering who will write the chilling stories they crave. OUTline magazine has found the answer: Scott Nicholson!"
OUTline magazine

SCOTT NICHOLSON

THE MANOR

PINNACLE BOOKS
Kensington Publishing Corp.
http://www.kensingtonbooks.com

PINNACLE BOOKS are published by

Kensington Publishing Corp.
850 Third Avenue
New York, NY 10022

First Pinnacle Books Printing: September 2004

10 9 8 7 6 5 4 3 2 1

Printed in the United States of America

For my mother, Delores, who sees

"If you can dream, and not
make dreams your master . . ."

—Rudyard Kipling

"I'll eat your dreams."

—Ephram Elijah Krane

CHAPTER 1

Mason Jackson stared at the large oil painting that hung on the wall above the fireplace. It stared right back, as severe as any of Mason's former art instructors. The scowling face of the portrait dominated the room, ten times life-size. The flesh tones of the oils were so realistic that Mason could imagine the figure bursting free of the ornate wooden frame. A brass plate beneath the painting was etched with the name EPHRAM KORBAN.

Mason studied the black eyes. They were the only features that lacked the realism of the rest of the painting. The eyes were dead, dull, completely unanimated. But Mason wasn't a painter himself, so he had no grounds for criticism. Critics be damned, and he was actually more interested in the frame than the painting. It appeared to be hand-carved.

Mason glanced behind him at the people milling in the foyer. Through the open door, he could see two men in overalls unloading the wagon. A busty, fortyish woman wearing a long black dress seemed to be everywhere at once, giving orders, distributing drinks in long sweaty glasses, shaking hands. Mason moved closer to the fireplace. Though the day was warm for late October, a fire blazed in the hearth, all yellow and orange and other bright autumn colors.

The fireplace mantel was also hand-carved. Bas-relief cherubim and seraphim, plump Raphaelite forms winging among the thick curls of clouds. Mason checked his fingers to make sure they were clean, then felt among the smooth shapes. As his hands explored, he noticed someone had left a half-filled glass of red wine on the mantel. He thought of the rings the glass might leave on the white paint, like blood on virgin snow. No respect for the work of a craftsman.

He again looked at the eyes in the painting. Now Ephram Korban seemed to be gazing out across the room, brooding over these people who had dared to cross his threshold. The face was alternately compelling and repulsive. Mason touched the frame—

"Lovely, isn't it?" came a woman's high voice.

Mason spun, his satchel nearly knocking over the wineglass. Before him stood the buxom woman in the black dress, her dark hair tied in a tight bun. Her smile was fixed on her face as if chiseled.

"Yes," Mason said. "Whoever carved this must have spent a few weeks on it."

She giggled, a thin, artificial sound. "I was talking about the *painting,* silly," she said.

She toyed with the strand of pearls around her neck, the pearls unfashionably interrupted by a small brass locket. Her dark eyes sparkled with all the life that Korban's painted ones lacked. Mason wondered if that was something you could practice. He could picture the woman before the mirror, fastening her pearls, checking her teeth, adjusting the sparkle in her eyes.

The woman held out her hand. Mason took it, wondering if he was supposed to bow and kiss it like some French dandy in a period film. Her skin was cool. She turned his hand over and looked at his fingers, nodding. "Ah, so you're the sculptor."

"Huh?"

"Calluses. We don't get many calluses here at the manor." She leaned forward, like a conspirator. "At least among the guests. The hired help still has to work."

Mason nodded. He looked down at his tennis shoes with the scuffed toes, the hole in his blue jeans. The other people who rode up with him in the van wore leather pumps, Kenneth Coles, open-backed sandals, clothes out of catalogues that bore New Hampshire names. He didn't belong here. He was dirt-poor southern mill-town trash, no matter what sort of artistic airs he put on.

"You're our first sculptor in a while," she said, her cold hand still clinging to his. "Let's see if I have the copy memorized: 'Mason Beaufort Jackson, honors graduate from the Adderly School of the Arts, currently employed at Rayford Hosiery in Sawyer Creek, North Carolina. Winner of the 2002 Grassroots Consortium Award. Commissioned by Westridge University to create a piece for their Alumni Hall.' Now, what *was* the title of that piece?"

She finally let go of his hand and pressed her hand against her forehead as if reading a page in her mind, then snapped her fingers. "*Diluvium.* Of course. How terribly lovely."

Mason groaned inwardly. He hadn't realized exactly how pretentious the title sounded until hearing it pass those well-bred lips. "Well, it was the crowd I was in at the time. Avant-garde, but still meeting for lunch at McDonald's."

The woman emitted her bone-rattling laugh, then pointed to the canvas satchel slung over his shoulder. "Are those your tools?"

"Yes, ma'am."

"I'm looking forward to seeing you use them," she said. "I'm Mamie Goldfeld. I insist that you call me Miss Mamie."

He glanced at Korban's portrait, then back to Miss Mamie.

"Ah, you noticed," she said.

"The eyes."

"I'm the last living relative of Ephram Korban. I run the manor, keeping it as an artists' retreat just the way he wanted. Master Korban always appreciated the creative spirit."

"Was he an artist himself?"

"A frustrated one. A dilettante. He was mostly a collector."

Mason took in more of the architectural details of the foyer. The arch over the front entrance was ten feet high, with leaded squares of glass set in a transom overhead. The foyer had a high ceiling, the white walls and trim accentuated with an oak-paneled wainscoting as high as Mason's chest. Two Ionic columns in the center of the room held a huge ceiling beam aloft.

"This is a pretty place," Mason said, because Miss Mamie clearly expected him to say something. He'd nearly said "lovely," an adjective he'd never used before. Five minutes at an expensive artists' retreat and he was already putting on airs, developing a persona. God forbid he should ever actually accomplish anything. He'd be insufferable.

"I'm pleased you like it," she said. "Colonial revivalist. Master Korban was proud of his heritage, which is why his will stipulated that the manor be preserved intact."

"Korban. That's Jewish, isn't it?"

"In name only. Not in spirit. He borrowed his heritage, bought what he couldn't borrow, and stole what he couldn't afford. He ended up with everything, you see."

Mason looked at the portrait again, measured the tenacity and arrogance of the features. "Looks like your ancestor was the kind of man who didn't take no for an answer."

"Yes, but he was also highly generous. As you know."

Mason smiled, though he felt as if a lizard were

crawling in his throat. He was here on the dole. He could never have afforded such a retreat on his factory pay. When you got right down to it, he was a token, invited so the Korban estate and the arts council could revel in their magnanimous support of the underclass.

Miss Mamie looked past him to where a small group of guests stood talking. "There's dear Mr. and Mrs. Abramov. The classical composers, you know."

Mason didn't know, but he kept smiling just the same. The token grin of gratitude.

"Excuse me, I must say hello. Lilith will be along to show you to your room, and I do hope you enjoy your stay."

She glanced at Korban's portrait with an expression approaching wistfulness, then was gone with a bustle of fabric. Mason gazed at the portrait again. The fire popped, sending a thick red ember up the chimney. Korban's eyes still looked dead. Mason was about to turn away to find his luggage when the fire snapped again. For the briefest of moments, the face in the portrait was superimposed over the flames like a sunset's reflection on a lake.

Mason shrugged and rubbed his eyes. He was tired, that was all. A five-hour Greyhound ride from Sawyer Creek to Black Rock, then a half hour in a van winding up mountain roads. He got dizzy all over again thinking about the views from the van window, how the rocky slopes dropped hundreds of feet on either side. They'd disembarked at a narrow wooden bridge that seemed to be the only connection between the civilized world and Korban Manor. The suitcases and bags were loaded onto a horse-drawn wagon and the guests had to walk the rest of the way to the manor.

His first step on the bridge was like a leap of misplaced faith. He'd almost lost the sausage biscuit he'd had for breakfast, even though he'd kept his eyes fixed straight ahead and a sweaty palm on the bridge rail.

The great gap of space surrounding him, the soft wind rising from the valley, and the lost weight of the world hundreds of feet below all pressed against his skin. His chest clenched the breath out of his lungs and he tried to tell himself that acrophobia was an irrational fear. But only one thought kept his legs moving: this was one of those paths to success, a strait gate and narrow way that all true artists had to navigate, this scared-sick stagger was leading him closer to recognition.

Before he knew it, he was on solid ground again, though he had to lean against a tree for a moment to let the blood return to his brain. Then he joined the others on the dirt road, following in the wake of the wagon, passing through a dark forest that could have harbored any number of endangered species. The other guests chattered and laughed, as smug as tourists, and Mason wondered whether they'd even noticed the isolation of their new milieu.

Then the forest ended and Korban Manor stood before them like something out of an antique postcard. The open fields fell away to a soft swell of orchard, a patchwork of meadows, and two barns stitched together with fencing. The manor itself was three outsized stories high, tall the way they were built in the late 1800s, six Colonial columns supporting the portico ceiling at the entrance. Black shutters framed the windows against the white siding. Four chimneys puffed away, the smoke swirling through the giant red oaks and poplar that surrounded the house.

Atop the roof was a widow's walk, a flattened area with a lonely railing. He wondered if any widows had ever walked those boards. Probably. One thing about an old house, you could be sure that somebody had died there, probably a whole lot of somebodies.

A painter or photographer would probably kill for the view the widow's walk afforded. Mason might even commit a lesser crime for the privilege, except he knew he'd grow dizzy with all that open air around him and that deadly depth stretching below. At least he'd have an opportunity to study Korban Manor's intricate scrollwork from the safety of ground level.

He fought a sudden urge to pull a hatchet from his satchel and swipe it across Ephram Korban's disquieting smirk.

"You look like you could use an eye-opener," came a voice beside him. It was Roth, the photographer who had shared a seat with him on the van. The man spoke with a clipped and not entirely authentic British accent, alcohol on his breath. A martini was poised in one wrinkled hand.

"No, thanks," Mason said.

"It's afternoon, and we're all grown-ups here." Roth's eyes crinkled beneath white eyebrows. His face was sharp, thin, and full of angles. Mason saw it as a natural sculpture, the weathered topography of skin, a crag of a jawbone, the eroded plain of forehead. He had a bad habit of reducing people to essential shapes and forgetting that some sort of soul might exist within the raw clay of creation.

"I don't drink."

"Oh, you a religious nut?"

"I'm not any kind of nut, as far as I know. Except for that part about hearing God's voice in a burning bush."

Roth laughed and drained some of the martini. "Don't get your knickers in a twist. You're terribly young to throw in with this lot," he said, nodding toward the people that Miss Mamie was greeting. "What's a pip like you doing on a getaway like this?"

"I'm here on a grant. North Carolina Arts Council and Korban Manor." Mason looked at the fire again. No faces swirled among the bright colors. No voices arose, either. He forced himself to relax.

"A real artist, eh? Not like these," Roth said, rolling his eyes toward Miss Mamie's well-dressed guests.

"Most of them need an artists' retreat like they need another mutual fund. A bunch of tweeds whose highest endeavor is gluing dried beans to a scrap of gunny-sack."

Another critic. Passing judgment on the unrevealed talents of others. At least they'd paid their own way, unlike Mason. "What part of England are you from?"

"Not a pint of Brit in me," he said. "Was over there in the military for a while and picked up a little of the accent. Comes in handy with the birds." He winked one of his smoky gray eyes.

"You came here to shoot, I suppose." Mason had dated a girl at Adderly who'd had a book of Roth's work. Roth did nature, wildlife, architecture, and the occasional portrait. He couldn't touch the gritty glamour of Leibovitz or the visceral sensibility of Mapplethorpe, but his photographs possessed their own brand of blunt honesty.

"I got bankrolled by a few magazines," Roth said. "I'm to do some house-and-garden stuff, scenic mountain shots, that sort of tripe. I do want to shoot that bridge, though. Highest wooden bridge in the southern Appalachians, they say."

"I believe it. Makes me spin just thinking about it."

"You bugged by heights?"

"Where I come from, the highest building is two stories, if you don't count silos. I can handle stairs okay, but I'm not much good on a ladder. Looking down three hundred feet—"

"Drop-off like that one on every side," Roth said, taking another drink, relishing Mason's face going pale. "Korban liked his isolation. Wanted his place to be like one of those European castles."

Roth lifted a toast toward Korban's portrait. "Here's to you, old sod."

Mason's satchel was getting heavy. He was anxious to get settled in, finish planning the pieces he wanted to work on. And Roth's accent was annoying.

A pretty woman in black came down the stairs, her dress just short of authentic Goth, a lace shawl over her thin shoulders. She appeared to be a receptionist of some kind. She led a couple away from Miss Mamie's group. The man was in his fifties, double-chinned, wearing a scowl, the woman blue-eyed with a clear complexion who could have walked off the cover of *Seventeen.* They went up the stairs together, the man clearing his throat, his enormous jowls quivering.

"Might get him later," Roth said. "Maybe at a roll-top desk with a quill pen in his hand. I'm not keen on personality work, but I could get a tidy bundle for that."

"Who?"

Roth smiled as if Mason had just fallen off a turnip wagon. "Jefferson Spence."

"You mean *the* Jefferson Spence? The novelist?"

"The one and only. The last great southern writer. Faulkner and O'Connor and Wolfe all rolled into one, if you believe the jacket copy."

Mason watched the writer labor up the stairs. "What's *he* need with an artists' colony?"

"Fodder. You don't know much about him, do you?"

"Never read him. I'm more into Erskine Caldwell."

"One critic called Spence's style 'stream-of-pompousness.' "

Mason laughed. "Well, it was nice of him to bring along his daughter."

Roth shook his head. "I suppose you don't read the tabloids, either. That's not his daughter. That would be his latest, I presume."

Miss Mamie's voice rose, her laughter filling the foyer. To her right stood a small, dark-haired woman, about Mason's age. Mason stared at her two seconds longer than what could pass for polite interest because her cyan eyes were startling. She met his gaze, gave him a half smile, then turned her attention back to Miss Mamie.

Roth had noticed her, too. His eyes were as bright as a wolf's. "Cute bird."

Mason pretended not to hear. "Excuse me. I've got to stretch my legs a little."

Roth gave a faux gentleman's salute and went to refill his drink. Mason adjusted the satchel strap across his shoulder and went toward the open door. The wagon was gone, the squiggles of its tracks leading toward one of the barns, dark heaps of horse manure dotting the sandy road. The Korban Manor brochure had delighted in the fact that no motor vehicles would be around to "disturb creative impulses." Likewise, no distractions such as television, telephone, or electricity existed at the estate. A regular Gilligan's Island, Mason thought, only without the canned laughter and unexpected plot twists.

Mason overheard one of the group say, "Let me tell you about this lovely idea I had for a novel. It's about this writer who—"

Mason gave a last look back at Korban's face, then entered the autumn sunshine. The fields were golden green sheets stretched to the surrounding forest. Great ridges of earth rose along the horizon, carved and chipped and smoothed by that master sculptor, Time. Mason now knew why these mountains were called the Blue Ridge, though the changing leaves splashed such an array of colors that he almost wished he'd stuck with painting.

Pumpkin orange, summer squash yellow, cornsilk gold, beet purple. Van Gogh would have given his other ear to paint this place.

Except such a thought smacked of that dreaded ideal of artistic sacrifice. He wondered if the esteemed historical roster of insane artists had not been schizophrenic or poisoned by the lead in their paint, but had instead been driven mad by the whispering of demanding Muses. Mason drove the thought from his head because it seemed like an option only a nut would consider. And he'd given up painting not because of a lack of desire or talent, but because of its visual nature. His mother could feel the sculpture with her fingers, but a painting was nothing to her but an endless piece of darkness.

A few horses and cows grazed in the meadow that sloped away from the front of the house. The open land must have been about twenty acres, cleared of boulders and carefully tended. Mason found it hard to believe that these soft grounds gave way to steep granite cliffs on all sides.

Not even a jet trail marked the blue autumn sky, as if the manor were remote from modern civilization not only in distance but in time as well. Majestic hardwoods spread their limbs at carefully spaced intervals along a carriage trail that wound toward the west. An apple orchard covered a rise beside the pasture, the trees dotted with pink and golden fruit. Lush grass swayed softly in a hayfield beyond, ending at the edge of a dense forest.

A soft voice interrupted his reverie: "Now you know why artists trip over their egos to get up here. Especially in the fall."

It was the dark-haired woman with the cyan eyes. She crossed the porch and leaned over the railing, then closed her eyes and inhaled through her nose with an exaggerated flourish. "Ah. Fresh air. A nice change from the stench of pretension inside."

"You a painter?" Mason asked, still looking across the fields, irritated by her jab at artists.

"No."

"Me either."

"What are you, then?"

"Does everybody have to *be* something?"

The woman tilted her head back toward the house. "If you listen to them, you'd think so."

"Well, this is a retreat, after all. Back up and go,

'Whoa,' I reckon." He didn't want her to know he felt out of his element. He already missed Sawyer Creek's dirty little streets with their utility poles and peeling billboards. Back home, he'd be heating up the teakettle and tuning the radio to Mama's favorite conservative talk show right about now.

"What's in the bag?"

"This satchel? Nothing. Just some tools."

"I thought you were one of the staff," she said. "Too bad. Because I despise artists. I think they're full of themselves. Nothing personal."

Mason tried not to look at her too closely, though that was all he wanted to do. She was pretty, sure, but there was also the sense that she wouldn't let him hide behind his dumb bumpkin act, the one he'd used to bluff his way through art college. Those cyan eyes pierced too deeply, saw beyond the slick face of first impressions. He came up with a snappy comeback a couple of seconds too late. "Then why are you making it personal?"

"Because you're probably worse than the rest. You're so attached to what's inside your satchel you wouldn't trust it with the rest of the luggage."

He wished he could tell her. The tools were not all that expensive, but they had come at great cost. He thought of Mama alone at their cramped apartment in Sawyer Creek, sitting in her worn recliner, a cat in her lap. Eyes never blinking.

This woman he'd only just met was too damned insightful and saw his self-doubt with uncanny clarity. He *was* worse than the rest, even while pretending he was apart from other artists, not buying into their wankish and vain prattle. He wasn't sure whether his work revealed anything about the world, but he was determined to shove it in the world's face and make it notice anyway.

Mason adjusted the satchel on his shoulder, feeling

the woman's eyes on him. "Sculpting tools," he said. "A hammer, hatchet, chisels, fluters, gougers, some blades."

"You do wood?"

"I've done a little of everything." He finally looked her full in the face, forcing himself not to blink against her gaze. "Except here I'll be doing wood."

She nodded as if she'd already forgotten him. "Six weeks is not very long. It would be hard to tackle something stone in that time."

Her accent was almost rural, as if she'd tried to be country but somebody had sent her off to college to have it squeezed out of her. One of the horses, a big roan, galloped across the pasture. She smiled as she watched it.

"Some place, huh?" Mason said.

"I've seen pictures, but they certainly don't do it justice." Again she sounded distracted, as if Mason were as boring as Miss Mamie's well-heeled gang in the foyer.

Mason stepped between the shrubs and fingered the mortised joints of the railing. Grooved columns held up the portico, the paint thick and scaly where the layers had built up over the decades. The stone foundation of the manor wore a fur coat of green moss. A sudden juvenile urge to impress the woman came over him. "Colonial revivalist architecture," he said. "This Korban guy must have had the bucks."

"Do you know anything about him?"

"Only what I read in the brochure. Industrialist, made a fortune after the Spanish-American war, bought out this mountain, and built the manor as a summer home. Two thousand acres of land connected to civilization by nothing except that wooden bridge."

He hated himself for blathering. He hadn't come to Korban Manor to mess around. He needed to get serious about his work, not spar with someone who seemed about as interested in him as if he were a piece of lint. Besides, artists were supposed to be aloof.

"So you only have the sanitized biography," she said. "I did a little research on him myself. That's my line."

"You're a writer?"

"Something like that."

"Figured. They're more stuck-up and screwed-up than artists, if you ask me."

"Nobody did. As I was about to say, Korban set down in his will that the place be kept as a period piece from the end of the nineteenth century. He stipulated that Korban Manor become an artists' retreat. While he was alive, he encouraged the servants to fill the house with handmade mountain crafts and folk art. Maybe he liked the idea of his house being filled with creative energy. Sort of a way to keep himself alive."

"That portrait of him is a bit much, though," Mason said. "He must have had a hell of an ego."

"He probably was an artist, then." She looked tired and gave him a dismissive and maddening half smile. "Excuse me, I have to go to my room."

Mason fumed inside. Stupid self-obsessed girl, distracted and abrupt, as snotty as any of those Yankees chattering in the foyer. He should have faked it a little better, acted like a heartbreaker. Maybe he'd start wearing a beret, appear sophisticated, grow one of those wimpy little Pierre mustaches. That would get a laugh out of the boys back at Rayford Hosiery.

"See you later," he said, trying hard not to sound optimistic. Then, without knowing where the words came from, he added, "I hope you find what you came here for."

She turned, met his eyes, serious again. "I'm looking for myself. Tell me if you see her."

Then she was gone, swallowed by the big white house that bore Korban's name.

CHAPTER 2

Anna Galloway pulled back the lace curtains of the bedroom window. A bit of dust rose from the windowpane at the stir of air. Sunlight spilled on her shoulders, the October glow warming the floor beneath her feet. The mountain air was chillier than she was used to, and even the roaring fire didn't quell her shivers. A painting of Ephram Korban hung over the room's fireplace, smaller than the one downstairs but just as brooding. The sculptor with the kicked-puppy aura was right about one thing: Korban had been thoroughly in love with himself.

She looked out over the meadows. Here she was, at long last. The place she was supposed to be, for whatever reason. This was the end of the world, the logical place for endings. She drove the fatalism from her mind and instead watched the roan and chestnut galloping across the pasture. The display of freedom and peace warmed her.

"It's so pretty, isn't it?" the woman behind her said. She'd told Anna that her name was "Cris without the *h*" as if the lack of *h* somehow made her harder and less flexible. And since they were going to be roomies . . .

"It's wonderful," Anna said. "Everything I dreamed it would be."

Cris already had her makeup kit, watercolor brushes, and sketch pads scattered across the bed nearest the door. Anna had nothing but a slim stack of books piled neatly on her dresser. Her attitude toward material possessions and earthly comforts had undergone dramatic changes in the past year. You travel light when you're not sure where you're headed.

The pain swept across her abdomen, sneaky this time, a needle poking in slow motion. She closed her eyes, counted backward in big fat numerals.

Ten, round and thin . . .

Nine, loop and droop . . .

She was down to six and the pain was floating somewhere above that far cut in the Blue Ridge Mountains when Cris's voice pulled her back.

"Like, what do you do?"

Anna turned from the window. Cris sat on the bed, brushing her long blond hair. Anna was glad the chemotherapy hadn't made her own hair fall out. Not just because of vanity, but because she wanted to take all of herself with her when she went.

"I do research articles," Anna said.

"Oh, you're a writer."

"Not fiction like Jefferson Spence. More like metaphysics."

"Science and stuff?"

Anna sat on her bed. The pain was back, but not as sharp as before. "I worked at the Rhine Research Center in Durham. Investigator."

"You quit?"

"Not really. I just got finished."

"Rhine. Isn't that ESP, ghosts, and weird stuff? Like on *X-Files?*"

"Except the truth isn't 'out there.' It's in *here*." She touched her temple. "The power of the mind. And we don't do aliens. I was a paranormal investigator. Except I became a dinosaur. Extinct almost before I even got started."

"You're too young to be a dinosaur."

"Everything's electronic these days. Electromagnetic field detectors, subsonic recorders, infrared cameras. If you can't plot it on a computer, they don't think it exists. But I believe what I see with my heart."

Cris looked around the room, as if noticing the dark corners and flickering fire-cast shadows for the first time. "You didn't come here because of—"

"Don't worry. I'm here for personal reasons."

"Aha. I saw you talking to that muscle guy with the canvas satchel, out on the porch."

"Not *that* kind of personal reason. Besides, he's not my type."

"Give it a few days. Stranger things have happened."

"And I'm sure you're here to throw yourself into your art?" Anna pointed to the sketch pads. "I won't give you my lecture on the artistic temperament, because I like you."

"Oh, I think my husband is plooking his secretary and wanted me out of the house so they could use the hot tub. He sent me to Greece over the summer. New Mexico last spring to do the Georgia O'Keeffe thing. Now the North Carolina mountains."

"At least he's generous."

"I'll never be a real artist, but it gives me something to do on retreats besides chase men and drink. But my Muse allows me those little luxuries, too. Speaking of which, I noticed a bar in the study. Care for one before dinner?"

"No, thank you. I believe I'll rest a little."

"Well, just don't walk around with a sheet over your head. I might mistake you for a ghost."

"If I die, I promise you'll be among the first to know."

Anna lay back on the pillow. A feather poked her neck. The door closed, Cris's footsteps faded down the hall, dying leaves whisked against the window. The smoke-aged walls gave off a comforting aroma, and the oil lamp's glow added to the warmth of the room. She felt at peace for the first time since—

No. She wouldn't think of that now.

The pain was back, a rude houseguest. She tried the trick of numbers, but her concentration kept getting tangled up with memory, as it so often did lately. Ever since she'd started dreaming of Korban Manor.

Ten, round and thin . . .

An image of Stephen slid into her mind between the one and the zero. Stephen, with his cameras and gizmos, his mustache and laugh. To him, Anna was the parapsychologist's version of a campfire girl. Stephen had no need for *sensing* ghosts. He could prove them, he said.

Their graveyard dates ended up with her wandering over grass and headstones while Stephen focused on setting up equipment. The night she'd sensed her first ghost, shimmering beside the marble angel in the Guilford Cemetery, Stephen was too busy marking down EMF readings to look when she called. The ghost didn't wait around for a Kodak moment, it dissolved like mist at sunrise. But before those evanescent threads spooled themselves back to whatever land they'd come from, the haunted eyes had stared fully into Anna's.

The look was one of mutual understanding.

Nine, loop and droop . . .

That had been her first investigation with Stephen. But the ghost-hunting circle was small. Her frustration was outweighed by her loneliness. They'd slept together on the floor of Asheville's Hanger Hall on a winter night when the wind was too brisk even for ghosts. And two weeks later, she'd overheard him at a party calling her a "flake, but a lovable flake."

So after six years of study and field research, she was little more respectable than an 800-hundred-number phone psychic. There were plenty enough skeptics out in the real world, between the hard scientists and those who were always up for a good old-fashioned witch burning. But the laughter of her own peers was enough to drive her to big, spooky, empty places where she could chase ghosts alone.

Eight, a double gate . . .

Then the pain came, and the first of the dreams. She had stepped from the forest, her feet soft on the damp grass, the lawn as lush as only dreams could paint it. The manor stood before her, windows dark as eyes, the trees around the house twisted and bare. A single strand of smoke rose from one of the four chimneys. The smoke curled, collected, gathered on the roof just above the white railing.

And the shape formed, and the woman's whispered word, "Anna," woke her up, as it had so many nights since.

Seven, sharp and even . . .

That was what the pain was, a seven, sticking in her intestines.

Stephen came over the day she found out the colon cancer had metastasized to her liver. He held her hand and his eyes managed to look dewy and glazed behind his thick glasses. The mustache even twitched. But he was too practical, too emotionally void to realize exactly what the diagnosis meant. To him, death was nothing more than a cessation of pulse, a change in energy readings. So much for soul mates.

Even after Anna had talked the doctors out of a colectomy, accepting the death sentence as the cancer raced to other organs, Stephen still acted as if science would intervene and save her. He probably even prayed to science, that coldest of all gods. She refused his offer of a ride home from the hospital. She'd come to accept that loneliness was a natural state for someone soon to be a ghost.

Six, an arc and trick . . .

Miracles happen, one of her oncologists had told her.

But she didn't expect them to occur in a hospital, with tubes pumping radiation into her, blades removing her flesh a sliver at a time, doctors marking off her dwindling days. And she had stopped dreaming in the hospital. It was only back home, in the wee hours of her own quiet bed, that Korban Manor once more stood before her.

Night after night, as the dream grew longer and more vivid, the shape on the roof gained substance. At last Anna could clearly see the distant face, diaphanous hair flowing out like a veil. The cyan eyes, the welcoming smile, the bouquet held before her from the forlorn stage of the widow's walk. At last the face was recognizable.

The woman was Anna.

Five, a broken wing . . .

The pain was softer now, snow on flowers.

She'd conducted some research, knowing the manor was familiar to her through more than just dream visitations. She found a few items on Korban Manor in the Rhine archives. Ephram Korban had spent twenty years building his estate on the remote Appalachian crag, then had leapt to his death from the widow's walk in an apparent suicide. Some locals in the small town of Black Rock passed along stories of sightings, mostly disregarded as the gossip of hired hands. A field investigation, shortly before the house was restored as an artists' retreat, had netted zero in the way of data or enthusiasm.

But maybe Korban's pain, his anger, his love, his hope, his dreams, were soaked into these walls like the cedar stain on the wainscoting. Maybe this wood and stone and glass had absorbed the radiant energy of his humanity. Maybe the manor whose construction had obsessed him was now his prison. Maybe haunting wasn't a choice but an obligation.

Four, a north fork . . .

She drifted in the gray plane between sleep and thought, wondering if she would dream of the mansion now that she was actually here. She closed her mind to her five senses, and only that other one remained, the sense that Stephen had ridiculed, the one Anna had hidden away from her few friends and many foster parents. The line between being sensitive and being a freak was thin.

Three, a skeleton key . . .

For just a moment, she was pulled from sleep. Something wafted behind the maple baseboard, scurried along the cracks between dimensions. She didn't want to open her eyes. She could see better if her eyes were closed.

Two, an empty hook . . .

She felt eyes on her. Someone was watching, perhaps her own ghost, the woman spun from the smoke of dreams who held that bouquet of fatal welcome.

One, a dividing line . . .

The line between some and none, here and gone, bed and grave, love and hate, black and white.

Zero.

Nothing.

Anna had come from nothing, was born to nothing, and walked toward nothing, both her past and future black.

She opened her eyes.

No one was in the room, no ghost shifted against the wall.

Only Korban, dead as dry oil, features shadowed by the flickering firelight.

The sunlight's angles had grown steeper in the room. The pain was gone. Anna rose and went outside to wait for sundown, wondering if this was the night she would finally meet herself.

"Have you seen George?" Miss Mamie asked Ransom Streater. She hated to mingle with the hired help, with the exception of Lilith, but there were times when orders had to be given or stories set straight. The best way to head off gossip was to originate it.

"No, ma'am." Ransom stood by the barn, his hat in his scarred hands, sweat clinging to his thin hair. He smelled of the barnyard, hay and manure and rusty metal. Around his neck was a leather strap, and she knew it was attached to one of those quaint charm bags. These rural mountain people actually believed that roots and powders had influence over the living and the dead. If only they knew that magic was created through the force of will, not by wishful thinking.

Magic was all in the making. Like the thing she held cradled in her arms, the poppet she had shaped with great love and tenderness.

"I need someone to help the sculptor find some wood tomorrow," she said.

"Yes, ma'am." The man's Adam's apple bobbed once.

"When was the last time you heard from George?"

"This afternoon, right after the last batch of guests come in. Said he was going up Beechy Gap to check on things."

Miss Mamie hid her smile. So George had gone to Beechy Gap. Good. Nobody from town would miss him for at least a couple of weeks, and by then it wouldn't matter.

And she could count on Ransom to keep his mouth shut. Ransom knew what kind of accidents happened to people around Korban Manor, even to those who wore charms and muttered old-timey spells. And a job was a job.

Everyone had a burning mission in life.

Some missions were more special than others.

She took the little doll from its bit of folded cloth. Its apple head had shriveled into a dark and wizened face, the mouth grim with animated pain. The body was made from whittled ash and the arms and legs were strips of jackvine. Ransom drew back from the doll as if it were a rattlesnake.

"Will you take care of George for me?" Miss Mamie asked.

"He was my friend. It's the least I can do." A shadow crossed his face. "I need to wait till morning, though. I don't go up Beechy Gap at night."

"First thing, then. I don't want to upset the guests. You know what's coming, don't you?"

"A blue moon in October," Ransom said. His eyes shifted to the barn door. A horseshoe hung above it, points up, the dull metal catching the dying daylight. As if luck mattered.

"You've been with us a long time."

"And I aim to stick around a lot longer."

"Then you won't let me down?"

"I'll bury him proper, silver on his eyes. I take pride in my work."

"Ephram always said, 'Pride will walk you through the tunnels of the soul.' "

"Ephram Korban said lots of things. And people said lots of things about him."

"Some of it might even be true." Miss Mamie stroked the doll, suffering her own moment of pride at its skillful rendering. Folk art, they called it. The little poppet contained far more folk than anybody knew. "Excuse me, I have a dinner to host."

Ransom gave a little bow and tugged the strap of his overalls. Miss Mamie left him to feeding the livestock and headed toward the manor. She carried the doll as if it were a precious gift to a loved one. Even though the house was as familiar to her as her own skin, to see it from a distance always brought a fresh rush of joy. The fields, the trees, the mountain wind seemed to sing his name.

This was her home.

Their home.

Forever.

CHAPTER 3

Pain comes in many colors, but fear comes in only one.

George Lawson thought he'd experienced all the colors of pain in his fifty-three years. White pain, like the time he'd raked the tip of a chain saw across his shinbone while clearing out some locust scrub a few summers back. He'd gotten acquainted with dull sky-blue pain when rheumatoid arthritis had painted a strip along his spine. And the invisible gray gut-punch had hung around for months after Selma dropped him for a rug-weaving hippie back around the end of the Reagan years.

He'd felt pain in a hundred colors, oranges and candy-apple reds and sawgrass greens, and pain had taken just as many shapes and sizes. But he was damn near positive he'd never felt pain like the kind that bear-hugged him now. This was all of those combined, a rainbow of pain, an oil slick in a mud puddle, everything a nerve ending could jangle at a fellow, and then some.

But the *fear*—

The fear was nothing but black. Bigger, darker,

blinding and suffocating, growing like a shadow over those other colors. Black fear lodged in his throat like a grease rag, like a clot of stale molasses, like a lump of coal. He sucked in a gasp of that autumn-sweet Appalachian air.

George tried to move his left arm just as an experiment. Mistake.

Two twenty-penny nails had pinned his biceps to the floor. He even tasted the nails, though he was pretty sure the only things in his mouth were some dust, a little blood, and a few loose teeth. And the fear. The taste was metal and rust and the kind of smithy, gunpowdery bitterness that filled the air when a fixer-upper worked a hammer. The collapsed shed settled around him with a splintering groan.

George knew he'd better open his eyes. Because inside his head, he was looking down a long dark tunnel, and the deeper he got, the farther away he was from the light pouring in from the mouth of the tunnel. He was riding down into that tunnel as smoothly as if he were on miners' rails. And part of him wanted to slide on away, down into that cool airless place just around the bend.

But the other part of him was taking over. The part that had pulled his hind end through the jungles of Vietnam, the part that had rolled him out of that hospital bed when the doctors told him he was a heartbeat away from the Big One, the part that had lifted him into the sunshine after the foggy months of loneliness. It was the part that George thought of as Old Leatherneck. Sort of a secret identity that he took on when times got tough. And he really needed Old Leatherneck now, because times didn't come any tougher than this.

Another bad thing about closing his eyes was that he kept seeing *her.* The Woman in White.

So he forced his eyelids open, thanks to his secret identity. Wood splinters sprinkled down and stuck to his tears. Something warm and wet trickled down his right temple, but he wasn't too concerned with that at the moment. First he wanted to figure out what that purplish, raggedy thing was, the thing speared on a split two-by-four a few feet over his head. It was oddly familiar, but out of place, like a sailboat in the middle of a cornfield.

The purplish thing wriggled. No, it had only slid down a little on the broken tip of the board, making a sound like Jell-O dropping onto the floor. Even in the gloomy light and swirling dust, George could make out five little stubs dangling like the teats on a cow's udder. That's when Old Leatherneck kicked in like a dozen cups of percolated coffee.

"So it's a goddamned hand, Georgie-Boy. What's the problem? How many people in this world was born with no hands at all? Why, you saw Joes in Nam that lost every frigging limb they had, and all they could do was lay around flopping like beached puppyfish. So get the hell over it."

George gulped, and the imaginary broken glass in his mouth worked its way down his throat. The dead fingers above were splayed out as if waiting for a high five. George hoped Old Leatherneck didn't cut him one inch of slack this time. Because he didn't believe there was an inch to spare.

"And since you're the only bozo laying around down here in this crap heap of a fallen-down shed, then odds are pretty good that it's *your* hand, soldier."

George turned his head a little so that he couldn't see the hand. He rolled his eyeballs down to look at his body. He couldn't see anything past his chest because a pile of hemlock ceiling joists were spilled like jumbo tiddlywinks across his gut. He tried to wriggle his shoulders and pain erupted in flaming colorbursts.

"Okay, soldier. You gonna whine like a little girlie-boy, or are you gonna stand up and haul your wrinkled rump hole out of here?"

George didn't see any way he could stand up. For one thing, he couldn't feel his legs.

"Excuses, excuses. Well, Georgie, it could be a *whole* lot worse. 'Cause in case you didn't notice, there's a slick sheet of roofing tin about four inches away from your main neck-vein, and that could have just kited on down and done some business. Then we wouldn't even be having this lovely little chat."

The sharp edge of the tin caught the dying sunlight. As he watched, the piece of roofing slid closer with a metallic squeak. More cracking came from high above in the invisible carnage of the eaves. Something slithered in the soft shadows.

"No, it ain't no snake. Never mind that the copperheads and rattlers get active this time of year, doing the last twist before going off to hibernate. Ain't no *ssssnakes* in here, Georgie."

George thought of that old Johnny Cash song, about how the snakes crawl at night. But the song had it wrong. Snakes slept at night because they were cold-blooded. George knew, because he'd looked it up.

George gulped again, trying to squeeze a little of that mountain air into his bruised lungs. A small drop of liquid fell between his eyes. More blood collected at the ruined wrist hanging above him. The swelling teardrop of blood dangled from the end of a stringy bit of tendon. He wondered if the hand was his left one or his right one.

"Hell of a wonderer you are, Georgie. But I'll tell you, since you've always needed to know things. It's the old hammerer, the crap-wiper, the hand that shook the hand of Senator Hallifield at that Republican barbecue in Raleigh. Yep, them fingers there used to grip the two-seamer curve ball that took you fourteen-and-three back in your senior year. Them are the knuckles that got one good sock to the jaw of that hippie Selma run off with. But, hey, it's dead weight now. Water under the bridge. Let's worry about the meat that's still *attached*."

George wished he could feel his feet. Then he wouldn't be so afraid that he was turning into one of those puppyfish. Something inside his crushed gut spasmed and gurgled. With every shallow breath, broken rib bones reached deeper into his chest for a scoop of fresh organs. And who did he have to blame?

"Nobody but you and that snoopy nose of yours, soldier. Just got to poke into things that ain't none of your business. Just got to goddamned *know*, don't you? Always did, and always will. But if you don't get off that fat rump of yours, *always* ain't even going to last till sundown."

Sure, George liked to know things. He wanted to know why dragonflies were called "snakefeeders." He wanted to know why Selma had worked the springs of their old brass bed with a flea-ridden liberal longhair. He wanted to know why that picture of Ephram Korban that hung in the manor gave him seven kinds of creeps. He wanted to know why that old bat Abigail and his buddy Ransom had warned him away from this neck of the woods. Most of all, he wanted to know why the Woman in White had been dancing in the shed the moment before it fell down around him.

"Ain't no earthly good dwelling on what you can't figure out," came the distant voice of Old Leatherneck. "You'd best get back to the situation at *hand*, if you know what I mean."

Another drop of blood plopped onto his face, this time on his chin. George started to reach up and wipe it away, then was reminded that the arm that did his wiping was severed at the wrist. Pain lanced up his shoulder, as bright and yellow red as Napalm.

George squinted through the jagged and crisscrossed lumber overhead. A few muted shafts of light spilled through the rubble, dust swirling slowly in the air. That meant a bit of daylight was left. Time had taken on a weird, stretched-out quality, kind of like in Nam when the grunts hunkered down for incoming even before the first mortars whistled through the air.

"Hey, Georgie, give me a little credit here. I pulled you out of that mess, didn't I? So don't give up on me yet. But I need a little help. You've got to have a little goddamned *hope.*"

Hope. Hope got you up in the morning. Hope put you to bed and tucked you in. Hope was the last thing you held on to when everything else was gone. The thought chilled George, or it may have been the cold sweat that covered his face.

"I'm holding on," George whispered. He usually didn't talk back to Old Leatherneck. He figured only crazy people talked back to the voices inside their heads. But then, there sure were a hell of a lot of crazy people around Korban Manor. Ransom Streater claimed to see people who weren't there, or those who had passed on long before. George wished one of them would have a vision now, do that Sight thing Abigail was always going on about, see him trapped under the old shed.

But Korban Manor was nearly a mile away, and not many messed around in this neck of the woods. Chances were, nobody was in shouting distance even if George could balloon his lungs up enough for a good scream. Chances were, the other hired help was busy around the house, packing in the latest batch of rich artists, Miss Mamie glaring at them if they dared to rest for even a minute. Chances were, even if he managed to crawl out from under three tons of wood and steel and glass, he'd leak away the rest of his blood before he made it back to the trail, let alone to the wagon road or manor.

But first he'd have to get free. Then he could worry about the rest of it. He looked to his right, to the side of his body that was missing a part. A section of the roof that was more or less intact sloped down from a point just above his waist to the ground fifteen feet away. The rubble above him was held up by a single bowed rafter.

If *that* gave way . . .

"Then it's 'Sayonara, Cholly,' " Old Leatherneck said, coming back from whatever shocked pocket of George's brain that the ornery bastard had been hiding out in. "Now move it."

A two-by-four rested near George's cheek, the grain rough against his skin. If he could maneuver it, maybe use it as a lever, he could pry his left arm free. He moved his arm, and the bone of his elbow clubbed against the wooden floor. His right arm must have been asleep, because now it came to tingling life.

He scooted the two-by-four against his side, and the payoff came. The end of his arm exploded in a bright burst of agony. This was *orange* pain, the color of orange that shot out of the Human Torch's hands in those Fantastic Four comics he'd read as a kid. Still, he pushed the two-by-four along until he could cradle it in the crook of his injured arm.

"There you go, Georgie-boy," said his one-man chain of command. "Give 'em hell. Only, what are you going to use as a fulcrum for your little make-do seesaw?"

Old Leatherneck had a point, as much as George hated to admit it. But if he gave up now, then surviving Nam and Selma and the stroke and stepping on a copperhead was all for nothing. Sliding down along those miners' rails in the dark would be that much easier. Just as an experiment, because he needed to know, he closed his eyes.

And he was deeper inside the long dark tunnel. The

light at the living end was fainter now, fuzzier. And he was accelerating, sliding fast and smooth as if sledding on snow. The air was thin and cool as the final bend came nearer.

George relaxed, though he was shivering and his blood was starved for oxygen and his heart was hammering like a roofer trying to beat a rainstorm. Because in here, in the tunnel, it was *okay* to give up hope. Nobody in here would hold it against him. He sensed that others were waiting to welcome him, huddled in the shadows, those who had ridden the rails before him. And he was rounding the bend, hell, this was easy, this was *fun,* and then, the soft slithering sound pickaxed him in the skull.

What if there are SNAKES around the bend?

George opened his eyes and fought back to the mouth of the tunnel and saw that the sun was still hanging stubbornly in the sky somewhere above, and the AWOL hand was splayed out stiff and livid, wearing a bracelet of splinters and dirt. He'd almost gone under, and knew that shock was setting in.

Back in An Loc once, some of the grunts had been sitting around knocking down Schlitz tall boys with George Jones on the record player. A young medic named Haley stubbed out a joint as big as a rifle barrel and told them why shock was a dying soldier's best friend.

"Some kinds of pain, even a plungerful of morphine won't touch," Haley said, a wreath of blue smoke around his head. "But shock, man, it shuts you down nice and easy. Blood pressure drops, breathing gets shallow, you get all sweaty, and you don't even know your Mama's name. Crash and bleed out, man, then drift off."

They'd told Haley to shut the hell up. And George had dodged his own run-in with fatal shock, at least so far. But lying under the crush of wreckage and running down Haley's list of symptoms, he was three-fourths of the way there. He still remembered Mama had been named Beatrice Anne.

The torn hand was slipping off the broken tip of lumber. A drop of blood hit his cheek. George gritted his loose teeth and flipped the two-by-four onto his chest. He pushed with his stump of a forearm until one end of the board was under the joist that had his left arm pinned.

He tried not to look at his ruined wrist. Blood ran down the underside of his arm. If he didn't get a tourniquet on it soon—

"Don't wait for that weed-brained Haley to swoop down in his Huey, Georgie-Boy. Some things, a man's gotta do for hisself. And a fixer-upper like you, somebody who's a real handyman—course, you're only *half* as handy as you used to be, ain't you?"

George wanted to scream at Old Leatherneck to shut up and go away. But George needed him, needed that taunting inner voice as badly as ever. Walking the lonely roads and horse trails of the Korban estate, he'd taken what companionship he could find. Sure, some of the folks down at Stony Hampton's café whispered about spooks and such around the manor, but after Nam, George figured the scariest spooks were the kinds that sent their sons into battle.

So when he'd seen the flicker of pale movement inside the shed, he hadn't given the whispers much of a thought. He'd figured it was a possum or maybe a screech owl. Nothing that would have caused much damage. But George was paid to keep the place up and the critters out, or, as Miss Mamie said, "Just the way things were when Ephram was still lord and master here." So George had lifted the old metal latch and pushed open the creaking door, hoping that any snakes were scared away by the noise.

"But it wasn't no possum, nor no screech owl, was it?" whispered Old Leatherneck.

George's eyes popped open. He must have drifted off. That was another one of Haley's signs. The two-by-four across his chest rose and fell with his shallow breathing. The sun had slipped low, the dark angles of shadows sharp and thick in the carnage.

Fear gave him a burst of energy, and he levered the two-by-four. His stub of a wrist screamed in fire-juice red.

"Hear that? Wasn't no possum, was it, Georgie?"

Now he wished the old bastard would shut up. He needed to focus, get the job done in a hurry, he didn't need—

"Might be *sssnakes.*"

Or it might be—

—the long white slithery shadow—

—whatever trick his eyes had played on him as he'd stepped inside the shed. Because if a fellow couldn't trust his own eyes, his days as a to-the-sixteenth-inch handyman were numbered. But right now, all that mattered was—

—that slippery shadow that you could see right through—

—the next push, prying that ceiling joist off his left arm. His chest erupted in hot blue sparks of pain, hell-blazer blue, a blue so intense it was almost white. But the joist gave a little groan and inched upward, awakening the nailed nerves in his biceps.

"She's moving, soldier! She's a-moving! And the pain ain't nothing, is it? Hell, we been through boo-koos of this kind of hurt. This is like a pansy-assed waltz through the daisies."

A waltz. The long white shadow had been doing a waltz. Like a worn linen curtain blowing in the wind, only . . .

"Sure wasn't no screech owl's face, Georgie-Boy."

The shadow had a human face.

George gurgled and the spit trickled down his cheek. He pried again and the joist lifted another cruel and precious inch. New colors of pain came, pus yellow, electric green, screaming violet, crazed ribbons of agony. A big section of the roof quivered and the amputated hand worked free of its wooden skewer, fell and bounced off his forehead and away.

But George barely noticed, because he was back in the tunnel, riding the miners' rails. And he was rounding that slow curve into darkness, that final turn away from the bothers of breathing.

And suddenly he knew what was around the bend.

She would be waiting, the white shadow with the large round begging eyes, the thing with arms spread wide, one hand holding that dead bouquet of flowers. She looked even more afraid than George. Just before the shed collapsed, he'd seen the long see-through tail wriggling under the lace hem of her gown, a tail as scaly as a—

"The snakes crawl at night, Georgie."

"No, they don't," George said, voice hoarse and weak. "I know, because I looked it up."

He was weeping because he realized he couldn't remember his mama's name. But sorrow didn't matter now, neither did the pain, nor the nails in his flesh, nor the missing hand, nor the dust filling his lungs, nor the creeping night. Even Old Leatherneck was nothing, just a distant jungle ghost, a cobweb, an echo.

All that mattered were the miners' rails and that turn in the bend, and the tunnel opening into a deeper, airless blackness. A black beyond the colors of pain.

She was waiting. With company.

Johnny Cash was right, and the encyclopedia was wrong.

The snakes *did* crawl at night.

CHAPTER 4

Mason was tired from his walk along the wagon trails. He'd spent the afternoon trying to clear his head, relishing the solitude and quiet of the mountain forest that surrounded the estate. Out there, under the ancient hardwood trees, nobody had any expectations of him. He didn't have to be a hot new artist, he wasn't the repository for his mother's hopes and dreams, he had no obligation to prove his worth to the world's most unforgiving father. On the grounds of Korban Manor, he was just another loser with a bag of tricks.

The foyer was nearly empty when Mason returned to the manor just before sunset. He nodded at an elderly couple who wore matching jackets, their shirtsleeves laced, drinks poised. Roth and a dark-skinned woman were talking, Roth miming as if he were snapping a photograph. The gaunt maid stood at the foot of the stairs, hands clasped behind her back, staring at the portrait of Korban. Mason waved to Roth and crossed the room, careful to avoid looking into the fireplace. He was afraid he'd see something that probably wasn't there.

He touched the maid on the shoulder. She spun as if

electrocuted, and Mason stepped back and held his hands apart. "Sorry to startle you. Are you the one showing us our rooms?"

She forced a smile and nodded. Mason squinted to read the brass nameplate fixed to her chest. *Lilith.*

"Name, please?" Her voice was barely above a whisper. Roth's laughter boomed from the other end of the room, no doubt fueled by one of his own jokes.

"Jackson," Mason said.

"Mr. Jackson, you're late." She tried a smile again, but it flitted across her pale face and settled into the shadows of her mouth. "Second floor, end of the south wing."

"I hope we've got bathrooms," he said, trying for bumpkin humor. "I know we're supposed to go back in time, but I didn't see an outhouse anywhere."

"Shared baths for adjoining rooms only," she said, already heading up the stairs. "You have a private bath. Follow me, please."

Mason took a last look back at the fireplace, then at Korban's giant face. Even with dead eyes and confined to two dimensions, the man had charisma. But then, so had David Koresh, Charles Manson, and Adolf Hitler. And Mason's father. The gallery of assholes. Mason shook his head and started up the stairs. Lilith hadn't offered to carry his satchel. Maybe she'd noticed how possessively he clung to it, or maybe the chivalry and manners of the nineteenth century still held sway here.

Lilith glided over the oak treads with a swish of her long dress. If she was going for big-city Goth, she certainly had the sickly complexion for it. She moved with a grace that belied her brittle features. Judging from her bony hands and the angles of her skull, Mason expected her to clatter when she walked.

The second floor was as grand as the first, with the same high ceiling and wainscoting. A pair of chandeliers hung above the great hallway, each with cream-colored candles stuck in a silver ring and surrounded by crystal teardrops. Astral lamps burned at eye level every twenty feet, the flames throwing enough light to shrink the shadows along the wood trim. Rows of three solid maple doors lined both walls, and oil landscapes were set at intervals between the rooms. The art was of high quality, all of manor scenery. One of the paintings was of the wooden bridge that Mason and the guests had crossed, and the image brought back memories of his light-headed panic. It, like the other paintings, bore no artist's signature.

Huge portraits of Korban, with different lighting effects than the one in the foyer but possessing the obligatory scowl of the era, hung at each end of the hall.

"Nice paintings," he said to Lilith.

"Mr. Korban lived for his art. We all did."

"Oh, are you one of *us?*" He meant it as humor. Either he was too worried about his imminent failure as a sculptor or she was preoccupied, but the joke fell as flat as canvas.

"I used to be," Lilith replied.

They passed an open door and Mason looked inside. Jefferson Spence's bulk was overwhelming a wooden swivel chair as the writer unpacked papers and spread them across a desk. Miss Seventeen was nowhere in sight. Mason noticed that the room only had one bed, then quickly looked away, chiding himself for being nosy.

Lilith led him before a door at the end of the hall. It creaked as she pushed it open. She stood aside so Mason could enter, her eyes on the floor.

"Thanks," Mason said. His battered suitcase, a Sampsonite with electrician's tape holding the handle together, was already inside the room. The suite was large with a king-sized wooden poster bed, cherry desks, matching chestnut bureaus, and round-topped nightstands. Tall rectangular windows were set in the south and west walls, and Mason realized the room would get sunlight throughout the day. That was a luxury at a place that had no electricity. The setting sun suffused the room with a honey-colored warmth.

"Wow. This must be one of the better rooms," he said.

The maid still waited outside, as if afraid to breathe the room's air.

"It's the master suite," she said. "It used to be Ephram Korban's bedroom."

"Is that why his portrait's on the wall?" Mason said, nodding to the painting that hung above the bedroom's large fireplace. It was a smaller version of the painting that hung in the foyer, of a slightly younger Korban. The eyes, though, were just as black and bottomless, and the faintest hint of a smile played across those so-cruel lips.

"Miss Mamie chose this room especially for you," Lilith said without emotion. "She said you've come highly recommended."

Mason tossed his satchel on the bed. The tools clinked dully together. "I hope I can live up to her expectations."

"Nobody has yet." Lilith still waited outside the door. If she was joking, there was no sign of it in her wan face.

"Uh, I don't know much about places like this," he said, putting a hand in his pocket, falling back on his "Aw, shucks" routine. He'd learned that people were more forgiving if they thought he was a dumb hick because their expectations were lower. He achieved the same effect with his southern drawl, though that was mostly unintentional. He secretly suspected his success at Adderly had been due to the sophisticated instructors' amazement that a country rube could break the confines of his heritage and actually compete in the ranks of the cultural elite. "You might think I'm stupid, but am I supposed to tip you?"

"No, of course not. And Miss Mamie would kill me if you tried." Lilith managed a smile, relieved at being dismissed. She was even attractive, in a nervous, pallid way, like a princess whose head was due to roll. She wasn't as pretty as the stuck-up woman with the cyan eyes, but Lilith probably wasn't contemptuous of artists if she herself was one.

Lilith pointed to the door on the west wall. "The bathroom's in there."

"Fine." He sat on the bed.

"Is that all?"

"Unless you want to take off my shoes for me."

She took a hesitant step forward, staring at the floor.

"Hey, I was just kidding." He gave a laugh that sounded like a horse choking on an apple.

Lilith flashed her feverish smile again, then said, "Dinner's at eight sharp, Mr. Jackson. Don't be late. Miss Mamie wouldn't like it."

Then she was gone. Mason turned his attention once more to the furnishings. A lamp stood on each nightstand, an oval glass base filled with heavy oil and encased in brass workings. A fire crackled away in the hearth, a stack of split locust and oak piled near the stonework. It was a miracle the old place hadn't burned down in all these years. Mason leaned back on the pillows and stared at the hand-swirled patterns in the gypsum ceiling.

Okay, Mase, this is what you wanted bad enough to go to all that trouble for. You did everything but stand naked in front of the Arts Council grant committee and shake your goodies. You swayed the critics, sold your brand of snake oil, and now you've taken maybe the biggest step of your career. Maybe even your life. Because if you don't produce any salable work here, you're looking at another foodstamp Christmas in Sawyer Creek.

And you'll have to look Mama in the eye, even if she

can't look back at you, and tell her you failed, that your dreams weren't strong enough, that you didn't believe in them enough.

Diabetic retinopathy. A rapid deterioration of her vision, except she'd never said a word even as the tunnel closed in. She'd lied to the doctors long enough for the condition to pass the point of no return, and Mason had only found out when it was too late. She was too young for Medicare and not poor enough for Medicaid, but still could have gone ahead and run up the bills and then declared bankruptcy later. However, that would have depleted the meager savings she'd set aside for his education. Mason had wasted the money at Adderly, beating on hunks of wood and metal, trying to turn them into dreams.

The worst part was that Mason didn't know whether to admire her for her sacrifice or despise her for being so noble. Now she was scraping by on disability and whatever little bit Mason could afford to give her out of his factory paycheck. But that job was gone now, lost because of his pursuit of art. And still Mama was his greatest fan.

"Don't ever let go of your dreams, honey," she said through teeth she couldn't afford to repair. "That's all we got in this world, is dreams."

Mason rolled to his feet and paced the room. It was the same way he paced when he was anxious about an idea, when he felt the itch in his fingers, when some new sculpture began to take shape in his mind. It was the same mixture of excitement and dread, excitement that the new idea was the best ever, and dread in knowing that the finished product could never match the dream image.

Except, this time, the anxiety wasn't the by-product of exhilaration.

This retreat was the biggest of his big dream images. He'd already decided that if no direction or recognition came from his time at Korban Manor, he would toss his tools off the old wooden bridge that separated Korban Manor from the rest of the world. Sure, the heights would give him trouble, but he could crawl blind if necessary. He'd listen to the metal clanging and clattering off the far rocks below, then he'd allow the blisters and calluses to heal while he found a real job.

He always knew that creativity came at a price. You had to pay the price even for a chance at failure. Doctors and lawyers spent ten years in college and paid tens of thousands of dollars. Criminals paid with the risk of lost freedom. Priests gave up pleasures of the flesh. Soldiers faced an even greater cost. Artists paid with other things, the cheapest of which was pain. Not that he minded suffering for his art. He just didn't think Mama should suffer for it. He looked down and saw that his fists were clenched into angry hammers, the rage nearly making him drunk.

He stopped pacing and leaned against the window, looking through the old-fashioned rippled glass to the manor grounds. Even though he was only two stories up, he had to grip the molding to keep the dizziness at bay. The woman he'd talked to earlier stood by the fence, petting a horse. The sunset gilded the horizon and the gentle light made her ethereal and beautiful, a fairy-tale princess floating above the grass. The green rolling fields, the shimmering sky, the sparkling lake at the foot of the pasture, and the seemingly weightless woman all seemed locked away in a dream.

And, according to his father, dreams were a goddamned waste of good daylight.

Mason went into the bathroom. The plumbing was primitive, though the fixtures were as ornate as the rest of the house. A cast-iron tub sat in the corner. The sink was marble, with gleaming chrome spigots and a framed mirror.

He faced the ceramic toilet and relieved himself,

noting the small siphon tank set high on the wall. The pipes behind the wall jumped and quivered when he flushed. He washed his hands at the sink, glancing in the mirror. Though the water was cold, the mirror fogged.

He wiped at it with the sleeve of his shirt. Still the haze remained. He frowned at his bleary reflection. The face in the mirror seemed a little slow in responding, the sad and tired face of a condemned prisoner.

When he returned to the room, his tools were spread across his bed. They almost seemed to taunt him, daring him to take them up and fail. He didn't remember taking them out of the satchel. Was he that uptight and distracted?

The portrait of Korban glowered down at him, the imagined smile gone. Korban was just another taskmaster, a demanding and cold critic. An observer, outside the creative process, but ready to judge something that no one but the creator could understand. Just another asshole with an opinion.

Mason went to the tools, drawn as always by their power. He bent to them, touched the fluters, chisels, hammers, and gouges, took comfort in their edges and weight. They ached to feed, they needed Mason's fingers to help them shape their world. And Mason needed them in turn, a symbiotic addiction that would create as much as it destroyed. He turned his back to Korban's portrait, then wiped the tools with a chamois cloth until they gleamed in the firelight.

"We can just push the beds together," Adam said.

"Yeah, and when you roll over in your sleep, *you'll* be the one whose ass falls into the crack."

"Wonder what kind of bed the married couples got."

"Probably a swinging harness rigged to the bedposts, with a mirror on the ceiling."

"Don't act so persecuted, Paul. This will be romantic, like in the old days when we used to snuggle on your sister's couch."

"Yeah, until Sis found out. *That* was a scene that won't make it into a Disney family special."

Adam sighed. If only Paul weren't so hardheaded. They would make do. They always had. And God wasn't out to punish people like them, despite the vehement rants of the rabid right wing.

"Listen," Adam said. "We'll push both beds sideways against the wall, and you can have the back. If anybody rolls off in the night and knocks his head on the floor, it'll be me."

Paul rubbed his hair in exasperation. A few strands of it stood up, dirty-blond and wavy, young Robert Redford hair. That, combined with his half-lidded eyes and thick eyelashes, made him look sleepy. Adam liked that sleepy look. It was one of the things that had first attracted him to Paul.

"Okay," Paul said. "I'll quit griping now. This *is* supposed to be a second honeymoon."

Adam smiled. Paul's tirades never lasted long. "Does this mean I get my virginity back?"

Paul pulled one of the feather pillows from under the blankets and threw it.

Adam knocked it away easily. "Say, did you get a load of Miss Mamie?"

"She could pass for a drag queen if she had a little neck stubble."

They laughed together. Adam said, "You don't mince words. And you don't mince anything else, either."

"I'll mince your meat if you're not careful. And that's why you love me."

"Well, that's one of the reasons."

"Let's get unpacked. I want to go out and meet some people."

"That's exactly like you," Adam said. "We go eight

hundred miles to get away from it all, then you have to swing right into the middle of the social scene."

"Live to party, Princess."

"Hey, it's *my* inheritance we're throwing away here. And don't think I'm going to let you forget it."

Paul gave his fake pout in reply.

Adam carried their luggage to the closet. Paul had three matching suitcases and a heavy-duty case for his video camera. Adam had only a gym bag and a backpack.

"Besides," Adam said, "when the money runs out, we can always rent that tremendously gorgeous body out for Calvin Klein commercials."

"As long as I don't have to pose nude with Kate Moss. She gives me the willies."

"If she gets a look at you, she'll want to carry your baby."

"Like *that* will ever happen."

"Hey, come on. You'd make a cute dad."

"Don't start that," Paul said.

Adam began putting Paul's cotton shirts on hangers, careful to keep his back turned. He didn't want his disappointment to show. Paul was dead set against adoption, against that ultimate long-term commitment. And nobody could be as dead set as Paul.

"Sorry," Adam said, his words muffled by the closet. "I just thought, out here in the wilderness, away from our old life and all the pressures—"

"I *said* not to start."

"You said we could talk about it when we got here."

"But I didn't mean right away. I want to relax a little, and you're making me all tense."

"Let's not fight. It's a bad way to start a vacation."

"I need to work some, too. How can I get anything done if you're bugging me about that 'settling down' crap?"

Adam sighed into the dark hollow of the closet. He

finished putting away the clothes, then pretended to be interested in what was going on outside the window. Paul would have fun getting some footage here. A nice, peaceful nature documentary for an uptight Boston boy.

They had a room on the third floor, smaller than the ones he'd seen while the maid was leading them upstairs. The window was set in a gable. The entire upper floor, including walls and angled ceilings, was covered with varnished tongue-in-groove boards. On the way up, Adam had asked the maid about a narrow ladder that led to a small trapdoor in the roof. She told them it went to the widow's walk and that guests weren't allowed up there. She said it with what Adam thought was nervousness and a dismissive haste. He wondered if, during some past retreat, a guest had suffered an accident there.

He turned from the window, ready to make peace. If he could get Paul talking about video, the spat would soon be forgotten. "So, do you think you brought enough tape?"

"Got enough for eight hours. Too bad the budget didn't allow for me to get a Beta SP camera. I'm stuck with crappy digital."

"Well, you're freelancing for public television. What do you expect, the budget for *Titanic* minus Leo DiCaprio's dialogue coach?"

"Hey, I'd be happy with his hairstylist's budget. Documentary grants are at the bottom of the list for funding these days. Maybe I should go into 'Mysteries of the Unexplained Enigmas and Other Offbeat Occult Phenomena.' With all this talk about the manor being haunted, who knows?"

Adam smiled, counting a victory whenever Paul slipped into sarcastic humor. Paul wouldn't take any money from Adam to subsidize his videos, but otherwise he had no qualms about being a "kept man." Paul stretched out on one of the narrow beds and stared at the ceiling. Maybe he was visualizing the edit of some sequence.

"Tell you what," Adam said. "I'll see if I can arrange to be abducted by space aliens while you roll the camera."

"I hear they do all kinds of bizarre sexual experiments."

"Sounds better every minute."

"Hey, what can *they* do that I can't do better?"

Adam crossed the room. Paul had that sleepy look again. "Kiss me, you fool."

Paul did. Adam felt eyes watching them. Strange.

"What?" Paul asked, his voice husky.

"Don't know," Adam said. He looked around. No one could possibly see in the window from outside, and the door was locked. Besides the furniture, the only thing in the room was an oil painting, a smaller replica of the man's portrait that hung in the foyer.

I'm not going to be paranoid. It's okay to be gay, even in the rural South. It's OKAY to get back to nature. This love is as real as anything in this world.

He slid into bed beside Paul, wondering if the old geezer Korban would disapprove of two boys boffing under his roof. Who cared? Korban was dead, and Paul was very much alive.

October was a hunter, its prey the green beast of summer. The wind moved over the hills like a reluctant hawk; wings wide, talons low, hard eyes sweeping. Beneath its golden and frosty skin, the earth quaked in the wind of the hawk's passing. The morning held its gray breath. Each tender leaf and blade of grass trembled in fear.

Jefferson Spence looked down at the keys of the old manual Royal. "Horse teeth," the keys were called.

George Washington had horse teeth, according to legend. Spence knew he was wasting time, finding any distraction to keep him from starting another sentence. He stared into the bobbing flame of the lantern on his desk.

He looked up at Ephram Korban's face on the wall. In this very room, twenty years before, Spence had written *Seasons of Sleep,* a masterpiece by all accounts, especially Spence's own. All his novels since had fallen short, but maybe the magic would return.

Words were magic. And maybe old Korban would let slip a secret or two, bestow some hidden wisdom gleaned from all those years on the wall.

"What," Spence said to the portrait, his voice filling the room, "are you trying to say?"

Bridget called from the bathroom in her soft Georgia drawl. "What's that, honey?"

"To have and have not," he said.

"What is it you don't have? I thought we packed everything."

"Never mind, my sweet. A Hemingway allusion is best saved for a more appreciative audience."

Spence had collected Bridget during a summer writing workshop at the University of Georgia. He had led the workshop during the day and spent his evenings cooling off in the bars of Athens. Most of the sophomore seminar students had joined him for the first few nights, but his passion for overindulgence and his brusque nature had caused the group to dwindle. By Thursday of the first week, only the faithful still orbited like bright satellites gravitating toward the black hole of Spence's incalculable mass.

Three of those were eligible in Spence's eyes: a bronze-skinned African goddess with oily curls; a hollow-cheeked blonde who had a devilish way of licking her lips and an unhealthy appetite for the works of Richard Brautigan; and the tender Bridget. As always, a couple of male students had also crowded his elbows and plied writing tips from him in exchange for drinks. Spence had little patience with writers. His best advice was to spend time in front of the keyboard instead of in front of bar mirrors. But, to Spence, women's minds were simpler and therefore uncluttered with literary pretensions.

He had selected Bridget precisely because she was the most innocent, and therefore would be the least corrupted of the three choices. With her fresh skin and clean hair, her simple and naive speech, her down-home manners and belle grace, she was everything that Spence wasn't. She was a lamb in a world of wolves. And Spence was pleased that he'd gotten the first bite.

He'd lured her to his hotel room that weekend with the promise of showing her his latest manuscript. "Not even my agent has seen it," he'd said, swimming in a haze of vodka. "Consider yourself blessed, my sweet."

She stayed the night, clumsily undressing as he watched. She shyly turned her back when she unsnapped her bra, and Spence smiled when she faced him with her arms covering her breasts. His was a smile of approval, but not for her physical qualities, as delightful as those were. He was pleased with himself for such a perfect conquest, such a decadent notch in his triggerless gun.

She hadn't complained or expressed surprise when he didn't attempt intercourse. A few women had actually ridiculed him, *him,* Jefferson Davis Spence, the next last great southern writer, just because he was impotent. But Bridget only lay meekly next to him while he stroked her as if she were a pet cat. Her warmth was comforting in the night. After a few weeks, she'd even stopped trembling beneath his touch.

That had been four months ago, and he figured she was probably good for at least another half a year. Then, as with all the others, the scales would fall from her eyes, the sexual frustration and the endless servitude would wear her down, until going back to college and getting a degree seemed a much better career choice than watching the great Jefferson Spence barrel headlong toward his first coronary. Then Spence would find himself alone, desperately alone, with nothing but himself and his thoughts, himself and words, himself and the monster he had crafted inside his own head.

He looked down at the paper that was scrolled into the Royal. Six years. Six years, and all he had to show for it was this paragraph that he'd rewritten three hundred times. It was the same paragraph with which he'd lured Bridget that first time, the one he didn't even dare show his agent or editor. He'd known the time had arrived to get away from it all, seek a fresh perspective, summon those arcane Muses. If there was any place where he could recapture the magic, it was Korban Manor.

He placed his fingers on the keys. The shower came on in the bathroom, and Bridget began singing in her small, pretty voice. "Stand By Me," the old Ben King song. He typed "stand by me" under his opening paragraph, then clenched his teeth and ripped the page out of the carriage. He tore the sheet of paper into four pieces and let the scraps flutter to the floor.

Spence leaned back in his chair and looked out the window. The treetops were swaying in the wind that had arisen with the approaching dusk. He imagined the smells of autumn, of fallen apples bruised and sweet under the trees, of birch leaves crumpling under boot heels, of cherry bark splitting and leaking rubbery jeweled sap, of pumpkin pies and chimney smoke. If only he could find the words to describe those things.

Spence turned his attention back to the portrait of Korban on the wall. He thought about walking into the bathroom and watching Bridget soap herself up. But she might try to excite him. Each new beauty always thought she would be the one, out of dozens who had tried, to overcome what he called "the Hemingway curse." And with each fresh failure, Spence felt angry and humbled. Though he welcomed anger, he loathed humility.

He cursed under his breath and rolled a fresh sheet of paper into the typewriter. The paper was heavy, a twenty percent cotton mix. Worthy paper. The words would come. They had to come. He commanded them to come.

Spence stared into the face of Korban. "What should I write, sir?"

The portrait stared back, its eyes oil-black.

Spence's fingers hit the keys, the clattering motion vibrated through the desk and echoed off the wooden floor, the carriage return's bell rang every thirty seconds.

The house sat amid the breasts of hills, among swells, above rivers, above all Earth, reaching where only the gods could dwell. And in the house, in the high lonely window from which he could see the world that would be his, the man smiled.

They had come, they had answered his call, those who would give him life. They would sing his songs, they would carve his name into their hearts, they would paint him into the sky. They came with their poetries, their images, their fevered words, their dreams. They came bearing gifts, and he would give unto them likewise—

Spence was so lost in his writing, lost as he had not been in years, that he didn't notice when Bridget walked nude and steaming into the room. He worked feverishly, his tongue pressed against his teeth. The gift was returning, flowing like blood through forgotten veins. He didn't know whom to thank, Bridget, Korban, or some unseen Muse.

He'd worry about that later. For now, the words carried Spence beyond himself.

CHAPTER 5

Anna looked down at her plate. The prime rib oozed juices and steam, and ordinarily would have been tempting enough to challenge her vegetarian principles. The softly boiled broccoli sprouts and red potatoes had elicited several exploratory stabs of her fork. The apple pie's crust was so tender it flaked all over the china plate.

As she watched the sugary lava of the pie filling flow between the crumbs, she wondered what it would be like to worry about dieting. She glanced across the dining room at Jefferson Spence and saw no hesitation in that man's fork. She took a few hasty mouthfuls of the vegetables, then pushed the food around a little so it would look as if she had eaten well. The way Miss Mamie fussed over dinner proceedings, Anna almost felt guilty about not appreciating the food.

The dining room was a long hall just off the main foyer. The room contained four tables, a long one in the center occupied by the people that Anna secretly thought of as "the *über*culture." The other, smaller tables were relegated to the corners. Apparently Miss Mamie had tried to match people of similar interests when she made out the seating charts. That meant putting all the below-fifties at the smaller tables.

Anna was sitting with Cris and the dark-skinned woman whom Anna had seen carrying a camera earlier. To her left was the guy she'd talked to on the porch, the sullen sculptor. Though his face was plain, something about his green-brown eyes kept drawing her attention. A secret fire buried deep. Or maybe it was only the reflection of the two candles that burned in the center of the table. Or an illusion created by her own desperate solitude.

Cris had mumbled a prayer before dinner. The dark-skinned woman had also bowed her head. Anna wasn't compelled to join in their ritual and instead took the opportunity to study their faces. The sculptor had kept his head down but his eyes open. Then Anna had seen what he was looking at: a fly circled the edge of his plate, dipping a tentative feeler into the brown gravy.

She'd hidden her smile as he surreptitiously tried to blow it away. When Cris said, "Amen," he quickly whisked his cloth napkin out of his lap and waved it with a flourish. The fly headed toward the oil lamps that burned in the chandeliers overhead. Anna watched its flight, and when she turned her attention back to dinner, the sculptor was looking at her.

"Darned thing was about to carry off my dinner," he said. "Evil creature."

"Maybe it was Beelzebub," she said. "Lord of the flies."

"Beelzebubba's more like it. It's a southern fly."

Anna laughed for the first time in weeks. Her tablemates looked at them with furrowed brows. The man introduced himself to them as Mason and said he was a retired textile worker from the foothills. "I'm also an aspiring sculptor," he said. "But don't confuse me with Henry Moore or anything."

"Didn't he play James Bond?" Cris asked.

"No, that was *Roger* Moore."

He politely waved off the wine when the maid, Lilith, brought the carafe around. Anna took a glass herself, though she had no intention of taking more than a few sips. The conservatism that came with a death sentence had surprised her. When you only have a little time left, you try to heighten your experience, not dull it.

Her eyes wandered to Mason again. He was watching Lilith as if he was interested in more than just a second helping of hot rolls. She was both annoyed and surprised when a flare of jealousy raced across her heart. She despised pettiness and, besides, possessiveness was the last vice a dying person should suffer. Stephen had taught her that you could never understand another person, much less own one, and the idea of soul mates was best limited to romance novels. She took a gulp of wine and let the mild sting of alcohol distract her, then introduced herself to the dark-skinned woman.

The woman was named Zainab and had been born in Saudi Arabia. She was Arabian-American, but only indirectly from oil money; her father had been an engineer at Aramco. Zainab came to the U.S. to attend Stanford, back before everyone from the Middle East had to jump through flaming hoops to immigrate here, and now wanted to be a photographer "when she grew up."

"In America, you get to be grown up when you're fourteen," Anna said. "At least if you believe the fashion magazines. Of course, when you reach forty, you're expected to look twenty-five."

"Hey," Cris said, polishing off her third glass of wine. "I'm thirty going on twenty-nine. Guess that means I'm headed in the right direction."

Anna chopped at her pie a little more, then pushed the dessert plate away. Cris leaned toward Mason, her eyelashes doing some serious fluttering.

"So, what do the guys in the foothills do for fun?" Cris asked.

"We go down to the Dumpsters behind the local café

and throw rocks at the rats. The rats in Sawyer Creek eat better than the welfare families."

"I bet the rats live well around here," Cris said.

Not a smooth move, Anna thought. *Talk of rodents does not a bedmate beckon.*

"We call it 'living high on the hog' back home," Mason said, shuddering in mock revulsion. "I was talking to one of the handymen today. He told me about setting out steel traps, and burying the food scraps to keep the rats down. Garbage disposal is a big chore here."

"It's amazing the things we take for granted in a civilized society," Anna said.

"Who's civilized?" Cris said, giggling. "Sounds like we're heading for one of those 'walked four miles through the snow to get to school' stories."

"It was 'four kilometers over sand dunes without a camel' where I grew up," said Zainab.

"I saw one of the maids with a basket of laundry. Not *her,*" Anna said, frowning toward Lilith, who was uncorking a wine bottle at the main table. "Imagine what it must be like to hand-wash all these table linens and curtains, not to mention the sheets."

"Seems the sheets get a good workout around here, if you believe the rumors," Cris said.

"You mean the ghost stories?" Mason said.

Anna's breath caught in her throat. If she managed to contact any ghosts here, she didn't want a bunch of would-be necromancers holding midnight séances and playing with Ouija boards. She believed those sorts of disrespectful games sent ghosts running for the safety of the grave. And if she had a mission here, a last bit of business before her soul could rest, she preferred to handle it undistracted.

"I was talking about sex, but the ghost stories are interesting, too," Cris said. Her sibilants were starting to get a little mushy.

Strike two, Anna said to herself. *A man who's an ar-*

rogant, tee-totaling prude probably doesn't want to swap tongues with someone whose mouth smells like a barroom.

She knew she was being catty. The last entanglement had cured her of desire. And she definitely had no romantic interest in the sculptor. Even if he did have strong hands, thick, wavy hair, those dreaming-awake eyes. Maybe what she had taken for sullenness was actually insecurity. A shyness and hesitancy that was refreshing compared to Stephen's self-righteousness, and—

Stop it right there, girl. Find something NOT to like about him.

There.

He chews with his mouth open and he has pie crumbs sticking to his chin.

Mason said, "According to William Roth—"

"Oh, I *met* him." Zainab's brown eyes lit up as she interrupted. "I actually got to talk to him. I've always admired his work, but he's not at all like you'd think a famous person would be. He's so down-to-earth. And he has the most wonderful accent."

"He's quite a character, all right."

"I think William is charming," Zainab said, looking at him seated at the main table where he seemed to be engaged in three conversations at once.

"What were you saying about ghosts?" Cris said, as if she'd just realized the subject had jumped track. "Anna does that stuff—"

Anna cut her off with a look and a subtle shake of her head. She didn't want everyone to think she was a flake, at least not right away.

"Roth says Korban Manor is haunted, and he's going to try to take some pictures," Mason said. "And the handyman I met today sure seems a little spooked."

"Has anything weird happened to you guys since we got here?" Zainab asked.

Mason frowned. "I don't know about ghosts. I'll believe them when I see them, I suppose. But old geezer Korban's pictures all over the place sure give me the creeps." He nodded to the portrait on the wall above the head of the main table.

"A big old place like this," Anna said, "you always have creaky boards and sudden drafts blowing from everywhere. And all these lamps and candles throw a bunch of flickering shadows. It's no wonder stories make the rounds."

"Sure," Mason said. "If there really *were* ghosts, do you think all these people would keep coming back year after year?"

"And how could they keep any employees?" Anna said.

"Well, I wouldn't mind seeing a ghost or two," Cris said, her cheeks bright. "Might liven the place up a bit. I like things that go bump in the night." Cris smiled at Mason in lewd punctuation.

Anna watched his reaction. *This is it. Right over the heart of the plate. Strike three, or the long ball.*

Mason shrugged, seemingly oblivious to Cris's come-on. "I don't know. I'll believe it when I see it."

A small, cheap glow of victory burned in Anna's chest. Then she despised herself for the feeling. What business was it of hers if Cris hooked up with this country boy? After Stephen, men didn't exist, anyway. Ghosts were far more solid and reliable than men were.

The conversation was broken when Miss Mamie rose from her seat at the head of the main table. She tapped her wineglass with a spoon, and the clatter of dishes and small talk died to a whisper. Lilith and the other maid stood at attention near the foyer, each holding a silver pitcher.

"Ladies and gentlemen, lovely guests," Miss Mamie said, her voice filling the hall. She looked at the faces lining the main table, clearly enjoying the moment. "Friends."

Anna was already bored. She hoped the speech would be short. Miss Mamie drew in a breath as if she were a soprano about to leap into an aria.

"I'd like to welcome all of you to Korban Manor," Miss Mamie said. "As most of you know, this house was built in 1902 by my grandfather, Ephram Korban. After he passed on, God rest his soul, it came into my father's hands. We turned the manor into an artists' retreat to fulfill Ephram's final request. Now it's my duty to carry on the legacy, and I do that with great pride and joy."

"And profit," cut in a British accent, and an uncertain laughter rippled across the room.

Miss Mamie smiled. "That, too, Mr. Roth. But it's more than just a way to fund the estate's preservation. It's a labor of love, a continuation of Ephram's vision. He himself was an admirer of the arts. And I hope each of you finds fulfillment during your stay here, and in so doing, you'll help keep Ephram's dreams alive in your own way."

Anna sneaked a glance at Mason. He was staring at Miss Mamie with blatant curiosity.

Hmmm. Maybe he's not as handsome as I first thought. His nose is a little long in profile. And his fingers are too thick. I'll bet he's clumsy with women.

Satisfied that she had found enough flaws, she sipped her wine. Miss Mamie was in the middle of stoking the collective artistic fires.

"—so I propose a toast, my friends," the hostess said, twiddling her pearls. She raised her wineglass toward the vaulted ceiling, then turned and tipped it toward the portrait of Korban. Most of the room joined her. Anna reached for her glass again, then changed her mind. Mason saw her and smirked.

Asshole. Probably one of those "holier than thou" types. An artist with a superiority complex. Now, THERE'S a rarity.

She grabbed her glass. When Miss Mamie drank, Anna took a large gulp. It was house-bottled muscadine, a little too sweet for swilling. But she took an extra swallow for good measure.

"You're welcome to join me in the study for after-dinner drinks and conversation," Miss Mamie concluded. "There's a smoking porch off the study as well. Again, thank you for allowing us the pleasure of your company. Good evening."

The room erupted in chatter and rattling silverware. Cris wobbled slightly as she stood, and she put a hand on Mason's shoulder to balance herself. Anna pretended not to notice. She was after *ghosts,* damn it. Ghosts didn't make a fool out of you the way men always did.

She slipped away up the stairs. The lamps along the hall threw a warm glow over the woodwork. She entered the dark bedroom and stood by the window, looking over the dark manor grounds. The sky was fading into a deep periwinkle, soon to be smothered by the blackness creeping from the east, the moon rising faint and blue in the east.

She took her flashlight from the nightstand. At least one modern convenience had been allowed, probably on the demands of the manor's insurance provider. She turned the light on and played it across the walls, half expecting to see a restless spirit, but revealing only a spiderweb crack in the plasterboard.

She sighed. Ghoulie-chasing. That was what Stephen called it.

"Leave me to do the serious investigating," he'd say. "You can play at ghoulie-chasing."

A ghost lived in this house. She knew it as surely as she knew that she was dying. And she would chase it to hell if she had to, because she wanted to be right for once in her life. At least, she wanted Stephen to know she had been right. Even if it was only her own ghost she found.

She collected a sweater and put the flashlight in her

pocket. A long walk alone with the night would do her good.

Rubbish.

Rubbish and poppycock.

Rubbish, poppycock, and swill.

William Roth ran through the derogatory nouns in his mind as he studied the books that lined the study walls. The books were all hardbacks, many with leather covers and gilded titles. The dust on them was proof of their dullness.

A jolly good put-on for the intelligentsia. Because the books are all poppycock and . . . claptrap. Yes, CERTAINLY claptrap.

Précis of the French Revolution. The Diary of Sir Wendell Swanswight. Talmud. Juris Studis.

They would make rather bully paperweights. The only thing they had going for them was that they fit the shelves perfectly. Roth sipped his scotch-and-water as he worked his way toward the small crowd that had gathered around Jefferson Spence. The great man's tremulous voice held forth on some didactic opinion or other. Spence went unchallenged by his admirers.

The Arab bird stood across the room, her ever-present camera around her neck. He mentally practiced her name, because it was difficult to fake a British accent while saying it. *Zay-ih-nahb.* He would have to teach her a few things about photographic codes of conduct. You don't blunder about like a rhino through the veldt. You stalk, you wait, you seduce your subject with infinite patience and care, you lull, you caress, and then—flick, click, thank you, prick.

But he could get Zainab anytime. She was easy meat waiting to be culled from the herd. She was a crippled gazelle, and Roth was a lion. First he had bigger game to snare.

Wait a minute, bloke. Bad metaphor. You know from your time in Afrikker that a lioness does all the hunting while the lion lies around licking his balls. But the bloody Yanks don't know that. King of the Jungle, and that bit.

He was thinking in his Manchester accent. He had descended into Liverpudlian in the mid-nineties during that brief Beatles revival, then had gone Yorkshire in the wake of "The Full Monty." Fads came and went, and so did his accent. He occasionally slipped in a "righty-right" or "bit of the old what for," but Americans didn't notice his errors. The only time he had to be careful was when he met a real Brit.

And a fat bloody chance of that here, he thought, smiling to himself. He had reached the edge of Spence's circle now.

"And they say there are hermeneutic elements in *Look Homeward, Angel,"* Spence said, his jowls quivering for emphasis. "I submit to you that Gant is no more than a symbol for the human heart. A flimsy extended metaphor propped up by a billion adjectives. If you sent that to an editor today, she'd say, 'Wonderful, now can you make it read like Grisham?' "

The eyes of the onlookers brightened with awe. This man was a master, a snake charmer. His ego was as ample as his belly. None dared to dispute his ephemeral pronouncements.

Spence drained half of his martini before continuing. "The worst book of the twentieth century? Perhaps not. That jester's crown must go to Hemingway's *A Moveable Feast.* The critics raved about the undercurrent of tension that supposedly wends through the novel. Claptrap. It is nothing but Hemingway-in-a-bottle, quintessential Ernest. Too earnestly Ernest, one might say."

Spence paused for the requisite laughter. It came.

Roth smiled. Spence was as great a deceiver as Roth himself. And he played the celebrity game just as successfully. Roth was constantly amazed by people's hunger for idols. Bring on your false gods. The masses needed an opiate, and that bit.

Roth worked his way to Spence's left, edging between a blue-haired biddie and an old chap with a hunched back. The cute little bird with the nice knockers was at Spence's side. She hadn't spoken a word all evening, even during dinner. Roth knew, because he had watched her and Spence at their private table. Roth calculated the chances of working her for a bit of the old in-out. That would be a dandy feather in the cap.

Spence blathered on about the moral instructions encodified in *The Great Gatsby*. The crowd nodded in approval, and occasionally dared to murmur. Roth figured the time was right to make his presence known. "I say, Mr. Spence, didn't some editor supposedly say, 'Fitzgerald, get rid of that Gatsby clown and you'll have yourself a good book'?"

All eyes turned to Roth and then back to Spence. The writer looked at Roth as if measuring the reach of an adversary. Then Spence smiled. "Purely apocryphal. Though it contains the seeds of possibility. Sir William Roth, is it?"

"Yes, a pleasure to meet you, my good man," Roth said, extending his hand. A tingle of pleasure surged through him as the "little people" oohed and aahed at this meeting of the gods.

Spence polished off his drink and handed the empty glass to his shapely companion. "So what do you think of my analysis of Gatsby?"

"Scintillating. And I agree that Wolfe's book is absolute poppycock." Out of the corner of his eye, Roth watched the girl's shimmering rear as she walked to the bar.

Spence turned away from his admirers and squared off with Roth. The photographer nudged Spence toward the corner of the room. The crowd took its cue and broke into small groups, some stepping onto the porch for smokes, others refilling their drinks.

"What brings you to Korban Manor, Mr. Roth?"

Roth rolled his scotch-and-water between his hands. "Business, sir. Always business with me."

"The devil, you say. That's just what the world needs, another four hundred negatives of this place. Or are you hired for a publicity shoot?"

"I'm freelancing."

"Hmmph. I'm working, too, if you can believe it."

Roth knew that Spence hadn't finished a novel in years. He had blustered his way through some opinion pieces and essays, and had penned a scathing introduction to *The New Southern Voices Collection* that had likely driven some of the anthology's contributors to tears. The critics had given him up. He was like a beached whale—fun to poke while blood could be drawn, but shunned after becoming a bloated, gassy corpse.

"I would think this place would be rather inspiring for a man of your genius," Roth said, barely disguising the taunt.

Spence didn't rise to the bait. He'd probably read too many of his publisher's press releases, the ones that kept promising a coming masterpiece. "This is the one, Mr. Roth. This is the work that will earn the Nobel Prize for Literature. It's about time an American brought home that particular piece of hardware. Nothing personal, mind you."

Roth turned up one palm in submission. His British accent had fooled even Spence, a man who had trained himself to observe human behavior. Spence's girlfriend brought the writer his drink, put it in his hand, and dutifully returned to his shadow.

Roth smiled at her and then began the laborious task of drawing Spence into his trust.

CHAPTER 6

I'm a ghoulie-chasing fool.

Anna let the yellow beam of the flashlight lead her as if she had no will of her own. She found herself heading up a forest trail, onto one of the narrower worn paths crowded by laurel. The waxy leaves brushed against her face and hands. Crickets and katydids launched their choruses from the obscurity of the dark forest.

You follow and you follow and you never catch up. You reach out and they dance away. You run and they run faster. You look in the dark and see nothing but darkness.

Ghosts played by their own rules. Anna had a hunch that ghosts didn't need to unravel secrets, didn't demand explanations. Life's great mysteries must mean very little to those no longer living. Undoubtedly all spirits received the necessary explanations as a gift to welcome them to the afterlife. But perhaps the dead needed amusement. Eternity surely got tedious after a while.

Anna wasn't worried about getting lost in the woods, even though Korban Manor's lighted windows had disappeared from view. After leaving the house, she'd stopped by the barn and found four horses in their stalls. She had massaged their necks and stroked the bristling hairs above their noses.

She was comforted by their warm animal smell. The aroma of straw and manure brought back memories of one of her foster families, who had kept a farm in West Virginia. Anna had grown into a woman that summer. Her first sexual experience was with the handsome but dull boy who came every other day to collect the eggs. She'd also spent hours in the weedy local cemetery, sitting among the crumbling, illegible markers, wondering about the people under the ground and the part of them that might have survived the crush of dirt and decay.

And still she wondered, her curiosity sending her into anthropology at Duke University and parapsychology at the Rhine Research Center, and now out into the night woods. Roads that never ended, a seeking that never found. The moon and a sprinkle of starlight gave vague shape to the landscape. She followed the ridge to the point where the ground sloped rapidly away. Boulders gleamed like bad teeth in the weak light. Beyond the field of stone was a yawning gap of black valley, dusted silver by an early frost.

The ribs and ripples of the Blue Ridge Mountains rolled out toward the horizon, the distant twinkle of the town of Black Rock set among them like blue and orange jewels. A jet's winking red light cut a dotted line in the east. A little flying tin can of humanity, some passengers probably afraid of a crash, some munching stale peanuts, others longing for a cigarette. Most with thoughts of relatives, spouses, and lovers recently visited or waiting at airport terminals ahead.

All with places to go, things to look forward to. People to belong to. Hopes, dreams, futures. Life. She thought of that Shirley Jackson line, "Journeys end in lovers meeting."

Yeah, right. Journeys end in death, and lovers never meet.

She turned from the lights that were starting to blur in her vision and put aside her self-pity. She had a forest to explore. And she felt a tingle in her gut, an instinct that she had learned to trust even if Stephen couldn't prove it was real. There were dead among these trees and hills.

She sometimes wondered if the cancer was a progression of that instinct. As if death were her true natural state, and life was only an interruption to be briefly endured. As if, by rights, she belonged to the dead, and that her sense of them grew stronger the closer she got to becoming one of them.

That was morbid thinking. Still, she couldn't ignore the Jungian symbolism of turning her back on those dim, distant lights of civilization to enter the dark forest alone. In search of herself.

This is my life's work. If I can leave just one thing behind, if I can shed a little light into the ignorant and blind caves of the human consciousness, then maybe it's worth it. Or maybe I'm more vain than any artist, politician, or religious zealot in thinking that my beliefs matter.

Wouldn't it be nice to love, to belong, to be connected? To know that there was more to your time of breathing than the rush toward its end? What if it WERE possible to meet another spirit, touch someone, share the science of souls, to create something that has a life beyond living and dying? Or is such wishing only a more grotesque form of vanity?

She stared at the cone of battery-powered light as it bobbed ahead of her on the trail. The older she got, and the closer to death and the deeper into her search she found herself, the more alone she became. And if there was anything that frightened her, that *could* frighten someone who had seen ghosts, it was the thought that any soul or consciousness or life force that continued beyond death would do so alone, forever isolated, forever lost.

Anna figured she was about a mile from the manor now. She was beginning to tire. That was one of the things she hated most about her illness. Her strength was slowly draining away, slipping from this life into the next.

She paused and played the flashlight along the ridge ahead of her. Night noises crept from beneath the canopy of hardwoods, the stirring of nocturnal animals and the restless mountain wind. A breath of pine-cleansed air and the cold dampness of the early twilight revived her. The trail had intersected with several larger ones, and she had earlier crossed another wagon road. She followed her instinct, the one that carried her through the night like the moon pulled a restless tide.

The trail widened under a copse of balsams, then opened onto a meadow of thick grass. A shack overlooked the clearing, frail and wobbly on its stilts of stacked rock. A crumbling chimney, gray in the dim starlight, penetrated the slanted tin roof. The glass sheets of the windows were like dark eyes watching for company.

This was what Anna had been sent to find. She waded through the meadow, her pants cuffs soaked by the frosted grains of grass. A large rounded stone was set at the foot of the porch, as pale as the belly of a fish. She stepped on the stone and peered into the dark doorway.

The house wanted her.

Maybe not the house, but whoever had lived and then died here. Something had bound a human soul to this place, an event terrible enough to leave a psychic imprint, much the way light burned through the emulsion on a photographic negative.

The air hummed with inaudible music. The tiny hairs on the back of Anna's neck stood like magnetized needles. Despite the chill of night, her armpits were sweaty. A preternatural fear coursed through her veins, threatening to override her curiosity.

Something hovered beyond the door, wispy and frail as if unfamiliar with its own substance.

Or perhaps it was only the wind blowing through some chink in the board-and-batten walls.

Anna shined the flashlight on a knothole just above the door handle. A flicker of white shadow filled the hole, then dissolved.

Anna put her other foot on the stone porch. A form, a face, imprinted itself in the grain of the door.

A small voice skirled in on the wind, soft and hollow as a distant flute: "I've been waiting."

Anna fought the urge to run. Though she *believed* in ghosts, the sudden strangeness of encountering one always hit her like a dash of ice water. And this one . . . this one *talked.*

Anna backed away, the flashlight fixed on the door.

"Don't go," came the cold and hollow voice. Anna's muscles froze. She fought with her own body as her heartbeat thundered in her ears. The voice came again, smaller, pleading: "Please."

It was a child's voice. Anna's fear mixed with sympathy, melded into a need to comprehend. Did young ghosts stay young forever?

Anna stepped up onto the porch. The boards creaked under her feet. Something fluttered under the eaves and then joined the night sky. A bat.

"What do you want?" Anna said, trying to keep the tremor out of her voice. Her flashlight beam on the door revealed only wood and rusted hardware.

"Are you her?"

"Her?"

"Help me," came the plaintive voice again, fading now, almost lost. "Help us."

Anna lifted the iron catch and pushed the door open, playing the flashlight's beam into the house.

She glimpsed a tiny figure, a young face outlined by long locks of hair, a few folds of soft fabric flowing beneath the begging eyes. The threads of the vision were unraveling.

"Stay," Anna said, both a request and a desperate command.

But the shape faded, the ghostly lips parted as if to speak, and then there were only the eyes, floating, floating, becoming wisps of lesser shadow, then nothing. The eyes had burned into Anna's memory. She would never forget them. The eyes had looked—*haunted.*

"Hello?" Anna called. The word died in the hollow shell of the shack. She moved the light across the room. A few shelves stood to one side, a rough beam of wood spanning the black opening of the fireplace. A long table marked off what had been the kitchen area. A row of crude, hand-carved figurines stood on the table, their gnarled limbs protruding at grotesque angles.

Anna touched one of the figurines. It was about a foot tall, not lacquered or painted, the wood dark and bone-dry with age. The body was made from a chopped root, the arms and legs shaped from twisted jackvine. The head was a wrinkled piece of fruit, brown like dried apple, the eyes and mouth set in a deformed grin.

They appeared to be folk art, something an early Scots-Irish mountain settler had carved during long winter nights to amuse the children. But the figurines were arrayed on the table like religious relics. One was wrapped in a peeling sheet of birch bark that appeared to emulate a dress. Another wore a garland of dried and dead flowers.

Anna shined the flashlight on the nearest stooped statue. The crude opening of the mouth held a gray, papery substance. Anna scratched at it with her fingernail and it fell to the table. Anna identified the object instantly by its mottled markings and coarse, pebbly grain.

Snakeskin.

Anna moved behind the table, facing in the same direction as the figurines. An old fireplace was directly across the room, its stones blackened by the smoke of ten thousand fires. The heap of ashes gave no evidence of when the fireplace was last used. The corners of the room were thick with cobwebs, which drifted like diaphanous sails against the breeze that leaked through the log walls.

One upper half of the room was covered by a loft. Anna climbed the rickety ladder, but saw only thick dust and the scattering of leaves that marked a rodent's nest.

She was checking the primitive kitchen when she heard a noise outside. The moonlight at the window was briefly interrupted. Had the ghost returned?

Anna ran outside, holding the flashlight at chest level. A stooped human form crossed the meadow, heading for the thicket of hardwoods behind the shack. A ragged shawl trailed out behind the figure in the night wind that had arisen.

"Wait!" Anna took a step and tripped over a loose piece of planking. She tumbled off the porch and landed on her wrist in the packed dirt. An electric shock of pain raced up her arm. By the time she got to her feet and collected her flashlight, the person or thing had disappeared into the black trees.

Anna followed. When she reached the edge of the

forest, she waited and strained her ears. The night made a hundred sounds: the wind moaning through the branches, limbs squeaking, leaves scraping against bark, animals disturbed from sleep, unseen birds chittering. Any hope of hearing footfalls was futile.

It must have been human. Anna sensed no ethereal thread she could follow. She wondered if the person in the shawl had also seen the ghost. Or was it someone who had arranged the primitive figurines in a strange mockery of ritual? Had she really seen the ghost or was she victim of an elaborate trick? Was she so desperate to find proof of afterlife that her own mind was deceiving her?

Anna rubbed her wrist for a moment. No one, not even Anna herself, had known her destination that night. The ghost had been real, she was certain. The figurines were probably the handiwork of one of the manor's guests and left behind as a gift or tribute. Or maybe it had been the idle tomfoolery of one of the manor's workers.

She turned to follow the flashlight back toward Korban Manor, bothered by the strange sensation that she was heading home.

She realized why she had come to Korban Manor. She had been fooled into thinking it had been her choice, that she needed to make contact for her own reasons. Out of all the reputedly haunted places she could have spent her final days, she hadn't simply picked this mountain estate. She hadn't dreamed of this place because of some long-forgotten paranormal journal she had once read.

No, she had been *summoned.*

The snapping of a twig brought her out of her reverie. Something large emerged from the forest shadows. Anna raised the flashlight, ready to use it as a club if necessary. The beam flashed across the looming black shape.

"You!" she said.

Mason held up his hands as if to ward off her anger. "I saw her."

"The ghost?"

"What ghost? I saw an old woman spying on you, then she took off running through the woods. I tried to follow her but she must know these old trails pretty well."

"How dare you follow me? What are you, some kind of slimy pervert stalker?"

"No, I just . . . well, Miss Mamie's little party was boring me to death, and I couldn't help being curious after all that talk about ghost stories. When I saw you leave the manor—"

"You arrogant bastard." She shoved past him and headed down the trail, not caring that she was leaving him in darkness. She only wished that ghosts really *were* evil, so that one might bite off his stupid oversize head. With any luck, he'd wander off the trail and have to spend the night in the forest, then wake up cold, sore, and miserable. She broke into a run and told herself it was the wind and not anger and embarrassment that filled her eyes with tears.

Miss Mamie took off her pearls and placed them on the dresser among the purple velvet ribbons and bottles of rosewater. She looked in the mirror, bringing the lamp closer so she could check her skin. Anyone seeing the faint beginnings of wrinkles around her mouth and the streaks of silver at her temples would think she was fifty years old. Not bad, considering she was going on a hundred and twenty.

Ephram had promised to keep her young. Ephram always kept his promises. He was the perfect gentleman. That was what had first attracted her, why she'd fallen in love with him. His was a complete and perfect possession.

She opened the locket attached to her necklace. Inside the locket was Ephram's young face in sepia, with its sharp cheeks, a narrow angle of nose, thick beard and sideburns burgeoning over a high stiff collar. Oh, and those dark eyes, those cold, burning eyes that had swept her heart away and caged her soul, that had sparked the tinder of her desire. He'd always had power, even back when he was a mortal.

But now, *now* . . .

"Now we are ready," he said from the mirror. "Just as I promised."

Her heart accelerated and her palms grew moist. She placed a hand on the mirror's smooth surface. Ephram's face coalesced in the reflection of the firelight. A row of peeled apples hung drying on a string by the fire, carved into heads, with protruding ears and noses. The eyes and mouths glistened like scars. The faces would take shape as they dried, taking on their own unique features.

"How do you like them?" she asked.

"You've chosen well." Ephram's voice was low and sibilant.

"They will feed you, given time." Miss Mamie looked into those seductive eyes. She felt a flush of warmth. Her love had never faltered.

Her dead husband's eyes flared in a storm of red and gold. "Even now, their dreams give me strength. And the blue moon is coming again."

"Just like the night you died."

"Please, my love. You know I don't favor that word. It sounds so . . . permanent."

"What about Sylva?" Miss Mamie said, lowering her eyes, anticipating his anger.

"What of her? She's just an old witch-woman with a sack of feathers, weeds, and old bones. Her power is nothing but the pathetic power of suggestion. But *mine*"—his voice rose, thunderous, until she was afraid that the guests upstairs might hear—"mine is the power that shapes *both* sides."

"So many years." Miss Mamie ran her hands over the neckline of her lace nightgown. "I don't know if I can wait much longer."

"Patience, my heart's love. These are special. These are true makers. They carve me, they write me, they draw me into life. Their hands give me shape, their minds give me substance. They make me just as you make them. And soon, Margaret—"

Ephram reached up through the mist that swirled inside the mirror and placed his palm against the glass. Miss Mamie put her fingers on the mirror, craving the cruel and arousing electricity of his touch. Her dead husband smiled.

"Soon all those we have sacrificed will find their home, their true eternal life, in me. I will have what any lord and master deserves."

"What any lord and master deserves," she repeated in a whisper. Then the mists faded. Ephram collapsed into an ethereal smoke, and the mirror was again clear.

She studied her own face. She was a lucky woman. Her own hopes and dreams were about to be reborn. Soon Ephram could escape the mirror, these walls, this house. Soon she could touch his flesh again.

She went to bed, alone with her lust. *Patience,* she told herself. Ephram had promised her. And Ephram always kept his promises.

CHAPTER 7

"I need something stronger."

"You ain't supposed to come out here in broad daylight, Ransom. What if somebody seen you?"

"I'm scared. I ain't coming out here in the dark. It's bad enough when you can *see,* and it's getting worse."

"Was you followed?"

"Not by none of the guests. Miss Mamie told them they ain't allowed up Beechy Gap. But the others"—Ransom lowered his voice and hunched his head as if afraid that the cabin's knotty walls were listening—"you know, *them*—they's everywheres now."

Sylva Hartley bent and spat into her fireplace. The liquid hissed and cracked, then evaporated against the flaming logs. She ran the back of her leathery hand against her shriveled mouth. She looked past Ransom, staring down the decades that were as dark as the smoky stones beneath the hearth.

"Lord knows it's getting worse," she finally said in agreement. She pulled her frayed shawl up around her neck.

"The last charm worked right fair for a while. Kept

them scared off. But now, they just laugh at me when I do my warding."

Sylva thought Ransom ought to have a little more faith. That was the key: faith. All the charms in the world didn't amount to a hill of beans if you didn't *believe.* Ransom had been raised Christian, and that was all fine and dandy. But when you got right down to it, some things were older and ran deeper than religion.

It was too bad about George Lawson. George was an outsider, not born on the mountain. He didn't know what he was up against. With the proper charms, he might have dodged Ephram's little games.

But maybe not. Ransom was right. They were getting stronger. Ephram was getting stronger. And now George was on their side, too. Along with all the other people Ephram had fetched over in the last hundred years.

"You mind flipping them johnny cakes?" she said.

Ransom crossed the floor of the cabin to the little blue steel cookstove. He turned the cakes in the skillet. The smell of scorched cornmeal filled the room.

"They don't stay invisible no more," he said, his back to her. "It used to be just Korban, and you only seen him in the Big House once in a while. But the others, they been *walkin'.*"

"The blue moon in October. A time of magic. Right magic and wrong magic."

"What are you gonna do?" Ransom's voice trembled.

She didn't blame him for being scared. She was scared, too, but she didn't dare let it show. "First off, I'm going to have me a bite to eat. After that, I guess we'll just have to see what the cat drug in."

Ransom handed her a plate made of hammered tin. He had laid a fried piece of side pork beside the johnny cakes. Liquid fat pooled in the bottom of the plate and dripped out a small hole in the metal. Sylva put the plate on one arm of her rocker so the grease wouldn't stain her clothes.

"It's the people, ain't it?" Ransom asked, the firelight glittering in his eyes. "The people staying at the Big House."

Sylva said nothing, just worked the pig gristle between the stumps of her teeth. There was a generous hunk of meat in the fat. Ransom always made sure she got one of the better slabs whenever they slaughtered and smoked one of the manor's hogs. She figured she ate almost as well as the fancy guests.

She swallowed the pork, then drained a cup of sassafras tea. Finally, she spoke, gazing into the fire, at the yellow and orange and bright blue. "It's the people. And the girl. The one with the Sight."

Even though her voice was soft, the words were as thick as thunder in the damp air of the cabin. The whole forest had grown quiet, as if the trees were bending in to listen. She was sure a catbird had been warbling out a happy sunrise song only minutes before.

"First he claimed the dead ones, now he's going after the live ones," Ransom said. "They's got to be some kind of ritual or other you can use against him."

"You forget. We got to play by the rules. But Ephram Korban, he ain't beholden to nothing. Not man nor God nor none of my little bags of stoneroot and bear teeth and hawk feathers."

Ransom touched the pocket of his coveralls.

"But just keep right on believin'," she said. "The ashes of a prayer are mightier than the highest flames of hell."

"I'd best be getting back. Got the livestock to tend to. And Miss Mamie's been watching me awful close."

"Get on, then."

"You sure you'll be okay?"

"Been okay all along, ain't I? But it's good to be looking out for each other."

Ransom nodded. His face was in the shadows beyond the reach of the firelight and she wasn't able to see his expression. The sun filled the room as he opened the door and went outside. She winced at the intruding light and waited for the sound of the falling wooden latch. Then she turned her gaze back to the fire and forked up another chunk of corn cake.

The fire . . .

If only they had listened to Sylva's mother. She had tried to warn everybody about the strange Yankee with the well-bottom eyes and the pocketful of money and the sneer that lurked between his lips, the snakish smile that you only saw when he'd let you.

But they fell under Ephram Korban's spell, the menfolk who were after the jobs he promised, the women who came calling on him while their men were out clearing trees or sawing firewood or laying stone walls. None of those women were able to resist him for long. Even the children were drawn to him. Whenever Korban got a few of the young ones together, he would throw a penny on the ground just to watch them scratch and claw each other as they fought over it.

Sylva's mother had resisted Ephram. At least that's what she always told Sylva. But Sylva herself, she went to work in the manor when she was just fourteen. Daddy made her. Said you was never too young to learn the pain and glory of a hard day's work, that there was no reason to laze around the house while he had to get up before the roosters and mix sulfur-and-lime solution to spray on the apple trees.

She started out keeping the manor's fireplace ashes swept up, then was put in charge of the laundry as well. Her spine ached with the memory of hauling those big woven baskets a quarter mile down to the creek, where a barrel of lye-water would be waiting. She'd let the clothes soak a while, then drag them dripping and heavy up to the top of the washboard. Up and down, over and over, while the alkaline ate away at her skin.

And heaven help her if she got a cut. That soapy juice burned like a slice of hellfire.

Sylva looked down at her knotty fingers, at the burls of her knuckles. The scars still wove among the blue road maps of her veins. These same hands had betrayed her, all because she had to touch the fire.

Ephram always had to have a fire blazing. The men were ordered to keep the firebox in the back room full at all times. One hired helper was assigned to the furnace room downstairs to make sure the main chimney stayed stoked around the clock. But all the other fireplaces had be lit, too, even in the summer. And, as one of the house girls, Sylva was responsible for the fireplaces on the second floor.

That meant going into the master bedroom. She had always hated the room, especially at night when, as her last and most dreaded chore, she carried an armful of heavy oak and ash and white pine to the fire. She would rest the logs on the hearth, then pile them stick by stick on the bed of embers. She tried to concentrate on her work, but she couldn't help looking around at all the fine things, the oval cut-edged mirror over the bureau, the velvet drapes that plunged from the top of the windows like lush purple waterfalls, the soft silk lace rimming the edge of the poster bed.

She had touched that lace, of course. She knew the fabrics of the master bed better than anyone. She had seen the secrets written in the stains of sleep, and her job was to scrub them away. To erase all hint of corruption.

Sometimes the mistress would already be in bed when Sylva came in. Margaret would watch her without speaking, a little smile of triumph on her face that she tried to hide behind the books she pretended to read. Sylva mumbled "yes'm" or "no'm" if Margaret said anything.

Ephram himself was never in the bedroom during her nightly stoking. She called him "Ephram" in her secret heart of hearts, but she wouldn't dare call him that aloud. No, he was "master" or "sir" or, in a pinch, "Mr. Korban." She had wondered if he ever slept. Some of the help said he paced the widow's walk, especially when the moon was near full. They said his shadow stretched two miles across the mountains in every direction. Even then, the whispers had started.

But young Sylva didn't believe the rumors, of how he laughed whenever one of the horses threw a rider, how he made the hog and cattle butchers save a pail of fresh blood in the springhouse, how he burned black candles in the dark of the basement when the only sound in the sleeping manor was the whisper of the grandfather clock's pendulum. They said that if you passed him in the dead of night, his eyes changed colors, gold, red, then yellow, the shades of fire. But that was what the men said. The house girls said other things, which Sylva equally refused to believe.

Until the night his fire went out.

Sylva had been late, her mother had a fever and Sylva had to feed her little brother and sister. Daddy was gone overnight, taking a wagon load of apples down the narrow trail that was really just a long scar in the side of the cliffs. So Sylva had whipped up some porridge, splashed it out into two bowls for the children, then changed the herb poultice on her mother's forehead. By that time, the fingers of dusk were scratching at the frosty November ground.

Sylva ran the half mile to the manor, holding her skirts high, her breath silver in the twilight. The briars whipped at her knees and her long hair tangled in the laurel that lined the trail. She knew the way well enough, but she felt as if she were slogging through molasses. The manor seemed to be slipping farther away from her, as if the snake-belly trail had gained new curves.

Sylva finally reached the house, her heart lodged in her throat and her pulse hammering. She quietly gathered some logs from the firebox and crept up the back stairs. She remembered that Margaret was away on a trip somewhere, to a place called Baton Rouge, fancy-sounding. If only Sylva could hurry, maybe no one would notice her tardiness.

The bedroom was dark. She was afraid to light a lantern because, if any guests were visiting, one of them might look in. Sylva closed the door behind her, hoping the embers still cast enough glow for her to see. But the hearthstones were cold and the room was filled with the pungent stench of the spent fire.

Kneeling, she put the wood on the floor and groped for the newspapers and the tin box of matches that she kept beside the poker. Even sheltered from the cold night air, she felt smothered as if by the waters of a deep dream, and the smallest movement took a great effort. The matches rattled when she knocked over the container. She balled up some pages of the newspaper and stuffed them under the fire irons. As she did, a harsh, low sound came from somewhere in the room.

She struck a match and it flared briefly and died. In that split second of light, she had seen movement out of the corner of her eye. Trying to hurry, though gravity worked against her, she struck another match. A winter wind blew across the room and extinguished the flame before she could touch it to the paper.

She wondered why the windows were open. Ephram never allowed the windows open in his room. Her fingers were like water skins as she fumbled for another match. The low sound came again, a rattling exhalation followed by the unmistakable creak of the poster bed. She squeezed her eyes closed, even though the room was pitch-black, and concentrated on the match that she wanted to scratch across a stone. The dark had never frightened her until that moment.

A voice came, muffled and desperate and everything but dead.

"Fuh . . . fire," it said.

Sylva's heart gave a jump like a frightened rabbit. Ephram Korban was in the room, in the bed. She dared not look in his direction, but the same power that seemed to be weighing down her limbs made her neck turn slowly toward the bed. She opened her eyes and saw nothing but blackness.

"Spell me," he said, a little more forcefully, almost angrily, but still muffled as if speaking through blankets. She nodded slowly, though he couldn't see her in the dark. Nor could she see him. And yet . . .

As she looked at the bed, its form taking shape in her mind from the memory of it, she could picture Ephram lying there, his face stern and his hair and beard flowing onto the pillows. Handsome Ephram, who had never been sick. Ephram, who stayed young and strong while the workers and natives had faded away with their wrinkles and stories and tired, failing breath. Ephram, who was said to never sleep.

Two small dots of light hovered in the darkness of the bed, weakly glowing, the only thing in the room she could see. She tried to turn her head away, tried to strike the match, even though she had now been pulled from mere waking sleep to a helpless awareness. She knew which side of the bed was his. The dots expanded, hovering in the area near the headboard where the pillows were. Where Ephram's eyes should be.

The eyes smoldered the deep red color of a dying ember.

"Call in the fire," he rasped, as a sharp flicker of yellow glinted among the red dots. The glowing eyes blurred in her tears, then she jerked the matchstick along the stone. It caught and she applied the flame to the paper. At last she could look away from that terrible bed, those impossible eyes. But she had to say those awful words, the ones Mama had taught her.

The spell.

She whispered them, hoping to weaken their power through lack of volume. "Go out frost, come in fire. Go out frost, come in fire. Go out frost, come in fire."

The fire leapt to life and she put some kindling on the grate. As the wood crackled and heat cascaded onto her face, she found that her limbs were regaining their strength.

Not daring to turn now that the room was bathed in firelight, she busied herself stacking a night's supply of logs onto the irons. Her tears had dried on her cheeks, but she felt their salty tracks. She was afraid she was in trouble, that she had committed the most unforgivable of offenses. She could only stare into the flames as they rose like yellow and red and blue water up the chimney.

A hand fell softly on her shoulder. She looked up, and Ephram was standing above her. He was smiling. His eyes were deep and dark and beautiful, alive in the firelight. How silly she had been, thinking them to be red.

"I'm sorry," she said, her words barely audible over the snapping of the hot logs and the hammering of her heart.

Ephram said nothing, only moved his hand from her shoulder to her cheek, then up under her long hair until his thumb brushed her ear. She shivered even though the fire was roaring.

"Thank you," he said. "We burn together."

She didn't understand, all she knew was that she had wished for this moment so many times while lying on her straw mattress back home. Those dreams had come to her, taken over her body, brought her skin alive. Ephram's hands on her flesh. But in her fantasies, she hadn't been this scared.

Then she realized what was wrong. He was behind her and above her, his face lit by the fire. She was kneeling on the hearth, looking up. But, somehow, his shadow was on her face. She couldn't fix on the thought, couldn't make sense of it, because other sensations were flooding her. His fervid hand traced the soft slope of her neck.

And again Sylva was smothered in a dream, only under a different power this time, as she rose and let him put his arms around her, as the hellish heat of his lips pressed against hers. She was lost in his warmth, his strength, his great shadow. When he took her hand in his and brought it to the flames, she didn't whimper or beg. He was the master, after all.

Their hands went into the flames, merged, combusted, and skin and bone were replaced by smoke and ash. There was no pain. How could there not be pain?

The next thing she knew, she was removing her coarse house-girl skirt and homespun blouse and they merged once more, this time on the floor in front of the fire, the spell lost from her lips, and only Ephram in her senses.

Sylva looked down at her withered hands.

If only she had felt pain. The wounds without pain were the slowest in healing.

The tin plate sat empty in her lap. The fire had gone out. She shivered and spat into the ashes. She wasn't sure which pain was greater, Ephram's loving or his leaving her.

She had known Ephram would come back. But then, he had never really left. He didn't die when she had pushed him off the widow's walk. He just went into the house. Because she'd killed him under the October blue moon.

As he had promised, wood and stone became his flesh, the smoke his breath and the mirrors his eyes, the shadows his restless spirit's blood. And his heart burned in the fires of forever.

She shivered in the heat of the day and reached for the matches.

CHAPTER 8

The house threw a sunrise shadow across the backyard. Mason was tired, his face scratched from his midnight wanderings. He'd slept poorly, his brain invaded by feverish images of Anna, his mother, Ephram Korban, Lilith, a dozen others whose faces were lost in smoke. He shivered as he walked behind the manor, following the worn path that wound between two outbuildings. He climbed a row of creosote railroad ties that were terraced into the earth as steps leading into the forest.

The door on the smaller building was open. An old man in overalls emerged from the darkness within. Mason waved a greeting. The man rubbed his hands together, his breath coming out in a mist.

"Brrr," he said, creasing his wrinkled jaws. "Cold as a woman's heart in there."

"What is it?" Mason asked. He'd assumed it was a tool storage shed or something similar. The shed, like its larger counterpart, was constructed of rough-cut logs and chinked with yellowish red cement. A smell of damp age and cedar spilled from the doorway.

“ ’Frigeration,” the man said. When his mouth opened on the “gee” sound, Mason saw that the old man had about enough teeth left to play a quick game of jacks. His overalls threatened to swallow him, his back hunched from years of work. The man cocked his head back toward the door and went into the shed. “Take a look-see.”

Mason followed. Cold air wafted over his face. A mound covered the center of the dirt floor. The old man stooped down and swept at the grainy mound with his hands, revealing streaks of shiny silver.

“Ice,” said the man. “We bury it under sawdust so it will keep through summer. You wouldn’t think it would last that long, would you?”

“I wondered how you kept the food cold without power,” Mason said. “What about the food safety police, the health inspectors?”

“They’s rules of the world and then they’s rules of Korban Manor. Two different things.”

The old man pointed through the door to a western rise covered by tulip poplars. Wagon tracks crossed the meadow, curving up the slope like twin red snakes. “They’s a little pond up yonder,” he said. “A spring pops out ’twixt two rocks. The pond’s fenced off from the animals so it stays clean. Come the third or fourth long freeze in January, when the water’s good and hard, we go up and cut out big blocks of it.”

“Sounds like a lot of work. I understand that heavy machinery isn’t allowed on the grounds.”

“Oh, we got machines. A wagon is a machine. So’s a horse, in its way. And, of course, they got *us,* too.”

Mason went out into the sun and the man closed the door behind him. His gnarled hand fumbled in the front pocket of his overalls as if he were looking for a cigarette. He pulled out something that looked like a knotted rag with a tip of feather protruding from one end. He waved the rag in the sign of the cross over the front of the icehouse door. The motion was practiced and fluid, appearing natural despite its oddness.

Mason expected the man to comment on the ritual, but the knotted rag was quickly squirreled away. "What's in the other shed?" Mason asked after a moment.

"That's the larder. Keep stuff in there that doesn't need to be so cold, such as squash and cucumbers and corn. A little spring runs through there, gets piped out into the gully yonder."

Mason looked where the man had pointed and saw a trickle of water meandering through a bed of rich, black mud. Blackberry briars tangled along the creek banks, the scarlet vines bent in autumn's death. "Do you pick the berries, too?"

"Yep, and the apples. They's hells of apples around here. You gonna have something apple every meal. Pie, turnovers, stewed, fried apples with cinnamon and just a dash of brandy. We keep up a vegetable garden, too, and—"

"Ransom!"

They both turned at the sound of the shrill voice. Miss Mamie stood on the back porch, leaning over the railing.

"Yes, Miss Mamie," the man responded. The last bit of starch seemed to have gone out of him, and Mason was sure the old man was going to disappear inside his overalls.

"Now, Ransom, you know you're not to trouble the guests," Miss Mamie said in a high, artificially cheerful tone.

"I was just—" Ransom swelled momentarily, then seemed to think better of it. He studied the tips of his worn work boots. The sun lit the silver wires of hair that were combed back over his balding head. "Yes, Miss Mamie."

The hostess stood triumphantly at the porch rail and turned her attention to Mason. "Did you sleep well, Mr. Jackson?"

"Yes, ma'am," he lied. He sneaked a glance at Ransom. The man looked as if he'd been beaten with a hickory rod. "Um . . . thanks for setting me up in the master bedroom. It's very comfortable."

"Lovely." She clasped her hands together. Her pearls shifted over her bosom. "Ephram Korban would be so pleased. You know our motto: 'The splendid isolation of Korban Manor will fire the imagination and kindle the creative spirit.' "

"I read the brochure," Mason said. "And I've already got a few ideas. I might need a little help getting started, though. Is it okay if Ransom helps me collect some good sculpting wood?"

Miss Mamie frowned and her thin eyebrows flattened. Her face wore the same expression that glared from the portraits of Korban. Mason realized he had challenged her authority, if only mildly. He was suddenly sorry he had dragged Ransom into the spotlight of her stare. She folded her arms like a schoolmarm debating the punishment of unruly students.

After a moment, she said, "Of course it's okay. As long as his chores are finished. Are your chores finished, Ransom?"

Ransom kept his eyes down. "Yes, ma'am. I'm done till dinner. Then I got to curry the horses and see to the produce."

Miss Mamie smiled and adopted her cheerful voice again. "Lovely. And that sculpture better be perfect, Mr. Jackson. We're counting on you."

"I'm kindled and fired up," Mason said. "By the way, is there a space where I can work without bothering anybody? Sometimes I work late, and there's no way to beat up wood without making enough noise to wake the dead."

"There's a studio space in the basement. I'll have Lilith show you after lunch."

"No need to bother her. I'm sure she'll be busy with the other guests. Why not let Ransom show me?"

A shadow passed across Miss Mamie's face and her voice grew cold. "Ransom doesn't go down there."

Mason peeked at Ransom and saw the corner of the man's mouth twitch. *My God. He's scared to death of her.*

Miss Mamie turned back toward the manor, her heels clattering across the wooden porch. Door chimes jingled as she went inside. Ransom exhaled as if he had been holding his breath for the last few minutes.

"What a wonderful boss," Mason said when Ransom finally looked him in the eye.

"Careful," he said out of the side of his mouth. "She's probably watching from one of the windows."

"You're kidding."

"Just follow me," he whispered, then said, more loudly, "Toolshed's right through them trees."

After they had gone down a side trail far enough that the house was out of sight, Mason asked, "Is she always like that?"

Ransom's confidence grew as they moved farther from the house. "Oh, she don't mean nothing. That's just her way, is all. Everything's got to be just so. And she got worries of her own."

"How long have you worked here, Ransom? You don't mind if I call you 'Ransom,' do you?"

"Respect for elders. I like that, Mr. Jackson."

"Call me Mason, because I hope we're going to be friends."

Ransom looked back down the trail. "Only *outside* the house, son. Only outside."

"Got you."

"Anyways, you was asking how long I've been working here, and the answer to that is 'Always.' I was born here, in a little cabin just over the orchards. Place called Beechy Gap. Same cabin my grandpaw was born in, and my daddy, too. Cabin's still standing."

"They all worked here?"

"Yep. Grandpaw held deed to the north part, way back when Korban started buying up property around here. Grandpaw sold out and got a job thrown in as part of the deal. I guess us Streaters always been tied to the land, one way or another. Family history has it that my great-back-to-however-many-greats-grandpaw Jeremiah Streater was one of the first settlers in this part of the country. Came up with Daniel Boone, they say."

"Did Boone live here, too?"

"Well, he tried to. Kept a hunting cabin down around the foot of the mountain. But they took his land. They always take your land, see?"

Ransom didn't sound bitter. He said it as if it were a universal truth, something you could count on no matter what. The sun comes up, the rooster crows, the dew dries, they take your land.

"Toolshed's over yonder," Ransom said, heading for a clearing in a stand of poplars. He continued with his storytelling, the rhythm of his words matching the stride of his thin legs.

"Grandpaw went to work right away for Korban, clearing orchard land and cutting the roads. Him and two of my uncles. They leveled with shovels and stumped with iron bars and a team of mules. Korban was crazy about firewood right from the start. Had them saw up the trees with big old cross-saws and pile the logs up beside the road.

"And Korban had a landscape scheme all laid out. People thought he was a little touched in the head, wanting to turn this scrubby old mountain into some kind of king's place. But the money was green enough. Korban paid a dollar a day, which was unheard of at the time. He was big in textiles."

"I've worked in textiles myself," Mason said. "Can't say I ever got too big in it, though. I mostly just swapped out spindles for minimum wage."

"No need to be ashamed of honest work." Ransom paused and looked in the direction of a crow's call. The smell of moist leaves and forest rot filled Mason's nostrils. He noticed himself breathing harder than the old man, who was nearly three times his age. Ransom began walking again and continued with his story.

"When they got the road gouged out, they set to work on the bridge. In the old days, the only way to get up here was a trail that wound up the south face of those cliffs. You seen that drop-off driving up here."

"Yeah. Down to the bottom of the world." Mason's stomach fluttered at the remembered majesty and terror of the view. He was embarrassed by his shortness of breath and tried to hide it.

"That trail was how the early pioneers, Boone and Jeremiah and a handful of others, made it up in the first place. They say the Cherokee and Catawba used it before that, communal hunting grounds. The whites brought livestock up here, fighting and pushing the animals along the cliffs. But Korban wanted a bridge. And what Korban wanted, Korban always got."

"Kind of what I figured." A thick-planked building stood ahead of them, tucked under the branches of a jack pine. Its shake roof was littered with brown pine needles. Ransom led Mason toward it.

"They was about eight families that owned this piece of mountaintop. Korban bought them all out and put them to work building the house and gathering field stones for the foundation. He hired the womenfolk to set out apple seedlings and weed the gardens. Even the kids helped out, at a quarter a day plus keep."

"Didn't anybody notice that they were doing the same work, only now they had a master?"

The trail had widened out and wagon ruts led into

the heart of the forest from the other side of the clearing. Ransom stepped onto the warped stairs leading into the shed and paused. Mason was glad that the uphill walk had finally tapped the old man's stamina.

"You ain't from money, are you?" Ransom asked, raising a white eyebrow.

"Well, not really. Both my parents had to work all week to get by." Mason didn't mention that his dad worked only two days a week and drank four and a half. Dad faithfully took off every Sunday morning to give thanks for the evening's pint. No other prayers ever passed his lips that didn't reek of bourbon. Except maybe from his hospital bed, when cirrhosis escorted him to the self-destruction he'd spent a lifetime toasting.

"People around here, they fell all over themselves to get Korban's money. They was scrub poor, these people. The only cash they ever saw was once or twice a year when they loaded some handmade quilts or goods on the back of a mule and took down to Black Rock to trade. So when Korban come in with his offers, nobody blamed them for selling out."

"I guess I would sell out, too, if I got the chance," Mason said. He was thinking of *Diluvium,* his first commissioned piece and the worst thing he'd ever fabricated. Also the most successful.

Ransom fumbled in his overalls pocket and again pulled out the feathery rag ball. He waved it in the strange genuflection before lifting the cast-iron latch on the shed door.

"Um—what's that feather for?" Mason asked.

"Warding off," Ransom said, as if everybody carried such a charm. He pushed the door open. Before entering, he kicked the doorjamb so hard that his overalls quivered around his bony frame. "Yep, still sturdy."

Mason wanted to ask what Ransom thought he was warding off, but didn't know what words to use. He chalked it up as one more of the manor's oddities. Compared with ghost stories, Korban's ever-watchful portraits, the jittery maid, and hearth fires burning in the heat of day, what was one old man's eccentricities? Next to Anna, Ransom was practically a model of sanity and reason.

They went into the small shed, Ransom peering up at the rafters. Light spilled from the two single-paned windows set in the south wall. Workbenches lined the back room, piled high with broken harness and rusting plows, millwork and buckets of cut nails. Worn-handled shovels, picks, and axes leaned near the door. A long cross-saw dangled from wooden pegs, a few of its jagged teeth missing. The corner was a mess of wooden planes, hammers, and block-and-tackle tangled in yellowed hemp rope. The room smelled of iron and old leather.

"Don't have to lock up tools," Ransom said. "What would a thief want with a tool? Then he'd have to work."

Mason began picking out the equipment they might need. If he was lucky, they would find a chunk of walnut or maybe a maple stump. More likely, they would have to hack a piece out of a fallen tree. He was checking the heft of a hatchet when he noticed Ransom studying the dark ceiling again. "Sky's not about to fall, is it?"

"Never know."

"What are we, about four thousand feet above sea level? A lot less sky to fall on us up here."

Ransom didn't even smile, just scratched at one weathered cheek. Maybe Mason had misjudged the old man. Those sparkling and tireless eyes suggested Ransom was no stranger to humor. But maybe the man had his own reasons for becoming solemn.

"Found what you need?" Ransom asked, waiting near the door.

"Sure. You mind grabbing that maul over to your left? We might need to do some heavy hitting."

When they were back outside, they stood in the clearing and arranged the tools for easier carrying. Ransom wore an expression that Mason could only call "relieved."

"What's the matter?" Mason asked.

"Man's got a right to be scared, ain't he?"

What was there to be scared of out here? Did wild predators still stalk these woods? "Scared of what?"

"Miss Mamie said not to tell." Ransom sounded almost like a child. Mason wondered what kind of hold the woman had over Ransom. The man even said her name with a kind of frightened reverence, his hand moving up his overalls bib toward the pocket that held the rag-ball charm.

"Look, if there's some kind of danger, you owe it to your guests to warn them. Plus, I thought we were friends."

Ransom looked off toward the trees at the sun that was starting its downward slide to the west. "I reckon. Don't ever let on to Miss Mamie, though."

"Of course not."

Ransom exhaled slowly. "You know we have four gatherings of guests each year. We take a month between each batch to get things fixed up, 'cause we're too busy when the guests are here to do repairs. Somebody has to go around and check on all the little outbuildings and cabins, original homesteads that can't be torn down. Korban set it in his will that everything stay like it was.

"Three of us was keeping up the grounds. We always switched off, one keeping up the livestock, one tending to the flowers and gardens and firewood, and the last playing handyman. Miss Lilith, the maid, and the cook see to the kitchen and the house."

"I've met Lilith. Pretty girl."

Ransom wobbled his knot of a head. "Not hard on the eyes. Anyways, last night, one of the men, George

Lawson, was up Beechy Gap checking on the old Easley place. That was another of the original settler families. The last Easley girl worked at the house until she married off down to Charlotte with one of them artists a few years back.

"Well, my friend George, he went into that old Easley shack. I don't know what happened, I didn't find no tools or nothing, so I can't say he was doing carpentry work. But the whole blamed shack fell on him." Ransom's jaw clenched. "Died real slow."

"I'm sorry, Ransom. What did the investigators say?"

"Like I said, they's rules of the world and they's rules of Korban Manor."

Mason didn't understand. This place was remote, but an accidental death ought to require some kind of inquiry.

"George was a good man. And he wasn't stupid. Made it through Vietnam, so he must have had some kind of sense. He just crossed the wrong threshold, is all." Ransom looked like he was about to add something to that last sentence, then changed his mind.

"Which way's Beechy Gap?"

Ransom jerked his head toward the north. "Over the ridge yonder."

"I wouldn't mind having a look sometime."

"Nope. Guests ain't allowed up there."

"Rough terrain?"

Ransom looked him full in the eyes for the first time since they'd left the tool shed. "Some things just ain't part of the deal. You'll find a lot of places are off-limits at Korban Manor."

Ransom pulled the charm from his pocket and motioned at the shed with it. "Now, about that wood of yours. I got to be getting back soon."

They gathered the tools and veered off the trail into the forest.

* * *

Adam walked along the fence, his head full of the wilderness smells. He felt sure that Manhattan's pollutants had permanently clogged his sinuses, but maybe the fresh mountain air would add a year back to the six the city had stolen from his life. The near-perfect silence was eerie, and he had almost gone through a physical withdrawal in the night as his sleeping self yearned for those constant sirens, car horns, and burglar alarms. And all this wide-open space was unnatural. No wonder hillbillies were stereotyped as crazed and grizzled outcasts. There was nothing to impose the insanity of civilization upon them, so they had to make up their own rules of order.

Paul was off somewhere shooting video, no doubt wrapped up in the latest project, the world reduced to the narrow scope of his viewfinder. That was for the best. Though solitude was kind of creepy in itself, especially in the sprawling expanse of the manor, he needed a break from Paul's company. He'd talked briefly with the weird photographer Roth on the porch, and had recognized the same artistic self-absorption that plagued Paul.

Adam saw a man by the barn dressed in worn work clothes. It wasn't one of the handymen who'd helped unload the van. Probably someone in charge of the stables, or else the tender of the long garden that stretched in stubbled rows in the low valley. The man waved Adam over. Adam stole a glance back at the manor a hundred yards away, then approached the barn.

"Morning, there," the man said. His hands were tucked deep into the pockets of his loose-fitting jeans. A shovel leaned against the wall beside him.

"Hi," Adam said.

"You're one of the guests, I reckon."

"We just got in yesterday."

"What do you think of the place so far?"

"It's . . . different from what I'm used to. But that's part of the adventure."

"Yep, the unknown is always scary at first. But once you get used to it, you start to like it."

Adam looked down at a set of wire-enclosed pens beyond the garden. A grunting sound rolled across the hills.

"Hogs," the man said. "About time of year to get out the boiling kettle and have us a slaughter."

Adam's face must have shown his revulsion.

The man laughed. "Don't worry, son. You won't get no blood on your hands. But meat don't get on the table by itself."

"I prefer my meat boneless," Adam said.

"Miss Mamie serves it up however you like. Careful, though, she's been known to take a shine to the guests. Especially them that's young and male. I reckon even an old crow like that needs a play-pretty once in a while."

"Thanks for the warning, but she's not my type," he said.

The man leaned forward like a conspirator, his face emerging from the shadows of the barn's overhang. "Say, can you do me a favor?"

"What's that?" Adam looked back at the manor again. Smoke rose from its four chimneys, but other than that, it appeared devoid of life. Even the breeze seemed to have died.

"Dig me a hole. I'll pay you."

"I don't want to get you in any trouble. Miss Mamie seems to have this thing about the guests being kept apart from the staff."

The man licked his lips. "Let me worry about Miss Mamie. But I got a sore arm and I'm a little down in the back. Pain's hellfire blue this morning."

"Okay, then," Adam said. He took the shovel and tested its balance.

The man took his right hand out of his pocket and pointed to the base of a dying gray apple tree that stood alone in a slight clearing. "Right there between the roots," he said. "About big enough to hold a hatbox."

The man followed Adam to the spot, and Adam slid the bright blade into the earth, turned the dark soil. In a couple of minutes he'd shaped the hole to the man's satisfaction.

"That's fine and dandy," the man said. "I can handle the rest. Appreciate it."

"What are you burying?"

"Covering up for old Ransom. He's no-account, but he's been around so long he gets away with murder. I got to finish a job for him."

"Well, have a good morning. I need to get back to my room."

"Here," he said, his right hand dipping into his pocket again. "A little something for your trouble."

"No, really," Adam said, holding up his hands in protest. The shovel handle had heated up the flesh surrounding his palms, a hint of possible blisters to come.

"You don't want to hurt my feelings, do you?" the man said. "Us mountaineers can get mighty prideful about such things."

"Sure, then."

The man held his fist out, then opened it over Adam's palm. A small green thing dropped into it.

"Four-leaf clover," the man said.

Adam smiled. "I'm going to need all the luck I can get."

Adam started back toward the barn, then turned and said, "I'm Adam, by the way."

"Lawson," the man said, now hunched over the hole as if his bad back had undergone a miracle cure. "George Lawson."

CHAPTER 9

Anna awoke with light slanting through the window, and for a few moments couldn't remember where she was. Then it all came back, Korban Manor, Mason, the cabin in the woods with its mysterious figurines, the pained spirit of the girl she'd encountered.

Why had the ghost asked for Anna's help? And who was the person in the shawl who had fled into the forest? Anna shook away the spiderwebs of memory. She hadn't dreamed last night, unless that whole walk in the woods had taken place solely in her imagination.

"Did you have a good night's sleep?" Cris asked from her bed across the room.

"I slept like the dead. Haven't slept that well in years. I guess even a city girl benefits from the peace and quiet."

Cris, her voice raspy from sleep and hangover, said, "I know what you mean. In Modesto, a siren wakes you up every fifteen minutes. It's kind of weird, though."

"What's weird?" Anna looked at Korban's portrait, then at the fire that must have been stoked and banked by one of the servants in the night.

"For the first time since I was a little girl, I remembered my dreams."

"Really?" Anna thought of her own recurrent dream, of her ghostly self on the widow's walk, holding that forlorn and haunted bouquet.

"Yeah. I was running across the orchard out there, I had these long bedclothes on, billowing out behind me. You know, all that lacy Victorian stuff you see on the covers of Gothic novels? I was running in slow motion, like the wind was pushing me back or something."

"The old 'running but never getting there' dream," Anna said. "I had them during final exams or sometimes when I submitted a research paper."

Or like the last time I dreamed about Stephen. What was that, nearly a year ago?

"I wasn't running away." Cris's voice faded a little as she recalled the details of the dream. "I was running *to* something. Waiting in the shadows, right at the edge of the trees. It was so real. I could feel the dew on my bare feet, the cold air against my face, the warmth—"

Anna raised herself up on her pillow and saw Cris, hair tangled, eyes bleary, but a blush apparent on her cheeks.

"—the warmth down *there,"* Cris finished, as if startled by the force of the memory. "And I just kept running. I could feel the house behind me, almost like it was watching, like it wanted me to . . . then I was all the way across the meadow. The shadow thing, it moved out from under the trees, it touched me, but I couldn't see its face. Where it touched my shoulder, the warmth sort of expanded, filling me up . . ."

Cris's widened eyes stared past the room into the remembered dream. "It was pretty intense," she whispered.

Anna wasn't used to people sharing intimate details with her. Being an orphan had taught her to maintain a safe emotional distance. She'd kept secrets even from the few romantic interests in her life, keeping a deep part of herself hidden. Now this woman she'd only met yesterday was sharing a sensual dream. But maybe it was something else. "You found some company. Mason, I'll bet."

Cris grinned. "No, I definitely would have remembered if something had happened with him. I wasn't *that* drunk."

Anna forced herself to show interest in Cris's dream as penance for thinking of Mason. "What do you suppose it means?"

"That I'm a basket case?"

As if dreams had meaning. Dreams were nothing but a mistake of the synapses, a firing off of excess electrical energy much the way sparks jump off a cracked distributor wire in a car. Dreams were random brain waves, no matter what the professors in the Duke behavioral sciences program had taught her.

Basically, dreams were nonsense. Both the sleeping and the waking kind. Especially when they compelled you to visit a big manor tucked high in the Appalachian Mountains, where you searched for your own ghost. Especially then.

"Maybe it's just your subconscious reveling in your newfound sense of freedom," Anna said, scrambling up a solipsism from one of her old psychology classes. "After all, you have all kinds of time, no deadlines, no husband to please. Nothing but yourself and what you want to do. Maybe it's only natural that this relief should express itself in romantic imagery."

"Wow. That's good. I can't wait to get back home and tell my analyst."

Anna was going to add something about sexual frustration due to the dream's Victorian overtones. But that was too cynical and obtuse even for Anna.

"Or maybe it was just a dream," she said, dreading the coming bout of bloody diarrhea that welcomed her to each new day.

"Probably," Cris said.

Anna pushed off her quilts and sat up, shivering inside her cotton nightgown. "Dibs on the bathroom."

"Go ahead. I need to lie here a minute and get my wits together. I'm going to sneak downstairs and score a caffeine fix. Want anything?"

"No, thanks."

When Anna returned to the room, Cris was gathering her sketch pads, a cup of coffee steaming on the nightstand. "I ran into Jefferson Spence. You know, the fat writer. It's kind of cool to be here with actual famous people."

Anna shrugged. "We had to study his *Seasons of Sleep* in American lit. About put *me* to sleep, let me tell you."

"He wrote that one here, at the manor. They say he writes about real people, only he changes the names so he won't get sued. I wonder if we'll be in his next book."

Anna went to her dresser to pick out some clothes. "I'll be the ghost-hunting flake with the big nose, and you can be—"

"—the bimbo housewife who has wet dreams."

"Except it wouldn't be that simple in the book," Anna said, then sniffed daintily. "You'd be a 'trembling Venus, clutching and grasping at the sheets, back arched toward the dark ceiling of heaven, the endless roof of forever, the prison of night,' et cetera and so on."

Cris laughed so hard that she snorted into her coffee. A knock came at the door. Anna crossed her arms, not sure if the nightgown was revealing or not. She avoided mirrors these days.

Cris apparently had little modesty, having gone downstairs in the yellow slip she still wore. "Enter," she shouted. "We're all decent here."

Miss Mamie came into the room, her hands clasped, a smile on her face that could have been carved in wood. "You ladies sleep well?"

"More or less," Cris said. "The beds are very comfortable."

"And you, Miss Galloway? You were out late last night?" Miss Mamie's eyes reflected the warm flickering light of the fire.

Was Miss Mamie chiding her, or merely making conversation? The hostess knew that Anna was a parapsychologist. Anna hadn't seen any reason to lie on her retreat application. In fact, she'd learned to take a stubborn pride in her peculiarities.

So she saw no reason to lie now. "I took a walk," she said. "On that ridge to the east."

"Did you find what you were looking for?" There was no mistaking the challenge in the hostess's voice.

"No." Not a lie. She wasn't sure yet what she was looking for, besides her own ghost.

"Maybe it will come to you, Miss Galloway. Keep your spirits up." Miss Mamie pursed her lips in a reptilian smile and looked at the portrait of Ephram Korban.

"You've got a very strange house," Cris said.

"The house is his," Miss Mamie said, with a slight bow toward the portrait. She touched the locket that hung from the strand of pearls that circled her throat. "I just keep the home fires burning."

She left them to dress and to speculate about the meaning of their hostess's cryptic manner.

"This way, Mr. Jackson."

Lilith headed down the narrow stairs. Mason repositioned the twenty-pound chunk of red maple in his arms and followed her. The musty, moist air clung to the skin of Mason's face. He stared down into the dark basement, making sure each step was solid before fully shifting his weight.

Lilith waited at the bottom of the stairs, holding the lantern at shoulder level. When Mason finally reached the basement floor, he peered into the gloomy and shifting shadows, trying to get a feel for the basement's layout. Tiny wedges of windows were set high in the walls just above the ground, but only a graying of starlight leaked through. The aroma of dry rot gave way to a deeper, older decay.

He stumbled and his tool satchel banged against his hip. The handle was starting to dig into his skin where the satchel dangled from his shoulder. Lilith led him past a couple of thick wooden beams, a cluster of old furniture, and a small doorway. The lantern's firelight glinted off rows of dusty wine bottles tucked in the narrow alcove.

"Why is it so hot?" Mason asked. His voice was swallowed by the dead space.

"Central heating," Lilith said. "Mr. Korban insisted on having his fires."

Mason wondered if he would be able to work down here for long stretches. Sculpting usually sent the sweat gushing from his pores. The work was as much muscle as it was inspiration. Only the final touches, the thin detailing and polishing, were not so physically demanding that they wore him out.

"Where's the stove?" he asked.

Lilith pointed into the darkness toward the left end of the basement. "There's a separate room over there so the workers can keep the fire stoked from the outside. The ductwork runs all through the house."

She lifted the lantern higher and Mason saw the dull metal sheeting of the ducts.

"Air-circulated heat," he said. "That was pretty sophisticated for its time, wasn't it?"

"I'm not a historian, Mr. Jackson. Miss Mamie would be the one to answer such questions."

Lilith led him into an area that wasn't exactly a room. It was more like a bit of floor space divided by timber posts and shelving. A rough-finished cabinet flanked the near side of what he guessed was going to be his studio.

"I hope this will do," she said. "We've only had a few sculptors at the manor, but many painters. And one old gentleman who did acid etchings and woodblock prints. We've all managed to work just fine down here."

"Oh, do you paint?"

"I used to."

He didn't want to comment on her career change. His own might be coming soon enough. "Maybe a little of that creative spirit soaked into the walls."

"Maybe so, Mr. Jackson. Maybe more than we know."

She was an odd one, Mason decided. If she weren't so frosty, he would risk getting to know her. But he was better off focusing on his work. Besides, he was positive that Miss Mamie wouldn't approve of the hired help cavorting with the guests, no matter how much the guests cavorted with each other.

A thick table stood in the center of the studio space. Mason set down the bulky maple with a solid thump. He shook the satchel from his arm onto the table as well. It would stay dark down here even during the day. He didn't mind, though. He worked mostly by touch and instinct, anyway.

"Will that be all?" Again Lilith seemed to be in a hurry to get away from him. Or perhaps it wasn't him. Maybe she wanted to be away from this dim, claustrophobic place where Mason was going to spend his time.

"So will I have to curse the darkness?" he answered.

"Excuse me?"

He pointed to the lantern. "I assume you're taking that with you."

"Oh, I see." She stepped toward the shelves, and in the lantern light Mason saw a clutter of half-melted candles. "There are matches in that cupboard."

She waited until Mason lit two of the thick candles. He found an oil lamp on the bottom shelf and rolled up the wick. He had just touched the tip of a candle to the wick when she called, "Good luck," then she was gone.

As her echoing footsteps receded up the stairs, he muttered to himself, "Jeez, no wonder people make up stories about this place."

Mason lit an extra candle and spread his tools across the table. He studied the sharpened edges of the blades before turning his attention to the red maple. Then he paced, his mind drifting into that mysterious well-spring from which ideas bubbled forth.

His foot caught on something, causing a muffled crash. He brought the lamp down low to see what he had tripped over. It was a stretched canvas, the back graying with age. He turned it over.

On the canvas was a perfect reproduction of Korban Manor on a stormy night, done in the same thick oils as the other paintings that lined the walls of the house. The manor was drawn to precise scale, seeming such a natural part of the landscape that it looked as if the house had grown out of the soil like a living thing. In the painting was the knothole that Mason had noticed earlier that morning in the siding beneath a second-floor window.

But the photographic realism wasn't the only quality that made the painting so powerful. The manor was vibrant, as if it were shaking with the force of the fantasized gale. The trees were wild with wind, and black clouds hovered around the manor's flat roof. Mason gently touched the canvas and a cool electricity surged up his arm. He wondered why such a beautiful work was relegated to the corruptive air of the basement.

He leaned it against the table and brought the lamp closer, careful not to let the heat sear the finish. He scanned every inch of the artwork, softly running his fingers along the furrows made by the brushstrokes. The angles of the gables were geometrically accurate, the shading well proportioned, the range of colors as true as the human eye. Even the bark of the trees had a sophisticated complexion.

He was looking at the top of the house, at the white railing of the widow's walk, when he spotted the painting's sole flaw. The artist had inadvertently smudged the colors together. A grayish blotch marred an area on the widow's walk. The artist could have easily fixed the mistake, but for some reason hadn't. Still, the painting was far too skilled to remain hidden away in darkness.

Mason didn't know how long he ended up staring at the painting. It had such mesmerizing power that it seemed to soak him into its maelstrom. Finally, he shook his head, realizing that if he didn't get started, he would waste the first day of his last chance. He leaned the painting out of the way against a support timber, promising himself that he would ask Miss Mamie about it later.

He had been putting off the start of his own work, the hewing of the bark from the section of maple. He was annoyed to find his mind drifting back to the painting.

"Come on, you bastard," he chided himself. "This is it. Think of Mama back in Sawyer Creek, shriveling away because she made the sacrifice. Alone in the dark."

He heard her voice in his head, telling him to hold on to his dreams. He rearranged his tools, laying out his fluter, his gouge, his hatchet, his adze, his mallet, his half-dozen chisels with their different edges and angles. Still no idea came to him. He looked around at the shadows sent leaping by the candlelight.

Someone was in the surrounding darkness, watching.

A faint rustle in the corner. Mason lifted the lamp. A small, dark thing separated itself from the lesser darkness and skittered toward the wine rack.

A mouse. Mason's toes curled inside his shoes. He'd always hated rodents. When he was young, just before his father had died, the family had lived in a rented mobile home. The trailer park was next to a trash dump, and rats multiplied fruitfully thanks to the wealth of garbage.

One night, he heard scratching sounds inside the couch that he slept upon. He turned on the light, and watched with horror as tiny newborn rats spilled from a tear in the couch's fabric. Equally repulsive was the family's old gray cat, which swallowed the rats whole, one by one, as they emerged blind into the world. The mother rat must have been sick or something, because the couch stank of her death for weeks afterward. By then, Mason had taken to sleeping in a reclining chair on the other side of the living room.

And another, older memory rose, but he pushed it back into its dark chink of slumber.

This creature in the basement had been only a mouse. Mason could handle that. Mice were timid. Rats were the ones to despise, with their long tails, deliberate manner, and those eyes that shone with a defiant intelligence.

He tried once again to focus on his work. Maybe the mouse had been his Muse. Other artists talked about the spirit moving them, moving *inside* them. Mason didn't understand. All he had was stubbornness and anger to drive him.

He addressed the chunk of wood that Ransom had helped him cut from a fallen tree. "Okay, what kind of secrets are you hiding inside you?"

He studied the pattern of the growth rings and caressed the grain of the wood. The dead sap pulsed. A draft of air whistled through the heating ducts.

"What do you want to become?" He picked up his hatchet. The draft turned into low laughter. He felt a hand around his own, a warm pocket of guiding air.

His voice rose. "What in the hell do you want from me?"

Mason sank the metal blade deep into the flesh of the maple. The flat single echo of the blow sounded almost like a sigh of contentment.

CHAPTER 10

Roth was irritated. He had shot three rolls of film, framing the house first in the soft, low-angle morning light and then in harsher, steeper shadows as the sun climbed the eastern sky. He had walked a good distance down the sandy road so he could do a series of approaching perspectives through a telephoto lens, working off a tripod. He achieved a rather nice depth of field, manipulating the f-stop so that the house seemed small against the surrounding forest. Then he did some closer, handheld work to get the opposite effect, to make the manor appear to tower over the trees and hills.

And that was all top-shelf, spot-on and all that, but then he wanted to try something different. He'd wanted to photograph the bridge. The narrow, weather-beaten bridge would make a jolly center spread for a coffee table picture book, what with all the dramatic cliffs and foggy vistas.

He was positive he *wanted* to photograph the bridge, but by the time he'd walked under the canopy of trees down the road, the idea didn't seem all that wonderful. The day was so warm that, even in the shade, his forehead beaded with sweat. A spasm of nausea and dizziness passed over him. Before he came around the final bend where the manor grounds gave way to the plummeting rocks, he'd decided that the bridge would be a bloody waste of good stock.

So he walked back toward Korban Manor. By then a little breeze sprang up, and he felt better as the sweat dried. He snapped more pictures of the house from the exact same locations as before. It was all such a bunch of poppycock.

"I'm going daft, is all," he muttered under his breath.

"What's that you said?"

The female voice had come from somewhere to his right. He squinted into the shadow of the trees, hoping he'd maintained his British accent while he'd been muttering. One mustn't slip.

"I was saying, 'What a lot of bother,' " he said.

He saw her now, sitting on a stump beside a sycamore. She had a sketch pad in her lap and a charcoal stick clutched between her fingers. Roth eyed her long legs, appreciating that the day was warm enough for her to wear shorts.

"You taking pictures?" she asked.

Pictures. Gawps and ninnies took *pictures*. Roth framed the vital, captured the essential, immortalized the utterly proper. *Stupid bird,* he thought. Still, in his experience, the emptier the space upstairs, the tighter the compartment below.

He was getting frustrated with his work anyway. Maybe the time was right to line up an evening's companion. "Yes, my dear," he said, raising the camera and pointing it at the woman.

She looked away.

"Don't be shy, love. Make my camera happy. I won't even make you say 'cheese' or anything of that sort." He zoomed in on her cleavage without her noticing.

She looked up and smiled, he clicked the shutter,

and then put the camera away. "Say, didn't I see you at Miss Mamie's little after-dinner last night?"

"Yeah. I saw you. You're William Roth, right?"

Roth loved it when they pretended not to be impressed by his celebrity, but she couldn't hide the small sparkle in her eyes. Maybe he wasn't a famous movie star, but name recognition definitely came in handy for bedding the birds. "I'm every inch of him," Roth said. "And to whom do I have the pleasure?"

"Cris Whitfield. Cris without the *h.*" She held out her hand in greeting, realized it was smudged by the charcoal, and put it back in her lap.

"Charmed." He arched his neck as if to look at her drawing, but was actually peeking down her halter top. "What are you drawing?"

"The house," she said, nodding toward it.

"Mind if I've a look?"

She shrugged and turned the sketch pad toward him. He took the opportunity to stand over her.

"I'm not very good," Cris said.

Looked quite good from the little peek I got.

"The house isn't an easy subject," he said, reaching for the pad. "I can hardly get a decent framing for it. I can't imagine how frightfully awful drawing the thing would—"

He'd expected a stick-house drawing, something that the Big Bad Wolf could blow over with a half a breath. But not this . . . this *asylum* the woman had sketched. Not coming from this little ponytailed girl who looked like a Malibu beach bunny, who probably studied EST or reiki or whatever New Age pap was all the rage now.

Because the drawing was definitely of the manor, but was of much *more* than that.

It was all droopy and dark and pessimistic, a cross between Dali and that Spanish artist, Goya. They'd found some of Goya's paintings after he'd died, hidden away in his house because no one could bear to look at them. Roth fought a sudden urge to touch the sketch.

The charcoal was as thick as fur on the paper. The shadows of the portico were sharp and steep, and Roth could almost imagine winged creatures fluttering in that darkness. The windows of the gables were leering eyes, the large front door a ravenous maw. He glanced from the drawing to the house, and for just a second, so short a time that he could convince himself that it was a trick of suggestion, the house *looked* the way she had drawn it, swaying and throbbing like a live, growling beast.

"Bloody hell, girl," he finally managed. "Where did that come from?"

She looked shyly down at the tips of her hiking boots. When she shrugged, he only half noticed her jiggling breasts. "I don't know," she said. "It just sort of happened."

Roth shook his head.

"I've never done anything that good," she said. "I mean, I'm not that good at all."

"Looks ace to me."

"Not this picture. I know *it's* good. But it's not because of me. It's because of the house."

"The house?" Roth thought about how he couldn't manage to make himself photograph anything but the house. And how he'd felt a little queasy when he'd been walking down the road toward the bridge. At least until he got back within sight of the house.

"It's like it's got this . . . energy," Cris said. "When I was drawing, the charcoal almost seemed to be moving by itself."

"Like hypnotic suggestion and that rot?" he snorted, then regretted it. Scorn wasn't the way into a woman's heart, or any of the other warm parts, either.

Cris's lip curled. She slapped the sketch pad closed.

The haunting, warped drawing still lingered in Roth's mind.

"Everybody's a critic," she said. "Why don't you just go back to pushing your silly little buttons?"

She stormed past him, kicking up leaves. Roth watched her walk onto the wagon road and toward the house. He shifted the strap that was digging into his neck, then checked the camera that was perched on the tripod.

Blew a go at *her,* he thought. *What do I care about any twopence line drawing, anyway? Artists are a pack of fools, going on about "meaning" and "creative spirit" and such nonsense.* All it came down to was money, power, and sex, and how to secure more of each.

He peered through his viewfinder at the manor. Cris bounced up the wide steps leading to the porch. As she disappeared through the front door, Roth couldn't shake the feeling that the house had swallowed her whole.

The forest looked different in the daytime. Its edges were blunter, the branches less menacing, the shadows under the canopy less solid and suffocating. Anna took in the afternoon air, feeling alive, fresh, renewed. Korban Manor and the mountains were bringing back her appetite, making her forget the long darkness that the cancer pushed her toward.

She took a right at the fork in the trail, remembering that Robert Frost poem about the road less traveled, because the right fork was little more than an animal path. But the trail led to an opening on a knoll, a soft rounded skull of earth wearing a cap of grass. In the middle of the opening stood a square section of iron fence, and white and gray gravestones protruded from the dirt within it.

"So this is where you keep your dead," she said to the sky.

Anna made her way to the fence. She looked around, but the forest was still and silent. This wouldn't be the first cemetery she'd committed trespass against. She heaved herself over, gripping the wrought floral design and scrollwork of the fence to keep from spearing herself on the sharp-tipped ends.

Two large marble monuments, beautiful though worn with age, dominated the graveyard. The first read EPHRAM ELIJAH KORBAN, 1859–1918. TOO SOON SUMMONED. The one beside it, slightly less ornate, said simply MARGARET. Anna knelt and pressed her palm to the soil above Ephram's final resting place.

"Anybody home, Miss Galloway?"

Anna looked up. Miss Mamie stood by the fence, somehow having crossed fifty feet of open field without Anna noticing.

"I was just out for a walk, and I got curious."

"You know what they say about curiosity and the cat. Most of our guests respect fences."

"Do you mean the guests who walk, or the ones who float?"

Miss Mamie's giggle echoed off the monuments. "Ah, those ghost stories. I couldn't resist approving your application, you know. Paranormal researcher. That's too perfect."

"It's just as much an art form as painting and writing. It's all about seeking, isn't it?"

"Clever. And just what are you seeking, Anna?"

"I suppose I'll know it when I find it."

"One can only hope. Or perhaps you won't have to search. Perhaps it will find *you.*"

"Then you don't mind if I prowl in your graveyard?"

Miss Mamie looked at Korban's monument. "Make yourself at home."

"Thanks."

"Don't be late for dinner, though. And be careful if

you're caught out after dark." Miss Mamie started to leave, then added. "You're one of those, aren't you?"

"One of what?"

"What the mountain people around here call 'gifted.' Second Sight. The power to see things other people can't."

"I'm not so special."

"Those ghost stories are so delightful. And good for business, too. What artist who fancies himself living on the edge could possibly pass up an opportunity to come here? If you see anything, you'll tell me, won't you?"

"Cross my heart and hope to die."

"Don't hope too hard. Not yet, anyway."

Anna watched the woman cross the grass and enter the forest, then she headed toward the rest of the grave markers that stippled the slope. She explored them, reading the names. Hartley, Streater, Aldridge, McFall. Then the names gave way to simple flagstone markers, in some cases chunks of rough granite propped toward the heavens as a forlorn memento of a long-forgotten life.

Would her own death be so little noted? Would her mark be as insignificant? Did it even matter?

At the edge of the scattered stones, where the rear of the fence met the woods, a pale carved tombstone stood in the shade of an old cedar. Anna went to it, read RACHEL FAYE HARTLEY etched in the marble. An ornate bouquet of flowers was engraved above the name.

"Rachel Faye, Rachel Faye," Anna said. "Someone must have loved you."

And though Rachel Faye Hartley was now dust, Anna envied her just a little.

Sylva watched from the forest until Miss Mamie left. Anna looked small and lost in the graveyard, talking to the stones, looking for ghosts among the blades of grass. The girl had the Sight, that much was plain. And something else was plain, that dark aura around her, hanging around her flesh like a rainbow of midnight.

Anna was fixing to die.

Sylva drew her shawl close together, holding it with one knotted hand. The other held her walking stick, which she leaned on to rest for the trip back to Beechy Gap. She didn't get out much these days, especially now that Korban's fetches were walking loose. Things were mighty stirred up, and part of that had to do with the coming blue moon.

The other part had to do with that girl in the graveyard, the one who stared a little too long at the grave of Rachel Faye Hartley.

"You'll be joining her soon enough," Sylva whispered to the laurel thicket around her. "If Ephram will let you, that is."

The sun was sinking by the time Anna climbed back over the fence, full of vinegar for such a sick person. Anna didn't know the old ways, was weak in the power of charms and such. The girl wouldn't understand the power of the healing roots, bone powder, and special ways of spelling. But maybe the talent was only buried in her, not lost forever. Because blood ran thick, thicker than water. And magic ran through tunnels of the soul, Ephram always said.

But Ephram was a liar.

Both before and after he died.

A screech owl hooted, a sound as lonely as a night winter wind. Sign of death, for one to hoot during daylight. But lately signs of death were everywhere, coming at all hours. Sylva said a spell of safe passage and slipped into the woods, hurrying home as best she could before the sun kissed the edge of the mountains.

CHAPTER 11

"Honey?"

Spence pounded on the typewriter keys, pretending not to hear her.

"Jeff?" Bridget put a hand on his shoulder.

He stopped typing and looked up. "You know not to bother me when I'm working."

"But you didn't even come to bed last night."

He hated the plaintive note in her voice, her eagerness to please. He despised her concern. Mostly, he was annoyed by the distraction.

"I hope the typewriter didn't keep you awake." He didn't really care whether it had or not. He was making progress, chasing the elusive Muse, and that was all that mattered.

"No, it's not that," Bridget said. "You just need your rest."

"There will be plenty of time for rest after I'm dead. But at the moment, I'm feeling particularly and effusively alive. So be a dear and let me continue."

"But you missed lunch. That's not like you."

Spence wondered if that was some kind of barb at his weight. But Bridget never criticized. She hadn't the imagination to attack with words. Spence was the reigning master of that genre.

"It's also unlike me to interrupt my work to have a little romantic chat," he said, then stretched his vowels out in his Ashley Wilkes accent. "Now, why don't ya'll make like Scahlett and get yosef gone with the wind?"

"Don't be mean, honey. I'm only trying to help. I want you to be happy. And I know you're only happy when you're working on something."

"Then make me ecstatic," he said. "Leave."

A small sob caught in Bridget's throat. Spence ignored it, already turning his attention back to the half-finished page and the thirty other pages stacked beside the Royal. He would do some revision, he knew, but it was excellent work. His best in many years. And he didn't want it to end.

The door opened and he called to Bridget without looking. "I'll see you at dinner," he lied.

The door closed softly. Spence smiled to himself. She didn't have enough self-esteem to slam the door in anger. She would be apologizing by this evening, thinking the little scene was all her fault.

She was by far the most enjoyable of Spence's corruptions, out of all the English majors and married professors and young literary agents and assistant editors who thought they'd fallen in love with him. But, in the end, they were nothing, just meaningless stacks of bones, scaffolds to prop him up when the loneliness was unbearable. When he was working and working well, he needed no one's love but his own.

"And yours, of course," Spence said to the portrait of Korban, lest his creative benefactor frown.

Spence picked up the manuscript and began reading. The grace of the language, the tight sentence structure, the powerful description were all superb. He'd never been shy about patting himself on the back, but now he had topped even his own lofty literary standards. He would shame them all, from Chaucer to Keats to King.

He didn't question the origin of the words. That was a mystery best left to those whose livelihood was derived from the scholarly vivisection of the humanities. But he'd never before written with such ease as he had last night and today.

Automatic writing. That's what it felt like.

What Spence always called, during those few occasions when the ink flowed so freely, "ghostwriting." As if the paper and typewriter themselves were sucking words out of the air. As if his fingers knew the next word before his brain did. As if he were not even there.

Appropriate to the manuscript, to call it ghostwritten, he thought. It had a Gothic feel, somewhat darker than the southern-flavored literature that had once made him the darling of New York. And then there was the protagonist, the handsome, bearded, and odd man whose name he still hadn't decided upon. That was strange, to be so far along in the manuscript and not even know the main character's name.

He caught himself looking, for the tenth time, at the painting of Korban that hung on the wall above the desk. Then he closed his eyes. After a moment, he resumed ghostwriting.

"Did you hear that?"

"Hear what?"

"A thumping sound."

Adam strained his ears. Paul was probably just being paranoid. He had slipped outside and smoked a joint after dinner. Paul was two things when he was stoned, paranoid and horny.

"Probably that fat writer banging his chippy in the room below us," Adam said.

"If it is, they're the most uncoordinated couple in the history of the human race. Quickest, too."

"All I care about right now is us," Adam said, resting his head on Paul's shoulder. "Thanks for the good time."

"No, thank *you.*"

"And I promise not to bring up the subject of adoption for at least a week."

"You just brought it up."

Paul. "Forget I said anything."

Adam pulled the covers up to his chin and curled his body against Paul's warmth. Adam was afraid he'd have trouble sleeping. The mountaintop estate was too quiet for a city boy, and Adam had never experienced such near-total darkness. He still missed the bright lights, traffic, and aggravation.

"Do you feel like getting out the radio?" he asked.

"Did you bring batteries?"

"Yeah. Figured we might need a little contact with the outside world. The radio's in my bag."

"I'd have to crawl over you to get it."

"I won't bite."

"I'm too tired, anyway. 'Fagged,' as that phony-assed photographer would say."

"You just drank too much wine, that's all. And you know what pot does to you."

"Tonight was for fun. Tomorrow, I'm going to be working again."

Adam collected the radio, brought it back to bed, and switched it on. He twisted the dial, switched bands from FM to AM. Nothing but weird static. "I guess radio waves get blocked by the mountains."

"Or else cool-freaky pop gets censored up here."

They lay for a moment in the darkness. The house was still and hushed. The embers had grown low in the fireplace, and Adam didn't feel like fumbling for a match to light the oil lamp on the bedside table.

"I've been thinking," Paul said.

"News flash. Stop the presses."

Paul elbowed Adam in the ribs. Adam tickled him in return.

"But seriously," Paul said. "I'm thinking of doing a documentary on this place."

"This place?"

"Korban Manor. It's pretty unique, and I could get a lot of scenic footage. Ephram Korban's history sounds pretty interesting, too. An industrialist with a God complex."

"A historical documentary?"

"Something like that?"

"What about all the footage you've already shot, all those weeks in the Adirondacks and the Alleghenies?"

"I'll keep it in the can. I can use it anytime."

"I don't know, Paul. The grant people might get upset. After all, you signed on for an Appalachian nature documentary."

"To hell with the grant committees. I do what I want."

Paul was pulling his Orson Welles bit. Even in the dark, Adam could visualize the famous "Paul pout."

So what if Paul spent months on footage, and still had weeks of postproduction, editing, and scripting left? Those were only technical details. Paul wanted to be the artist, the posturing auteur, the brash visionary. Stubbornly refusing to sell out.

No matter the cost.

But Adam wasn't in the mood to argue. Not after the good time they'd just had.

"Why don't you sleep on it, and we can talk about it in the morning?" Adam stroked one of Paul's well-developed biceps. Lugging a twenty-pound camera and battery belt through the mountains all summer had really toned him up.

"I mean, this is like an alien world or something,"

Paul said. "No electricity, people living like they did a hundred years ago. And the servants, all of them still live here, like serfs around the castle."

Adam was drifting off despite Paul's excitement. "Uh-huh," he mumbled.

He must have fallen asleep, because he was standing on a tower, the wind blowing through his hair, dark trees swaying below him—

No, it wasn't a tower. He recognized the grounds of the manor. He was on top of the house, on that little flat space marked off by the white railing—now, what had the maid called it? Oh yeah, the widow's walk—and Adam found himself climbing over the rail and looking down at the stone walkway sixty feet below, and the clouds told him to jump, he felt a hand on his back, pushing, then he was flying, falling, the wind shook him, why—

"Adam! Wake up." Paul was shaking his shoulder. Paul had sat up in bed, the blankets around his waist. A decent amount of time must have passed, because a little moonlight leaked through the window.

"What is it?" Adam was still groggy from the dream and the after-dinner drinks.

Paul pointed toward the door, his eyes wide and wet in the dimness. "I saw something. A woman, I think. All dressed in white. *She* was white."

"This is the southern Appalachians, Paul. Everybody's white." Adam shook away the fragments of the nightmare.

"No, it wasn't like that. She was *see-through.*"

Adam gave a drowsy snort. "That's what happens when you smoke Panamanian orange-hair. It's a wonder you didn't see the ghost of J. Edgar Hoover in drag."

"I'm not joking, Adam."

Adam put a hand on Paul's chest. His boyfriend's heart was pounding.

"Get back under the covers," Adam said. "You must have fallen asleep and had a weird dream. I think I had one myself."

Paul lay back down, his breathing rapid and shallow. Adam opened his eyes momentarily to see Paul staring at the ceiling. "No drinks or smoke tomorrow, okay?"

There was a stretch of silence, one that only a noise-polluted New Yorker could truly appreciate. Finally Paul said, "I told you I'd be working."

Adam knew that tone. They'd argued enough for one vacation. Adoption, Paul's video, his drug use. And now Paul was seeing things. Adam suddenly wondered if their relationship would survive six weeks at Korban Manor.

He turned his back on Paul and burrowed into the pillows.

"She had flowers," Paul said.

Mason's hands ached. Sawdust and wood shavings were scattered around his feet. Wood chips had worked their way down the tops of his tennis shoes and dug into the skin around his ankles. He tossed his chisel and mallet on the table and stood back to look at the piece.

He had worked in a fever, not thinking about which grain to follow, which parts to excise, where to cut. He wiped his forehead with the sleeve of his flannel shirt. The room had grown warmer. The candles had long since melted away, and the oil was low in the base of the lantern. He must have worked for hours, but the soreness in his limbs was the only evidence of passing time.

Except for the bust before him on the table.

He'd never attempted a bust before. He brought the lantern closer, examining the sculpture with a critical eye. He could find no flaws, no features that were out of proportion. Even the curves of the earlobes were natural and lifelike, the eyebrows etched with a delicate awl. The sculpture was faithful to its subject.

TOO faithful, Mason thought. *I'm nowhere near good enough to produce this caliber of work. I've had successes along the way. But this . . . Jesus Henry Christ on a crutch, I couldn't do Korban's face this well if I'd KNOWN the old geezer.*

But it was Korban's head on the table, the Korban that filled the giant oil paintings upstairs, the same face that hung above the fireplace in Mason's room. Most amazing of all was that the eyes had power, just as they did in the portraits. That was ridiculous, though. These eyes were maple, dead wood.

Still . . .

It was almost as if the figure had life. As if the true heart of the wood had always been this shape, as if the bust had always existed but had been imprisoned in the tree. The face had been caged, and Mason had merely inserted the key and opened the door.

He shook his head in disbelief. "I don't have any idea where you came from," he said to the bust, "but you're going to make the critics love me."

The love of the critics meant success, and that meant money. Success meant he'd never have to step foot in another textile mill as long as he lived, he wouldn't have to blow chunks of gray lint out of his nose at every break, he wouldn't have to wait for a bell to tell him when to take a leak or buy a Snickers bar or race the other lintheads to the parking lot at quitting time. Sure, he still had years of carving ahead, but success started with a single big break.

He was already planning a corporate commission, the gravy train for artists. He'd buy Mama a house, get her some advanced text-reading software and an expensive computer, and then find all the other ways to pay her back for the years of handicap and hardship. Best of all, he could make her smile.

Or maybe he was being suckered by the Dream Image, the high that came after completing a work. He still had to treat the wood, do the fine sanding and polishing. A hundred things could still go wrong. Even as dry as the maple had been after years in the forest, the wood could split and crack.

Mason rubbed his shoulder. His clothes were damp from sweat. The weariness that had been building under the surface now crested and crashed like a wave. Even though he was tired, he felt too excited to sleep. He took one last look at the bust of Korban, then covered his work with an old canvas drop cloth he'd found in the corner.

The first red rays of dawn stabbed through the ground-level windows. Mason's stubble itched. Back in his old life, he'd be on his third cup of coffee by now, waiting on the corner for Junior Furman's pickup to haul him to work. The start of another day that was like a thousand other days.

Mason traced his way back across the basement, ducking under the low beams and stepping around the stacks of stored furniture. He finally found the stairs and went up to the main floor. The smell of bacon, eggs, and biscuits drifted from the east wing, and kitchenware clanged in some distant room. Mason's stomach growled. An older couple passed him in the hall, steam rising from their ceramic coffee cups. They nodded a wary greeting. Mason realized he probably looked bleary-eyed and unkempt, like an escaped lunatic who'd broken into the medicine cabinet.

When Mason reached his room, he looked at the painting of Korban again, marveling at how closely his sculpture resembled that stern face. But the face seemed a little less stern this morning. And the eyes had taken on a little more light—

Don't be bloody DAFT, he chided himself in William Roth's accent.

Mason took a long, hot shower, then lay in bed as dawn sneaked through the cracks in the curtains. In his mind's tired eye, he saw Korban's face, then that dissolved away and he saw Anna. Then his mother, features worn, made even sadder by the pathetic light of hope that somehow still shone in her diseased eyes. Then he pictured Miss Mamie, with her haughty lips. Ransom, clutching his warding charm. Korban, dark pupils holding wretched secrets. Anna, soft and somehow vulnerable, harboring her own secrets.

Korban. His mother. The bust. Anna.

Miss Mamie. Ransom.

KorbanAnnaMissMamieAnnaKorban.

Anna.

He decided he liked Anna's face best, and thought of her until he slept and dreamed of wood.

CHAPTER 12

Anna woke before the first rooster's crow broke the black silence. Across the room, Cris rolled over in her sleep. The darkness behind Anna's closed eyes wasn't as total as the room's darkness. Streaks of blue and red flared across the back of her eyelids.

She slipped into her robe and went into the bathroom. The antique plumbing used gravity to flush the toilets, and the water pressure was inconsistent, though the central heating ensured plenty of hot water. She lit a globed lantern before extinguishing her flashlight, then stepped into the shower and turned the taps.

Under the dull drumming of the water, she forgot the pain in her abdomen. She hadn't dreamed last night, though the questions had swirled around and around as she spun down the drain of sleep.

Where was her ghost? Who was Rachel Faye Hartley? Why was Miss Mamie so curious about Anna's "gift"? How much time did she have left? What would happen after that time expired?

And the biggie, would anyone even care?

She peeled back the shower curtain and wrapped a towel around her. The room had grown colder, and with the water turned off, the steam hung heavy on her skin. It coated the mirror above the sink, and though she wasn't in the mood to gauge the darkness of the circles beneath her eyes, she wanted to make sure she could pass for hale and hearty.

She was about to reach up a corner of the towel to wipe the mirror when the room grew even colder, as if a wind had crept through the crack beneath the door. Her blurred face in the mirror breathed mist.

Then the water collecting on the mirror ran in streaks, and Anna didn't believe her eyes. Because even somebody who saw ghosts didn't see things like this.

Letters formed, as if drawn by the tip of an invisible finger, the symbols silver in the soft glow of the lamp.

G-O.

Anna saw her own wide eyes reflected in the word, as the second set of letters etched itself against the surface of the mirror. O-U-T.

"Go out?" Anna whispered, now that her mind translated the symbols into words.

Was this a message of some sort? From whom? Go out from where? Did something want her out of the house?

But another word was forming, even as the steam threatened to turn to ice and shivers stretched her skin tight.

F-R-O-S-T just above the rim of the mirror.

Anna fought down a breath, though her lungs were like frozen stones. Then the letters blurred, the cold steam collected and ran down the smooth glass in rivulets, and the words were gone.

"Go out frost," Anna said.

She toweled quickly and hurried back into the room to stoke the fire.

"It's going to be beautiful."

Miss Mamie gazed lovingly at the bust that Mason

had carved. The sculptor was gifted. Ephram had chosen well. But Ephram had always chosen well, in love, in life, and now in death.

"Mr. Jackson worked late," Lilith said, holding the lantern higher so the light caught the angles of Korban's hewn features. "He won't be down for a while."

Miss Mamie ached to fondle Korban's face, but she didn't dare risk drawing any of its energy away. That wasn't for her. That was for Ephram. She would touch him again soon enough. The blue moon was only two nights away.

Lilith went to the corner of the studio space and lifted an oil painting. "This was my favorite," she said.

"Put that down. You're done with painting. And so is he. Know your place."

Lilith returned the painting to the shadows. Lilith was just another servant, another tool that helped build Ephram's bridge back into this world. But Lilith's spirit still hung in the air, an echo of the dreams she had created, dreams that fed Ephram and fueled his sleeping soul. She was like the others, too hungry for her own return, too obsessed with her own escape from the tunnel.

She didn't know that she would never escape.

"You may go now," Miss Mamie said. "Help see to lunch. I'll be along shortly."

Lilith took another forlorn look at the painting.

As if she would ever be as gifted an artist as Ephram, Miss Mamie thought. Oh, Lilith had tried, she'd sacrificed, but she was just starting to learn the basics when she'd drowned in the pond below the barn. Her tunnel of the soul always led back here, to this dark basement where she had once dared to create.

Lilith climbed the stairs and closed the basement door.

They were alone.

"Oh, Ephram," Miss Mamie said to the bust. "It's better than I ever dreamed."

The oak flexed and stretched, the eyes twitched between their wooden lids. Then the lips parted. "Yes. The fit is rather nice."

She squatted so that she was at eye level with him. She stroked the rough cheek, ran the back of her hand along the engraved beard.

"It's working," she whispered. "Just as you said."

The stiff brow lifted. "It's going to take a little getting used to. Soon, Margaret, my love, I'll have arms to hold you again. Hands to paint with, eyes to see the world anew, legs to walk beside you. But the sculptor must work harder. I need to be finished in time."

"I'll make him start this evening." She wondered what those arms would be like, once Mason Jackson finished the life-sized statue. They might be crude and clumsy. But even wearing wooden flesh was better than being trapped in the damp stone, bleak walls, and cold glass of the manor. Ephram could eventually use his magic to soften the wood, tame it, and make it tender.

He was gaining power as the blue moon approached. She could sense it, as if he were a bed of embers on the edge of erupting into hot flame. He was summoning his fetches, those who had died under his spell, those who feared the dark slithery things in the tunnels of their souls. He ate their dreams and fed them fear. And she had helped by carving their poppets, which were hidden away in that old cabin on Beechy Gap, and their souls could never leave the mountain.

"Soon," Miss Mamie said, the word like an ache, a long promise.

This was the end of decades of waiting, of dark deeds and death, of plotting, stealing, enslaving. Time was nothing to Ephram, but Miss Mamie still clung to the impatience of mortality. Possession worked both ways, its tug equally strong on the living and the dead.

Ephram's wooden lips pressed together, then stretched into a smile. "It weakens me to leave the walls."

"You'll be whole again. Two more nights."

"And Anna?"

"She's weak. Dying."

"Ah. Sweet dreams."

The bust grimaced, eyes closed, forehead creased in concentration. "Make him finish me," Ephram said with effort.

"Mr. Jackson has passion," Miss Mamie said. "He loves you. He worships you. He wants to please you."

"He worships only the flesh of his work. But no matter. His spirit is mine."

"We all belong to you. They dream of you."

"As they should."

"And after you've lured Sylva to the manor—"

"You're not to mention her name." The bust's eyes opened, flickering in bands of orange and red. She cringed, waiting for Ephram to punish her, give her back the years, steal away the gift of youth. She knelt, head bowed, tears streaming down her face.

"Do you know why I've never led you through your tunnel of the soul?" Ephram said, voice cold, long dead, and almost weary.

Miss Mamie wiped her eyes and sniffed in hope. "Because you love me?"

That was the only dream worth having, the only dream that would last beyond death. Love absolved them of evil, made the killings and the soul tricks and the torture of dead things all worthy and noble. Love forgave what God could not.

Ephram's laughter was abrupt and harsh, crowding the stale air of the basement. She looked into his cruel, hot eyes.

"No, no, no," he said, more comfortable now in the wood, seeping into the angles and grooves and shaved spaces until it was *his* face. "I spare you because I need you. You're the one person I know will never betray me."

Sylva had betrayed him, though Miss Mamie wasn't going to remind him. His anger at Sylva might become misplaced again, as it so often did. But Miss Mamie might find out the one thing that bothered her, if she asked the right questions.

"I have to know," she said, breathless, the room stifling. "Do you love me the most?"

The bust sighed. Miss Mamie wondered if a dead man was capable of lying. No, not Ephram. He never lied, and he always kept his promises.

"Margaret, there is only you. Forever. Why do you think I've lingered here, chained my soul to this house with you?"

If only she could be certain. But a house of love wasn't built on a foundation of doubt. "Then why have you kept Sylva alive, too?"

Silence filled the basement, the shadows waiting impatiently at the edge of the lantern's glow. She had only dared challenge him because she knew, with the blue moon approaching, that Ephram needed her more than ever. And she wanted them to possess each other, mind, body, and spirit. No secrets.

"I kept her old," Ephram said. "And I've never brought her into my heart. There's only room for you here, on the inside, the dead side. And soon, when I have legs, we will walk both sides, together."

Miss Mamie blinked back tears. How could she have doubted him?

She couldn't help herself, she leaned closer, held her face against the wood, scorched her skin against her lover's searing lips.

Then he was gone, back into the walls where the fire could warm his soul.

Mason woke just in time to miss lunch. His mouth felt as if it had a dirty sock stuck in it. Someone had stoked the fire while he'd slept. He dressed in his other pair of jeans and a plain red flannel shirt. He thought about the sculpture as he brushed his teeth, wondering if he'd really finished it in a single night.

His studied his reflection in the bathroom mirror. Dark wedges haunted the flesh under his eyes. He wasn't used to keeping odd hours. He usually followed the "slow and steady" theory of work, but he'd never before been swept up in such a creative storm as he had while fashioning the bust. No wonder so many of the so-called "true visionaries" crashed and burned at an early age.

"Oh yeah, I'm a real visionary, all right," he said to his bleary reflection. "Double visionary."

His reflection shimmered a little and he rubbed his eyes. A wave of dizziness struck him and he reached out to balance himself. One hand gripped the sink and the other pressed against the mirror. The glass was warm beneath his palm. For the briefest of moments, Mason saw the bust he'd sculpted instead of his own reflection, then the hallucination passed. Mason frowned and splashed some water on his face. It was bad enough seeing Korban everywhere on canvas, but if the bastard was going to swim nonstop before his eyes, then maybe Mason needed a break. Or a shrink.

The upper floors were quiet. Walking down the stairs, he heard clattering noises rising from what he figured was the kitchen. Maids had carried food through the door to the left of the stairs. He wondered if anybody would mind if he ducked in for a snack.

Mason poked his head through the swiveled door. A plump, dour woman wrestled with a cast-iron skillet at the sink. A froth of soap bubbles clung to one cheek.

"Hey there," Mason said. "Is it okay if I grab a quick sandwich?"

She glared at him, through him. He looked over his shoulder. When he looked back, she gave a terse nod to a counter by the stove. A loaf of homemade bread sat on a cutting board, three or four white slices stacked to the side.

Most of lunch had been cleared up and put away, but the odor of fried trout still hung in the air. Mason passed a long cookstove with its thick metal grill. There was a door on each side for stoking wood, and a wide door in the middle for a baking oven. A smaller stove stood off near the corner, its pipe running up and making an elbow through the wall. Mason marveled that anyone could cook at all on these primitive appliances, much less create feasts lavish enough for the manor's pampered guests.

Mason picked up two slices of bread. "Anything to put between these?"

The cook glowered and wiped a butcher knife with her towel. "There, in the icebox," she said in a thick Bavarian accent, pointing the knife toward what looked like a squat highboy with doors instead of drawers.

Mason opened one of the doors, and cool air wafted over his face. On the metal shelves were some eggs in a basket, a thick wheel of cheese, a pitcher of cream, a boned chunk of cooked ham, and assorted fruits and vegetables. A block of ice sat on the highest shelf, its corners rounded from melting. Water dripped into a catch pan at the bottom of the icebox.

Mason pulled out the cheese and ham and placed them on the counter, then took a small knife from a wooden holder. He cut a couple of slices from each, then stacked them on a piece of bread. He could feel the cook's eyes on his back.

"Don't worry, I'll clean up after myself." Mason's smile evoked no change in her hard eyes. He pulled a couple of leaves from a head of iceberg lettuce, added it to the sandwich, topped it with bread, and mashed the whole thing flat.

"That's how we do it down in Sawyer Creek," he said, taking a bite.

The cook frowned and returned to the dirty dishes. That's when Mason saw the painting on the wall above the door. Another portrait of Korban. This one done in deep shadows, those eyes as cold as in all the other paintings. Was there a room in the house that didn't have that man's unrelenting scowl?

A coffeepot rested on the small cookstove. Ceramic coffee mugs hung from hooks on a rack near the sink. Mason stepped around the counter and reached for one.

"Pardon me," he said, as the cook flinched. Mason lost his balance, still groggy from his cheated sleep. He put out his hand to avoid falling into her.

When he touched her shoulder, she gave a screech and dropped a plate. It shattered on the floor. Mason stepped back and looked at his hand.

No. That couldn't have happened.

The door swiveled open and Miss Mamie entered the room. She wore a bulldog mask of disapproval.

"Sorry, it was my fault," Mason said. He was about to add that he'd be happy to pay for the broken dish, then remembered that he didn't have any money.

"Gertrude?" Miss Mamie said. Her eyes seemed to grow even darker as the cook's face paled. The cook glanced at the portrait of Korban above the sink.

"No, really, it was me," Mason said. "I was just getting a cup—"

"Guests normally aren't allowed in the kitchen area, Mr. Jackson, for reasons I'm sure you'll understand."

"Uh, sure. I was just leaving." He collected his sandwich and made for the door.

"Back to work now, Gertrude," Miss Mamie said. The cook immediately plunged her arms into the soapy dishwater, too afraid to stop long enough to sweep up the shards of broken ceramic.

Miss Mamie held the swivel door open so Mason could pass, then followed him into the hall. "How do you like working in the basement?" she asked, once again cheerful, as if the incident in the kitchen had never happened.

"It's perfect," Mason said, continuing down the hall, still uneasy. "It's private, with enough room so I can swing my elbows around, and the walls and floor are insulated so I don't have to worry about bothering anybody."

"Lovely," she said. "Master Korban would be pleased."

"Stays a little warm down there, though."

"Well, we simply must keep the central fire going. We pride ourselves on having hot water available twenty-four hours a day."

"Sure, I understand. It's not intolerable or anything. The worst part is that I get all sweaty and stinky, and I wouldn't want to scare off the other guests."

"That's why we have the hot water, Mr. Jackson."

Mason had reached the door to the basement. He had to go down there and see if he had actually sculpted the bust of Korban or if the night before had been a dream. He wondered if Miss Mamie was going to follow him down.

"Well, I'll see you at dinner, I reckon," he said, waiting by the door.

She put a cold hand on his arm. "You'll be getting some more wood this evening, won't you? I'll have Ransom hook up the wagon."

"Well, I need to finish something first."

"Oh, I thought you were going to do a life-sized piece."

Mason searched his memory. Had he mentioned such a thing? A human figure? Had he even thought about it? Maybe his big dream images were getting so oversize that he was babbling about them before he could even get started.

"Yeah, I was thinking of something like that," he said.

"You're going to be successful. But you have to have the fire. Master Korban always said hard work is its own reward. You know what they say about idle hands."

Mason held up the hand that wasn't holding the sandwich. "Well, I'd better get to work, then."

Miss Mamie wore a look of anticipation as he reached for the doorknob. Mason didn't want to show anyone the work until he was sure it was finished.

"And I'll get up with Ransom about that wood," he said, slipping through the door. He closed it behind him, stumbling a little in the dark. By the time he'd inched his way down the steps, his eyes had adjusted to the daylight trickling through the small, high windows.

He reached the workbench and lifted the drop cloth. From the table, Korban stared back at him.

No, not Korban. Just a highly detailed replica.

But for just a *moment . . .*

Easy, guy. You're just a little short of sleep, is all.

Then Mason looked down at his hand, remembering how it had felt when it had touched the cook. When it had passed through the cook.

Remembering how his hand had sunk into her flesh as if she were made of soggy, store-bought white bread. Remembering how his hand had burned.

Okay, so you're more than just a little short of sleep. You must have hit yourself in the head with the mallet last night.

Maybe hunger was the culprit. He took another bite of his sandwich.

Yeah, hunger. He'd better fatten up during his stay. There might be lean days ahead.

Unless he kept producing work like *this.*

The sculpture was solid proof of his ability. Fine, lifelike detail. Each eyelash defined. The lips set in a soft sneer between the thick mustache and beard, ready to part in speaking. Even when he turned away, he felt as if the eyes were following him.

He found an old broom in the corner and swept the wood shavings into a pile near the corner. Then he saw the oil painting where he'd left it leaning against the cabinet. He'd forgotten to ask Miss Mamie about it.

Mason picked up the finished view of the house. He held it high so he could admire the brushstrokes in daylight. Yes, beautiful, if only the artist had fixed that little smudge.

The smudge had grown larger since the night before. The gray area had stretched wide enough to cover two balusters of the railing.

It must have been a flaw in the paint. But Mason had never heard of oil paint deteriorating so rapidly. Though thoroughly dried, the paint was far from ancient.

Or maybe this was all in his imagination.

The incredible expanding stain, Ransom and his charms, Anna and her hints of ghosts, the creepy Lilith, the insubstantial cook. Sure, he could chalk all those odd things up to his imagination. But better to blame that good old standby, the all-time fave.

Stress.

Because this was it, the last hurrah, the whole enchilada, the really big shew, the last grab for the brass ring. The last big dream. Because if he didn't produce here, it was back to the textile mills, probably for good.

And THAT would make Mama proud, wouldn't it? After all her sacrifice.

Mason finished his sandwich, even though he'd lost his appetite. This bust couldn't be his masterpiece. Miss Mamie was right. Bigger was better.

CHAPTER 13

"Did you get any footage this morning?" Adam leaned against the bureau and folded his arms.

Paul put away his camera. "I have to save my batteries. I only have four. That gives me about eight hours of juice. And there's no way to recharge them out here."

Adam watched Paul stack the equipment in the closet. His partner had a cute body, he had to admit. But Adam sometimes wondered if their relationship was built on anything besides the physical. Paul liked Times Square, and the place gave Adam the creeps. Paul liked coffeehouses and parties, and Adam liked curling up on the sofa with a good book. When it came right down to it, Paul was late-night MTV and Adam was weekend VH-1.

And there was the issue of adoption. Adam was ready to raise a child, to share the wealth of love in his heart. He had plenty of money from his inheritance. Enough to pay the adoption fees and lawyers, enough for the courts to be satisfied that Adam had that most-desired parental quality: that Adam would be able to afford whatever outrageously expensive toy was trendy each Christmas, so the child wouldn't grow up as a social outcast, snubbed by peers and forever despised by advertisers.

Adam was afraid in some small part of himself that he only wanted a child to tie Paul down. Paul was a bit of a free spirit, and even unknowingly hurt Adam by going on a weeklong cruise with an older man before Adam had mustered the courage to share his feelings. Paul had been faithful since, but Adam wondered if perhaps the right temptation had never arisen. In fact, he thought maybe you couldn't even call it "faith" until that faith had survived a test.

"What do you want to do tonight?" Paul said. "Go down for drinks?"

"You could have joined me for lunch."

"Look, we don't have to spend every damned second together, do we?"

Adam didn't answer, because something shifted in the mirror, a flicker cast by the fireplace.

"What's wrong?" Paul said.

Adam rubbed his eyes. "Nothing. I'm just a little messed up, I guess."

Paul grinned. "Oh yeah. Maybe you saw the woman in white. And you thought I was lying."

"Too many other weird things are happening. I just saw—"

"Saw what?"

"I don't know. Just the reflection of the painting. I feel like . . . like everything's going out of control. I mean, we're fighting all the time and I'm supposed to care about your stupid video when you won't even listen to a word I say. And this place, it's getting on my nerves."

"Come on, this is only our third day here."

"And these problems are supposed to just go away?"

Paul's face clenched in anger. "I don't have time for this right now. In fact, I never have time for these pointless arguments. All you want to do is talk in circles."

"Look, I don't mind paying for this vacation, but I thought you were going to be working on your project—"

"Oh, here we go with that crap again. You and your money."

Adam was on the verge of tears. Paul scorned tears and would say Adam was being a silly little girl. And Paul would say it with the smug superiority of someone whose emotions were always in check. Except the emotion of anger.

"Oh, Princess," Paul said, coming to him, hugging him. "Did someone upset the tea cart? Do you need another forty mattresses so you won't feel the pea?"

"Go away." Adam pushed Paul's arms from around his waist. "You bastard."

Adam's vision blurred from rage. This was crazy. He never lost control like this.

"Fine, Princess," Paul said. "Don't bother waiting up for me."

Adam sat on the bed as the door slammed. He wished they'd never come to Korban Manor. He stood and grabbed the bedstead, then started pulling the twin beds apart. When he had them in separate corners of the room, he looked up at the portrait of Korban.

"Paul can have the woman in white, and I'll have you."

The fire roared its approval.

The horses were beautiful, sleek, their muscles bunched in grace. No wonder they were Anna's favorite animals. Once, before the fatalistic oncology report, she had dreamed of owning a stable and boarding horses. But that dream was as fleeting and insubstantial as all the others, whether the dream was of Korban Manor, Stephen, or her own ghost.

She heard an off-key whistle, what sounded like an attempt at "Yankee Doodle," and turned to see Mason walking down the road toward the barn. He waved and stopped beside her at the fence, then looked across the pasture as if watching a movie projected against the distant mountains.

"So, how's the ghost-hunting going?" he asked.

She didn't need this. Stephen was bad enough. At least Stephen believed in ghosts, though his ghosts had energy readings instead of souls. But Mason was just another self-centered loser, probably a blind atheist, cocksure that nothing existed after breath ceased. Atheists were far more proselytizing and smug than any Christian Anna had ever met.

"You know something?" she said. "People like you deserve to be haunted."

Mason spread his arms in wounded resignation. "What did I say?"

"You don't have to say it with words. Your eyes say plenty. Your eyes say, 'What a lovable flake. She's bound to be impressed by a great artist such as myself and it's only a matter of time before she falls into my bed.' "

"You must have me confused with William Roth."

"Sorry," she said, knowing she was taking her frustration and anger out on a relatively innocent bystander. But no one was completely innocent. "I'm just a little unraveled at the moment."

"Want to talk about it?"

"Yeah. Like you'd understand."

"Look, I've seen you taking your long walks, sneaking out at night with your flashlight. So you like to be alone. That's fine. So do I. But if weird things are happening to me, they're probably happening to you, too. Maybe even worse stuff, because no way in hell would I go out *there* in the dark." Mason nodded to the forest that, even with the explosion of autumn's colors, appeared to harbor fast and sharp shadows.

"What weird things are you talking about? I thought you were a skeptic."

"Ah. I figured I'd arouse your scientific curiosity, if nothing else. Have you seen George around?"

"George?"

Mason moved closer, lowering his voice as if to deter an invisible eavesdropper. "How long does somebody have to be dead before he becomes a ghost?"

Anna looked at Korban Manor through the trees, at the widow's walk with its thin white railing, where her dream figure had stood under the moonlight. "Maybe it happens before they're even dead."

"Okay. How about this one? Can you be haunted by something inside your own head? Because I'm seeing Ephram Korban every time I close my eyes, I see him in the mirror, I see him in the fireplace, my hands carve his goddamned face even when I tell them to work on something else."

"I think the shrinks call it 'obsessive-compulsive disorder.' But that describes every artist I've ever known. And ninety-nine percent of all human males."

"Hey, we're not all assholes. And I wish you'd get off your personal vendetta against everybody who has a dream. Some artists are normal people who just happen to make things because we can't figure out how in the hell to communicate with people."

"And some of *us* are normal people who search for proof of the afterlife because this life sucks in so many ways and humans always disappoint us. Ghosts are easier to believe in than most of the people I've met."

"Truce, then. Obviously we're both crazy as hell. For a minute there, I was afraid we didn't have anything in common."

That brought an unfamiliar smile to Anna's lips. "All right. Let's start over. I guess you've heard all the ghost stories. About how Ephram Korban jumped to his death off the widow's walk, though the best legends claim that one of the servants pushed him to his death because of the usual reasons."

"What reasons are those?"

"Unrequited love or requited love. Why else would you want to kill somebody? And, according to gossip and even a few parapsychology articles, Korban's spirit wanders the land, trying to find a way back into the manor in which he invested so much of his time, money, and energy."

"You don't believe it?"

The horses heard a call from the barn and took off at a gallop. "I wish I were that free," she said. "Maybe I'll get to be a horse in the next life."

"The downside is, you'd have to die first. Like Ephram Korban."

"Well, he has a grave site up over that ridge, but a grave's nothing but a hole in the ground. I haven't seen his ghost."

"You really think ghosts are here?"

"I know they're here. When your life burns up, you leave a little smoke behind. And don't ask me to prove it, or you'll remind me of someone I've spent the past year forgetting."

"I'll take your word for it. Maybe I'll ask Ransom to let me borrow one of his charm bags. Says they keep restless spirits away."

"Can't hurt," Anna said. "I'm going down to the barn. Care to join me?"

"I'm heading there anyway. Miss Mamie has all but demanded that Ransom help me find a whopping big log to turn into a life-sized statue."

"Ah, you poor suffering artists. Always having to please the critics."

"You poor critics, always having to fake that world-class cynicism."

By the time they reached the barn, Ransom had led the horses under an open shed built onto one wing of the barn. He hooked the cinch under the belly of the big roan, whose ears twitched as if this were a familiar game. Two lanterns blazed inside the barn, dangling from the dusty rafters. Leather straps and gleaming bits of metal hung along one wall, and four saddles were lined on a bench beneath the pieces of harness.

"Well, hello there, young 'uns," Ransom called in greeting. He looked a bit longer at Anna and glanced at the sky with a frown.

"Need any help?" Anna asked.

"Don't need none, but I sure do like company. You know your way around a horse?"

"One end eats and the other doesn't," Mason said.

"And one end might kick you in the crotch, if you send off vibes of stupidity." Anna rubbed the nose of the chestnut, and in seconds it was nuzzling her neck, blowing softly through its nostrils. If only she were that good with men. Back when she cared about such things, anyway. Or ghosts. It would be a welcome change for them to rush out of the land of the dead with open arms and a smile.

She snapped the reins on the bridle and fed the leather through the steel rings. "These guys are great," she said to Ransom.

"They sure took a shine to you."

"I was raised around horses once."

"Once?" Mason asked.

"A long story, one of many," she said.

"Watch out, Mason," Ransom said. "A woman with secrets is generally bad news. Will you folks give me a hand hauling out the wagon?"

They headed for the interior of the barn, Ransom pausing to push the sliding wooden doors farther apart. He was about to step inside when he looked above the barn door and grabbed the rag-ball charm from around his neck. He waved it and closed his eyes, whispering something rhythmical that Anna couldn't hear.

"Danged if they ain't changed it again," Ransom said. He rolled a wooden barrel to the door, climbed on it with trembling legs, then stood and turned the horseshoe that was nailed above the door. He hung it so that the prongs pointed up, toward the sky.

"Does the luck not work the other way?" Anna asked.

"That charm is a heck of a lot older than what you might reckon. It's come to mean 'luck' to most people, but signs get watered down and weakened 'cause people forget the truth of them. Same as a four-leaf clover."

"Sure, they're magically delicious, like the cereal."

"Used to be, it gave the person carrying it the power to see ghosts and witches. Back when people believed."

Anna caught Mason's look. "So points-down on the horseshoe is bad, right?"

"It's practically throwing open the door to every kind of dead thing you care to imagine. I like for the dead to stay dead." He again gave Anna that sad, distant look. "Too bad not everybody around these parts feels the same way."

Mason helped Ransom down from the barrel. Anna tethered the horses to a locust post and followed the men inside the barn. Horse-drawn vehicles were lined against a side wall. The hay wagon stood nearest the door. Beside it were two sleighs, a surrey with its top folded down, and a fancy carriage with a lantern at each corner. All of the vehicles were restored and maintained in the kind of condition that would send antique dealers scrambling for their checkbooks. The aroma of cottonseed oil and leather fought with the hay dust for dominance of the barn's air.

A large metal hay rake sat in the far corner, slightly red from rust. There was a single seat for the operator, and a coupling in the front to yoke the draft animals. The large steel tines of the rake curled in the air like a claw.

"That's a wicked-looking machine," Mason said.

"Yep," Ransom said, unblocking the wheels of the wagon. "That's the windrower, that sharp part that looks like an overgrown pitchfork. And you can see the hay-cutter arm. Works by the turn of the wheels. We still do hay the hard way around here."

"I'll bet the horses love it," Anna said.

"Yeah, and they's smart enough to know they get to eat the hay, come winter."

"You going to cut any while we're here?" she asked, thinking how much fun it would be to help. Hard physical labor did wonders for the depressed and self-pitying mind. "Some of those meadows around here are getting pretty high."

"We had to hold off for a while because the signs were in the heart."

"The heart?"

"Ain't a good time for cutting oats or wheat or any reaping crop. It's a time fit only for the harvest of dead things."

Mason cleared his throat and spat loudly. "Ugh. Hay dust choking me." He looked at Anna and said, "Sorry for being crude. That's the way we do it in Sawyer Creek."

"In case you ain't noticed, this ain't Sawyer Creek," Ransom said. He motioned them to go to the rear of the wagon and he picked up the tongue. "Throw your shoulders in, now."

They maneuvered the wagon out the door and under the shed. As Anna and Ransom hitched the team, Mason explored the barn. A few minutes later, he poked his head outside. "Hey, what's under the trapdoor?"

Ransom stroked the mane on the chestnut mare.

"Taters, sweet taters, cabbage, apples, turnips. Root cellar for stuff that don't need to be kept so cold."

"Can I look?"

Ransom went to the bench and tugged on a pair of rough leather gloves. "Help yourself."

Anna followed Mason to the corner of the barn, where the trapdoor was set in the floor between two stacks of hay bales.

"Got doors on the bottom floor, where the barn's set against the hillside," Ransom said. "We can haul from the orchards and gardens straight up to here, save a lot of handling. Then there's a tunnel goes back to the Big House. Ephram Korban had it dug in case a blizzard struck or something. He was always going on about 'tunnels of the soul,' for some reason. I expect he was about half crazy, if some of them legends are true."

"Or maybe all the legends are true and he was all the way crazy," Anna said.

Mason knelt and lifted the heavy wooden door. The cellar smelled of sweet must and earth, with a faint scent of rotted fruit. The darkness beneath had a weight, like black oil. A makeshift ladder led down into the seemingly bottomless depths.

"Ain't much of interest down there," Ransom said. "Unless you like to sit and talk to the rats."

"Rats?" Mason let the door fall with a slam, knocking dust loose from the rafters. Anna fought a sneeze.

Ransom grinned, his sparse teeth yellow in the weak lamplight. "Rats as big around as your thigh."

"I hate rats," Mason said. "I grew up with them. Sounded like cavalry behind the walls of my bedroom. What I hate the most is those beady eyes, like they're sizing you up."

"Don't worry," Ransom said. "They get plenty to eat without having to gnaw on the guests."

"Miss Mamie would probably scold them for having bad manners."

Anna laughed. Maybe Mason wasn't so bad. At least he wasn't afraid to show weakness. Unlike her.

Mason stood and wiped his hands on his jeans. Something fluttered from the rafters and brushed Anna's face, and she wiped at it as if it were cobwebs.

"Jesus, don't tell me that was a bat," Mason said, ducking. "Bats are nothing but rats with wings."

"That was a bluebird," Ransom said. "Lucky for you, young lady. If a bluebird flies in your path, it means you're going to be kissed."

"Great," she said. "And I thought I earned my kisses by casting magic spells on unsuspecting men."

"Believe what you want," Ransom said. "I reckon you see through the signs better than anybody. Now, I'd best get on with the chores."

Mason wiped his hands on an old horse blanket hanging from the rafters. "So, Ransom, do you have time to help me find an overgrown log that's just right for statue-making?"

"Why do you think we hitched up the wagon? Miss Mamie always gets her way with things."

"So I'm starting to find out."

"Let's get on before dark. Might have to go below Beechy Gap, where we had a big windfall a few winters back. Want to come along, young lady?"

"No, thanks. I've got some chores of my own."

"I reckon some things got to be done alone," he said.

Anna wasn't sure what to make of Ransom. He kept dropping hints but a deep fear was hidden behind his eyes. Maybe he had secrets of his own. She waited until Mason and Ransom climbed up onto the buckboard seat, then she passed Ransom the reins.

"See you later tonight?" Mason asked her.

Anna felt the half smile on her face, and wasn't sure which way she wanted the corners of her mouth to point. "We'll see."

Ransom flipped the reins and the team headed up

the road, where the wide sandy ribbon threaded between the trees into the forest. She slid the barn doors closed, then looked up at the horseshoe.

It was points-down again.

Dead things come in.

She looked at the forest.

Under the fringe of shadowed underbrush, amid the laurel and locust and briars, the woman in white stood, the bouquet held out in challenge. The ghost stared at Anna like a mirror, then turned and drifted among the trees.

"All right, damn you," Anna said. "I'll play hide-and-seek with you."

As she entered the forest, she wondered how you could ever catch up to your own ghost. And why it would hide from you in the first place. Ransom was right about one thing. A woman with secrets generally was bad news.

CHAPTER 14

And the night spread, seeping like warm oil over the hills, expanding, filling the valleys, and rising up the gray Appalachian slopes. The night became an ocean, an ink-stained bloodbath. The night became the sky. The night became a mouth that swallowed the night before, all the previous nights, all the nights to come, the night—

Spence rattled on, fingers pounding the slick keys. He was an automaton now. There was no world, no room, no smell of lantern smoke and sweat and sweet Bridget nearby, only the glowing battlefield of the half-empty page. No outer night lurked beyond the window, only the night that came to life through words, the night that swelled and surged through his veins, that pumped darkness through his extremities, that burned in the ebony furnace of his heart.

He was dimly aware of the strand of drool running down one side of his cheek. He grinned, and the drool leaked onto his cotton shirt. The saliva was from another plane, a reality so flat and dull and senseless compared to the magical land unfolding beneath his keystrokes. His wrists ached and his fingers were stiff, eyes watering from strain, but those problems were of the flesh, and this work was of the Word.

The master, the paper, urged him on. Commanded him forward. Trumpeted reveille with a Joshua horn. Ordained him a god, albeit a lesser god.

Because he was a servant to the great god Word, the one true god. Word who giveth and taketh away, Word who gave his only begotten suffix so that Spence shall not perish but have everlasting metaphor, Word who spewed forth from burning bush and graven tablet and mighty cloud. In Word we trust.

A hand dropped on his shoulder, an intrusion from somewhere on that dreary plane of soil and substance. Ah, that must be the Muse, who was also slave to Word, made Word from dust and bit of bone, Muse who offered the fruit, Muse who served as adjective to his improper noun.

"Jeff," she sang, and lovely was her music. He wanted to weep, but the tears would blur the glorious page. His page. And Spence's moment of vanity broke the spell, angering the god who was Word.

He stopped typing and glanced around, blinking.

"Come to bed, honey," Muse said. "You haven't slept in thirty-six hours."

A thick ream of manuscript was piled on his desk. His eyes burned and he forced his dry eyelids to close. Muse was drawing him away from the world of Word, down from the soft high temple. Perhaps Muse was no friend after all, but an enemy. "What do you want?"

She was no longer Muse, only Bridget, a Georgia sophomore shivering in a sheer nightgown, her nipples hard from the chill in the air.

"I'm worried about you." She leaned over him from behind and wrapped her arms around his chest. Spence let the swivel chair sag backward. Now that the spell of Word was broken, anxiety sluiced through his limbs. One corner of his eye twitched.

Bridget kissed him on the neck, just below the line of his newly grown stubble. "You're working so hard. Why don't you come to bed?"

"I can't work if I'm in bed." His irritability returned now that the letters had stopped flowing.

"I'm lonely for you, honey."

She had forgiven him for the previous day's mistreatment. Or had that been last night? A hundred years ago? Time lost all meaning at Korban Manor.

"Dear, dear, dear," he said, letting each word dangle in the air like a noose. "What is your loneliness compared to the great loss the world would suffer should my work go unfinished?"

"I know it's important. I'm not like you, though. I need a little companionship now and then."

"Surely you can turn your not inconsiderable charms toward procuring yourself a bedmate. You can play your illusory games of love elsewhere, with my blessing."

Bridget pulled her arms from his chest. Spence swiveled the chair so he could admire his latest bauble. Her comely curves undulated beneath the clinging fabric of her gown. A treasure. A pretty, useless thing.

"Jeff, I don't want anybody else. I love *you.*"

This distraction was getting interesting. Perhaps Word would forgive him a moment's idleness. Surely even Ephram Korban played emotional games in his day.

"Love," he said, and the word flowed as if spoken by Sir Laurence Olivier himself, the liquid of the phonic dripping off Spence's tongue. A classic oratory was coming on, rising from his bones to his chest, through his lungs and throat, air made wisdom. The only thing that ever changed was the audience.

"Love, the ultimate vanity," he said. "All love is self-love. Motherly, brotherly, sexual, puppy, religious, sacrificial. All love is masturbation. And so, I give you permission to love yourself, since that seems to be what you require of me."

"Honey, don't be so . . . so . . ."

"Obdurate. From the Latin 'to harden.' Synonyms: firm, unbending, inflexible. Oh, how I wish that were true. But the mind embraces what the flesh shrinks from in shame."

"Don't do that. You know I don't care about your—about *our*—problem."

Spence laughed, his girth wiggling from the sheer ecstasy of his self-love. He reached up and stroked her hair, a romance-novel cliché, silken tassels, spun gold. Her cheeks were pink with hoarded passion, lips slightly parted as she gasped at his touch. Her skin glowed like honey in the firelight.

"Our problem," he said.

She had crossed the line. This demanded a response.

His hand closed into a fist around her hair. He pulled her head forward, reaching behind him to grab the manuscript. He flung the loose pages at her face, pleased at the slapping sound the paper made against her skin. The pages kited to the floor as she grunted.

"Pick them up," he said, twisting her hair, forcing her to her knees. She was petite, no match for his great bulk. She sobbed as she fumbled among the papers. He jerked her to her feet, though she had collected only a small sheaf of pages.

"Read," he said, with cold menace.

Her eyes were wide, cheeks wet with tears, lower lip quivering.

"Read," he said again. Calm now.

Her eyes flicked across the page, shoulders shaken with sobs, breasts swaying miserably against the confines of satin.

"Aloud." He was once again Jefferson Davis Spence, the legend, the genuine article. No more illusions of Muses and far-off literary gods, no more lofty aspirations, no more symbiosis with the Royal typewriter. Now he could focus on the art of cruelty.

" 'The night spread its f-filth like spies, like flies,' " she said, voice trembling. " 'The n-night walked the night, climbed its own spine like a ladder, the night rattled the bones of its own cage . . .' "

Spence relaxed his grip on her hair, and now stroked her. He closed his eyes, lost in the precious rhythm of his own prose.

" '. . . the night growled, hissed like a snake, sputtered like a black firework, the night entered itself, laved itself with its own tongue, swallowed its own tail . . .' "

Ah, the Muse was singing again. All she needed was the proper sheet music.

" '. . the night tastes of charcoal and ash, the night tastes of licorice, the night tastes of teeth—yes, of cold teeth . . . go out frost . . .' "

Her voice trailed away, but Spence still rocked back and forth in his chair like a babe lulled by its own sonorous babble.

"Jeff?" She took a careful step backward.

"You stopped reading. I didn't tell you to stop."

"This stuff is . . . this stuff is . . ."

Spence smiled, his face warm with satisfaction at this small but tender tribute the peak of self-love. He braced for the paroxysm of bliss, awaiting her ejaculation of praise.

"This is just so awful." She dropped the section of manuscript to the floor. "You've been wasting your talent on *this?* This . . . *maggot mess?"*

Spence, anticipating the rush of sweet validation, didn't register her words at first. But the tone was clear. Even with their southern flavor, the words were exactly like those of Mrs. Eileen Foxx, his fifth grade teacher. Foxx in Socks, the kids called her, because they weren't clever enough to come up with something lewd or connected to bodily functions.

Mrs. Foxx had berated him in front of the whole class because he'd had the temerity to misspell the word *receive.* He stood at the chalkboard, breathing the dust of a thousand mistakes, while the other children howled with laughter, relieved because it wasn't *them* this time. And the warm wetness spread beneath his waist, his small bladder voided, and the laughter changed in pitch, rose to the level of schoolhouse legend.

And on that sunny spring afternoon at Fairfield Elementary school, a new grammar rule was formed: *I* before *E* except after *P.*

Born as well that day was Jefferson Spence, the writer. The one who would out-obtuse Faulkner, who would out-macho Hemingway, who would out-wolf Tom Wolfe. And though he couldn't reach back through the halls of time and grab Mrs. Foxx by the frayed seams of her cardigan sweater and smash those ever-pursed lips, he could act now. He could vent against the critics and the sneerers and the pretty popinjays, all the other Eileen Foxxes of the world who deserved retribution.

He swept his hand hard against the cheek of the faux Muse. She moaned and collapsed back onto the bed, an arm bouncing against the brass bedstead, another arm flopping across her chest. A trickle of blood leaked from her mouth, and one nostril clotted red as well. As the flesh of her cheek warmed from the blow, her eyes stared back at him with all the severity of Eileen Foxx's.

He turned from her gaze.

Ah, Ephram smiled. Ephram, who had offered support during *Seasons of Sleep.* Ephram, an ally in a universe of small-minded fifth graders who would never understand.

It wasn't that he always failed with women, or that his literary output was uneven. It wasn't a flaw in the equipment. It was *them.* It had always been them.

They stood between him and the true light, the bright shining path, the burning Word. Who needed mere physical pleasure? What one needed was the shedding of pleasure, the removal of distraction.

One needed to become the Word, a communion reduced to its simplest form.

Spence placed his fingers on the cold keys of the typewriter. The lantern hissed in approval, the fireplace rumbled with hot delight. He looked at Ephram again, and then at the blank page, his greatest ally and his most dreaded enemy.

He scarcely heard the door close behind his back. He pressed his fingers down, seeking the approval of the true god Word. His hands moved of their own accord, as if encased in living gloves.

Anna stumbled through the trees, tired but determined, the ghostly figure always just on the edge of her vision. The moon had risen in synchronicity with sunset, only a small curve sliced from its white roundness. The flashlight was unnecessary in the clearings and stretches of meadow, but the moon couldn't penetrate the cold shadows beneath the forest canopy.

The ghost woman faded in and out of view, as if fighting to keep its constitution. Anna had called out to her several times, but not even the wind responded. The forest was silent, and even the crickets seemed to be huddling in dread. The air was chilly and dew hung heavy on the maple, laurel, and birch leaves that brushed her face and shoulders. The game of hide-and-seek seemed eternal, as if Anna would forever have to chase this spirit, the two of them bound in a shared purgatory of loneliness.

Anna thought the ghost was leading her to the cabin where she had seen the ghost of the young girl on her first night at the manor. But her dead tour guide turned up the ridge when they reached the meadow below the cabin, heading higher into the steep hills of Beechy

Gap. Anna weaved her way among granite boulders that angled from the ground like worn fossils. The trail steepened and narrowed, and the vegetation changed as well, from leafy deciduous to stunted balsam and jack pine.

Anna scooted across a long flat jut of stone. She was on the highest part of the rocky ridge. The great sea of mountains stretched out toward the horizon. A whisper of wind tried to stir itself, then gave up and settled back to earth.

The trees were thinner here, and her breath plumed from her mouth like the smoke of her soul. The few stars hung in the cold sky, shivering and twinkling. Even the familiar Dog Star and the orange wink of Saturn gave her no comfort. She was alone, except for the translucent woman who hovered above the cold dirt and stone of the ridge. The ghost beckoned her forward with a wave of the haunted bouquet.

Anna's flashlight played over a mass of fallen posts and splintered boards scattered in a treeless stretch of ground. The ghost woman was among the ruins of the old shack, her ethereal figure penetrated by a dozen ragged pieces of wood. The ghost opened her mouth, trying to form a lost language. Bits of broken glass glinted in the flashlight's beam.

Anna slid off the rock toward the twisted debris. One thick piece of timber jabbed forlornly at the sky. Anna stepped closer, answering the summons of the ghost. The woman stood waiting, eyes vacant, the bouquet held out in either welcome or apology.

Then the night fell in.

One of the broken timbers lifted from the ground and cut an audible arc in the air as if swung by an invisible giant. The heavy wood slammed into her stomach. The flashlight fell at her feet, its beam sending a thin streak of orange into the underbrush.

Anna doubled over, spears of fire wending through her gut, rusty nails driving into her temples, her teeth biting tin roofing. But it was more than the agony of cancer. This pain was bone-deep and deadly serious. Her right wrist was squeezed in a knife-edged vise.

Anna closed her eyes and collapsed.

No slow-motion countdown would take this pain away. Through the hammering of her pulse, she could hear tremors in the building's rubble. Wood rot and corruption assaulted her nostrils as she writhed in the muddy fallen leaves.

In the jumble of ruin, she saw a tunnel, a long, dark, cold mouth opening up before her. A stale breeze blew up from the depths of the tunnel, but it had to be her imagination, because the tunnel led down into the earth. Her sweat was slivers of ice on her face, the cold swabbing her bones, and she thought of those words from the bathroom mirror. Go out frost.

Then she heard the voice, a soft mournful wail that stretched over the hills.

Anna opened her eyes with effort, vision blurred by tears of pain. Two forms drifted among the ruins, the ghost woman kneeling, a second ghost swelling and hovering over the first. The other ghost was a man in blue jeans, flannel shirt, and workman's leather boots, his clothes as translucent as his sick milk of skin. A few shreds of nebulous flesh hung from one sleeve of the shirt. His one hand held the piece of timber that had struck her. He looked down at the ghost woman, his eyes as deep as the cold black tunnel had been.

A radiance shone around the dead man, an aura of malevolent energy. His ectoplasmic face was twisted in rage, the lips peeled back to show jagged teeth. He dropped the timber and put his lone hand around the woman's throat, and Anna could see the strength in his fingers as they tightened around surreal flesh. Anna's throat burned in sympathetic pain. The ghost woman screamed soundlessly, struggled for a moment like a wind-driven linen caught in a briar vine, then faded from view, again a corpse, dead a second time, the bouquet falling from her fingers and dissipating into mist.

Anna rolled onto her hands and knees and started to crawl away. The caustic fires still scorched her insides, but now a black surf of fear washed over her, momentarily dousing the raw ache. She glanced back and saw that the man's aura had grown brighter, as if the spirit murder had fueled some infernal fire. He smiled at her, his tongue slithery as an eel and his eyes spilling forth a darkness that rivaled the black night.

The mouth parted. "That you, Selma?"

At least this ghost remembered language, though its tone was crazed.

"It's me," it said. "George. I knew you'd come back. Korban promised me."

Come back? From HIS side or hers?

"I'm not Selma," Anna said, trying to rise, but the weight of the night sky was too great.

"I got a present I been saving just for you. We got tunnels of the soul, Selma."

The ghost held something in his hand, something that dangled like a small kill from a hunter's belt. Anna thought at first it was the bouquet. Then it wiggled.

It was his other hand, the one that had lost its place at the end of his right arm.

As she struggled in the dirt, the spirit tossed the hand toward her. It landed on its fingers and scrabbled after her like a spider. The ghost's laughter echoed across the dismal hills. "Hand of glory, Selma."

Anna turned, tried again to regain her feet, but the pain had made her drunk, awkward, confused.

The severed hand closed around her ankle.

That was impossible. Ghosts had no substance, at least a substance that could take solid form in the real world.

But this IS the real world. And sometimes, it's not what you believe, but how MUCH you believe.

She believed in ghosts. They existed. You couldn't turn faith off and on like water from a spigot.

Too bad.

Because now she had what she'd always wanted.

Physical contact with the dead.

Her ankle was numb, hot ice, liquid fire, ringed by dull razors.

The fingers pressed into her meat. Anna was jerked flat on her stomach. She flailed at the air, grabbing for a nearby pine branch. The hand pulled her backward before she could reach the branch. Toward the rubble. Where *he* waited.

"Come on, now, Selma. Don't keep old Georgie-Boy waiting." The ghost's voice had changed, deepened.

She dug her fingernails into the ground, clawing at the sharp stones and pine needles. She grunted, realizing for the first time since she'd witnessed the spectral struggle that she was still breathing.

Breath.

That meant she was alive. Not a ghost yet. But if this spirit had the power to murder ghosts, what would it do to the living?

The hand tugged again, sliding her across three feet of damp dirt. Wet leaves worked their way underneath her shirt, chilling her belly.

A strange sound spilled across the ridge, like the scream of a dying mourning dove. Anna looked at the ghostman, his smile stretching and leaking red, orange, yellow, the colors melding into a malchromatic aurora that surrounded him as if he were lit by hellfire.

Anna slid another couple of feet closer to the ruins, desperately kicking at the hand. It was like kicking a rotted fish. She was pulled again and the sharp end of a piece of wood pressed into the back of her leg. The thing was dragging her into the spiked tips of broken timber and the sawteeth of the ripped tin roofing. She was about to be sacrificed at the stake.

But why?

Why would a ghost want to kill *her?*

"Snakes crawl at night, honey," it said. "Snakes crawl at night."

More backward pressure.

The sharp wood against her leg dug into flesh and sent bright sparks of pain shooting up the chimney of her nervous system. A board knocked against her vertebrae, drumming her spine as if it were a xylophone. Broken glass dug into her knee, cutting through the corduroy of her slacks and stinging like acid. The flames in her abdomen expanded into her chest, into her head, sent lava through her limbs. She closed her eyes and saw streaks of light against the back of her eyelids, like popping embers or shooting stars. Behind the streaks was the black tunnel, expanding endlessly outward, and shimmering at the far end was the woman in white.

So this is what it feels like to die.

She had come to Korban Manor to find her ghost, pushed by the prophetic power of her dreams. This was what she wanted. Except she'd never expected it to be so painful. More shards, splinters, and crooked nails worked into her skin as the rubble shifted with her weight.

Silly girl. Guess you were wrong about everything. You thought death would be cold, but it's hot, hot, and that tunnel is so deep—

The hand on her ankle yanked, insistent, tenacious. Then a hand gripped one shoulder.

And words came from somewhere above her, like the voice of an insane angel: "Go out frost, go out frost, go out frost."

The pain fell away, and only darkness remained.

CHAPTER 15

Getting the log onto the wagon, then to the manor and down the stairs to the basement, had been a real bitch. Ransom refused to help carry the log through the house, but Miss Mamie had roused some drinkers from the study, enlisting their help. Paul, Adam, William Roth, Zainab, even Lilith. It was a miracle they hadn't dropped the log on their toes, but at last it stood upright, supported by scrap lumber and wires tied to nails in the joists overhead.

"That had better be some statue, after all this trouble," Miss Mamie had called from the head of the basement stairs before slamming the door and leaving Mason alone.

No. Not alone.

He lifted the sheet of canvas. The face of Ephram Korban stared at him. Had Mason really carved such smug perfection? But the work wasn't complete. Now that Korban had a face, he needed legs, arms, hands, an oak heart.

This would be the sculpture that earned Mason Beaufort Jackson a mention in the magazines. Forget *The Artist's Magazine* or *Art Times*. This baby was going to land him in the pages of *Newsweek*. Mason began writing headlines and article leads in his head, a feature in *Sculpture* to start with.

MILLTOWN BOY MAKES GOOD

If you heard that an artist was named "Mason Jackson," you'd automatically assume that he'd adopted a nom de plume.

(Wait a second, "nom de plume" is only for authors. Okay, call it a pseudonym then. The article writer would work that bit out.)

But there's nothing put on about this up-and-coming sculptor. Jackson has been called "the Appalachian Michelangelo." This young southern artist may have his feet planted in the land of moonshine and ski slopes, but his hands have descended from a more heavenly plane. Jackson's sculpture series, The Korban Analogies, *is opening to wide acclaim at the Museum of Modern Art in Philadelphia and will soon cross the ocean to London and Paris, where critics have already rested the heavy crown of "Genius" on the unprepossessing man's head.*

Jackson's tour de force is the powerful Korban Emerging *(pictured, left), which Jackson calls "a product of semidivine guidance." The Rodinesque muscularity and massiveness of the work has impressed even the most jaded critics, but there's also a singular delicacy to Jackson's piece.*

No less a discerning eye than Winston DeBussey's has found the work faultless. He calls Mason an "uncanny master" of wood, a medium in which so few top artists dare to work these days.

"It is as if there is no difference between the

pulp and human tissue," raves DeBussey in a rare moment of expansiveness. "Jackson breathes organic life into every swirl of grain. One almost expects to look down and see roots, as if the statue is continually replenishing itself from the juice and salt of earth."

But Jackson takes the praise in stride, offering little insight into the mind behind the man.

"Each piece is conceptualized through a dream image," Jackson said, speaking from his farmhouse-cum-studio in Sawyer Creek, a small mill town nestled in the North Carolina foothills. "And I have absolutely nothing to do with that part of the process. My job is to take that fragile gift and somehow not misinterpret it through these clumsy human hands. Because the dream is the important thing, not the dreamer."

If Mason started talking like that, Junior would elbow him in the ribs and Mama would make him stop watching public television. Such nonsense would earn him some funny looks at the hosiery mill, where he was more at home than in any art museum. He could fool himself into thinking he was good, but fooling others was much harder. If he wanted to fool the entire world, this monstrous piece of oak before him needed to be turned into the most beautiful dream image ever conceived.

First he'd have to skin the bark.

Then find the man inside.

He lifted the hatchet, looked at the dark spaces in the corners of the basement. He didn't belong in the mill. This was what he was born for, the reason he'd come to Korban Manor. He'd never felt so alive.

He thought of Anna's words, how Ephram Korban's spirit lived on in these walls. How a soul might be nothing more than the sum of a person's mortal dreams.

How dreams could lie. How dreams could turn to ash.

No. This dream was real.

The hatchet bit into the wood.

The bony hand on Anna's shoulder tugged her shirt, lifted her. So the ghostman had her now. She was finally going to find out what it was like to be dead. Or maybe she was already a ghost, because the worst of the pain was fading.

Anna tried to stand, but her legs were like damp smoke. She knelt on one bloody knee, feeling for purchase among the broken boards. She opened her eyes to face the dead thing, resigning herself to crawl into the dark tunnel.

But it wasn't the leering spirit that held her. It was an old woman.

"Ought to watch yourself a mite better," the woman said.

Her face was wrinkled, the moonlight revealing her swollen veins, her eyebrows as white as ice. But the blue eyes set among those sagging folds of skin were bright, young, intelligent. And Anna recognized the shawl that was draped around the woman's stooped shoulders.

"You were at the cabin—"

"Hush yourself, child. I seen what you seen, and we both seen way too much. Let's get away from here, then we can have us a long chat."

Anna got to her feet, pushing the broken boards away from her legs. The pain was gone, and the ring of fire around her ankle had faded. The moon was higher now, approaching the zenith of its arc.

Anna studied the rubble. It could all have been a dream, except for the tearing of her clothes and skin.

"Come on away from there. George got fetched

over, but that don't mean you got to go yet," the woman said.

The old woman led Anna from the fallen building. The woman had surprising strength for someone who appeared to be in her eighties. Anna watched her climb over the flat rocks with the agility of a mountain goat, even though she used a thick walking stick to steady herself. Anna looked for her flashlight, but it must have rolled into the thorny underbrush and out of sight. She hurried after the woman.

The old woman paused on a table of rock, looking out over the great expanse of mountains. The sky was woolen gray, but Anna could make out the ripples and swells of earth stretching out to the horizon.

"Korban about snatched you," the woman said without turning toward Anna. "Thought I'd get a chance to warn you first. But old Ephram's always been the impatient sort."

"Ephram Korban, you mean?"

"The master of these here parts. Or, at least, he likes to think so."

"But you're talking in present tense. He's dead."

"Like that matters much." She spat off the rock into the tops of the trees below.

"Who was that woman I saw?" Anna's head was clearing a little. "And the little girl at the cabin?"

The old woman laughed, but it was a broken gargle, heavy with cynicism. "You got the Sight, all right. Knew it when I first laid eyes on you. Now, no more questions till we get away from this place. 'Cause this place is *Korban's.*"

Anna followed the woman off the rock and down the narrow trail, amazed at the way the woman's hard leather shoes dodged over protruding roots and stones, the walking stick nimbly stabbing at the dirt in search of purchase. They headed off the ridge to the back side of Beechy Gap.

Anna paused to catch her breath, rubbing her abdomen. "One question. What does 'go out frost' mean?"

"Old mountain spell. Means 'dead stay dead.' "

Anna would have to remember that one. She hoped that, unlike what Ransom had said about horseshoes and four-leaf clovers, this little piece of magic hadn't been worn thin by time.

Adam had spent the long hours of insomnia trying to nab the thoughts that orbited his head like space junk. And most of the thoughts were about asking Miss Mamie if there was a way he could cancel his stay at the manor. He didn't care about a refund. Paul could remain with his camera and his pouty lips and his arrogance for the rest of the six weeks, as far as Adam was concerned. All Adam needed was a ride out of this place.

They'd had another argument, this one in the study after carrying the log into the basement. Paul was showing off for William Roth, who was hitting on several women at once, and Adam tried to get Paul aside for a chat. Paul had sneered and said, "Why don't you go to bed, Princess? I know how bored you get talking about anything besides yourself."

Adam had finally fallen asleep sometime around what felt like midnight, though the moon was so bright that time hadn't seemed to pass at all. And again he'd had the dream, the dream of the fall from the widow's walk. But this time he recognized the man who was trying to push him off the top of the house. It was the man he'd imagined seeing in the closet when Paul was putting away his camera. The man in the portrait. Ephram Korban.

And again Korban had Adam leaning over the railing. The hard wood pressed against the small of his back. Even as he was dreaming, he realized that you weren't supposed to feel pain in your dreams.

But all his senses were working: he could smell the sweet beech trees, hear the aluminum tinkle of the creek, taste the rancid graveyard stench of Korban's breath, see the stars spinning crazily above as the man pushed him backward over the rail.

"You have no vanity," Korban said. "I can't eat your dreams. They're made of air."

Adam's fingers tangled in the man's beard, desperately gripping the coarse hairs. But as Korban pushed him away, the hairs ripped out at their roots. And just as Adam fell, losing his grip on Korban's woolen waistcoat, he stared into the man's eyes.

The eyes flickered from charcoal black to a sizzling amber. Korban's cold iron hands released their grip on Adam's upper arms and Adam screamed as he hurtled to the packed ground sixty feet below.

The air whistled like a teakettle in pain.

The great gulf of space yawned overhead, farther and farther away, its softness lost to him even as he grasped for a handle on the stars.

The house's windows gleamed in streaks, the shutters blurring in his peripheral vision. His blood rushed to his feet. This dream was stranger than any he'd ever had. Because you were supposed to wake up when you fell in your dreams.

But Adam was aware of the impact as his head pounded into the circle of the driveway. He clearly heard the crunching of bone as his spine folded like a paper bird, he gasped as his breath whooshed from his lungs, he bit his tongue in half and the amputated tip squirted from between broken teeth, he tasted his own warm blood, then vomited as his shattered pelvis speared his stomach and kidney.

As his ruined flesh lay sprawled and leaking on the ground, he clearly saw his own eyeballs lying beside his head. The eyeballs glowered at him, their brown irises helpless in the ovate globes of white, the pupils large with shock and fear, no sockets or eyelids to hide their twin disapproval. Even dreaming, he recognized the absurdity of seeing his own eyes. He couldn't wait to tell Paul about this.

Except you also weren't supposed to feel pain in a dream, either. And what else could this be but pain, this sheet of red that dropped on him like a hundred sulfuric guillotines? Ribbons of electricity shot through his broken body, his nerves screaming like four alarms at a firehouse. Adam tried to laugh. Wasn't this funny, experiencing this hellburst of orange that flooded his brain, when he was surely dead?

But wait a second. Can you dream that you're dead?

But how would you *know* if you were dead . . . this was the kind of thing that would give you a headache if you didn't know you were dreaming. But Adam had a headache anyway. He knelt to scrape his spilled brains together, scooped them up, and put them back in their broken shell.

As his fingers stirred through the steaming wrinkles of his own cerebrum, he realized that his body was splayed out before him. This was odd, surreal, Daliesque. He expected to awaken at any moment to find himself giggling into his pillow. But he didn't wake up. He stood, looking at the pool of red that seeped from beneath his body and the sour bile around his head. A splinter of femur protruded from one thigh, angling out from a rip in the gray pajamas. The bone gleamed bright and wet in the pale light. The body's head was turned away in the direction of the wide stone steps that led into Korban Manor.

But his *real* head, at least the one that housed his soul, was staring higher, at the black portal of the door.

Shapes spilled out of the maw, white wispy forms

like bits of shredded cobweb being swept along by the breeze of a broom.

Some coalesced into more or less human figures, men, women, and small children, their faces blank, their eyes as black as the interior of the foyer. Some of them were in coarse crinolines, or trousers with button-up flies, a few men in overalls and felt hats, the women in bonnets or with their hair pinned up in buns. The young boys were in knickers, mended stockings sagging over square leather shoes, the girls in plain shifts, ribbons in their pigtails. An infant materialized at the feet of one of the women, its ragged diaper mingling with its ragged legs.

Adam stepped backward as they walked toward him. Except they weren't *walking,* they were flitting, floating, flying, arms wide, mouths slack with grim purpose. There were about two dozen figures, and he saw Lilith among them, the maid with the flowing dress, but she was as misty as the others. The plump cook, whom he'd seen earlier pouring dishwater off the back porch, was wiping her hands on her apron.

He screamed, but no one could hear you when you were dead.

It was long past time for waking up.

He tried to run, but stood transfixed, frozen, as cold as a December tombstone.

The crowd gathered around the body that lay on the ground, the ghosts—*yes, of course they're ghosts, if I'm going to have a bad dream I might as well go for broke*—the ghosts merged and intertwined, showing no concern for the social constraints of personal space. And Adam, now more fascinated than frightened, also looked down at the object of their attention.

It was he, himself, the person formerly know as Adam Andrews. There was the mole on his cheek, the small white scar above his elbow where he'd fallen off his bicycle at age nine, the awkward bend in the second toe of his kicking foot that he'd severely dislocated playing high school soccer. There was his hand, the nails unevenly trimmed, a few threads of Korban's beard hair still clutched in the rigid fingers. There was the silver ring with the garnet stone that Paul had given him.

There lay his blood, his flesh, his body.

A low sound filled the lawn, stretching across the hills, a funeral dirge that reminded Adam of recordings of whales he'd heard. It was a bizarre language, sonorous and sad. The syllables of the tuneless sound phased into aural chaos, a thick clotted noise. It was emanating from the manor, as if the foyer were the building's throat.

The ghosts turned toward the door, solemn as only the dead could be. Adam gulped, looked down at his hands, and saw he was made of the same mist as the others, spun from the same insubstantial threads. He was a ghost. That meant . . .

He was really dead.

He smiled to himself. He closed his dreaming eyes. He'd have to forget being mad at Paul at least long enough to tell him about the dream. He wondered if he was snoring, then remembered that he'd pushed the beds apart, so he couldn't count on Paul giving him a nudge in the ribs. And right now, he'd love to be tickled, cuddled awake, to pull Paul's body close, to feel some human heat.

Because being dead was a chilly business. He must have kicked the quilts off in his sleep.

Yes, of course. Any crazy thing makes sense if you analyze it long enough. And deciding to leave Paul must have stirred up some funny things in the old Jungian jungle.

But why shouldn't your mind pull a trick or two on you while you're asleep?

And what could be a better vacation site than this theme park of the deceased? What was that old black-

and-white movie? Yeah, Carnival of Souls, *dancing with the dead, wake up and say, "It was all a dream." And old Ephram Korban IS a nightmare-inducing sort.*

So why not enjoy it, laugh it up, go along for the ride? You'll be awake soon enough, back in the real world with real problems. Like how to deal with Paul. For real.

He opened his eyes, and found himself still in his nightmare.

The ghosts were bending, lifting the corpse. Amused, Adam joined them. When one of the bloody arms lolled outward, Adam placed it back over the chest cavity. The ghosts hoisted the body toward the door of the house, pale pallbearers in a silent procession. Adam trailed after them as they wafted up the steps. Waiting at the door was his malefactor, Korban.

The man flashed a cold smile of triumph, his eyes like onyx marbles.

"Welcome to your tunnel of the soul, Adam," Korban said.

For a moment, Adam forgot he was dreaming. Korban held the door wide as the procession entered the darkness. Adam was unable to keep from following.

Korban's face loomed near, and the man held out a welcoming arm. As Adam drifted into the waiting murk, he realized that it wasn't the manor that was swallowing him. The foyer was a tunnel, a tube of frigid stone-glass walls, an ever-widening mouth, all darkness, beyond light and the things that light touched. Adam shivered, colder now than ghost-cold, unwilling to let his id play anymore.

Time to wake up now . . .

Because Korban was changing, his eyes turning from dead dark orbs into fiery hateful suns.

Because Korban was glowing with loathsome heat, Korban was reaching out to him, reaching in him, into his chest, into his heart—

Please, please, please wake up!

Korban's fingers squeezed and new pain erupted, a pain beyond human understanding, so intense that even the dreaming dead Adam screamed, and Korban pulled him deeper into the tunnel, and he knew that what was waiting ahead would be the worst thing that any part of his brain could concoct.

He screamed again, screamed and screamed, closed his dream eyes so that he wouldn't see what was ahead—

But he *knew* what was ahead, the thing he'd buried so deeply in his mind that he'd forgotten. Though like all true forced forgettings, it had only gained power during the long years of hibernation. And when a buried memory finally claws through its coffin, digs its way through the dirt to the surface, it's not going to look kindly on the undertaker.

This was a memory that had teeth.

So he screamed again, and the hand in his chest was shaking, shaking him—

"Wake up, Adam."

He opened his eyes, but he was still seeing the glimmers of his buried memory, the image making him throw his arms out in panic. He struck Paul in the shoulder.

"Hey!"

Paul stood beside Adam's bed in his underwear. Adam stared at him, unblinking. A faint fuzz of moonlight leaked through the window and the fire threw red light onto the walls.

"You must have been having a hell of a dream," Paul said.

Adam lay still, rolling his eyes around in their sockets, his chest sore from remembered pain. The quilts were bunched in knots around him. He glanced at the corners of the room, at the closet door, expecting the freshly exhumed memory to play out its image in the nearest available scrap of shadow. He looked at the portrait above the fireplace, watching for Korban's lips to part and welcome him into the tunnel.

"I mean, you even woke *me* up with your thrashing around," Paul said, then added, with the slightest hint of scorn in his voice, "and I was all the way across the room."

Adam flexed his fingers, reached up, and wiped the sweat from his forehead and upper lip.

He drew in a breath, a sweet living and waking breath, and nothing had ever tasted so fine, not the chocolate cherry sauce on his favorite sundae, not the driest Chardonnay, not a new love's first kiss.

Paul put his hands on his hips, impatient now. "Did you dream about my woman in white? Or are you still not talking to me?"

Adam opened his mouth, glad to find the tip of his tongue brushing reassuringly against his teeth.

"You were right about one thing," Adam whispered, the words dry in his throat. "It was one *hell* of a dream."

CHAPTER 16

Beautiful.

Spence held up the page so the moonlight from the window would flash fully on the words.

It had been waiting here. All these years. The Muse's blessing, the sweet inspiration, the sleeping dream of creation. The Gift.

The house had given him another masterpiece.

He leaned back in his chair and laughed. The sound echoed off the wood of the room, rattled the dresser on the mirror, mocked back at him from the wainscoting, curled around the cornice of the fireplace mantel, played off the cold rock hearth and swirled in the air like stirred dust. Korban's portrait grinned in the mischief of a secret understanding.

The room was much nicer now that it was empty. There was only Spence and the Royal. Spence and words. And the world beyond the words?

The world itself didn't matter. What mattered was the interpretation, the human reflection, the shaping of the illusion. The craft. Symbolism.

The words.

Spence's words.

So what if those latest novels had meandered off course, had failed to sustain themselves, had crept plotless into unresolved graves? The important thing was that Spence had been anointed. The critics loved him. The *New York Times Book Review* had him on the cover, not once, but twice. And the little people, the aspiring writers and the coffee-shop crowd and pathetic English majors, gobbled up his books like bottom-feeding fish. This was before the era of television talk-show best sellers fashioned their follow-the-leader tastes into a drab society of the mutually hip.

Not that the little people mattered, aside from providing the stimulus of mass adoration. Spence didn't write for them. He didn't write for the critics, either. They were as blind as Homer had been, puffing themselves up as if they had a hand in the creative process, hogs who couldn't recognize they were feeding at the same trough they spat in. Even editors were nothing more than intruders, more in love with the product than the act.

Ultimately, Spence's whole life and career had revolved around the search. There had to be a way to strip away the layers of symbolism, to get right to the heart of the meaning. To reach the truth of things without the distraction of the typewriter's clacking, without the clumsy fingers that served as the brain's agents. Surely a more simple clarity existed than the black and white of ink on pulp.

Soon, he would arrive. At that spiritual pinnacle, the moment when all human history, all universal laws, all theologies, every speck of dust and grain of matter and mote of thought could be condensed to its purest form. When all of everything could become the one.

One true Word.

Spence sighed. Until he achieved that godliness, that command of the essence, he had to work through these idiot tools of language. Poe always ranted about "unity of effect," how every word must contribute to the whole. That paranoid, absinthe-swilling madman was on the right path, but wouldn't it be much better to find the single word that *was* the effect?

At least he could love what he wrote, despite its mortal shortcomings. He read the last completed paragraph.

> *And he, becoming Night, found his limbs, his blood and joy, stretching across the hills. Seeping out beyond the cold dark stone that was his prison, the mountain that was his sepulcher, the house that was his heart. His fingers were now more than mere trees, his eyes more than mirrors, his teeth more than broken wood. He, becoming Night, could spread his inky waters, could lap his tides at far shores, could engulf and drown the surrounding nondarkness that no longer threatened.*
>
> *The Night walked both sides of dawn, once again bold and dreaming.*

Spence laid the page on the desk. He rubbed his eyes. Two days. Had he been writing for two days?

His stomach gurgled. He could use something to eat. Bridget would be waiting at breakfast. Maybe he would even deign to forgive her.

He rolled a blank page into the Royal before leaving the room so it would be waiting when he returned. He looked back at it from the doorway. The white paper glared accusingly at him.

"Don't worry, the Word will come," he said to it, to the room, to the house and whatever was waiting in its walls. Then he closed the door.

Sylva crossed the cabin floor and tossed a pinch of salt in the fire to keep the fetches away. Then she put the poultice on Anna's knee where the cuts were deepest. A little of the gummy mixture dribbled out of the cloth and ran down Anna's leg.

"That ought to mend you up right nice," Sylva said.

"What's in it?"

"The usual. Chimney soot and molasses mixed with a little pine rosin. It's best to wrap a cut with a cobweb, but ain't many spiders this high up."

"Won't that cause an infection?"

"Nothing's much cleaner than chimney soot. Made pure by the fire, you see."

The wound would heal fine. Sylva didn't think she could mend the other things that were wrong with Anna, the bad cells that burned inside her. And she didn't think she should, even if she knew what herbs to use. Part of having the power to heal was knowing when to let nature run its course. When to let the dead be dead, and when to let the living move on to other business of the soul.

Anna was marked, as clearly as if her fate had been written by a judge. The shame of it was, she was just getting started in her life, just beginning to grasp her mighty and frightsome gifts. But Sylva knew that the young woman's illness also made her powers stronger. That's why it had been so easy for Korban to summon her.

Anna pressed the poultice to her knee and drank from the hand-fashioned clay cup. "Thank you, Miss—"

"Sylva. Sylva Hartley."

"And thanks for the water. I've never tasted water as good as you have here on the mountain."

Sylva nodded and threw a stick of locust on the fire. Anna was putting off talking about it. Nobody liked to remember close calls. And Sylva had learned over the many years of waiting that patience was the only thing a body needed to be good at. She had waited a long time for the October blue moon.

"You about got fetched over."

"Is that what you call it when a ghost murders you?"

"Yeah. Call it bad luck, too." Sylva stood and fished her hanging kettle from its hook over the fireplace. She poured some of the steaming water into Anna's cup. Then she crossed to the cupboard and took some leaves out of a ceramic jar. She crumbled a few of the leaves into Anna's hot water.

"Smells good. Sort of like mint." Anna breathed in the aroma.

"Yep. Mint with a little wild cherry root mixed in. Might ease up your headache."

"How did you know?"

"They always give *me* a headache, when I'm spelling them off. Them fresh dead, they're easier to see but they're harder to beat back down into the grave."

Anna sipped at the tea and gave Sylva a sideways look. "How come they haven't 'fetched' you yet?"

Sylva gave a laugh that was more of a liquid hiccup. "Got my cat bones and my snakeroot and my lizard powder and a whole cupboard full of other roots and herbs and reptile skins. And here's my special piece of protection."

Sylva rummaged under her shawl to the place near her heart. She held out her palm to show Anna the small, shriveled white thing that Sylva wouldn't have traded for a cape of spun gold.

"Rabbit's foot?" Anna's dark eyebrows made arrow-tips on her forehead.

"Not just any rabbit's foot. This is the left hind foot of a graveyard rabbit, snared on a winter midnight."

"Another one of the old signs, like Ransom told me."

"They mean as much as you want 'em to. It's all about how strong you believe."

Anna set her cup on the rough-hewn table. She shivered despite the nearness of the fire. "What a night. I feel a thousand years old."

"Old? I expect you wouldn't believe that I'm a hundred and five myself, give or take a few. Then again, you might, but I hardly believe it myself. I keep up with my health and all, but I suspect it's got a little to do with Korban. Like he's stretching my years on out so I don't up and die a natural death before he's done with me."

Anna rested her chin in her hands. The fire reflected in her blue-green eyes.

Them eyes. Lord, she's Rachel's spittin' image.

"What does Korban want?" Anna asked. "I've studied ghosts for a long time, but most of them just seem to be trying to escape from here. This world, I mean."

Sylva stared into the fire along with Anna. The sun was trickling through the east window now, but still the room was dark, as if night was reluctant to leave.

"Korban wants it all back. Everything that was ever his, and then some."

"Why?"

"Why?" Sylva had thought about it many times over the years, but still didn't know the right answer. "Calling him evil would be too apple-pie easy. Maybe he was evil back when he was alive, but it's way beyond that now. He liked to own things, shape them up to fit his world. I reckon he still does. Is it evil to want to hold on to everything you ever loved?"

"I'm not sure I've ever been loved."

The words gripped Sylva's heart. Korban fetched Anna back for a reason. No matter what Rachel tried to do. Maybe nobody ever escaped from here, dead or alive.

"Ephram . . ." Sylva's voice fell, uncertain. She was sixteen again, awkward but with a flaming heart, as if both she and the world were young and still full of promise. "I loved Ephram. We all did, the women, I mean. He was mighty handsome in his way, but it wasn't just looks. There was something about him, some magnetism. Nobody could resist him for long.

"I took a job tending the house, like most other women that lived on the mountain then. The men were busy working to clear the land and keep the place up. Nobody really said anything when people started dying. Somebody's ax-head would fly off and cleave in their skull, a tree would fall on somebody's back, they'd find a body in one of the ponds, the skin puffy and their tongue all swollen blue. It was just accidents, in our minds. 'A run of bad luck,' we'd say to each other, though we all knew better."

Sylva squeezed her fists against her chest. She'd never told anybody this next part. She'd kept that all nice and unbothered and lying in the back of her mind like a lizard in a muddy crevice. But this child had way worse things to go through. Sylva's own suffering was nothing compared to that.

"One night, his fire went out. I was scared to death. That was my one main job, the thing that Ephram made a mention of every time I saw him, which wasn't that often. But every time you seen him, by God, you'd remember it, and you would play it back in your mind, his face, his hands, his voice, until your heart was aching. At least it was that way with me, and I'm pretty sure it was the same with the other womenfolk."

Sylva fell silent. Even across the decades, the moment still retained its vividness. She was filled with a warm flood of passion, mixed with that same gut-ripping dread. Her eyes were misty, and she didn't fight it this time, she just let the tears roll down her cheeks.

"Ephram, he was in the room. Except it was like his life was the fire. He just laid there on the bed, gasping, kind of. And I was so scared, child, you wouldn't know how scared I was."

Sylva sniffled. "But then again, maybe you would. I forget you just had your own run-in. And he made me light that fire and say those words I never shoulda said."

Anna touched Sylva's knee. The gesture gave her the strength to finish.

"When I finally got the fire lit, Ephram come to me. He took me up in his arms, and I looked into those black eyes, and I would have done anything for that man. And he kissed me and then did everything else he wanted. But the thing was, I wanted it as much as he did. After it was over, he sent me out. Didn't say a word, just buttoned up his trousers and jabbed at the fire a little, like I was a piece of meat he'd just killed for sport.

"I hardly ever looked at him again, I was so scared. Scared both that he'd want me and that he wouldn't. But a few weeks later, I missed my time of the month. Lordy mercy, I was really scared then. But there was no other signs, so I went on about my business, hoping and praying. Months passed, it got winter and then spring. Along about summer my belly first started to swell, but just the tiniest bit. That's when I knew. And I knew it was wrong, as slow as it was going."

Sylva's heart was thundering now. All the old anger and wasted love was filling her up, poisoning her again. Anna reached for her hand and squeezed it. That settled Sylva down a little. She had to do this, for both of them.

"Korban liked to get up on top of the house in the dead of night. Up there on the widow's walk. Folks whispered that he was calling out to the dark things, invisible creatures that slithered and floated around in the cracks of the night. But by then, I knew what he was really doing.

"He was calling up his fetches. Making them do his bad work. Spelling them. And I crept up them stairs one night. The moon was full, a blue moon in October, like what's coming tomorrow night. I remember the smell of sassafras in the air, and the dew so thick you could feel it on your skin. The little trapdoor that led to the roof was open, so I poked my head through and saw him standing along the rail, looking out over the moon-lit nothing."

The fire popped and exhaled a long hiss. Sylva closed her eyes and finished the story before Korban got up the strength to stop her.

"I eased my way up onto the widow's walk, and he still had his back to me. When I got my feet steady, I stood up, and Lordy, how the wind was blowing. Like it was the breath of the whole sky let out all at once. I ran toward Ephram, my clothes whipping all out behind me in the breeze. He turned just when I reached him."

Anna's mouth was open, her cup between her loose fingers. The fire spat, sending a coal toward Anna. Sylva reached out with her shoe and rubbed the ember into the floor.

That was a sign of being marked for death, sure as any. When the ember shoots at you, you're done for.

"What happened then?" Anna asked, her eyes wide. As if they were sitting on a front porch somewhere swapping made-up ghost stories. As if this weren't real.

"I pushed him over, off the rail. And he *let* me. Didn't raise a hand to stop me. Just smiled as he went over. You never heard such a scream. The kind of scream a rabbit makes when a horned owl digs its claws into the back of its neck. Except way longer and louder.

"But there was a laugh mixed in, too. That's when I knew getting rid of Ephram Korban wasn't going to be so easy."

Anna nodded. Sylva could see she was thinking about it, sorting it out, trying to make the pieces fit. It felt good to be telling after all these years. Maybe she could die with an unburdened heart when and if her time ever came.

"What about your baby?" Anna asked.

Sylva stared into the fire. She was tired, crushed by the weight of more than a century of haunts. Keeping tabs on them all these years wasn't easy, especially when they had her outnumbered. She hoped her conjure bags and her faith and her spells would be enough. There were a lot of poppets in that little cabin, a passle of dead folks.

"Sun's coming up," she said. "Ought to be safe enough now. You and me need to go for a walk."

Bloody birds.

William Roth hoped to catch a red-tailed hawk in flight, or at least something colorful like a blue jay or cardinal. Nature's way was to give color to the male of the species, while the female was designed to blend into the background. If only the human birds would behave that way, follow the order of things. Cris and that tight little wonder called Zainab were as elusive as any of these Appalachian avians. The only winged things about were ravens, black and ugly and watching from the trees as if waiting for a funeral.

Roth looked through his lens at the cusp of sunrise. The southern Appalachian mountains reminded him of Scotland's, rounded and rich. He would take a few rolls of scenic stuff, that was always fodder for travel magazines and the like. If he wasn't going to have any luck with the ladies, might as well carry the old lunch bucket.

He stepped out of the trees where the wooden bridge spanned the great valley of granite and scrub vegetation. Far below ran a silver stream, tumbling between boulders on its way to the ocean. Korban knew how to live, all right. Set up a mansion at the top of the world, have a house full of young serving girls, play artist, and enjoy the high life. Who'd blame the bloke for not wanting to let such pleasures go? If Roth were Korban, he'd certainly become a ghost and hang about.

Roth chuckled. Ghosts and that rot. He'd seen photos that people claimed depicted spirits. Roth could achieve the same trick by fuzzing a negative or playing with the light in the darkroom. Give him an hour and he could crank out a hundred different double- and triple-exposures, and he didn't need a digital file or computer to do it. He could put Elvis on the moon, he could have Ephram Korban drifting over the manor, he could stick Cris Whitfield's head on Marilyn Monroe's nude body.

Now, *that* was a project that might be worth pursuing. Or maybe Spence's chippie, whom he'd seen before dawn, walking the halls with a blank look in her eyes. Had a lovely blue bruise on her face, Spence must have played a bit rough in the sack. Maybe Roth could hide in their bathroom, get a firelit shot of the old bastard giving her what for. Blackmail him or sell it to the tabloids, either way a tidy bundle.

He walked out onto the bridge, switched to a longer lens, and advanced the film. The air stirred around him, that mountain wind that could cut right through a bloke's bones. But it wasn't just the wind. The ravens had swooped from the forest and lit on the rails of the bridge. Dozens of them. Staring at Roth with those beady black eyes.

Waiting.

"Bloody hell," he said.

"Hell is only in the mind, Mr. Roth."

He turned, and Lilith stood in the middle of the bridge. How in blazes? Where had *she* come from?

"I hope you're not thinking of leaving us."

"Um. I was just getting this vista." He held up the camera. "The views around here are perfectly lovely."

He gave her a closer look. That black dress clung to her in a rather dramatic fashion. She was a bit pale, reminded him of those girls from North England, the ones from factory towns where the smog and rain cut down on the sunbathing. Still, she was young and she had curves. If serving girls were good enough for Korban, why not Sir William Bloody Bollocks-Swinging Roth?

"Lots of lovely views around," he said. He smiled. Younger girls liked his smile. Or pretended to, which amounted to the same.

"Yes. I used to paint them. Before I went to work for Ephram Korban."

"Work for Korban? He died a long time ago, and you're just a pip."

She gave her own smile, a fleeting, mysterious thing. Coy bird, that one.

"Say," he said, gently stroking his lens. "Mind if I get the most lovely view I've found since I got here?"

"Be our guest, Mr. Roth."

He lifted the camera and aimed it at her, zoomed onto her breasts, focusing on one nipple. Bras weren't part of the uniform, apparently. Likely not panties, either. This girl was definitely quick to serve.

He took a couple of pictures of her face, framed up nice with that hair and eyes as dark as the ravens, skin fresh as rocks in the rain, lips quick and clever with a smile. When he'd devoted enough attention to thoroughly flatter her, he said, "You ever get any time off? I wouldn't mind getting to know you a bit better. Take some pictures in a more secluded environment."

"That can be arranged, Mr. Roth."

"Call me William, love."

She imitated his imitation accent. "Okay, William Love."

Had a sense of humor, too. She'd be a joy to tumble. Roth moved toward her, wanting to get close enough for her to marvel at the sparkle in his smoky eyes. Something crawled across his face and he brushed it away.

God save the bloody queen, it was a *spider.*

He stepped back and saw the web spun between him and Lilith, stretching across the bridge like golden wire, the dew catching the sunrise. He detested spiders. From the African veldt to the Arctic tundra, the little buggers jumped at you with their sharp pincers. He'd read somewhere that, no matter where you stood on the globe, there'd be a spider within six feet of you, and he believed it.

He looked down at the rough planks of the bridge. The yellow-striped bastard was making for a crack, its legs scrabbling, its arachnid brain no doubt having a laugh at Roth's expense. Roth brought a boot down on the spider, grinding it into the grain of the wood, sending its soul to spider hell, where hopefully God fed them nothing but DDT.

"Sorry, love," he said to Lilith. "Hope that didn't upset you."

The smile flitted across the thin lips, fast as insects. "You didn't kill it. You delivered it."

"What's that?"

"Living things never die, they just move on through deeper tunnels of the soul."

"Er, righty right."

"Now, if you'll excuse me, Miss Mamie will be wondering where I've gotten off to. I can't stay away from the house for long."

She walked past him, and he took a whiff of her fragrance. He liked that sort of thing, collected their scents the way some blokes collected phone numbers or underwear. This one smelled a bit like earth, ripe and lush. Fertile and moist. He could dig it, all right.

She stopped at the end of the bridge. "I'll see you later, then."

"Wouldn't miss it for the life of me," he said, and watched her delightful small arse shake as she walked up the sandy road leading to the manor. When she disappeared through the trees, he turned his attention back to the view. The ridges had lost their glow now that the sun was rising. He'd best pack away.

The ravens watched as he returned his lens to its case. Bloody birds had no fear. He thought about waving them on, sending them scattering over the valley. Oh, bother that. The day was looking up, with fair and tender Lilith on the agenda.

He was about to head back for the manor and breakfast when he saw the web again. Still spread out in those fine and sinister patterns, shipshape. Lilith had walked right through it. And still it hung there, whole and perfect, waiting to snatch things from the air.

This place was going to drive him daft if he wasn't careful.

CHAPTER 17

Mason hewed the flesh of the oak, excited by the tannic smell of the wood. He worked with his hatchet, scraping it around as if skinning an animal. The log was braced with a couple of old chestnut boards, a pain in the rump to work around, but art was never easy. With the wires adding support, the oak waited for his touch like a masochistic and naked lover in a torture chamber.

The reddish strips of peeled bark were piled around his feet, and he stumbled in them as he felt along the wood's smooth surface. Here would be the arms, one knee here, a strong spread of shoulder there. This knot could become the ball of one loose fist.

He hadn't lied to Miss Mamie. The statue would be worth the trouble. Nothing great was ever created without a little risk. Suffer for art, that was the ticket to the top. Sacrifice everything and everyone, especially yourself.

Mason drove the hatchet sideways, into the area that would be the neck. He drew back and struck again and again, the outline of the form burned into his mind, his hands sure of their work. He chopped until his right shoulder and biceps ached, removing the sections of dead wood that blocked the emergence of the true shape. The flames at the end of the candles bobbed as the air stirred with his blows and breath.

When he could no longer lift his arm, Mason stood back and pushed away the wood scraps with his shoe. He moved across the studio space and studied the log from different angles. The height of the shoulders, the angle of the elbow, the distance between the feet, all had to be perfectly measured. As he was taking a step back to get another view, he knocked over the oil painting that he'd leaned against the cupboard.

He knelt and picked it up. Again he was struck by its singular beauty. How would he feel if his own work never left the basement, if it stayed forever in the shadows, never to be appreciated and admired? His work would be better than this, but the painter had talent. The soft brushstrokes and colors, the off-white of the manor, the splendor of the night forest, the turbulent storm clouds as fresh as wet reality.

He looked closer, at the top of the house. The smudge along the widow's walk was brighter now and had spread several inches across the canvas. Mason peered into the mist and blinked. There were angles and shapes in the smudge. He brought the lantern from the table and tilted it toward the painting.

Mason traced a finger over one of the shapes. The shape was a deeper gray white than the smudge, suggesting a human shape. More forms hovered beyond it, behind the thick pale line that portrayed the rail of the widow's walk. People?

People would be out of place in the painting. The house was the subject, so dominating an image in itself that to besmirch it with humanity would be a cruel insult. Had somebody else made the same observation as

Mason, and tried to blot out those shapes on the roof? Or did the artist realize the mistake upon completion, and sought to correct it before the oils had dried?

Miss Mamie would know, or maybe Lilith, who'd shown an interest in the painting. Perhaps he'd be allowed to take it to his room and hang it beside that portrait of Korban. A master and his domain.

He leaned the painting back against the cupboard. His own work was more important. That was the artist's first tenet. Creative duty first, everything else second.

Besides, Mama was watching.

His wood called to him in the language of the unborn. He answered, with chisel and claw, tooth and hatchet, sharp blade and hungry soul.

Adam found Miss Mamie after breakfast. She sat in a wicker chair in the study with her hands folded in her lap. She was dressed in forest green today, her decollette gown showing the pale expanse of her upper bosom. She had foregone her pearl necklace in favor of a black silk choker.

She lifted her hands, revealing some small pieces of wood spread across a cloth. She had a knife in one hand, bits of wood clinging to the blade. As Adam watched, she sliced a length of thick vine and began wrapping it around what looked like the torso of a doll. The doll's head looked like a knob of dark, shriveled fruit, the features stretched and distorted from the act of drying.

The Abramovs were at the far end of the study, away from the fireplace and the sunlight that poured through the high windows. They were playing a minuet in *andante* that was reminiscent of Mozart. Their cello and violin trilled in counterpoint, then shifted into a descending harmony. The rich notes vibrated against Adam's skin.

He sat on the sofa across from Miss Mamie and

bowed his head in respectful silence. He watched the musicians' fingers glide over the strings. The duo increased their tempo, then went into the recapitulation, toying with the melody before finally sustaining the tonic and fifth notes as a finale. Adam joined Miss Mamie in applause.

"Bravo," she said. "How extraordinarily lovely. Ephram Korban would be pleased."

As the Abramovs started a new piece, Adam leaned over to Miss Mamie. "How are you today?"

"Just fine, Mr. Andrews. How do you like my little hobby? An old Appalachian craft, passed down by Ephram himself. They say when you whittle a poppet, you're building a house for a lost soul."

"Looks tough on the hands."

"But they make lovely gifts. What do you think of this one?"

She held up the gnarled figurine, the twisted limbs of vine making the poor thing look crippled. It was hideous, the eyes crude, one larger than the other.

"That's wonderful. I don't think Daniel Boone could have done any better."

"Are you enjoying your stay so far?"

"Actually, I wanted to talk to you about that. I've decided to cut my visit short. I have, um, pressing business to take care of."

Miss Mamie's brow darkened and she pursed her lips. She dropped the little wooden figure and it clattered off the hearth, the shriveled head rolling away. "Oh, dear, what a great fall," she said, so softly that Adam barely heard her.

Adam held up a hand. "I'm not looking for my money back. My roommate Paul will be staying on."

Miss Mamie looked out the window. A cloud must have passed over the sun, because the room grew darker. The Abramov melody shifted into a minor key and began twisting in *agitato.*

"Nobody can leave," she said.

"I know the van doesn't come back up for another couple of weeks. I was wondering if you could possibly make other arrangements."

"You don't understand. Nobody can leave. Especially you."

Mrs. Abramov's face clenched as she increased the tempo of her chaotic melody. There was little of the beauty that the couple had been squeezing out of the instruments only minutes before. Now the notes were more like tortured wails than music.

Adam looked out the window. "Can't one of the handymen take me down on horseback? I saw two of the guests out riding the other day."

"It's not time yet," Miss Mamie said, finally looking away from the window. Her eyes glittered with what Adam took to be anger. "The party is tonight. A lovely affair, up on the widow's walk under the full moon. It's something of a hallowed tradition at Korban Manor."

"I can pay extra for the trouble. I know what a bother this is."

Miss Mamie glowered and touched the locket that dangled unfashionably from her choker. "He—he doesn't want you to go."

"Paul?"

Miss Mamie seemed to recover just a little. "Black Rock is a half day's journey by horse. And you belong here."

The string music increased in intensity, fragmenting into chromatic chaos.

"I'll walk, then."

The music stopped abruptly, a diminished fifth quivering in the air, embarrassed at its isolation.

"No one leaves," she said.

Adam followed her gaze to the portrait of Korban above the fireplace, that same face that had whispered dream words to Adam about tunnels of the soul. Adam shivered. The house itself brooded, as if the walls were weary of darkness. The air was heavy, and even the blazing fire added nothing to the room's cheer. Adam moved to the hearth and rubbed his hands, trying to drive the remnants of the nightmare from his mind.

He looked down at the broken figurine. A scrap of fabric was tucked into a splintered crease in the torso. Gray cotton, like his pajamas.

"Play on," Miss Mamie said to the Abramovs.

Roth found Spence on the smoking porch, sitting in a hand-carved rocker whose legs seemed to bow outward from the stress.

"How goes the Shakespeare bit?" Roth asked.

The writer already had a drink, scotch, judging from its amber appearance. It was scarcely ten o'clock. Spence was certainly living up to his reputation. Roth had half suspected the writer had affected an alcoholic's indulgence that was as phony as his legendary womanizing or Roth's own accent.

"The best ever, as always," Spence said, face pale and eyes nearly pink from lack of sleep.

"You'd like to feed it to the critics with a shovel, wouldn't you, mate? I mean, they've been bloody hard on you these last few years."

Spence let out a wet sigh, his chins flexing like a grubworm. "There's only one critic I want to nail. My first one."

Roth sat in a swinging seat that was woven from thin reeds. He placed his camera case on the floor. If he worked it around right, a dissipated Spence would make a great addition to Roth's gallery of deceased celebrities. Because Spence was clearly running headlong toward some invisible cliff edge.

"Your old mum, I bet," Roth said. "They can be rather overbearing."

"My mother was a saint. The critic to whom I've alluded is long dead. But I have hopes that a merciful God will bring me face-to-face with her in the afterlife."

Roth grinned. "Yeah, what use is heaven if you can't have a go at all your old enemies?"

Spence took a long swallow of scotch. "You're boring me, Mr. Roth. I loathe boredom."

"Listen here, mate, I had this idea—"

"Let me guess. You have a book you want me to write and we'll split the money after I do all the work."

"Not quite that bald. I was thinking about a coffee table book on Korban. I'll take the photographs, dig up some old archival stuff, convert some of these portraits to digital files. All you have to do is put your name on the cover and type a few pages as a foreword."

"My name isn't what it used be."

"The project's a natural. Some eccentric bloke builds himself a rural empire, then dies by mysterious means. We can even play on the ghost angle. I've no qualms about inserting some transparent orbs or fairy dust on the film."

"Speaking of fairies," Spence said. Through the porch screen, they could see a young man carrying a video camera toward the forest.

"His friend let him go off alone like that? Seemed the jealous and clingy sort." Roth had occasionally been driven to experiment when no birds were available for plucking. Males were a bit too rough around the edges for his taste, but they offered an element of danger that no woman could match. Still, if Spence were that prim about such matters, best to play it straight. He made no comment.

"Ephram Korban would have despised such depraved moral weakness," Spence said.

"You talk as if you knew him."

"No, but I *understand* him. I can feel him. This house was his in more than mere ownership."

"Ah, you believe that ghost tripe?"

"I've felt the spirit move me."

Roth wondered how many drinks the man had downed with breakfast. "Then why not a book? We can do it as a tribute if you'd rather."

Spence lifted himself with effort. "I'd sooner write a trashy thriller, something with vampires and a Martian Pope and a government conspiracy. And an unlikely love interest. One must have a love interest to make the pot boil."

"Think about it."

"Excuse me, I have work to do. Real work." Spence carried his empty glass toward the study, no doubt for a refill.

Roth sat in the shade of the porch. Spence, dead in the bathtub, his fat, white gut displayed in a two-page tabloid spread. Moby dicked. That would be a picture worth a thousand words. And multiple thousands of dollars.

How to make that overtaxed heart explode? A ménage à trois with Bridget and Lilith? Or put Paul and Adam on him. With his homophobia, Spence likely had some serious bones in the closet.

Roth smiled. There was an easier way, one that wouldn't involve the complicity of outsiders.

If Spence were so bloody in love with his work, what would happen if the work went into the fireplace? Best of all, he could blame it all on a ghost. Who could ever prove otherwise?

The wind played through the trees that surrounded the graveyard, a lonely music for a dead resting place high on the edge of the world. Sylva leaned on her walking stick, watching from the fence, too brittle to risk climbing over. The old woman had knelt in the grass, searched the ground for a minute, then picked something and passed it through the fence to Anna. It was a four-leaf clover.

"Lucky charm?" Anna asked.

"Better than luck. Lets you see the dead."

"I already do."

"Only when *they* want. This here gives you the power over them." Sylva nodded toward the grave of Rachel Faye Hartley. "That's the one you'll be wanting to summon."

"Summon?"

"Come in fire, dead come back. Say it. Third time's a charm."

"I can't do that."

"It's in your blood. You just got to *believe*."

Anna stared at the cold stone, the flowers chiseled by some delicate hand, a bouquet that never wilted. She believed in ghosts, and so she saw them. And since she'd arrived at Korban Manor, she'd see them more clearly than ever before. Maybe it was always a question of faith. Part of the belief might originate from the dead spirit, and a ghost had to dream itself back toward the living world.

Perhaps Anna and the ghost had to meet halfway in a union of sad and enslaved souls, and if she only had to recite an old mountain folk spell, that wasn't so much to ask. The ghost, in this case the person who had lived by the name of Rachel Faye Hartley, had to put forth the real effort. After all, it would be Rachel who wrenched herself from the dark peace of eternal slumber to rise and return to a world perhaps best forgotten. A world that held only the promise of pain and loneliness.

Anna looked down at the clover. Could she believe in magic? With cancer eating her flesh, she had to put all her faith in the permanent existence of the soul, or else she might as well leap from the top of Korban Manor herself. Without faith, what was the point?

She closed her eyes and said the words: "Come in fire, come in fire, come in fire."

A chill caressed her, a soft immortal coldness. When she opened her eyes, the woman in white stood before her, the bouquet in her diaphanous hands. It was as if Anna were looking into a trick mirror, because she recognized herself in that pale and transparent face.

"Anna," the woman said, in that same whispered tone that had haunted Anna's dreams, had called to her from the trail, had led her into the woods where George Lawson's spirit seized her in its severed hand.

"You," Anna said. "You're the one who summoned me here. It's wasn't Ephram Korban at all."

"You grew up beautiful, just like I always figured." The words were like splashes of ice water.

"What are you talking about?"

"I hated to send you away. I thought it was the only way to save you from *him*. But I didn't know."

"Send me away?" Anna looked at Sylva, who pulled her shawl more tightly about her bony shoulders. Sylva nodded her knot of skull bone, her face tired, wrinkles deepening, as if she'd aged fifty years since arriving at the graveyard. Anna looked at the ghost of Rachel, back to Sylva, and again at the ghost. Their eyes had that same shape, the dark arch of brow, the same hint of mystery. Just like Anna's.

Just like Anna's.

"You're her." The realization sliced through Anna with the slow sureness of a glacier, more implacable than cancer, an impossible truth that was all the more horrible because the impossible had become ordinary.

Anna's blood froze in her veins, as hard as the frost that still sparkled beneath the patches of tombstone shadows.

"It's all my fault," Rachel said. "That's my sorrow, that's what haunts me in my tunnel of the soul. The fear that Ephram uses to control me."

"Ephram Korban. What do I care about him?" Anna's tears ran down her cheeks like the tracing of lifeless fingers.

The ghostly lips parted, Rachel's form glimmered under the sunrise. "It was hard on me to lose you, harder even than dying. Harder even than being dead. Because being dead is just like being alive, only worse."

"Hard on *you,"* Anna said. "Every night, in every new foster home, every time some stranger tucked me in, I prayed to God that you'd have to suffer. Even though I never knew you, I hated you. Because I never got to *belong."*

"I suffered, too."

"I hated you for not being there, for never existing. And now I find you, and you still don't exist."

"You don't understand, Anna. We need you."

"Need, need, need. What about me? I had needs, too." Anna flung the clover to the grave grass, the sobs shaking her. "Go away. I don't believe in you."

"Anna," Sylva said. "She may be dead, but she's blood."

"You can keep your blood. I'm done with it all." Anna moved between the stones, vision blurred by tears, scarcely aware of her feet, wanting only to be away, back in the world of ordinary pain, ordinary loneliness.

Rachel's voice reached across the grass, weaker, as if leaking from inside the mouth of an endless tunnel. "He haunts us, Anna. We're dead and *he still haunts us."*

Anna didn't even slow down. She had come here to find her own ghost. Now she had, and it was worse than she ever could have imagined. Her ghost didn't provide solace and the comfort of life beyond life. Her ghost brought the promise of eternal loneliness, proof that she would never belong, no matter which side of the grave claimed her.

"You don't know what it's like," Sylva shouted after her, the words swept by the October wind. "It's way worse to lose a daughter. I ought to know. 'Cause I lost Rachel."

Anna stopped near the shadow of Ephram Korban's monument. She turned, and her turning seemed as slow as the spinning of the earth, trickles of angry sorrow cold on her cheeks, flesh already numb to this new impossible truth.

Ephram Korban and Sylva.

Then Rachel.

And Anna.

Korban's name hovered before her in a watery haze, as if the chiseled letters on the monument gave weight to Sylva's words. Blood. Ephram Korban's blood ran through her, as tainted as that ancestral side which cursed her with the Sight, all bound up in this ridge of ancient Appalachian soil, a sorry dirt that couldn't even hold down its corpses.

Sylva called once more, but Anna wasn't listening. She climbed over the fence, her heart on fire with a single wish.

Dead stay dead.

Dead stay dead forever.

CHAPTER 18

Mason wiped the sweat from his forehead. He had removed his shirt, but still the room was too warm. Oak chips stuck to his chest and arms. His shoulders had passed the point of aching. The pain had transformed into a dull, constant drumming somewhere in the back of his mind.

His sculpting instructor at Adderly, Dennis Graves, had told him that the key to art was stamina. Mason's first assignment had been to carve the letters of the word *stamina* into a block of white pine. That clumsy effort now rested across Mama's dead television set. He'd given it to her like a kindergartner who'd brought home a finger painting. That was back before her blindness, though after her eyesight failed she often held it in her lap and ran her fingers over the letters.

Someday he was going to do another word just for her: *dreams*.

He would fashion it in bronze or copper, something durable. Maybe even granite. Except then the word would be too heavy. Maybe it would be too heavy even in balsa wood. Or air.

Mason had finished with the hatchet and adze. The

rough form was fleshed out. The sky had grown darker in the basement's small high windows. He didn't know if that meant rain or that dusk was coming. He'd long ago lost track of time.

Mason worked with his broad chisel and mallet, shaving off sections of the oak. The grain was cooperative, as if in a hurry to become its true shape. The statue was revealing itself too fast, and there was no way that he should be this far along already. It was almost as if the wood was pumping energy back through his tools into his hands.

Sure, Mase. Whatever you think. Artistic license.

And look here, the shoulders are squared, one of Korban's arms will be across his stomach, the other hand behind his back. An aristocratic pose. A man who knows what he's all about.

The dead space of the basement swallowed the sounds of metal on metal and metal into wood.

Come out, Korban. I know you're in there, somewhere inside this godforsaken hunk of oak. SING to me, you beautiful old bastard. Rise up and walk.

Mason squinted as a spray of sawdust skipped back toward his face. He drove the chisel's blade into a space beside the statue's left arm. Stamina. Dreams.

He'd have to send Dennis Graves another word.

Spirit.

You had to have spirit, or you were lost. The material had to have spirit. You couldn't squeeze soul out of a stone. It had to already exist, to have existed forever, waiting there for the artist to release it.

The breath of spirit wind blew from the four corners. That's where dream-images came from. They weren't really new ideas or visions. They were things that already *were,* that just had to be revealed to human minds.

Okay. Okay. Now you're losing it, linthead.

Artistic pretension is expected, and all that gibber-

ish might come in handy after you get "discovered." But right now, the reality is that you're working yourself into a lather and you can't make yourself stop. You should have taken a break to eat and rest.

But YOU CAN'T MAKE YOURSELF STOP.

Mason frowned and rammed the chisel off the flank of hip. He didn't think it was a good sign when people started having philosophical debates with themselves. He was *supposed* to be in a creative trance. He *wanted* it, searched for it, prayed to the gods of impossible dreams.

He looked at the bust of Korban, and it seemed to smile at him from the table. The wooden lips parted: "So why can't you stop?"

I can stop any time I want to.

"Certainly. I believe you, Mr. Jackson."

Look, you can't just turn creativity off and on at will. You've got to roll with it while you've got the wheels. You've got to take the Muse's hand when she wants to dance.

"Fine. No arguments. But let's just see you stop."

Okay. But I want you to know that my shoulders and arms and finger muscles are going to scream in pain because they're wound tighter than a spool of factory thread. Besides, I'm doing this for Mama, not me.

The bust said, "Excuses, excuses."

I'll show you. Here we go. . . .

Mason flailed at the chisel. Two inches of dark red wood peeled away from the section that would be Korban's left kneecap. He repositioned the blade and drew back the mallet for another blow.

The bust laughed, a sound like the shuffle of rodents. "You're not stopping."

Okay, already. Get off my case. I just had to get USED to the idea.

Mason curled another strip of oak away, then looked

down at his tools scattered around the floor among the shavings.

See? I can take my eyes off it if I want to. Just as an experiment, I'm going to think about something besides Ephram Korban's statue. Take, for instance, the lovely Anna Galloway. . . .

Mason paused, a drop of sweat hanging at the tip of his nose.

"Ah, so it's fair Anna that makes your heart sing," the bust said. "You can have her, you know. Once you finish. I promise. And I always keep my promises."

Mason clenched his teeth and gave the hammer an extra-hard swing. He could stop any time he wanted. He just didn't want to think about her right now. Didn't want to think, didn't want to think, didn't want to think—

"I say, who were you talking to?"

Mason spun, hammer in hand, raising it as if to ward off an attacker. William Roth stepped back, his gray eyes startled wide. He almost dropped the canisters of liquid in his arms.

"Easy, mate."

Mason lowered the hammer. The spell was broken. "Sorry. I was just getting carried away there for a minute."

"Looks longer than a ruddy minute to *me*. Have you been working on that thing nonstop?"

Mason nodded. The pain in the back of his shoulder blades sent its first red twinges to his brain. He rubbed his right biceps.

Roth looked past Mason at the statue. "Good Lord, how did you get so much done already? You must be working like a pack of beavers."

Mason looked at the statue and tried to see it as Roth did. All the limbs were clearly suggested in the mass of wood, and it was distinguishable as a human form. The head was a featureless block but in close proportion to the rest of the body. The legs rose up from the base with a vibrancy and strength.

"It's coming along," Mason said. "I promised Miss Mamie it would be lovely."

"What's the rush? You're going to bust a blooming artery if you keep at it like that."

"Say, can I ask you something?"

"As long as you put down the hammer."

Mason laid the hammer on the worktable beside the bust. "Take a look at this painting."

Roth set his canisters on the table and Mason lifted the canvas to the light of the nearest lantern.

Roth pursed his lips in approval. "Quite a piece of work."

"What do you see in that smudge there, at the top of the house? Along the railing of the widow's walk?"

Roth bent close and peered at the shapes. "Looks like people to me. Wonder who messed it up."

"Would you believe me if I told you those people weren't there two days ago?"

Roth looked at Mason and then back at the painting. "I'd say you're ass over teakettle from overwork."

"Well, maybe it's something to do with the chemicals in the paint. It just bugs me, that's all. As an artist myself, I know how it feels to come up short of perfection."

Roth gave his barking laugh. "Don't kid yourself with all that 'artist' rot. It's all about jack, selling out for whatever you can get."

Mason rubbed his chin and felt the scratch of stubble. He had been neglecting his hygiene. He could smell his own underarms. To Roth, the studio must have stunk like the laundry room at a gym. Mason knelt and retrieved his shirt, shook the wood chips free, and put it on. He glanced at the statue and felt guilty for thinking of abandoning it.

"What are you doing down here?" he asked Roth, before his mind could fixate on Korban again.

"Going to develop some negatives. Miss Mamie said I could use the wine cellar. Dark enough down here, don't you think?"

"And warm, too. They must be keeping the main furnace going full tilt. It's on the other side of the wall there. I hear them stoking it every three or four hours."

"This Korban bloke must not have been much of a save-the-trees sort."

Mason looked at the statue again. "Maybe in some crazy way, he *is* the trees."

"Get some sun, Mason. You're starting to go a bit dodgy."

"Maybe you're right."

"Loosen up, have some fun." Roth grinned, flashing his vulpine teeth. "Have a go at that quirky bird Anna. She's your style."

"No, thanks. I have enough worries. I'd better get some food in me so I can finish this thing."

From the stairs, Mason took a last look back at the statue that would be Ephram Korban. It was going to be wonderful. Dennis Graves would eat his mallet in jealousy. This creation was shaping up to be a god.

Spence wept.

The beauty, the elegance of the prose, was sweeping over him like the black tide in his novel. He could feel it approaching. With every sentence, every preposition, every punctuation mark, he was nearing the Word.

The keys sang as they slapped against the carriage, the ringing bell of the return heralded the coming glory. Spence could barely see the page through the blur of his tears, even with the sun pouring through the window, but he didn't need to see. The ghostwriter was compelling his fingers, sending them flying over the keyboard, the words no longer even remotely his own.

Spence wondered if that made any difference. The word *author* was derived from authority. He had always prided himself on his control and mastery of language, of juggling the alphabet, tricking verbs, nailing down nouns. But this was the uninhibited writing, the deeper language, the cracks between sound and thought. Communication that got to the heart of the truth.

He was dimly aware of Bridget on the bed. He would go to her later, when darkness came. New strength surged in his flesh, his blood was rejuvenated, his power to perform restored. The gift and blessing of the Word. The act of sacrifice always gave power back to the one making the sacrifice.

The room was cold, even with the fire leaping up the chimney as if yearning for the freedom of the sky. His fingers were like winter sticks, but still they rattled the keys, the music of ice cubes in a glass. Ephram Korban watched Spence from the portrait, the most encouraging of editors, his dark eyes suggesting plot twists.

Bridget could wait, impatient and aching in the warm bed. For now, there was only the page. The final page.

Spence sighed. The ending was always like a small death.

Those bittersweet words, *The End.*

Maybe End was the One True Word.

The only word that had ever mattered.

The manor welcomed Anna back, with its dark wainscoting and high ceiling and the fire roaring in the foyer hearth. And Korban, benevolent old Ephram, *Grandfather* Ephram, smiled kindly down from his vigilant perch above the mantel.

Maybe she did belong here. As much as anywhere.

She belonged nowhere else, after all. And Korban Manor was the end of the world, the kind of place where Anna deserved to pass her final days, walking these windswept ridges in the hard heart of the Appalachian winter. If she died here, her spirit would answer its true calling, her ghost would drift above the manor just as she'd seen so many times in her dreams.

And was that so bad?

As long as Rachel Faye Hartley stayed in the graveyard or haunted the trails of Beechy Gap, never crossing this threshold of stone and wood, then Anna could be as content as any dead and restless thing. To gaze from the widow's walk, a widow without a husband to mourn, nor even a mother for that matter, and wait for whatever came after the passing of forever. Could such an afterlife possibly be worse than her actual life, which she had drifted through without any positive effect, never knowing the full and mysterious power of love?

No. Death could never be worse than this life, the one that cancer had invaded, where she had been abandoned, where she had walked a million sad miles alone.

"Anna?"

God. Not him, not now. She wiped quickly at her eyes, pretending they had been stung by the smoke that came down the chimney as the wind turned. "Hi, Mason."

"I'm glad I found you. I've been meaning to ask you something."

"As long as it's not personal."

"Hey, are you okay? You look a little shook-up."

"Like I've seen a ghost?" Anna managed a bitter laugh.

"Well, that's sort of what I wanted to ask you about. Because there's a painting of Korban Manor down in the basement—"

Anna moved closer to the inviting warmth of the foyer's fireplace, rubbing her hands together. The action was designed to put distance between her and Mason, but he hovered uncomfortably near. He checked the hallways, then spoke, his voice lower.

"The painting has a smudge on the rooftop," he said. "And the way the paint's breaking down, it looks like the artist may have hidden some figures on an earlier layer of paint, sort of like a subliminal image. Because the smudge is starting to look like people."

"Don't artists sometimes recycle their canvases? Maybe the painter covered over a mistake or a rough draft."

"Well, that's what I thought, too. But now I can see their faces."

Anna looked up at Korban's portrait, wondered how many times that face had lived in a painter's fevered mind, how many hours her long-dead relative had sat in stiff repose as an adored subject. Even Cris had talked about how the manor and Korban's face kept creeping into her mind until all her fingers wanted to do was record him in charcoal, ink, and Conte crayon. And Mason had told Anna about the bust of Korban, how the dead man's image haunted his sleep and drove him into obsessive bouts of work.

"Let me guess," Anna said. "One of the faces is Ephram Korban's. Because you see him every time you close your eyes."

"One of them is Ephram Korban." He glanced sideways at the portrait, as if not quite trusting it enough to turn his back to it. "But that's not so strange, considering that nobody seems to do anything creative around here without invoking the old bastard in some way or another."

"He looks sort of charming, doesn't he?"

"As charming as a nest of snakes, maybe."

"Korban gets painted a lot around here. Big deal. What else is strange about the painting?"

"One of the other faces. I mean, the oil paint is dry, and from the dust on the frame, it might be a year old, or might be twenty. Maybe more. And you told me you'd never been here before."

"I never lie, unless I have a good reason." *Except to myself. I've been lying to myself since before I learned to speak.*

"Then, since you're a ghost hunter, you might be interested to know that *your* face is in the painting."

The fire spat an ember onto the hearth, toward Anna. Mason crushed it out with his foot.

"Show me," Anna said.

CHAPTER 19

William Roth pulled the negatives from the glass jar with practiced movements. He'd unwound hundreds of rolls of film, but this was the first time he'd done it in a wine cellar. A red light would have been handy, but this was no harder than developing in a tent in Sudan or a shack in the Amazon basin. He'd mixed the chemicals by the light of a lantern, doused the flame, done his business, and rinsed thoroughly.

All that remained was to let the film dry. The basement air was still, which might help keep the heavy dust off the emulsion. Dust hung everywhere about this place, what with the ashes of constant fires drifting about. And that fellow Mason with all his sawdust and grit.

Roth felt along the surface of the workbench, found the matches and the warm globe of the lantern, then stroked the match to life and touched it to the wick. He'd rigged a piece of twine across the small room, and now attached the six rolls of film to it using clothespins borrowed from the maid. After hanging the last strip, adding an extra clothespin at the bottom to take the curl out of the celluloid, he brought the lantern closer for a look at his work.

Ah, there were those shots from the bridge, and even colorless, and with black, white, and shades of gray reversed, he could tell the photos would add to the legend that was Roth. He scanned down the squares of images, coming to those of the bridge and Lilith.

"Bloody hell?" He brought the lantern closer, even though he risked warping the celluloid with the heat.

There spanned the length of bridge, where it disappeared into the trees leading back to Black Rock and civilization. Those creepy ravens were perfectly plain in reverse image along the bridge rails, and the frosted spiderweb hung in the pictures like a dark piece of lace. But Lilith didn't appear in any of them.

Roth wiped his eyes. Maybe he'd advanced the film too far, taken the shots of her after he'd reached the end of the roll. That was the sort of thing amateurs did, gawps and ninnies, not masters. When was the last time Roth had made a mistake?

"Bloody goddamned hell," he whispered, his accent a blend of Manchester and lower-class Cleveland. Maybe it was time for a drink, a comfy fireside, and a bit of rest. The fringe benefits of fame and fake charisma might prove to be fleeting if he kept on like this. Especially since Spence was proving to be a stone wall. If Roth's luck didn't improve soon, he might start blaming the curse of Korban or some such.

He lifted the lantern high, the dusty bottoms of the bottles surrounding him like ancient eyes. He pulled a bottle from the rack that lined one wall. The dark glass bore a plain label, corked right here at the estate. In ink, someone had handwritten *1909*. Probably a decent year. Decent enough to blot out that memory of the bridge, at any rate. And maybe decent enough to warm the heart and part the legs of the fair and tender Lilith.

Roth tucked the bottle under his arm and left the basement, his photographs consigned to the darkness.

"She won't let me leave," Adam said.

"Damn." Paul took another draw off his joint. The sweet smell of marijuana drifted across the back porch. "Too bad, Princess."

Paul's third joint of the day. Rational conversation would be impossible. But then, hadn't it always been? There wasn't much left to discuss anyway.

Adam stood against the rail, staring out at the mountains. Paul sat in one of the mule-eared rockers, not bothering to move his chair closer to Adam's. The noise of the piano leaked from the study, drowning out the morning song of birds. Someone laughed drunkenly inside the house, no doubt another suffering artist who had self-inflicted misery to drive away.

Adam didn't even have that pathetic excuse for his nightmares. Because he'd gone to bed cold sober, and his mind was far too clear, preserving every detail of his death and subsequent resurrection.

"You know something?" Paul's face looked sinister as he sucked in a lungful of smoke. He held it in, then exhaled toward Adam with an exaggerated flourish. "Maybe if you'd loosen up, you could get a little more joy out of life. Do you always have to be so damned serious about everything?"

Uptight city boy. That was Adam, all right. Worried about mutual funds when most people were worried about scoring the night's lover, deciding which band was the flavor of the month, or choosing a brand name clothes designer. But at least Adam wasn't selfish. That was why making the relationship work was so important to him. That was why he wanted to adopt a child.

He wanted to share what he had to offer, to give

himself away. He wanted a home in somebody's heart. Only he now feared it wouldn't be Paul's.

"Let it out," Adam said. "Go ahead and destroy me. That's all you've done since we got here, anyway. Might as well finish the job."

Paul giggled. "The martyr. Nails in your palms and a spear in your side. Poor boy. You've given me an idea for my next video. *The Noble Suffering of Adam Andrews*. Filmed in whine-a-vision."

Asshole. *Asshole.*

Adam clenched a fist, the anger merging with the fear, creating a hot mix that burned his gut. But losing control would be letting Paul have the final victory. Adam always lost with grace. And he'd had lots of practice.

He forced his voice to remain calm and quiet. "Look, since I'm stuck here for five more weeks, we may as well be civil to each other. That way, maybe we can look back at this one day and pretend it wasn't all bad."

The rocker squeaked as Paul stood up, and the ember of the joint stub arced into the damp grass beside the porch. Paul walked over to Adam, leaned forward until his face was so close that Adam could smell the marijuana and liquor on his breath.

"Now you're talking," Paul said. "Since we're stuck with each other, we might as well enjoy it."

Adam tried to slide away from the contact, but Paul hugged him, his breath hot on Adam's neck.

"Paul, I don't think—"

"Shh. You get all hot and bothered over Ephram Korban, talking about him in your sleep, but I'm probably a little more available."

"I can't, knowing you don't care about me. Now stop it, Miss Mamie might see us."

Paul stepped back, looked into Adam's eyes. Smiled. His damned hair was tousled, boyish, he was dead cute and knew it.

Suddenly his face changed, contorted, and Ephram Korban, that twisted, cruel face from Adam's nightmare, leered at him like a Halloween mask.

And the dream came back in all its brilliance and realism, Korban leaning him over the railing of the widow's walk, only kissing him this time, breath hot and foul, tongue like an insistent snake, mouth stealing the breath from his lungs. Then, drained and empty, Korban sucking him into the long tunnel toward the thing that Adam knew was waiting around the bend. The thing he feared most.

For Adam, there would be nothing. In Adam's part of the tunnel, after he passed through the row of ghosts, he would step into the pitch of his childhood nightmare. The one of suffocation, no sight, no sound, no touch besides the texture of the darkness pressing down around him. No taste besides the bland airless nothing.

No feeling besides the fear that came with isolation. And the dread of knowing that the bubble was complete, intact, unchanging. Eternal loneliness.

Was that why he was so desperate to adopt? To make someone need him? To make it so the child couldn't leave, at least for many years? Years that the awful colorless texture would be kept away.

He blinked and it was Paul who stood before him, not Ephram Korban. The piano notes were like needles of ice driven by the wind.

Only a flashback, he thought. *How old were you when you first had that dream of suffocation? Three? Two? Even before you knew about words?*

And this house has brought it back, the dream comes sniffing around your heels like a strange black dog that follows you home. That neither comes close enough to be petted nor gets left far enough behind to be forgotten.

Adam didn't know what the dream meant, and he

wasn't interested in a shrink's opinion, either. He only knew that he didn't want to be alone. Even if it meant surrendering, losing, grabbing and hanging on in desperation. He wrapped his arms around Paul, clung to him as if sinking in quicksand.

The death dream. Ephram Korban. The ghosts. All part of it. The house would take him in its jaws and then swallow him into its black stomach. Swallow him alone, unless he took someone with him into that airless silence.

"I care about you," Paul whispered in his ear. "Can't you tell?"

Paul cared about the flesh, the meat. But that was okay. That's all they were, anyway. They had no spirit. Two souls could never mingle as one, not even in dreams.

Adam let out a sharp breath. He hated the feelings that flooded his body, the passion that betrayed him. But love and hate were basically the same thing, and both were better than feeling nothing. Anything was better than the suffocation of solitude that waited in his tunnel of the soul. He pulled Paul closer.

"I have an idea," Paul said. "Let's go up on the roof. Up the little stairs. Fool around up there where you had your dream. And I promise not to push you off."

"That's what they all say," Adam said. "And the next thing you know, you're looking down at your own ghost."

"Trust me." Paul took his hand, led him inside.

As they entered the house, Adam realized that people never gave away their hearts, however willing or desperate or lonely they were. Hearts always had to be taken. By force or trickery. Love was murder, the infliction of death by cardiac theft, and the alternative was even worse.

Korban's painted eyes looked down at them, glimmering with cold empathy, wise to the futility of human dreams.

* * *

Anna held the lantern higher. The air in the basement smelled of wood and decay, the shadows creeping from the corners like solid things. Mason's statue skulked in the flicker of flame, the raw features suggesting an obscene strength. The bust of Korban was even more unsettling, because the face had grown comfortable in the polished grain. It had been fashioned with all the love God might have summoned in crafting Adam and Eve.

"What does it mean?" Mason asked.

"I think it means you're obsessed."

"I'm talking about the painting."

"You did all of this since *yesterday?"*

"Hey, the critics will love me, Mama will be proud, I'm the Mountain Michelangelo, the unsung hero of sculpture, blah, blah, blah. But look at this damned painting."

Anna looked. There, on the widow's walk, a host of figures stood in white relief against the dark background. Foremost was the woman Anna had seen in her dreams, the woman in the long flowing gown, the bouquet in her hands. The woman's mouth was open, caught in a scream or a whisper, the eyes imploring, pleading for deliverance from the grasping shapes behind her.

"That's you," Mason said.

"No. I thought it was, at first."

"You've seen this painting before?"

"In my dreams. For the past year, ever since I found out—since I decided to come to Korban Manor."

"If it's not you, then who is it?"

"You won't believe this."

Mason waved his arm to indicate his work. "I've turned into a genius practically overnight, every time I close my eyes Korban is right there telling me to get back to work, you and Ransom and half the guests are convinced that this house is haunted, and this picture has painted itself while nobody was watching. Now tell me what else I wouldn't believe."

"Okay, then. Promise not to laugh."

"I've not been in a laughing mood since I got here. I'm a serious artist, didn't you know that?"

"Oh yes. You've got 'suffering' written all over your face. It's your shield against the world. That's your excuse for keeping people away. You're as wooden as your goddamned statue."

Mason's eyes flashed anger, and for a moment Anna saw Stephen, his mask of barely suppressed rage at Anna's acceptance of approaching death, his calculation of what her loss would mean, his scorn when he'd learned she was going off to a "haunted" house that had never registered anomalous empirical data.

Mason grabbed her arm, squeezed hard enough to hurt. "Listen to me. When I was six years old, my mother bought be a package of modeling clay. It was like magic, digging my fingers in that stuff, twisting it and shaping it however I liked. For the first time in my life, I could control something.

"I made my mother a dinosaur, copying it from a picture in a book. I even put a row of little bony plates up its spine and spikes on its tail, two long horns and eyes that looked like they could stare down a T. Rex. Mama loved it. For the first time ever, I'd done something that really made her proud."

Mason squeezed harder, and Anna feared that he'd lost his mind, was going to snap her arm as if it were one of his whittling sticks. He talked faster, face red, eyes dark and faraway. "And my dad came in, saw the dinosaur, knocked it on the floor, and stomped it flat. Called me a goddamned useless daydreamer, a lazy-bones sack of crap. I can still see that imprint on the floor, the tread of his boot in the clay. Made me feel real special, all right.

"And *you're* special because you see things that don't exist. Well, let me tell you something, Little Miss Strange. This isn't one of your campfire tales. This is happening, this is real." He pulled her closer to the painting. "You can *see* it."

She twisted away, retreated with the lantern. The motion of the light made the shadows shift, gave the illusion that the statue had altered its position among the boards and wires that supported it. She gazed into the small flame of the lantern, where the orange gave way to blue and then to yellow. Maybe if she burned out her retinas, she'd never have to see another ghost in the short time she had left to live. Blinded to Second Sight or any sight.

"That's not me," she said, commanding her tears to evaporate. "It's my mother."

"Your mother?"

"She's here. She's dead. She's one of them now. And they can have her, for all I care."

"One of who? Wait a minute. You're losing me."

"Join the club. I've lost everybody else along the way."

She slammed the lantern onto Mason's worktable hard enough to rattle the glass. The shadows jumped as the flame bobbed, then the darkness began its slow crawl toward Anna. "Here. You're going to need this, because it gets awfully dark when your head's up your ass."

She headed for the stairs, welcoming the cool air that drifted over her skin like fingers of fog. The pain came again, in gentle prods, reminders of the sand that poured through the narrow hourglass gap between present and past. Soon the sand would run out and darkness would claim her. Soon but not nearly soon enough.

On each wooden step, she stomped out her ritual countdown.

Ten, round and thin.

Nine, loop and droop.
Eight, a double gate.
"Anna. Wait."
Seven, sharp and even.
Six, an arc and trick.
"I'm sorry."
She was sorry, too.
Five, a broken wing.
Four, a north fork.
"I'm scared."
Join the club.
Three, a skeleton key.
Two, an empty hook.
One, a dividing line.
"Help me."
Zero.
Nothing.

She opened the door and went down the hall, into the arteries of the house, aware of its patient and held breath, its warm and welcoming heart. Acceptance brought peace. This was the first and last place she had ever belonged. Sylva Hartley was right. She had come home.

She had come home. Sylva ground the dried bloodroot, pulse working her veins like a snowmelt busting through rocks at the tail end of winter. Only a handful of hours until sundown, and then the rising of the blue moon. Sylva had prayed for this night for nigh on a hundred years, and the ashes of a prayer were stronger than the hottest fires of hell.

The spirits shifted in the dirt, turned in their tunnels, restless, disturbed by Ephram Korban's rising power. She knew Ephram better than anybody, better than even Margaret did, or "Miss Mamie," as she'd taken to being called. Many was the night Ephram's voice haunted the wind of Beechy Gap, whispering to Sylva, sending her scuttling for the charms. And he was fetching up a storm now, had already called over George Lawson and one of them new guests, with more soon to follow. By the next sunrise, Korban would have them all. Even Anna. Especially Anna.

Sylva clutched the clay jar of catbone, sprinkled some on the hearth. Her hand ached from gripping the stone, but the powders had to be fine as grave dust. She crushed the mixture again, worked the dry herbs, trembling. The fire spat, which she took as a good omen.

Would her faith be enough? She had the spells down, all her life had been dress rehearsal for this one magic night. Mighty long had she walked these hills, collecting roots and legends, crossing over to commune with the dead, even when the dead just wanted to be left alone. The spell hung on her cracked lips like a fevered drool.

When the time was right, she'd say it. Frost and fire. Ephram Korban was frost and fire. Dead and alive. Both exactly the same, when you got right to the heart of it all.

She pulled a small cedar box from a chink in the log wall. The scrap of cloth was gray with age, stained with the soul juice of the one who had worn it. Sylva brought it to her lips, whispered, "Go out frost," kissed it, and placed it amid the pile of powder.

She ground the stone against the cloth, the threads fraying, ashes to ashes, dust to dust, frost to fire.

CHAPTER 20

Roth licked his lips. This was the good part. The bird had fallen for his line of poppycock. Swallowed it as if it were a worm. Which gave him an idea about what he would get Lilith to do when they got to her room.

She had led him through a small door in the pantry, a door he hadn't noticed before, a place of drafts and shadows that seemed spot-on for the common class. Come to think of it, the servants were ever-present, as if they never needed to sleep. He'd seen one of the maids tending the fire in the sitting room at three in the morning, and the hired hands were in at all hours with their loads of firewood.

Roth followed Lilith down a narrow set of stairs. This was a separate section of the basement, walled off from the part where Mason worked and where Roth had developed his negatives. When the door swung shut above them, they were in pitch-darkness. Neither had a lantern, and the inability to see excited Roth, made his skin tingle in anticipation. Or maybe it was the chilly dead air, the sense of enclosure, that caused his heart to pump faster.

She'd been easy and eager, all right. Most women acted like the old in-out in the middle of the day was an affront to the gods. Lilith didn't even need to finish her first glass of filched wine before she was leaning on Roth, giving him that special happy smile, looking into those smoky gray eyes that no woman in her right mind could resist.

He reached in front of him, keeping one hand on the wall so he wouldn't lose his balance. He touched Lilith's hair. He slid his hand down to where her shoulder should be, but she managed to stay a few steps ahead of him. She hadn't spoken since he'd made his suggestion, only smiled in submission and tilted her head to her secret door. She was one for games, she was.

Roth stepped off the creaking wood onto a hard, flat area. Then he heard a match strike a few feet away, and a tuft of flame erupted. Lilith's face was in the circle of light, but that was impossible, because she was beside him. Her black dress made her body invisible, and for a moment her face and hands appeared to be floating unattached in the air. He let go of her hair, or whatever he was touching, and jumped back as she lit a candle.

"We should have a fire," she whispered, her voice husky. Roth looked down at his hand and saw that it was covered with cobwebs. He yelped, then wiped his hand on his pants.

She giggled. "Did that scare you, Mr. Roth?"

"I hate spiders, remember? Ever since I was nine and got one in me mouth when I was crawling around under the porch. Had nightmares for a week after."

"Poor boy. You're safe with me."

"I hope not too safe, eh? I live for danger, and you're looking pretty bleeding dangerous, love."

As the candle caught and flared, he could make out the dim corners of the room, wondering if spiders lurked in the shadows. Six feet from anywhere, they said. As long as they *stayed* six feet away. He noticed an alcove that had another candle in it. How had she lit that one? He thought maybe the room led into another, but then saw Lilith's back and his own face. A mirror, as large as the bed beneath it, reflecting the room. Kinky bird.

He licked his lips and ran his tongue over his teeth. The room was small and the walls were stone masonry, so thick that no sound would escape. Maybe she liked to get in full voice while having a go. That was fine with Roth.

The room was empty of furniture besides the bed, and that bothered Roth for a moment. There were no blankets on the mattress, only an old linen sheet that looked like it could use a wash. The place was as dismal as a monk's cell. But he forgot all that when Lilith placed the candle on the hearth and sat on the bed, looking up at him with wanton eyes.

Black eyes. Deeper than a Newcastle coal shaft. He didn't see the things he wanted to see. He liked his birds to have a little fear, or at least a little performance anxiety. Made them try harder to please.

But he wasn't going to get particular. One was the same as another, when all was said and done. And her skin looked creamy enough. He would have thought she might blush a little, but she only smiled again, and something about the smile bothered him.

"You won't get in trouble, will you? Having it on with the guests?" he asked, more to break the suffocating silence than because he cared.

"Miss Mamie says guest satisfaction is the key to repeat business," she said, and again that devilish smile was on her lips. For a moment, Roth felt like the seduced instead of the seducer. But that was ridiculous. It was his fame, his charm, his aura of power that had swayed her. His name on a thousand glossy photo credits.

His heart pounded harder and he moved across the room to the bed. She lay back on the sheet, spreading her arms, opening herself to him.

"Am I as pretty as a picture, Mr. Roth?"

He gulped. Maybe it was all that wine he'd tossed back, but he was getting aroused too fast. He felt like an idiot schoolboy looking at a girlie mag. He didn't like to lose control. No bird could play with his emotions that easily.

Her breasts had flattened out beneath the neckline of her dress, and she raised her knees so that her legs were spread. Her dress slid along her thighs, and Roth couldn't tear his gaze away from the shadowy space between her hips. He'd never been this turned on.

Or maybe it was the house, the odd tingle he'd felt in the back of his head since he'd arrived. The tingle seemed to grow more intense and spread through his limbs. Fire, that's what it was. A mild flush of warmth expanding into a glow.

He knelt, wanting to touch her. He'd have to take it slow, or he'd become an animal. He didn't want to just have a slam, he wanted to go nice and easy. He liked that. He liked to hear them beg to be finished off.

But now he was afraid he was slipping, that the power and control had shifted, that she was the one calling the shots. His hands trembled as he reached for her, and he was suddenly angry with himself. He never trembled. He'd taken photos of charging rhinos from thirty feet, with a handheld camera, and they'd come out as clear and focused as an eye chart.

So he did what he always did when he wanted to prolong or deny his passion: he thought about his work. The batch of negatives he'd developed that afternoon. Something about them bothered him, but he couldn't remember at the moment. Definitely the wine had gotten him. And his anger at Spence had clouded his thoughts, too. Well, only one way to drive out the devil.

He put his hands on her bare lower thighs. Her skin was tepid, the same temperature as the room. Odd, but he'd warm her up soon enough. Nothing like a bit of friction for that. But not yet.

Roth climbed onto the bed, thought about removing his pants, then decided to wait. Lilith's hands were on his shoulders, around his neck, pulling his face to hers. What the hell, no use making her suffer any longer. For some reason, her lack of body heat excited him further. Maybe it was this blooming crypt of a room that chilled her. He took it as a personal challenge to stoke her fires.

His lips pressed against hers, her tongue uncertain in her mouth. For a bird with such a fast come-on, she was acting like she'd never kissed before. He hesitated, because something was wrong with the inside of her mouth.

Roth pressed himself down on top of Lilith, her body molding to his even through the dress. Her breasts compressed under him and he liked the feeling. But he was careful not to like it too much. Nice and easy was the ticket, even though his blood pounded hard through his flesh. What was it about the inside of her mouth?

It was just like the rest of her, a little too cool. What was the temperature under the ground, a constant fifty-six degrees or something? But surely her mouth should be hot, and not quite so dry. It was almost like shoving his tongue into a coat pocket. He hoped she wasn't this dry everywhere else.

Lilith moaned into his mouth. Didn't she have any juice?

She writhed under him, so he forgot about the awkwardness of her tongue. He reached out for the shoulder of her dress. He started to pull it lower, to expose more of her flesh to the candlelight.

"Yes," she gasped.

"Yes," came another voice.

Bloody hell?

Probably just an echo off the stone walls. A trick of the acoustics.

But the dead air of the room gobbled sound and swallowed it whole instead of bouncing it back and forth.

Roth caught a flicker of movement that distracted him from the blood rushing below his waist. Then he remembered the mirror and looked up at it. Maybe watching him and the lovely lass beneath him would rekindle his arousal.

In the mirror his face grew larger, as if he were watching himself through a fast-zooming lens. And why was that so wrong?

It was only a split second, but plenty of time for him to notice that the mirror was falling onto the bed, onto them, as if in slow motion. And that sheet of glass must weigh a hundred pounds. If it broke—

If it broke, he would be badly cut.

Badly.

But he couldn't move, Lilith had her limbs locked around him, and bloody hell, she was strong, he grunted as he tried to fight her off, but she had too many arms, too many, scratching and clutching at him, and he saw her reflection in the mirror and she wasn't Lilith, she was a black spider, squat and thick, pincers twitching near his lips, searching for a soul kiss.

Black widow, his mind screamed at him, *she always eats her mate.*

Looking up, he hardly recognized his reflection, eyes large, his mouth a black tunnel, the stems of Lilith's eight arms clasping him, the barbs of her forelimbs in his flesh.

But before the pain could spin its web, the mirror

was upon him, and as the glass shattered, it wasn't his face in the mirror, it was Korban's.

Then the silver shards sliced into his flesh and Lilith loosed her venom and he was in the long dark tunnel and Ephram Korban smiled at him, holding up a spoon that squirmed with the frantic scrabbling of spiders.

"Time for a spot of tea, Mr. Roth," Korban said.

"How is our statue coming along?" Miss Mamie hoped her impatience was buried deep, just as all her emotions were, except when under the naked gaze of Ephram.

"It's going to be lovely," Mason said, standing in the doorway of his room, eyes puffy, hair disheveled. "You want to come in?"

She and Ephram had spent many precious nights here, hours that seemed even sweeter with the distant years. But the room disturbed her because it always bore the stink and taint of Sylva, as if the walls still harbored the memory of Ephram's sin. She could forgive, all right. All women could forgive, that was how love worked, but she would never forget. Even if Ephram let her live to be a thousand.

Mason held open the door, and she peered past him to the fireplace, the dew drying on the windowsill, the smiling face of Ephram on the wall.

"I only have a moment," she said. "I'm busy preparing for the party."

"Party?"

"The blue moon party. It's something of a tradition at Korban Manor. Your presence is required."

"Sure. I guess I could spare the time."

"Not too much time, I hope. I know you're dedicated to your work."

"That reminds me. Do you know anything about that painting of the manor in the basement?"

Rage filled Miss Mamie, burned her, scorched her like her dead husband's love. She no longer cared if Mason saw the flames in her eyes. He couldn't escape anyway. He was as trapped here as she was.

She forced a smile, the good hostess. "Master Korban, I'm afraid. He once fancied himself a painter."

The anger opened a dark tunnel in her heart, the conduit through which Ephram kept his hold over her. An icy wind blew from the mouth of the tunnel, freezing her chest. Ephram's threat and Ephram's promise. He needed her fear as much as he needed the emotions of the others. She only wished her love was all he required. But love by itself was never enough.

"He was gifted." Mason must not have noticed her torment. She was good at hiding it, after all these decades.

"One of his greatest sorrows was that he never finished it," she said. "There's something melancholy about an artist's final work, even when the artist's talents are ordinary and mortal. One always hopes to make an impression that will live on after death."

"Our vanity," Mason said. "And I reckon it's what drives us crazy. Because we know we'll never achieve perfection."

"Perfection." Miss Mamie didn't need the painting before her in order to remember. She could close her eyes and see the house, the lighted windows, the low clouds, the widow's walk. She could taste the breeze that had blown from the northwest, crisp from its journey over Canadian tundra. String music quivered in the air, smoke poured from the chimneys as it rose into the round eye of the moon. And Ephram called them up, fetched his spirit slaves, and sent them after Rachel Faye Hartley.

Ephram didn't like his own family keeping secrets from him. Rachel had fled, leapt to her death from the widow's walk. Rachel had taken her secrets to the grave, but carried them back from the grave as well.

The hurt rose inside Miss Mamie, consumed her in a blaze of hatred. Ephram and Sylva were bound by blood. His illicit family would always hold the biggest place in his everlasting heart, no matter what sacrifices Miss Mamie made. No matter how deep her devotion. And that painting, the one Ephram called his work in progress, was an eternal reminder.

She turned away, into the hall, the portrait of Ephram close enough to touch. "That painting should have been burned long ago," she said.

"Anna said her mother was in the painting."

"Forget Anna. You're to think only of your statue."

"Anna says she's never been here before. How could Korban have known? He's in the painting, too. And somebody who looks like you."

"Illusions," Miss Mamie said. "Never trust an artist, because dreams lie and visions are temporary."

"Can I trust *anybody?*"

"Trust your heart, Mr. Jackson. That's the only thing worth believing in."

"My heart is getting pulled in three different directions."

She studied the young man's face. He was a lot like Ephram in some ways, stubborn and proud, afraid of weakness and failure. But Ephram had taken matters into his own hands, determined to leave none of his work unfinished. Obsessed with controlling his world. "I guess you'll just have to tear your heart into enough pieces to go around. As long as the biggest piece goes into your statue."

"Don't worry. I'll make you proud. I'll make them all proud."

"I'm sure you will. See you tonight. Don't be late."

The door closed. Miss Mamie touched the locket

that hung around her neck. When Ephram wore flesh again, he would prove that love never died. Sylva, Rachel, Anna, Lilith, and all the others would be forgotten, would be the embers of memories, fading, dying, and at last, lost to darkness. While Miss Mamie and Ephram burned on, together forever.

Anna sat on her bed, huddled in a blanket. The room had grown cold during the afternoon, the temperature falling as the fire burned low. She found herself staring at Ephram Korban's portrait, searching his face for genetic features that had been passed down to her. Korban, Rachel, Sylva. And somewhere in there, a faceless father, who'd slipped her off the mountain, abandoned her with only a first name, and died rather than return to the mountains. By his own hand and noose, according to Sylva.

She had drifted for so long, rootless and unconnected, and now she belonged to too many people. Her bloodline was too crooked, the generations skewed by whatever magic slowed the ravages of time here at the manor. Because if Sylva was a hundred and five, and Anna was twenty-six, then Rachel had died less than three decades ago. Or maybe when you died, you were ageless, and the years no longer counted.

There was a knock and Cris entered. "Hi, girl, what's up?"

"Just brooding."

"Hey, that's no way to spend an artists' retreat. Leave that to the idiots who think it's okay to starve for art. Or to pigheaded photographers."

"Ah, what's the point?"

"That's exactly the point. If it doesn't matter, if it's all a solo wet dream, then why not enjoy yourself?"

"Maybe you're right. I'm taking things a bit too seriously."

"That's the spirit." Cris slipped into the bathroom, paused at the door. "Excuse me. Time of the month. Full moon tonight."

"So I hear."

"And a big party on the roof. Miss Mamie says it's not to be missed. If Mason's there, maybe you'll get lucky." Cris winked, then closed the bathroom door. Anna pulled the blanket more tightly about her shoulders.

When Cris came out, she rummaged in her dresser for a sweater. "Hey, did you mess with my sketch pad?"

"I haven't been here today."

Cris held it up. Scrawled across a large sheet of paper, in slashing strokes of red crayon, were the words *Go out frost, come in fire.*

"Maybe it was one of the servants," Anna said. "A reminder note to put more wood on the fire."

"It's getting cold, all right. October in the mountains. If it wasn't for the falling leaves, I think I'd rather have Rio. See you tonight." Cris waved and left, tying her hair back in a ponytail as she went.

Anna watched the grain of the door as it swirled and bent inward. A shape superimposed itself against the dark oak panels. A pale hand, holding a bouquet, the woman with desperate eyes. And that one whispered word, "Anna."

Resting in peace was apparently not allowed for either the dead or the living.

CHAPTER 21

Mason wished he'd brought a lantern, since the afternoon had grown suddenly dark, heavy clouds sweeping from the northwest like smoke from a distant prairie fire. At least he was out of the house, having dodged the questioning gaze of Miss Mamie. He didn't want to go down into the basement, at least not until his head cleared. Anna was right, he'd become obsessed, and it was far more than just the pursuit of praise that drove him.

He headed down the road toward the barn. It was about time for Ransom to feed and put up the horses. Maybe Anna had gone to help him. Like Mason, she probably preferred the company of the old mountain man to that of the rowdy revelers in the manor. And she was nuts about the horses.

If he saw her, then he could apologize, talk plainly. Maybe try to understand her. She knew more than she let on, and unlike the other guests, she recognized that something seriously weird was going on at Korban Manor. And the two of them had something else in common.

Because, though she tried her best to hide it, a suffering ran deep inside her, turbulent waters beneath the calm surface. Or maybe he just liked looking into her cyan eyes and his imagination had done the rest. His imagination had always been his blessing and his curse, both his exit door from a lifetime in Sawyer Hosiery and the demon that rode his back in every waking moment and most of his sleeping ones.

He followed the fence line, stopping once to glance back at the house. There were several lighted windows, but much of its facade was dark and featureless. A few high piano notes tinkled in the breeze. He looked up at the roof, at the flat space above the gabled windows where the rail marked off the widow's walk. A few people moved about beyond the white railing, probably the servants setting up for the party. Mason compared the real thing to the painting in the basement.

No contest. The real thing was much creepier. He didn't buy Anna's lie about never having been to the manor, though Korban must have painted the picture decades before her birth. Mason had memorized her face well enough to know it was plainly Anna walking in that painted haze, complete with the bouquet and lace dress.

Miss Mamie didn't like that painting, either. She'd acted almost afraid of it, despite her obvious adoration of Korban. He shook his head. Why was she so adamant about his finishing the statue? She seemed even more anxious to get it done than Mason himself, as if she had her own critics to please.

He put his hands in his pockets. The forest seemed closer and darker, as if it had picked up and moved while no one was looking. An owl hooted from a stand of trees to his right. He walked a little faster.

Imagination.

Right, Mase. Big dream image. Korban on the brain.

The dream was a crock, a smelly pile of whatever it was that he'd just stepped in. The barn lay ahead, a faint square of lantern light leaking from the open door. Mason hurried toward it. He looked above the door and saw that the horseshoe was points-down on the wall. He couldn't remember if that was the good position or the ghosts-walk-on-in position. He almost wished he had a rag-ball charm to wave.

Mason stepped inside, his sneakers muted by the hay scattered across the planks. He didn't see Ransom or Anna. The smell of the leather harness and the sweet sorghum odor of the horse feed drifted across the air. The opposite door leading to the meadow was closed off. He swallowed and was about to call out when he heard Ransom's voice among the wagons: "Get away, George. You ain't got no call to be here."

The shadows of the surrey and wagons were high on the walls, and the staves and wheel spokes and the tines of the hay rake cast flickering black lines on the wooden walls. Ransom spoke again, and this time Mason located him, crouched behind one of the wagons.

"Got me a charm bag, George. You're supposed to leave me alone." The handyman's eyes were wide, staring across the buckled gray floor.

Wasn't George the name of the man who'd been killed in that accident? Had Ransom's belief in ghosts and folk magic finally driven him off the deep end?

Then Mason saw George.

And George *looked* dead, with his hollowed-out eyes sunk into the wispy substance of his impossible shape, the stump of one forearm held aloft. George looked so dead that Mason could see through him. And George was smiling, as if being dead was the best thing that ever happened to him.

"Been sent to fetch you, Ransom, old buddy." The words seemed to come from every corner of the room, rattling a few crisp leaves that had blown in during winters past. A chill ran up Mason's spine, his scalp tingled, he felt as if he was going to pass out.

Because this was no dream image.

He couldn't blame his imagination for *this*.

"Get on back, damn you," Ransom said, his voice shaky. He kept his eyes fixed on the George-thing and didn't notice Mason. George took a step forward.

Except that wasn't a STEP, was it, Mason? Because George didn't move a muscle, just floated forward like a windy scarecrow on a wire.

Cold air radiated off the George-thing, chilling the cramped space of the barn. Mason wasn't ready to call it a ghost. Because when he told Anna he'd believe it when he saw it, it turned out that he had lied. He *still* didn't believe it.

And he didn't believe what was dangling from the George-thing's lone hand. The missing hand, its milky fingers flexing as if eager to get a good grip around somebody's throat.

"Come on, Ransom," the cemetery voice said. "It only hurts for a second. And it's not so bad inside, once you get used to the snakes."

"Why, George? I ain't never done a thing to you." Ransom's eyes were wide with terror. "You was a good, God-fearing man. What you gone and got yourself into?"

Laughter shook the tin roofing. Mason's heart did a somersault.

"Got myself into the tunnel, old buddy. 'Cause I just had to *know*. Now let me fetch you on inside. Korban don't like to be kept waiting."

There was a rusty creak, and the hay rake rolled forward. Ransom's eyes shifted from side to side, looking for an escape. He saw Mason.

"The charm ain't working, Mason. *How come the charm ain't working?*"

George turned in Mason's direction, again without moving any of its withered, fibrous extremities. "Plenty of room inside, young fellow. The tunnel ain't got no end."

Ransom ducked between the wagon and the surrey and Mason turned to run. Too late. The barn door screed across its track and slammed shut.

Mason fled along the inside of the wall, making sure he kept plenty of distance between him and the ghost—*you just called it a GHOST, Mason. And that's not a good sign*—until he got beside the surrey. He dropped to his knees, his bones clattering against the floorboards. He crawled to Ransom's side. "What the hell is that thing, Ransom?"

Ransom peered between the spokes of the wagon wheel. Mason could smell the man's fear, salt and copper and greenbriar.

"What I been warning you about, son. He's one of *them* now. Korban's bunch."

"I don't believe in ghosts."

Ransom's rag-ball charm was clenched inside his fist. "That don't matter none, when the ghosts believe in *you.*"

The shape floated forward, arms raised, the ragged end of its amputation fluttering with the motion. Mason found himself staring at the stump, wondering why a ghost shouldn't be all in one piece.

Ghost—you called it a ghost again, Mason.

The hay rake creaked, rolling out of its corner toward the pair.

"Go away," the old man said in a high, broken voice. "I got warding powers."

"Come out and play, Ransom," said the George-thing. "Gets lonely inside, with just the snakes for company. We can set a spell and talk over old times. And Korban's got chores for us all."

Ransom held up the charm bag. "See here? Got my

lizard powder, yarrow, snakeroot, Saint Johnswort. You're *supposed* to go away."

George laughed again, and thunder rattled in the eaves of the barn. Horses whinnied in the neighboring stalls.

"Don't believe ever little thing they tell you," George said. "Them's just a bunch of old widows' tales. 'Cause it ain't *what* you believe, is it, Ransom?"

"It's how much," Ransom said, defeated, looking down at the little scrap of cotton that held the herbs and powder. The cloth was tied with a piece of frayed blue ribbon. White dust trickled from the opening.

Suddenly Ransom stood and threw the bag at George. "Ashes of a prayer, George!"

Mason was frozen by his own fear and a strange fascination as the bag came untied and the contents spread out in a cloud of green and gray dust. The material wafted over the ghost, mingled in its vapor, caught a stir of wind from the crack beneath the door, and swirled around the shape.

George shimmered, faded briefly, fizzled like a candle about to burn the last of its wax—

Jiminy H. Christ, it's working, Mason thought. *IT'S WORK—*

The cloud of herbs settled to the floor, and George wiped at its eyes.

"Now you boys have gone and made me mad," the ghost said, its voice flat and cold, seeping from the corners of the room like a fog. "I tried to do it nice, Ransom. Just you and me, taking us a nice long walk into the tunnel like old friends. But you tried to spell me."

George shook its see-through head. The motion made a breeze that chilled Mason to the bone. Ransom ducked behind the wagon wheel and tensed beside him. The ghost fluttered forward, steadily, now only twenty feet away, twelve, ten. A rusty metallic rattle filled the barn.

George held up the amputated hand. "They took my hammering hand, Ransom. *He* took it."

The ghost sounded almost wistful, as if debating whether to follow the orders of an absent overseer. But then the deep caves of the eyes grew bright, flickered in bronze and gold and blazing orange, and the face twisted into something that was barely recognizable as having once been human. It was shrunken, wizened, a shriveled rind with pockmarks for eyes. The voice came again, but it wasn't just George's voice, it was the combined voice of dozens, a congregation, a chorus of lost souls. *"Come inside, Ransom. We're waiting for you."*

The horses kicked their stall doors. A calf bawled from the meadow outside. The surrey and the wagons rocked back and forth. The lantern quivered on the floor and shadows climbed the walls like giant insects.

The calf bawled again, then once more, the sound somehow standing out in the cacophony.

"Calf bawled three times," Ransom whispered. "Sure sign of death."

Mason crouched beside him, wanting to ask Ransom what in the hell was happening. But his tongue felt like a piece of harness against the roof of his mouth. He didn't think he could work it to form words. Ransom looked at George, then at the closed door. The door was much farther.

Mason reached out to touch Ransom's sleeve, but came up with nothing. Ransom made a run for it. The ghost didn't move as Ransom's boots drummed across the plank floor. Mason wondered if he should make a run for it, too. Ransom moved fast, arms waving wildly.

He's going to make it!

Ransom was about six feet from the door when the hay rake pounced—*POUNCED,* Mason thought, *like a cat*—with a groan of stressed steel and wood, the rusty tines of the windrower sweeping down and forward. Ransom turned and faced the old farm machine as if to beg for mercy.

His eyes met Mason's, and Mason knew he would never forget that look, even if he got lucky and escaped George and managed to live to be a hundred and one. Ransom's face blanched, blood rushed from his skin as if trying to hide deep in his organs where the hay rake couldn't reach. Ransom's eyes were wet marbles of fear. The leathery skin of his jaws stretched tight as he opened his mouth to scream or pray or mutter an ancient mountain spell.

Then the windrower swept forward, skewering Ransom and pushing him backward. His body slammed against the door, two dozen giant nails hammered into wood. Ransom gurgled and a red mist spewed from his mouth. And the eyes were gazing down whatever tunnel death had cast him into.

The wagon and surrey stopped shaking, the walls settled back into place, and a sudden silence jarred the air. The old man's body sagged on the tines like a raw chuck steak at the end of a fork. Mason forced himself to look away from the viscera and carnage. The lantern threw off a burst of light, as if the flames were fed by Ransom's soul-wind leaving his body.

George floated toward Mason, who took a step backward.

"You're not here," Mason said. He put up his hands, palms open. "I don't believe in you, so you don't exist."

The ghost stopped and looked down at its own silken flesh. After a stretch of skipped heartbeats, it looked at Mason and grinned.

"I lied. It ain't what we believe that matters," it said softly, sifting forward another three feet. "It's what *Korban* believes."

The hand reached out, the hand in the hand, in a manly welcome. Marble cold and grave-dirt dead.

Mason turned, ran, waiting for the pounce of the hay rake or the grip of the ghost hand. He tripped over a gap in the floorboards and fell. He looked back at his feet. The root cellar.

He wriggled backward and flipped the trapdoor open, then scrambled through headfirst. He grabbed the first rung of the ladder and pulled himself into the damp darkness of the cellar. If potions and prayers didn't work, then a trapdoor wouldn't stop a ghost. But his muscles took over where his rational mind had shut down.

He was halfway inside when the trapdoor slammed down on his back. Stripes of silver pain streaked up his spinal column. Then he felt something on the cloth of his pants. A light tapping, walking.

Fingers.

He kicked and flailed his legs, grabbed the second rung, and heaved himself into the darkness. He was weightless for a moment, his stomach lurching from vertigo. Then he was falling, a drop into forever that was too fast for screaming. The door slammed into place overhead as he landed in the root cellar. The air was knocked from his lungs, but that didn't matter because he wasn't sure he'd breathed since he'd entered the barn.

The cellar was completely dark except for a few splinters of light that leaked through gaps in the flooring above. He experimentally moved his arms and something tumbled to the ground. He reached out and squeezed the thing under his hand, then felt it. He had landed in a sweet potato bin.

Mason rolled to his feet, then ducked behind the bin. He tried to remember what Ransom had said about another door at one end of the cellar, and a tunnel leading back to the house. George might already be down here. How well could ghosts see in the dark?

Boots, marching feet, fell loud and heavy above him, then he realized it was his pulse pounding in his ears.

He opened his mouth so he could listen better. The upstairs was quiet. Mason smelled the earth and the sweet apples. He tried to get a sense of the cellar's layout, to figure out where the exit was, but he'd lost his sense of direction in the dark.

He could find the ladder again, but a trapdoor worked both ways. What would be waiting for him if he went back up? The hay rake, its tines dripping red? George, ready to give him a hand up? How about Ransom, full of holes, now one of *them,* whatever *they* were supposed to be?

He thought of Anna, her quiet self-confidence, her hidden inner strength disguised as aloofness. She claimed to understand ghosts, and hadn't ridiculed Ransom's folk beliefs. She wouldn't freak if she saw a ghost. She would know what to do, if only he could reach her. But what can anybody who's alive really know about ghosts?

His racing thoughts were broken by a soft noise. At first he thought it was the creaking of the hay rake flexing its metal claw up in the barn. But the noise wasn't grating and metallic.

It was a rustle of fingers on cloth.

The hand.

He kicked and flailed, and more sweet potatoes tumbled to the cool dirt.

The noises came again, from all sides, from too many sources to be five ghostly digits.

Then he recognized the sound, one he'd grown familiar with while living by the Sawyer Creek landfill.

It wasn't a creaking, it was a *squeaking.*

Rats.

CHAPTER 22

"Go away," Anna said to the ghost that had stepped from the wall, that now stood before her in evanescent splendor.

Rachel drifted closer, the forlorn bouquet held out in apology or sorrow. "I never wanted to hurt you, Anna."

"Then why did you summon me back here? Why didn't you just let me die dumb and happy, with nobody to hate?"

"We need you, Anna. I need you."

"Need, need, need. Do you ever think I might have needed somebody, all those nights when I cried myself to sleep? And now you expect me to feel sorry for you just because you're *dead?*"

"It's not just me, Anna. He's trapped all of us here."

Did the dead have a choice about where their souls were bound to the real world? Did the doorway open on a particular place for each person, or did ghosts wander their favorite haunting grounds because they wished themselves into existence? Those were the kinds of questions the hard-line parapsychologists never asked. They were too busy trying to validate their own existence to feel any empathy for those spirits condemned to an eternity of wandering.

But Anna wasn't strong on empathy herself at the moment. "And if you were free, where would you go?"

Rachel looked out the window, at the mountains that stretched to the horizon. "Away," she said.

"And Korban has bound your soul here? Why would he do that?"

"He wants everything he ever had, and more. He wants to be served and worshipped. He has unfulfilled dreams. But I think it's love that keeps him here. Maybe, behind it all, he's afraid of being alone."

"Something else that runs in the family," Anna said. "Well, I don't mind being alone, not anymore. Because I found what I thought I'd always wanted, and now I see I never wanted it at all."

"We have tunnels of the soul, Anna. Where we face the things that haunted our lives and dreams. In my tunnel, I'm unable to save you, and I watch as Ephram twists your power until it serves him. Our family had the Sight, Sylva and me, but it's stronger in you. Because you can see the ghosts even without using charms and spells."

"Maybe the spells will help me," Anna said. "Isn't there one that makes the dead stay dead? 'Go out frost,' is that it?"

"Don't say it, Anna. Because soon you'll get fetched over, too, and Ephram will be too strong for any of us to stop."

Anna rose from the bed. "Go out frost."

Rachel dissolved a little, the bouquet wilting to transparent threads in her hand, her eyes full of ghostly sadness. "You're our only hope. It's Sylva."

"Go out frost."

Rachel faded against the door. "Sylva," she whispered.

"Go out frost. Third time's a charm."

Rachel disappeared. Anna looked up at Ephram Korban's portrait. "You can have her, for all I care."

Anna put on her jacket, collected her flashlight, and went for a walk, wanting to be as far away from Rachel as possible. If Rachel was going to hang out at Korban Manor, then Anna would take a stroll to Beechy Gap.

Rachel had said Sylva knew some sort of secret. Maybe Sylva knew a spell that would keep all ghosts away. Anna had dedicated a big part of her life to chasing ghosts. Now that they were everywhere, she never wanted to see another as long as she lived. Or even after that.

Mason kicked himself backward, pressing against the moist clay bank. Another sweet potato tumbled to the ground. At least he *hoped* it was a sweet potato. More squeaks pierced the darkness, a sour chorus rising around him.

He would rather face the ghost of George Lawson, stray hand and bloody hay rake and all, than what was down here in the dark. He thought about making a dash for the ladder, but he was disoriented. He was just as likely to run into the apple barrels or trip over one of the pallets that were scattered across the dirt floor. And falling would bring his face down to *their* level.

To his left came a clicking, a gnawing, a noise like teeth against tinfoil. Maybe five feet away, it was hard to tell in the blackness. The room was like a coffin, with no stir of air, no edge or end that made any difference to the one trapped inside. He huddled in a ball, looking up at the cracks in the boards, at the yellow lines of light that were his only comfort. He smelled his own sweat and fear and wondered if the salt would bring the rats closer.

Leaves whisked across the floor upstairs, then the barn door slid open with a rusty groan. That was followed by a dull thump and Mason pictured Ransom's body hitting the planks, limbs lolling uselessly. Then the lantern went out above, and Mason closed his eyes against a black as deep as any he had ever seen.

No. There had been a worse darkness.

Funny how things come back to you. Maybe this was one of those tunnels of the soul. A memory so long buried that the meat had rotted off its bones, that the skeleton had started its slow turn to dust, that the existence of it could no longer be proven. But always that spark remained, that hidden ember, just waiting for a breath of wind to bring the corpse back to full life, to resurrect the memory in all its awful glory.

Funny how that happened.

This was it, the memory. Only this couldn't be real. Or was the *first* time the one that was shadowy? It didn't matter. Because they were the same, past and present entwined in the same heart-stopping fear.

The squeaking.

The rats, tumbling in the dark like sweet potatoes or a child's toys. How many?

One was too many. How many squeaks? Mason held his breath so he could listen. Ten. Fifteen. Forty.

Mama was out of town. Somebody had died, that's all Mason knew, because he'd never seen Mama cry so much. And Mason sensed a change in her when Mama gave him all those extra hugs and kisses, held him in her lap for hours. Then she was gone.

And Daddy, Daddy with his bottles, was all Mason knew after that. He lay in the crib, his blankets wet, too scared to wail. If he cried out, maybe Mama would come. But if she didn't, Daddy might. Daddy would only get mad, yell, and break something.

So Mason didn't say anything. Time passed or else it didn't. There was no sun in the window, only the light that Daddy turned on and off. Daddy slept on the floor one time, and Mason looked through the wooden bars of his crib, saw him with his bottle tipped over, the brown liquid pouring out across the floor.

Daddy woke up, rubbed his eyes, yelled, looked in at Mason, left him wet again. Daddy turned out the light, and as the door closed, Mason remembered the vanishing wedge of brightness, how scared he was as it got smaller and smaller, then the door banged shut and the dark was big, thick, everything.

Time passed or else it didn't, Mason's tiny heart pumping, pounding, screaming. Crying would do no good. Mama wasn't here. And his cries might bring *them.* He closed his eyes, opened them. One black was the same color as the other.

Squatting in the root cellar, Mason closed his eyes, opened them, trying to blink away the memory. He covered his face with his hands. He remembered reading somewhere that rats always went for the soft parts first, the eyes and tongue and genitals. He didn't have enough hands.

This was the memory, the first time. The skittering in the dark. The scratching against the wall. The ticking of claws across wood. The squeak of pleasure at the discovery. So dark in the room that he couldn't see their shiny eyes when he finally forced himself to look.

Mason heard them, though, even with the wet blankets pulled tightly over his head. Soft whispers of tiny tongues against liquid. Daddy's bottle. The spilled stuff had brought them. Would it be enough to fill them? Would they go away?

Please, *please,* go away.

The squeaking sounded now like laughter, like a moist, slobbery snickering. Go away? Of *course* they wouldn't go away, this was the dark and they owned the dark. They crept toward the crib, the hush of their tails dragging behind.

No, *no, NO.*

This was *now* and not the memory, he wasn't a small

child, and he wasn't afraid of rats anymore. And because the root cellar was darker than the world outside, he might be able to see the outline of the door. All he had to do was open his eyes.

Mama's voice came to him, and he couldn't swear whether the words were spoken or merely imagined: *It's ALWAYS the memory, Mason. Big Dream Image. Don't ever let go of your dreams. They're the only thing you got in this world.*

And something quick and wet and warm flicked at his face, just under his left eye, it may have been only the corner of a blanket shifting, yes, of course, that's what it was, rats don't eat little boys, that's not tiny feet pressing against your legs, it's only your imagination, and you always had a good imagination, didn't you?

And you lived long enough to learn that the darkness doesn't spread out forever, that rats don't own everything, just your dreams, *AND DREAMS ARE THE ONLY THING YOU GOT IN THIS WORLD.*

And Mama came home finally and opened the door and turned on the light and held you but it was too late, days too late, years too late, the rats had *EATEN* you, eaten your eyes, now it's dark all the time and they own the dark and Mama can't open the door because they ate her eyes, too, and she's sitting in her rat's-nest chair back in Sawyer Creek and—

"Looks like you're in a right smart pickle."

The voice, from nowhere and everywhere, seemed part of the dark. And darkness had to have different colors, because the deep black tunnel opened like a throat before his closed eyes. Standing at the edge of the tunnel was Ransom Streater, dripping wounds and all, a perfect row of punctures across the chest of his overalls, one buckle bent. Ransom with his grinning possum mouth and old freckled bald head and dead, dead, dead eyes.

"Korban fetched me up to your bad place," Ransom

said. "You ought to see mine. I got it worse than you do, believe me. But Korban says if I'm a good helper, then I get out of my bad place for a little bit. All I gots to do is walk you out."

"Where am I?"

"Why, in the heart, that's where. 'Cepting Korban wants to send you back. Says you got chores to do."

"What chores?" Mason forced his eyes wide, even though the rats were hungry and eyes were soft and juicy. But the image didn't change, Ransom stood shimmering before him, the tunnel stretched out black and deep and cold, only now there was a light at the end, precious light, beautiful light, a ratless light, Mama was opening the door.

Mason stood, heard the rats slither back into their unseen holes. He said the only thing he could think of to say. "You're dead."

"And it ain't no cakewalk, let me tell you." Ransom touched his wounds, his eyebrows lifting as he fingered a hole in his ribs. "At least you got a choice."

Mason stepped closer, the light beckoned. He took one glance backward in the darkness, heard the noise of whiskers and claws and wet, sharp teeth. He shivered. Korban would keep this place waiting for him.

But the best thing to do was put your fears behind you, as least for as long as possible. Deny their existence. Bury them.

"Where does the tunnel go, Ransom?"

"Why, to the *end.* Where else would it go?"

Mason swallowed. He remembered Ransom, the old, living Ransom, had said the tunnel led back to the manor's basement. He thought about running for the ladder, but he heard a squeak and a whisper of tongue. Then, Mama's voice, unmistakable, poured from the dark throat of the tunnel. "Dreams is all we got, Mason. Now get in here and make Mama proud."

And it wasn't only Mama's voice, here in the damp,

dark dirt of Korban's estate, that bothered him. It was the suggestion of squeakiness in her words, as if they had spilled from between large, curved, rodent teeth.

Mason followed Ransom into the black tunnel, blinked as the light grew unbearably bright, then softened. A lantern was burning on the table. Mason was in the studio, his unfinished statue waiting before him.

"Tunnels of the soul, Mason," Mama said. "I'll be watching."

Mason turned just in time to see the long hideous gray rope of tail disappear into the dark tunnel. Ransom stood by the shadows of the basement. "We all got chores. My batch is waiting back in the tunnel. Yours is on *this* side, for now."

Mason knelt, trembling, and selected a fluter. He took up his hatchet and approached the statue, studied the rough oak form. Ephram Korban was in there somewhere, just as he inhabited everything. At the heart of it all.

Mama lied. She'd said dreams were all we had in this world. But we have nightmares, too. And memories.

And sometimes you can't tell the difference.

Mason attacked the wood as if his life depended on it.

CHAPTER 23

Sylva opened the door just before Anna reached the cabin. "Been expecting you."

Anna moved past her without waiting for an invitation. Sylva looked at the folded cloth on the mantel, the one that held her spelling charm. Every trick in the book, and a few she'd only heard whispered around long-ago campfires, were ground up and sprinkled inside the cloth, and words had been said over the concoction that few lips would dare speak. But this wasn't a time for the scared or the faint of heart.

"Warm your bones," Sylva said, motioning to an old cane chair by the fire. "Tonight's one of them that lets you know winter's right around the corner."

"You didn't tell me everything," Anna said, going to the hearth but kneeling instead of sitting.

"They's such a thing as knowing too much. Bad enough you got the Sight. But if you don't mind your step, you're going to end up too soon on the wrong side of dead."

"But why does my mo—no, not my mother, I mean *Rachel Hartley*—think I'm some kind of savior for the haunted? Why did she summon me here? If Korban's already got them, what can I do about it? Just because I can see ghosts doesn't mean I have any special powers."

"Remember what I told you about power. It ain't what you believe that matters, it's how much." Sylva kept her eyes fixed on the leaping flames, wouldn't let her gaze slide over to the folded cloth, no matter how hard they itched for a look.

"I don't owe Rachel anything," Anna said. "You said blood runs thicker than water. But that's not all that makes people belong to each other."

"Child, I know how it hurts. I've hated myself for my weakness, my sin with Korban. I tried a hundred times to tell myself that *he* caused it, he spelled me and made it happen. But it's always easy to lie to yourself, ain't it? It's easy to just push it down into the dark where you hope nobody will see the truth of it, least of all yourself."

Oh yeah, woman, you know the truth of it, don't you? Ephram let you kill him under the blue moon so his spirit could go into the house. But you never knew that Ephram would take up collecting, would fetch over everybody who died on his grounds. And you surely to goodness never knew he'd keep Miss Mamie young, turn love into poison like that.

"Your sin was a long time ago," Anna said. "You ought to be able to forgive yourself after all these years."

"I was always afraid to let loose and love him," Sylva said. "You don't know the times I wanted that night to happen again, at the same time I was knotted up inside with the frights. Maybe it was all Ephram's doing, one of his tricks. But it's a scary and wondrous thing when your heart gets plumb stole away. And it's scary and wondrous to burn with hate over something, too."

"But Rachel—"

"I loved her, same as she loves you. I reckon as much as Ephram loved me."

"You said Miss Mamie was keeping him alive. That, and the spirits of those he's trapped at the manor. The ones he uses for fuel, some sort of soul siphon, feeding on their pain and dreams."

"What do you reckon Ephram burns for?" Sylva bent and took up the poker, stabbed at the back log until sparks spat up the chimney. "The dead is just like living. They want things they can't have. Ephram's got unfinished dreams, a big appetite. That's why you're here."

Sylva felt the trembling in her old limbs, the rough coursing of her blood through narrowed veins. She had been old far too long. She had too many regrets, had been played for the worst kind of fool. If only she could close her eyes and rest in peace. But Ephram Korban wouldn't allow it.

Sylva was bound here come hell or high water, and Rachel had found out way too late that what belonged to Ephram always came back. Rachel's dying here was Anna's only chance. Because Ephram would find out where Anna was, that gift of the Sight would shine like a ghost beacon in a night sky.

"And my father?" Anna said. "Do you have any pictures of him?"

"Folks don't keep pictures around here, especially of them that want to stay dead. You ever heard of poppet magic? Where they steal your face and then steal your soul? You're the only one that can free them from Ephram."

"What do I care?" Anna said. "The dead will still be dead, and I'll still have nothing. At least if I die at the manor, I'll have a warm place to haunt."

Sylva let the tears come. That was a mighty fine weapon to have around. Anna fell for it, came close, hugged her.

"Rachel gave up her life so you could get away," Sylva whispered into Anna's ear. "If Ephram takes Rachel now, you'll lose her forever. And them that's bound to the house, not all of them are touched by sin. Like that girl ghost, Becky, you saw on your first night here. Tree fell on her, right out of the blue. That child never hurt a fly. If anybody's spirit deserves to be set free, it's hers."

Anna clenched her fists. "What am I supposed to do? I'm just one person. I'm weak, I'm dying, my soul's not in such hot shape in the first place. How in the hell am I supposed to *believe?*"

"You gotta follow your heart, Anna." Sylva went to the window. "Sun's about to set. You know what that means."

"Yeah, yeah, yeah. The blue moon."

Sylva crossed the room, stooped slowly, silently cursing Ephram for knotting up her bones and wrinkling her skin. She put a hand on Anna's shoulder, let a tear gather in her eye, then said, "You just follow your heart. That's what believing is all about."

Sylva gave her another hug, and this time Anna returned it, held on with a desperation that might have been born of a lifelong loneliness. Sylva finally let go and stepped back. "You'd best get back to the house, now. Miss Mamie's waiting."

Anna went out into the darkening forest. The wind was sharp, cold enough that the early dew was already turning hard. This was a night of frost, Sylva thought. A night for the dead.

She closed the cabin door and went to the mantel, caressed the folded cloth, and offered up ashes of prayers for its contents.

"You gentlemen are early," Miss Mamie said.

"Just enjoying the view," Paul said, feet propped on the rail, a glass of the house wine in his hand.

"A lovely sunset," she said.

Adam looked out at the edge of the world, the ridges capped with molten gold, the slopes rippling with alternating folds of color and shadow. The wind carried the promise of change, the air ripe with the last bitter-sweet odors of autumn. Maybe that was why he'd been so morose the last couple of days. Winter always felt like death to him, a gray wasteland to be endured, much like the nightmare from his childhood. And he'd blamed Paul for it, that seasonal shift that brought unease deep inside him.

"Aren't you glad you stayed, Mr. Andrews?" Miss Mamie said to him.

Adam and Paul exchanged glances. "Yes," Adam said. "I tend to get a little melodramatic at times. Right, Paul?"

"Sure, my little poppet." He patted Adam's hand, what Miss Mamie might take as a sign of moral support instead of a romantic gesture. "We're having the time of our lives."

Paul turned to Miss Mamie. "Is it okay if I bring my video camera up? This scenery is to die for."

Miss Mamie smiled. "Why not? I think tonight will be quite memorable, and well worth preserving."

Lilith came by, refilled Paul's glass, offered wine to Adam, who held up his hand in polite refusal. "No, thanks. I'm driving."

Miss Mamie's laughter carried on the wind. "Oh, you're a funny one. No wonder Ephram is so fond of you."

"Speaking of whom, I'm surprised there are no portraits of him on the widow's walk," Paul said.

"This was one of his favorite haunts, back when he was alive. He loved nothing better than a good party, especially under the full moon."

The Abramovs were seated against the railing near the impromptu bar, tuning their instruments. The drop in temperature affected the wood, and they had to constantly adjust the tension of the strings. As they ran through several series of scales, the shifting pitch gave the music a discordant, atonal quality.

"The Abramovs have promised an original duet," Miss Mamie said. "Written just for the occasion. Now, if you'll excuse me, I have preparations to attend to."

After she left, Adam leaned forward in his chair and gripped the widow's walk, daring himself to look over the side to the small slanting roof above the portico, and to the hard arc of driveway sixty feet below. To the spot where he had died. He swallowed and closed his eyes, leaned back in the chair.

"What's the matter, Princess?" Paul asked. "You've gone pale."

"Shouldn't have had that second glass of wine."

"How am I ever going to turn you into a party girl if you can't hold your liquor better than that? The night is young."

"Yeah, but I feel a hundred years old."

Paul patted Adam's knee. "You stay here and rest your ancient bones, then. I'm going to get my camera."

"And probably sneak a few hits off a joint?"

Paul gave that irresistible, mischievous grin. "Makes me creative. And all the rest."

"Save some for me."

"You haven't changed a bit, no matter what they say." Paul looked around, leaned forward, and kissed Adam on the cheek. "Like the lady said, it's going to be a night to remember."

Adam watched as Paul crossed the widow's walk and slipped through the trapdoor. Lilith and the dough-faced cook were setting up a buffet table. The Abramovs had returned their instruments to their cases and now stood near the railing, talking to the Mediterranean woman, Zainab. Smoke drifted from the four chimneys, rising above the trees that surrounded the manor.

Adam hunched into his chair, shivering. He wouldn't

mind a fire right now. Fall was dying and winter was coming on. Cold and gray and suffocating. Too bad this night couldn't last forever.

Sweat poured from Mason like blood from a shotgun wound, his muscles screaming as he ran the fluter under the slope that would be one of Korban's cheeks. He rammed his gouge down across the wooden shoulders with his left hand. He had never carved with both hands at the same time before, but anything was possible now. The wood seemed to peel away as if shucking itself. They were in a hurry, both he and his statue.

The voice came from the bust again, the voice that had been urging him onward, driving Mason into a frenzy of chiseling and chopping and planing. It had scared him at first, but now the voice was just that of another instructor, albeit the most demanding one Mason had ever worked under.

This was the most demanding of critics.

The tunnel was waiting if he failed.

The dark crib and the rats and his mama with the squeaky voice and long gray tail.

"More off the shoulder, you fool," said the bust.

Mason looked at the bust, at Korban, his creation, his first masterpiece. The lantern on the table threw the left side of the bust into shadow.

The wooden lips moved again. "Hurry. They're waiting."

"Who?" Mason's syllable was a whisper. The air of the basement was charged with an eerie static. The hairs on the backs of his hands tingled. Flames roared up the central chimney on the other side of the stone wall.

"Get on with it, sculptor."

"I need to rest."

"You'll have plenty of time to rest later."

Mason laid his tools on the table, wiped his brow, sagged to the concrete floor in exhaustion. Then he saw Korban's painting of the manor, the one someone must have altered while Mason wasn't around. Because the figures were clearly visible, dabbed in thick strokes of oil. The woman with the bouquet had moved into the foreground, beyond the railing, and her position had changed, her arms spread, eyes wide. She was falling.

And Mason didn't care what Anna said, all that nonsense about the woman being Anna's mother, because that was Anna's face and those were Anna's eyes and the woman wore that mysterious half smile that no other woman in the world could pull off.

"Ah," the bust said. "So it's the woman you want, after all. Precious Anna."

"What about her?" Mason was far past the point of doubting his sanity. Some artists claimed their work spoke to them, so maybe hearing Korban's voice wasn't unusual. But the dividing line, the step from mere genius into certifiable tortured soul, occurred when you started talking *back* to the object in question.

"You can have her, once you finish me. I've already promised you fame. And I always keep my promises."

Mason's response was to take his bull point from the table. He lifted his mallet, bent his elbow to test its weight. He thought about spinning and driving the thick iron point between Korban's eyes. A blow from the mallet would split the bust in half. But how could you kill something that was already dead?

The statue quivered before him, the rough-hewn limbs flexing. Grain split along one forearm, and the block of head tilted, a small knothole parting in the place where Mason had planned to carve the mouth.

"Finish me," moaned the knothole.

Mason dropped his hammer and stepped back, sweat and sawdust and fear stinging his eyes. The wooden arms reached for him, flecks of curled oak falling from the blunt hands. Mason stumbled against the table, knocking over the bust. He looked down and saw the eyes looking up at him. It was the same cold glare as in Korban's portrait upstairs. Too perfectly the same.

"What about Anna?" Mason said.

"I promise you two will be together. We'll all be one big happy family."

That made sense, as much sense as Mama watching from the tunnel, and probably a drunken and mean-eyed version of Dad as well. Just like old times, with rats in the walls and darkness all around and Dad passed out on the floor. So if he could drag Anna in there with him, the darkness might be a little more bearable. Korban always kept his promises. How could you not trust those wise and wonderful eyes?

Mason picked up the hatchet. The critics had spoken. More off the left. Finish it. Make it perfect. Big dream image brought to life. Create.

Wood.

Flesh.

Heart.

Dream.

CHAPTER 24

Anna felt as if she were back in one of her dreams, those that had filled her nights in the past year. As she had so many times before, in that lost land of sleep, she approached the manor from the forest. The house's hulking form rose between the trees that surrounded it like guardian beasts. The windows were eyes, glaring and cold even with the light of a dozen fires behind them. The chimneys spouted a breath of ephemeral transition, matter into energy, substance into heat. The front door whispered a soft welcome, the darkness inside promising peace.

But this waking dream had features beyond all those previous ones, as if a seventh sense had been added to her other six. The grass was thick under her shoes and glittering frost clung to the skin of the earth. The sky was bright on both the eastern and western horizons, painted with lavender and maroon by some large and ragged brush. The wind had settled like a sigh, and autumn's surrender hung in the cool air. The manor waited. Ephram Korban waited.

Is this where I belong? Anna thought. *Am I really coming home?*

Sylva said that Anna was fuel. That Korban would consume her, use her, leave her soul as ashes.

What did it matter? Let her love and hate and anger and pride flow out into the house. Into Ephram Korban. No one else wanted it.

She laughed, giddy as she crossed the porch, the raw static energy of the house flowing over her body, warming her, making her feel wonderful. Coming home. Home is where the heart is.

Miss Mamie was waiting. She opened the door and stepped aside, sweeping her arm out in welcome. "Ephram said you'd come."

Anna felt drunk. Even her pain was ebbing, the fires of cancer dying down inside her. She would offer everything. Korban could have her pain, her loneliness, her feeling of never having belonged. *Bon appétit.*

Yes, she had come home. This place had opened her soul, had allowed her to see ghosts. Given her what she wanted. She could die happy here.

"You're looking lovely this evening, Anna," Miss Mamie said to her. The words sounded as if they had come from far away. The fire roared and crackled at the end of the foyer. Anna looked at the portrait of Korban above the fireplace. Grandfather. With eyes so bright and loving.

How could she have resisted getting the family back together? Let the circle be unbroken. Did it matter if some were alive and some were dead? When you came right down to it, was there any difference?

One, a dividing line.

Then zero. Nothing. All the same.

Anna looked at the house with new eyes. The columns, the corners, the carving in the hearth, the reddish brown lower paneling, the polished oak floors. She didn't blame Korban for never wanting to leave this beautiful place. She didn't want to leave it now, either.

"You're just in time for the party," Miss Mamie said. "Up on the widow's walk."

Fuel.

Painting.

Something about the painting. Her standing here by the fire. Mason.

"What is it, dear?" Miss Mamie put a cool hand to Anna's cheek. "You're not feeling ill, are you?"

"Where's Mason?"

"The sculptor? He's busy right now, but he'll be joining us. As soon as he's finished."

Anna let herself be led to the stairs. Something about the walls bothered her, something she knew she should remember. But they were ascending now, Miss Mamie leading the way. They reached the second-floor landing and Anna looked down the hall toward her room. The astral lamps along the wall seemed to brighten and then dim, as if fed by a slow, even breathing.

They reached the third floor. Anna hadn't been to this part of the manor before, though threads of some dim ancestral memory tugged at her. The walls were covered with boxcar siding, cheap interlocking pine. No paintings hung here. There were doors that must have led to other bedrooms, and gabled windows at each end of the floor. A conductor's lantern on a handmade table near the stair rail was the only light.

The lantern.

Mason had one like it in the basement.

Where was Mason? She tried to picture his face, but it was lost in the mist inside her head, along with everything else. The walls throbbed, swelled, and contracted. The house was moving in rhythm with her breathing. She began to get dizzy, then Miss Mamie leaned her against a small ladder.

Anna looked up, as if through the eye of the world, at the clouds that caught the blue silver of the rising moon. The widow's walk. The top of the end of the world. Where her own ghost waited.

She forced her arms and legs to climb. It was time to meet herself.

Spence had found the Word.

He sensed—no, *knew*—it would be waiting at the end of this final paragraph.

Truth comes in unlikely packages. The One True God comes in the oddest of shapes. All gifts are weighty. Each gift demands its equal value in sacrifice.

The shifting and bulging walls of the house had distracted him at first. Just another evil, another thing to steal his attention, to turn him from the road to glory. Bridget gasped and screamed as they took form, as the misty shapes fell from the ceiling and rose from the oak flooring, as they drifted cold and hollow through the room.

Spence impatiently brushed them away. The True Shining Path beckoned him, and all else was superfluous poppycock and bombast, literistic excess. The True Path led to the next sentence that caused the next word to press itself into the wood pulp, as metal hammered ink into paper into existence.

The night was ready, breath borrowed and held prisoner, lungs of ebony and earth, feet of granite, arms sweeping seasons of sleep from the eyes of the sightless. October screamed, a carpet of frost, a turn of brown wind, the end of something. Time turned backward, cold to hot, hard water. Go out frost and come in . . .

He tilted forward in his chair, not caring if the chilled air sapped his strength. He needn't waste his flesh on Bridget. He had a better intercourse here, himself and the True Word. White shadows moved across the room in silence, the fire paused in consuming, his fingers itched.

Come in . . . what?

The Word hung there, teasing, waiting, drawing him body and soul onward, hovering ever out of reach.

"I say, chap, what are you waiting for?"

Spence thought at first the line had come from his own mind, a bit of clipped dialogue that was trying to force its way into the narrative. The fire roared, yet a frigid breeze skirled across the back of his neck. His fingers rested on the desk.

The voice came again, no Muse, no Bridget, no Korban. "Get on with it, man. It's not the bleeding end of the world yet."

Spence turned, glared at the photographer who stood in the corner of the room, face obscured by shadows. "Damn you, why didn't you knock? I can't abide interruptions when I'm working."

Roth's accent flattened, became nasally and midwestern. "We got tunnels of the soul, Jeff. And guess what's inside yours?"

"You're mad," Spence said. "Come out where I can see you."

The photographer waved a quick hand toward the portrait of Korban. "He said you can have a typewriter, but all the keys will be stuck."

Spence tried to rise, anger throbbing through him and sending a bright flash of pain across his left temple.

Roth laughed, his voice changed pitch, accelerated into that shrill and strident voice from Spence's past. The voice of Miss Eileen Foxx. *"I before E except after PEEEE,"* she said, Roth's body shaking with her gleeful laughter.

"F-f-foxx in socks?" Spence said, confused, his chest split with pain. A warmth spread around his groin, an unfamiliar wetness that was almost pleasant.

Roth moved back into the shadows and was gone. Eileen Foxx's last admonishment hung in the air like a threat: "You'd better make the grade, Jefferson, or I'll be waiting. Yessirree, you'll be staying after school with *me.*"

Spence stared into the fire until the dampness between his legs grew cold, then he faced the typewriter again, the words on the page almost like symbols etched by people from some lost civilization. They no longer had meaning, but he knew he wasn't finished. He needed that word.

The class would laugh at him if he didn't find the word.

Mason lifted the bull point again, the mallet in his slick right hand. The pile of wood shavings was ankle-deep around him, the statue hewn into a recognizable shape. The head needed a lot of work, but the arms and legs were there, the torso as strong and ugly as a stump. This was a hideous masterpiece, a raw stroke of genius, a creative vision that no eyes should ever see.

Eyes.

The thing needed eyes, so that it might see. And once it could see, then what?

"You're not working, sculptor," the bust said.

"I'm thinking," Mason said.

"You'll think when I tell you. Now finish."

Finish. And he could have it all, fame, fortune, Mama's approval. And the girl. Oh, don't forget the girl.

He looked at the painting again. The painted Anna had changed position, was definitely falling, and her arms were now spread wide, the bouquet slipping from her fingers, the half smile shifted to a dark, round tunnel of a scream.

Anna. Something about Anna that he should remember, if only he could think about anything besides the statue.

The whispers spilled from the corner of the basement, and he was afraid the tunnel had opened again, that Mama would come out and sniff at him with her pointy rodent nose, show her sharp teeth, wriggle her whiskers, and tell him about the power of dreams.

But the whisper stirred again, and the voice was Anna's: "Mason."

The voice was coming from the painting.

"Don't listen to her, sculptor," the bust said. "I need you. Give me my eyes. And my mouth. I'm hungry."

Anna spoke again from the painting. "He's burning you up, Mason. He's burning us all."

"Work," the bust commanded.

"Burning our dreams," Anna said. "The closer I get to being dead, the more I understand."

Being dead? Anna?

He had to find her. Something was wrong. Something was wrong with *him.* He looked at his blistered hands, the tools, the things that had shaped these monstrosities before him. Where had these graven idols come from? Not from his own imagination, that was certain.

"Dream me to life," the bust commanded. "Don't stop now."

Dream Korban.

No.

He wanted his own dreams. Good or bad, whether or not they ever brought him fame. Whether or not they made Mama proud.

He wanted his own dreams. Not Korban's.

Mason raised the bull point, pressed it into the hulking chest of the statue, swept his arm back, and smashed the mallet into the steel. The bust screamed. Mason flung the hammer at the bust, knocking it to the floor.

"Sculptorrrrr," Korban roared, voice like a thousand wildfires eating the air in the room, shaking the timbers of the house.

The statue quivered, its limbs moved with a groan of splinters, then it tore itself free from the nails that held it to the support boards. The wooden hands reached up and fumbled with the wires. The legs had been divided at the bottom, but the feet were not refined, mere dark clumps of oak covered in bark. The heavy feet scraped across the floor.

Moving toward him.

Mason kicked the table, tumbling the lantern over. The flame extinguished as the globe shattered. They were in darkness.

Both he and Korban.

Except Korban was used to darkness, Korban fed on darkness, Korban *was* darkness.

Mason groped in front of his face and headed toward where he thought the stairs were. He tripped over something metallic, then he fell into the arms of the animated statue, his bones knocking on wood—

No, it was only an old four-poster bed frame. But he was confused now, all directions the same, and he heard the twitching and squeaking behind him. Rodent noises.

No, no, no, not the crib.

And on the tail of that thought came another, equally frightful one. He had longed to create a lasting work of art. And he had done it. This was his undying success.

The statue's limbs snapped as it searched for its maker, the sound like dry bones breaking. Korban was stretching, trying on his new body in the darkness. His wonderful but clumsy body, crafted by Mason's loving touch.

"I'm blind," came Korban's muffled voice, as if he were chewing on sawdust. "You haven't finished my eyes."

Mason's fingers brushed one of the support beams. He ducked behind it and knelt in the dark. He tried to slow his breathing, but he couldn't. His pounding heart was going to give him away. The heavy wooden feet shuffled in his direction.

If he's blind, he's deaf, too. Unless part of him is still in the bust. Then maybe he can SMELL you.

Mason shuddered at the image of a rat leaning back on its haunches, whiskers quivering and nose wrinkling as it sniffed the air in search of sustenance. Korban was a rat, a rodent king, coming to get him. The thick tail slid across the cold concrete floor. Mason pressed against his eyelids until the pain drove the image away in a burst of bright green.

"Come here, sculptor," Korban said, and the voice was clearer now, more strident. Had Korban moved from the statue back into the bust?

The clumsy wooden feet shuffled closer, then moved away.

Where are the stairs?

"Don't betray me," Korban said. The voice filled the room, but the echoes were swallowed by the dead air.

The statue must have found the bust and lifted it off the floor. Which one did Korban inhabit? Or was he in both at the same time? If he could fill an entire house, then surely bouncing around between a couple of pieces of dead wood was no trick at all.

Two heavy steps forward. The rasping was either Korban's labored, unnatural breathing or warm air drifting through the ductwork overhead.

"We need each other," Korban whispered.

Fame, fortune, and the girl. And all Mason had to do was what he already lived and longed to do, what was in his blood, what he was born for and would risk death for.

To create.

To dream into life.

He was made to make.

He could make Korban, and Korban could make

him. What was it Anna had said? It was not what you believed, it was how much. He believed in his art.

Mason was tempted to reach out and touch it, caress the sleek muscle and wooden skin.

This would be his lasting work. It would be simple, really. Just transpose the features he had carved on the bust onto the statue. Bring Korban to full and final life.

He heard a clicking, a soft sound that might have been a chuckle. Or a rat's sigh.

"Finish me," Korban whispered.

Surrender would be so easy. Surrender to the dream. Why bothering running from the deepest desires of his heart, the calling of the fire in his soul?

Anna's voice came from the darkness, from the corner where the painting stood. "He'll eat your dreams, Mason."

Mason scrambled for the stairs, stumbled upward, the basement alive with the angry creak of wood and the slither of things unseen, the cold tunnel of darkness licking at his heels and threatening to swallow him forever.

CHAPTER 25

Sylva stood before the front door. She hadn't been in the house for many years. Not since the night of Rachel's death. A shiver swept over her, brought on by more than just the October chill. This was like entering a church, holy ground, a place where souls walked free.

She pressed the charm that was secreted inside her blouse, held it against the warmth of her heart. She was scared, but she had faith. The moon was rising, throwing cold light over the mountain as if a new sort of day was breaking. Maybe it was. A day of endless night, when things got reborn, when dark promises were kept and broken. When spells carried the weight of prayers.

Sylva pushed open the door without knocking. Ephram knew she was here, all right. No need to sneak around. And the others, they moved about in the walls, stirred in the basement, shifted among the cracks in the hearthstones.

Ephram's portrait nearly took the last of her breath away. She'd seen that face in a thousand dreams, half of them nightmares, the other half the kind that made you ashamed when you woke up.

"Look at me," she whispered.

Ephram stared at her with dark, painted eyes.

"I'm old," she said. "I spelled myself alive all these years. Sticking around, waiting for this blue moon of yours. Well, I'm here now, and I ain't sure what you plan to do about it."

The portrait fell from the wall, the heavy frame splintering, the canvas folding. When a picture fell, it was a sure sign that the subject was meant to die. But when a picture of a dead person fell . . .

The flames rushed out of the chimney, fingers of fire reaching toward Sylva, reminding her of that night on Korban's bedroom floor, the night he planted the seed of Rachel deep inside her. A night of cold burning.

And this was another night of forbidden heat, a night of frost and fire. She headed for the stairs, leaving Ephram's face lying on the wooden floor by the warmth of the house's heart. They were waiting up there on the widow's walk, under the rising moon. Anna and Miss Mamie and Lilith. Ephram would join them soon enough, and Sylva wouldn't miss this for the world. For more than the world, or any world beyond this one.

She squeezed the charm until her fingers ached, her heart pumping faith as she climbed the stairs.

Mason fell into the lamplight of the hallway as if it were a healing water. He slammed the basement door shut behind him, slid the metal bolt into its seat. Why was there a lock on the *outside?* What had been kept in the basement that required locks?

Now that he was out of the suffocating basement, his head cleared a little. And the thoughts that came were almost as frightening as the creative trance that had been consuming him from the inside out. He leaned against the door, heart pounding.

Smooth move, Mase. In case you forgot, this guy's

been dead for eighty years and you think a DOOR'S going to stop him?

But Korban had been clumsy and stiff when shifting into the statue. That's why the ghost or spirit or whatever moved into man-made objects. Because Korban needed that energy, that *made*-ness, before he could claim something as a vessel.

Then maybe he'll slip into the DOOR, sawdust-for-brains. It's not like he has to follow the rules or anything.

Maybe so. Mason slammed his fist against the door in frustration. The door thundered in response as wooden hands chopped from the other side. Mason looked down the hall.

"Help," he shouted. Surely someone would hear the hammering on the door and come see what was wrong. There was movement down the hall. The pantry door swung open.

"Thank God," Mason said, stepping away from the basement door. One of its wooden panels splintered and cracked from the pounding. "There's a—um—"

Mason was still searching for words when he realized they would be unnecessary. The cook came out of the kitchen, a cleaver in her chubby hand. He could see the utensil's raised wooden handle. All the way up to its gleaming tip. He was looking through the woman's hand.

She was made of the same milky substance as Ransom and George.

Which meant—

Mason looked to his right. The hall ended in a small closet door. He'd have to go past—or *through*—the cook to get to either the front or rear doors of the house. And he had a feeling that he needed to get out fast, because the walls were buzzing with that same strange static he'd felt in the basement.

The basement door splintered, gave way, and the golden red oak of Korban's hands stabbed through. The cook, suddenly solid, blocked the hall with her ethereal girth. Her lip was curled as if she'd just taken a whiff of rancid buttermilk. The cleaver danced in the air before her, its metal blade reflecting the flames from the lamps.

Mason backed away from her, though there was nowhere to run. Korban reached through the gash in the door, clubbing Mason with one crude stub of fist. A spark-filled darkness flooded his skull, and he fell to the floor. When he blinked himself awake, blood leaking down his scalp, he saw swirls in the grain of the wainscoting.

The wall was moving, or else his head was swimming. No, it wasn't the wall. It was something *inside* the wall.

A face took shape and emerged from the wood. The face split in a grin as it stepped into the hall. The ghost of George Lawson waved its spare hand and drifted toward Mason.

Korban shattered the latch and the basement door swung open. Mason forced himself to stand and ran toward the cook, hoping she was as soft as she looked. He ducked low and dived toward her knees, the way he'd been taught in peewee football back in Sawyer Creek. His bones jarred as he plowed into her chilly flesh, and he heard something pop in his shoulder.

Ghosts weren't supposed to be solid. But then, ghosts weren't supposed to *be* at all. The cleaver whistled through the air and he looked up just in time to see the cook's face, dead and unchanged. She could just as easily have been chopping carrots for a stew.

He tried to roll to his left, but the cleaver glanced off his upper biceps. He let out an agonized breath, and drops of blood were flung across his face as she raised the cleaver for another blow. He crawled like a crippled spider across the floor, skittering past her, Korban's massive feet thundering down the hall.

Mason leaped for the stairs, grabbing the rail to pull himself forward. His heart throbbed, sending fresh rushes of blood from his wound as he careened up the steps. The blood reassured him in an odd way, a reminder that he was still alive. In a world where dreams made nightmares, blood was welcome, and pain meant that he could still *feel.*

Mason reached the second-floor landing and peered down the hall to the master bedroom. William Roth stood in the shadows beside Spence's closed door.

"Run," Mason yelled, fumbling to close the torn gap in his arm. "The ghosts—Korban—"

Then all speech was lost as Roth stepped into the light of the astral lamps. The photographer's face hung in rags, a crisscross of fresh scars making a gridwork of his smile. His eye sockets were blank, like empty lenses.

The photographer held out a pale fist as Mason tried to shape his vocal cords into a scream.

"Hiyer, mate," the Roth-ghost said, the words mumbled and muffled. The sliced lips opened again, and wet spindly things fell from the dead man's mouth and began crawling down his ripped shirt. Spiders.

Both ends of the hall darkened. A harsh wind extinguished the lamps on the walls. It was the long dark tunnel, rushing at him from two directions, that would lead Mason back to the rats.

Ransom's voice crept from the walls. "We got tunnels of the soul, Mason."

The statue clambered up the stairs, awkward as a drunken mannequin. Mason peeked over the banister and saw the bust cradled in the statue's arm like an infant carried by its mother.

The bust's maple lips parted, and a cry echoed off the woodwork, as if the entire house joined voice with Korban: *"Finish MEEEEEE."*

Mason fled up the stairs. The third floor was dark. Only a milky spill of moonlight through the windows prevented Mason from running full-speed into a wall. He tried to suck breath into his lungs, but the black air was like a solid thing, a suffocating thickness. Mason heard voices and looked up, saw the square of lesser darkness.

The trapdoor to the widow's walk.

Where Anna's ghost had screamed from the painting.

The swollen moon rose, cutting through the tree branches. The forest glittered with frost, and Anna's breath hung silver before her. Miss Mamie led her to the railing, and Anna looked out across the land that would be her home. She belonged to this house, to this mountain, to Ephram Korban.

"You're beautiful," Miss Mamie said, lifting her lantern to Anna's face. "I can see why Ephram wants you so badly. For that, and for your gift."

The Abramovs sat in their chairs, drew their instruments to their bodies like the meat of lovers. Paul perched his video camera on a tripod, Adam watching him. Cris and Zainab chatted near the bar, Lilith laughing and filling their glasses. Other guests stood in a cluster by the far railing, talking in low, excited voices.

"You know why you're here, don't you, Anna?" Miss Mamie said.

"Because I belong here." The words were someone else's.

"So do I," Sylva said, and Miss Mamie turned, faced the old woman.

"No," Miss Mamie said, cheeks burning with rage.

"This is Ephram's night. He told me you'd never be back, that he had used you up."

"Ephram needs me more than he needs you."

"I kept him alive, and he kept me young. Look at you, you pathetic sack of skin and bones. And you thought he could ever love such as you."

"Love's like a door that swings both ways. And so's death. Frost and fire. But you wouldn't know that, would you? You don't know a thing about magic, or spells, or faith, or any of the things that kept Ephram's spirit here all these years."

"You're just a crazy old witch-woman, muttering over dust and herbs. I'm the one he needs. I know how to make the poppets."

"Well, he'll be along shortly, and you can just ask him for yourself. Now, what do we do about dear little Anna?"

"Anna?"

Anna lifted her head at the mention of her name, the night like water, the world in slow motion.

The Abramovs began a solemn duet, bows sliding across the strings with melancholy softness, the notes vibrating on the wind. This was Anna's house. She wasn't Anna Galloway, had never been. That life was a dream, the lethal cancer a bell that had sounded her home, death just a slow transition that carried her back to herself.

She was Anna Korban.

And she would walk these walls forever.

The cold of the world became the coldness inside her, the frozen heart of forever, as she stepped to that dividing line.

"What about her?" Sylva said.

"Oh, Anna dies," Miss Mamie said. "For the last time."

CHAPTER 26

Mason scrambled through the trapdoor and up into the cold night.

The presence of the great space around him, and the depth below, made his head swim and his stomach lurch. The sea of night and the distant rolling waves of the mountains took the strength from his legs, as if they were boneless. He forced himself not to think about the ground far below on all sides. A pathetic fear of heights paled in comparison to all the new fears he'd discovered.

Mason blinked the blood from his eyes and took in the unreal scenery of the widow's walk. Anna was by the rail, between Miss Mamie and an old woman in a filthy dress and shawl. They seemed to be arguing over Anna, who looked drugged or sleepy, swaying in the strange light cast by the moon. Mason's sweat cooled in the autumn air, and he touched the gash in his shoulder. The pain yanked him alert, and he ran to Anna.

"The painting," he said. "You were calling to me."

"Who are you?" Anna said.

"Where's the statue?" Miss Mamie asked him. "You didn't leave it down there alone, did you?"

He looked behind him, at the trapdoor. "We've got to get out of here, Anna."

Mason took her arm, and the coldness of her skin flooded through him like an electric shock. He looked into her eyes and saw a blackness inside that never ended. Tunnels. Her eyes were tunnels of the soul, leading down to death or opening from a deeper darkness inside her.

Before he could shake her, ask her what was wrong, the statue stuck its rough-hewn head through the opening. Shrieks erupted from some of the guests as the statue rose awkwardly onto the widow's walk, its heavy limbs clattering, Mason's chisel still in its chest, the bust tucked under its thick wooden arm. The Abramovs stopped in mid-arpeggio. A wineglass shattered. Miss Mamie gasped and rushed toward the brutish form. "Ephram!"

As the statue stood on unsteady legs, the cradled bust stared at Mason with hot anger in its eyes. Miss Mamie threw her arms around the wooden torso.

The old woman reached inside her shawl and pulled out a layer of cloth. She unfolded it and approached the statue with slow steps. "I brung you what you wanted, Ephram."

Mason looked from the old woman to Anna. They both had those same haunted cyan eyes, and Mason realized why they seemed so familiar. Because they were the eyes that he'd lovingly carved into the bust of Ephram Korban.

He reached for Anna again, to pull her toward the trapdoor, unable to think of anything besides making a run for it. Three flights of stairs, the house alive with ghosts. Korban would never let them leave. But they had to try.

Before Mason could order his legs to move, the ghost appeared near the railing, the spitting image of

Anna. She held a bouquet before her. Just like the woman in the painting.

"Mother," Anna said.

This wasn't the way Miss Mamie had imagined this night, the way she had wished it during all those thousands of lonely hours, when she had only Ephram's face in the mirror, his spirit in the hearth, his words coming from the portrait.

This night was supposed to be perfect, a union of two souls, all else forgotten. Ephram and his beloved Margaret, together again, joined in simultaneous life and death. With dreams to fill.

Yet there was the old hag Sylva, who had tempted poor Ephram so long ago. And now Rachel was here. Rachel, who was never supposed to be in the house. That was the reason she and Korban's servants had chased her, made her leap to her death. Ephram said those who betrayed him could never be free, but those who served would be allowed to die a second and final time. That's why Miss Mamie had carved the apple head dolls, the little poppets that housed the enslaved souls.

"The sculptor didn't finish," Miss Mamie said to the statue.

The bust answered. "He will."

Sylva knelt before the statue, unfolded the cloth, held up the collection of powders in both her wrinkled hands. "Ashes of a prayer, Ephram. I did just like you told me."

Miss Mamie clung to the statue, her beloved Ephram, who was wearing flesh after all those years of being reduced to smoke and shadow. "What's she talking about, Ephram?"

The statue swept its oaken arm, shoving Miss Mamie to the floor of the widow's walk. She rose to her hands and knees, her dress torn, the beautiful gown she'd been saving for the blue moon. For their second honeymoon.

"Ephram?" she said.

"He don't need you," Sylva said.

Miss Mamie crawled toward Ephram, hugged his chipped legs. "Ephram. You love me."

The statue kicked her away. "Spell me, Sylva."

"Give me her years first," Sylva said. "Make me young again. Like you promised."

"Spell me."

"You said you always keep your promises." Sylva held up the cloth full of folk potions.

"What's she talking about, Ephram?" Miss Mamie said. Suddenly she felt cold, as if a glacier had cut through her heart. She looked at her hands. Wrinkled flesh rose on her skin, deep creases carved themselves into her flesh, tiny rivers of age running dark in the moonlight. She touched her face, the skin drawing tight across her skull even as it sagged under her chin.

Oh God, she was growing *old*.

"You promised me, Ephram," she said. "Together forever."

The statue and bust joined in laughter. The guests ran for the trapdoor, but Lilith closed it and stood on it.

"Nobody ever leaves Korban Manor," she said, grinning like a skeleton.

Anna stepped toward Rachel, moving as if under dark water. "What are you doing here?"

"I tried to warn you, but you wouldn't listen."

"About Sylva?"

"She's always loved Korban. That's why she killed me, to please him. That's why she learned folk magic, the spells and potions that kept his spirit alive until she could finally bring him all the way back."

"This is all a crazy, screwed-up dream," Mason said.

Anna flashed him a half smile. Couldn't he see the obvious? Everything was so much easier when you were dead. Because the dead no longer have to dream.

"I'm seeing it, but I don't believe it," Paul said, head tilted into the viewfinder of his video camera. "This is great stuff. Romero on acid, John Carpenter on a budget."

Adam yanked on his arm. "We've got to get out of here."

"Shockumentary. I wouldn't miss this for the world."

"Damn you, Paul, this is like my dream. Don't you see? Everybody's *dead."*

Paul looked up from the camera, gave his boyish grin. "Not all of us, Princess. Just you."

"Don't be like that," he said.

"You're either working for the man on *this* side, or you serve him on the other side. You can be dead if you want, but me, I'd rather be the next Alfred Hitchcock, just like Korban promised me."

"I'm not dead, you stupid bastard."

Paul laughed. "Whatever."

Adam looked at the hand that gripped Paul's sleeve.

The fingers passed through the cloth, clutched on nothingness. He put a hand to his chest. When had his heart stopped beating?

Sweet Jesus, have mercy, when did my heart stop beating?

Paul pointed over the railing, to the hard patch of driveway below the porch. Adam couldn't help looking. There was a shape down below, prone, twisted, torn. Six feet long, dressed in gray pajamas that were dark with liquid. The shape was deathly still.

And alone.

Utterly alone.

* * *

Spence placed a quivering finger on the Royal. The ghosts had drifted past, their nebulous flesh throwing a chill around the room. Roth was gone, Bridget away somewhere.

Spence pressed a key.

F.

The One True Word, undressing itself, shucking its golden skin, opening its warm flesh to him. An invitation to enter.

The stir of ghosts ruffled the pages of his manuscript as the white shapes filtered into the ceiling. His greatest work ever. *The* greatest work ever. They could drag him back to Eileen Foxx's class, but this time he would have something to show them, to shut their slack little mouths and amaze their dull and cruel eyes. He had proof of his superiority.

His gut ached, sweat pooled under his armpits, his scalp tingled. The electric tension of the ghosts made the hairs on the back of his hands stand up. He pressed another key, and *i* slapped into place beside the *f.*

He thought the One True Word would be something rare and noble, something with seven syllables that only literary giants and dictionary-makers knew. Funny that the word was common, elemental. But Spence's opinions held no weight here.

He was only the instrument, the sword and scepter, the pen, the flint and steel. The Word was the beginning and end of things.

Go out frost and come in fi . . .

He slammed home the *r,* weeping at the finishing of his work, already feeling the old emptiness, already bracing himself to need Bridget again. Someone to save him from himself.

He looked up at Ephram Korban, at the kind face, the encouraging eyes, the generous lips that had given him every wondrous word of this magnificent manuscript.

"Thank you, sir," Spence said.

The ghosts were gone now. No distractions. No excuses. Just himself and Word and Korban. As he watched, the portrait faded to black, like the dying of an old tube television set.

He searched the keyboard, blind from tears, and put his clumsy, unworthy finger in the beautiful cup of the key.

Sylva felt the energy rush through her veins, the weariness falling away, the sweet juice of youth washing over her like a brisk waterfall. She tilted her head back and laughed. Let Miss Mamie fade to dust. Ephram loved only one, the one who had made the sacrifices. The one who had faith. The one who had crumbled the bloodied burial gown of her own daughter, who had crushed owl bones and raven feathers and stoneroot and a dozen other special substances.

The one who gave Ransom bad charms. The one who built Ephram's bridge back to this world on the ashes of a thousand prayers. The one who had said the spells, who had sent magic on the winds and summoned Anna, hooked her in the deepest meat of her heart and reeled her in, tricked her blind so that her death could complete the circle.

Oh, Sylva had the faith, all right, and she wanted all the fruits of faith.

She wanted Ephram back.

She rose, fourteen again, eager to give her restored virginity back to the man who had stolen her soul, who had lit an everlasting flame in her heart. She tossed a pinch of the special dust toward the statue, imagining those big arms loving her, those crude lips hot on her skin, those eyes burning into hers forever.

"Say it," the statue said.

She whispered, trembling, "Go out frost, come in fire."

CHAPTER 27

At Sylva's words, the four threads of smoke from the chimneys insinuated themselves, thickened into a great gray fog. The smoke sent its frayed fingers toward Anna, wending between Mason, Sylva, and the statue that housed part of the soul of Ephram Korban. The bust, which contained the rest of Ephram's invisible and eternal self, smiled at Anna with perverse affection.

Mason swatted at the smoke with both hands, but it slipped past him and the moonlit gray fingers crawled over Anna like cold earthworms. They found the soft part of her throat and became solid, squeezing in a gentle pressure that was almost erotic. She reached up to pull them away, then relaxed under their insistent caresses. Her lungs burned from lack of air and an icy dizziness rushed up her spine to the base of her skull. She tried to speak, Mason had her by the shoulders and was shaking her, she was dimly aware of movement on the widow's walk, but the gray tide was seeping in from the edges of her vision, pushed by a great black wave of nothing.

She didn't know when the change occurred. The line

had been thinner than she'd ever imagined. For the briefest of moments, she was on both sides, alive and dead at once, but the moment passed and she crossed over. She'd finally found herself, her true self. She'd become the ghost she'd always wanted to be.

The pain inside was gone. In its place was an unsettling hollowness, an empty ache. Loneliness. She was dead and she still didn't belong.

And death was just like life, because the world was the same: Sylva whispering something to the statue, Miss Mamie kneeling and wailing, her hands cupped over her face as if trying to hold her flesh in place, Lilith drifting under the moonlight, the Abramovs slumped with vacant eyes, now playing a funereal tune, Mason crouched before her, yelling at her, raving about a talking painting and Korban in the wood and dreams come to life and all sorts of nonsense. Couldn't he see that none of that mattered?

Death and life, all the same now.

Rachel hovered before her, holding out the bouquet. "I'm sorry, Anna. I failed you."

Anna reached for the bouquet. Her body collapsed.

"Anna!" Mason jumped toward her, tried to catch her and slow her fall, but the body she'd abandoned slumped beyond his reach. She heard her flesh slam against the wooden planks of the widow's walk, but her spirit kept falling. Through the house, through this place of dark emptiness that would be her home.

Death wasn't a release. Death, at least in Ephram Korban's version, was just another prison, this one full of the same suffering that shadowed the living. Only here, there was no escape, no hope, and still nobody to belong to.

"Anna." Rachel's voice, a moaning graveyard wind, a desperate fetching.

And still Anna fell.

* * *

Mason held Anna in his arms. Her face was pale, eyes glazed and protruding. He put his cheek to her mouth. No breath.

No breath.

Anger and fear rose in him, tears stinging his eyes. He looked up at the obscene, bloated moon. She was dead. And it was his fault. He'd failed her.

He gently laid her down, wiped the blood from his face, and turned to the statue. The old woman that Korban had called Sylva had changed, was now young, her face twisted in a sick rapture. Mason rose to his feet, though the long drop beyond the railing made his head swim, the sense of being on the top of the world caused his guts to clench in dread.

"Go out frost, come in fire," Sylva repeated, her skin vibrant and healthy in the moonlight. Hadn't Anna said something about frost and fire?

God, why couldn't he remember?

And did it even matter?

Because his statue, his creation, his big goddamned dream image, stood there on the widow's walk like a monstrous wooden idol, born of vanity and faith and love. Yes, love. Because Mason loved his work.

"You'll finish me, won't you, sculptor?" The bust spoke calmly, cradled in the thick arms of the statue. "You love me. Everyone loves me."

"You promised me Anna," Mason said.

"Oh, her. She's nothing. A necessary evil. And you'll learn that flesh is fleeting, but the spirit is for eternity. Isn't that right, my dear Sylva?"

"When you give somebody your heart, you owe them," the woman said. And though she now had a beauty that rivaled Anna's, the shadows around her eyes were older than the Appalachians, dark and cold and full of terrible secrets.

"Then pay your debt," Ephram said. "Finish the spell."

"Third time's a charm," she said. "But, first, they's one more promise you got to keep."

"Promise? What promise?" The statue raised its face to the moon, and the grain of the oak sparkled like a hundred diamonds. Frost. It had settled on the wood.

Frost and fire.

Mason wasn't sure of the connection between those two words. But he understood fire. Miss Mamie's lantern glowed near the railing, where she'd set it down upon Korban's arrival. Mason wondered if he could reach it before Korban decided it was time to start hurling bodies from the top of his house.

"Anna," Rachel called again.

Anna opened her eyes to darkness.

The darkness wasn't absolute. She blinked.

"Where am I?" she asked, her voice passing as if over a hundred tongues.

"In the basement."

"The house?"

"We all live here," said someone else, and a hand was in hers, small and cold.

"You," Anna said, "the girl ghost from the cabin, the one Sylva called Becky."

"You came to help us." And the girl smiled.

"I can't help you," Anna said. And now she saw Rachel, ethereal and shimmering against the curtain of darkness.

"I had to wait for you to die, Anna," Rachel said. "You have the gift, even stronger than mine. Korban killed me because he knew I was stronger than Sylva. But not like you. When you were alive, you had the Sight. Second Sight. But you had to die to get Third Sight."

"Third Sight?"

"The power to look from the dead back to the living.

The power to join us together. To hold our dreams, the way Ephram never could, because he wanted them for himself. He wanted our fear and hate. But he forgot about faith. Because we believe in you, Anna."

"Believe. So says the world's greatest liar." She wished she could laugh, but in this bleak, gray land of nothingness, such a sound couldn't exist.

"Believe," Rachel said. "Become the vessel. Hold our dreams, our real dreams. Let our dreams go into you, so we can finally die."

"You want to die?"

"More than anything," the girl said.

"Help us," came another voice from the gray smoke of this new dead world.

"Free us from Korban," said another, and then another. How many souls had Korban trapped here over the years? How many of Sylva's potions and spells had spun their sick binding magic?

"Follow your heart," Rachel said.

"My heart. It only leads me to hell."

"It belongs to the living."

"No. I belong here."

"Sylva lied, not me."

"I don't trust any of you. Why should I believe you?"

"Listen. I'm not your mother."

"Not my mother?"

"Ephram's power is that he lets you see what you want to see. He gives you what you wish for. Why do you think you can finally see the dead?"

Anna didn't think it was possible to descend into a chill deeper than death, but the revelation made her soul spin. She had been a fool. How could you ever find your own ghost?

"Sylva used you," Rachel said. "She used me, too. We're just pieces of driftwood to throw on her sacrificial fire."

"I hated you," Anna said. "When Sylva told me you were my mother, I thought I'd finally found somebody to blame. Now it's just me. I'm just as lost as ever."

"I'm sorry. I wanted to tell you, but Ephram controls me, too. All I want is to have never been born."

"That goes for me, too," Anna said.

"You're not alone, Anna. Something's happened. The binding spell has broken."

"The dolls," Adam said.

"Adam?" Anna said. Her soul eyes couldn't see him in the gloom. "Are you dead?"

"They say I am, so I must be."

"What about the dolls?" Rachel said.

"Miss Mamie made them," Adam said. "Carved, with little apple heads. I saw mine, only I didn't know what it was. I think she carved one for everybody who died."

"She's dead," Anna said. "I guess she never carved her own doll."

"Then she can't bind us anymore," Rachel said. "We're free."

"Not free," Anna said. "Not until Ephram's been killed for the final time."

"Save us," Becky said.

"Get us out of here," Adam said.

"You're the one," Rachel said. "You were fetched here for a reason."

Other voices came from the surrounding darkness, pleading, encouraging. Anna felt their energy flow around her, a current of heat that stirred her dead heart.

"Third Sight, Anna," Rachel said. "I'm not your mother, but I would be proud if I were. Because you're strong. Even stronger than Ephram."

"I don't know," Anna said. "What am I supposed to do?"

"Say it. What Sylva taught you. Only backward."

"Frost and fire?"

"Yes. And believe it. Living stay alive, dead go back."

Living. Maybe living wasn't so bad, even with its pain, sorrow, and failure. But at least life offered hope, second chances, choices. Was that the pain that rose inside her soul now? The pain of hope, the yearning for forgotten flesh, the regret of things left undone and words left unsaid?

She thought of Mason on the widow's walk, facing the wooden monster he had made, a monster that would haunt this mountain the way no ghost ever could. Haunt it like a god, with anger and power and arrogance, as if all things living and dead belonged to it.

"Go out fire, come in frost," Rachel said. "Say it."

Anna opened her dead and dreaming mouth. Dozens of voices joined hers, Becky's, Adam's, Rachel's, all blended into a chorus, a chant of hope, an ache for the final freedom. "Go out fire, come in frost. Go out fire, come in frost. Go out fire, come in frost."

One, a dividing line.

Two, an empty hook.

Three, a skeleton key.

Third time's a charm, opening the door.

To a room of hope. A house of faith.

A home for the soul of Anna Galloway.

She was Anna. She was alive.

She opened her eyes, saw the blanched circle of the moon, felt the October chill on her skin, tasted the smoke that skirled from the chimneys, smelled the decay of windblown leaves, heard the hollow distant roar of Ephram Korban's heart. She put a hand to her own heart. Beating. In rhythm with his. And with the spirits she carried inside her, the combined hopes and dreams of the unhappy dead.

Fuel.

Ephram wanted fuel, she would give him fuel.

She rose, and though her body still lay prone on the widow's walk, she didn't need flesh for this task. All she needed was faith of the spirit. Because she'd finally found something to belong to, something that offered more than just an endless darkness, something larger than herself.

Her house was full, and Korban's was a house divided.

Caught between frost and fire.

CHAPTER 28

Miss Mamie rose from her clatter of bones and husk of corpse.

Where was her flesh, the beauty that Ephram had given her? She wanted a mirror, because mirrors never lied. And neither did Ephram. Because Ephram loved her. He'd killed her for a reason, surely.

Maybe their love was meant for the *other* side, not the mortal side. That's the only thing that made sense. She still had eyes, she could see the mortal world, and could taste all the strange wonder of death, and death was the same as life, only better.

She would go to Ephram now, on his terms, the way he had made her.

But why was Sylva still alive? And young again, and beautiful?

Ephram could explain everything. After all, they had forever.

She went to him, though her spirit seemed stitched to the night sky, heavy and thick, and she fought to step from the fabric of darkness.

A dull aura shimmered around the rough cut of the

statue's shoulders. Ephram hoisted the polished maple bust aloft as if it were a trophy, showing himself the world, showing the world to the man who owned both sides of it.

"Make her go away," Sylva said to him. "Then I'll finish the spell."

"Sylva," Ephram said, the statue and bust speaking in unison. "I've given you everything."

"I want more than everything. It ain't enough that I get your heart. I want *her* out of your heart for good."

"You're the only one I ever loved."

"Yeah, but that's the same thing you said to her. Except you lied to one of us."

Miss Mamie fought the gravity that pulled her toward darkness. *Tunnels of the soul, Ephram said we all have tunnels of the soul. What's in mine, Ephram? What do I fear more than all the world?*

Sylva stared with wide loving eyes at the handsome hunk of oak. Her spells had brought out a misty horde, collecting around the statue like worshippers at the feet of a resurrected prophet:

Ransom, confused and sad, fingers fumbling for a charm that had no power.

George Lawson, offering his ragged hand in tribute.

The Abramovs, their instruments forgotten, the music playing on without them.

Lilith, fading in and out like a half-finished painting.

William Roth, dribbling spiders from his empty eyes.

The bust smiled at the night sky. "Good-bye, Margaret."

Miss Mamie moved her hand to the locket. But it was gone. It lay among her empty gown and the dust of her desiccated body. And she realized she was already in her tunnel. Because this was her greatest fear, and she must watch as her love spun unwanted down a dark drain, her sacrifice refused, a century of promises adding up to nothing.

She felt her soul scatter on the wind, to be carried off the mountain and away, where Ephram would be always out of reach.

No way.

No way in hell.

But Mason couldn't deny it. Anna's body had stirred beside him. Her eyelashes quivered. Her chest rose slightly beneath the splotch of Mason's blood on her blouse. Anna's breath cooled the sweat on Mason's palm. She was *back.*

And even in his fright and bewilderment, a surge of pleasure rushed through his bloodstream, a joy like none he had ever known. This was all a crazy dream, had to be, but dreams were everything now.

Mason looked at the lovely red wood of the statue he made, at the spirits gathered around it, at the maple bust that demanded Sylva finish her spell.

Anna's eyes opened, and her irises were no longer cyan. They were red, yellow, orange, glittering in the colors of fire.

And she rose, except her body stayed on the planks. She stood. A ghost. But still her body breathed.

She was on both sides at the same time, dead and alive.

"She—she ain't supposed to come back," Sylva whimpered, drawing into her old woman's hunch despite her youth. "You killed her like you did Rachel."

"I need her," Korban said. "She's part of the house. Now finish the spell. I kept my promise. Margaret is gone."

Anna's living lips parted in that glorious half smile, spilled words in a chorus of dead voices. "It's the *fire,* Mason."

He touched her cheek, and it was blazing with human heat. "Do you trust me?" he whispered, the kind of thing he would say in a dream. Nothing to lose.

Maybe this was the true art, the creation that gave back, the work that made itself. This was the biggest dream image of them all.

"Maybe," Anna said. "The fire."

"Maybe" was enough to risk everything. Mason knew what he had to do, what he should have done long ago. He eased toward the lantern, seeing Anna's eyes in its intoxicating flame.

Oh Lordy, something ain't right.

Sylva tossed the charm dust onto Ephram, pressed Rachel's burial gown to her heart.

Anna wasn't supposed to be back at all. She was supposed to be dead and haunting the house, serving Ephram, working as his blood and juice and power. But there she lay, breathing and blinking and whispering to the sculptor.

And Anna's eyes weren't right. Too many people looked through them, and every one was madder than a weasel in a hatbox.

She would make him get rid of Anna, too, just like Miss Mamie. And Rachel. Get rid of them all. Only her and Ephram.

She itched to try out this new body. A century of waiting was plenty long enough. She'd spent ten thousand charms on this man and it was time for a little payback.

The beautiful bust opened its mouth. It would be awkward kissing that thing, making love to this statue that didn't even have all its parts yet, but they always said that love would find a way. And she had forever to learn how. Forever to tame him and teach him the value of her spells and conjures and charms. Forever to be needed.

She opened her mouth to call in the fire a final time. "Go out frost and come in—"

Anna knew this was the moment, a time of eternal crossing. Of burnt offerings. A time for ghosts to die.

"Here comes your damn fire," Mason shouted above the mad music and rattling leaves. He grabbed the hurricane lantern, the flesh of his hand sizzling. He sprang at Ephram, screamed at the sky, and raised the lantern over his head, then swept it down toward the statue.

Anna led the leap out of her body, her spirit a conduit for the trapped dreams and lost hope of all haunted souls.

Fuel.

The lantern smashed against the statue, the thick oil soaking into the oak, orange and red and blue ropes of fire spreading across Korban's ungainly form. A blaze of yellow raced up one arm, igniting the dark maple of the bust. Twin screams splintered the night as the fire roared to full life, whipped by the frenzied wind.

Anna's chest emptied as the tortured ghosts of the manor routed through her, flew across the boards of the widow's walk, and swarmed into their hated master. Their fuel boosted the fire tenfold, twentyfold, and the statue stumbled and waltzed in blind agony. The bust dropped to the floor, the lips peeled back in endless pain. Mason kicked the flaming bust toward the statue, back into the hellish pillar of fire.

Anna scrambled backward, void of all spirits but her own, the conflagration too dazzling to watch even with Second or Third Sight. Acrid smoke belched from the manor's four chimneys, and rich red sparks cut tracers in the air.

The house swayed, its siding buckling and popping, the eaves snapping like dry bones. The gables themselves moaned in the anguish of collapse. Vines of smoke spilled from the manor's doors and windows, curling up the columns and darkening the sky.

Korban spun in the darkness, in a St. Vitus dance of overdue death, Sylva kneeling at his feet, the dead and alive scrambling to escape the fire that raged on both sides of the dividing line.

CHAPTER 29

A wall of flame stretched across the widow's walk, cutting off escape through the trapdoor. Mason squinted against the smoke, the nerves of his scorched hand screaming in alternating ribbons of red and yellow pain, his head and arm aching from their wounds. Mason stumbled to the railing and looked down at the dizzying darkness.

A hand touched him and he turned, ready to surrender, to let Ephram Korban pull him into the manor's endless nightmare.

It was Anna.

"The trees," Anna said. "I think we can reach them."

"I can't," he said, throat dry. "Heights."

"We all have to face our fears sooner or later. And you just burned your masterpiece. What else do you have to lose?"

"You."

"Okay, then. Come on, because I'm selfish as hell, too. And I don't want to survive this thing alone."

She climbed over the rail at the point farthest from the surging blaze. A poplar swayed in the fire's backdraft, its branches rattling against the railing. Glass shattered below, flames shooting out the windows and spewing from the screaming mouths of the chimneys. The entire house groaned and crackled in the throes of destruction.

"Ephram Korban," Anna said. "He's dying with the house."

She gripped the branches and pulled herself over, then reached back for Mason. "Hurry."

He took her hand, closed his eyes, then swung out and wrapped a leg around a thick branch. His stomach fluttered, feeling the space beneath him, the long, yawning gap between his body and the ground—

Don't think, Mason.

She came back from the dead, and you're worried about a little thing like falling.

But it wasn't the falling he was afraid of, it was the landing. The dying. Because he'd seen the hollow and vacant eyes of those who had stared down those black tunnels. He'd take blindness over any of the those deeply hidden horrors, those secrets of his soul that were stashed far away from the light.

He scrambled along the branch, her hand gripping his bloody shirt, and by the time they reached the thick trunk of the tree, he was gripping her in return.

The walls were collapsing. It was the end. Spence stared at the paper, at the Word.

F-i-r-e

Flames crawled along the cracks in the baseboard, smoke erupted from the fireplace. The window shattered outward and flames gushed from under the closet door like colored water.

A shrill voice pierced through the crackling of the fire: "Get out, Jeff."

The Muse? He looked up from the typewriter, confused. The work was beautiful. Out of place in this malefic chaos, this destruction, this Dantean inferno. But the Word—the word couldn't harm its maker, could it?

He had been wrong. The Word had lied.

Korban had lied.

The *writer* was the master. The language was the slave.

The room was filled with smoke now. Bridget, shouting from the hall, ducked out of sight. Spence sat forward with a squeak of chair springs. He tried to scoop up his manuscript, but hungry flames rippled up the back of the desk.

He stood, eyes bleary, fingers numb. Smoke filled his mouth and throat. He started toward the door. He couldn't leave his manuscript. He turned with effort, dazed from lack of oxygen. The pages had burst into a bright bonfire, the sentences now vapor, the Word lost in the heat of its own blinding glorious lie.

Spence blundered against the door frame, a tug of regret in his chest. He hadn't pressed the period, the final key. He hadn't finished the manuscript. He started back into the room, but the ceiling was falling, the house collapsing, the typewriter lost in a tide of yellow and red.

The fire sucked oxygen through the window, and the hot breeze sent a sheet of paper out the doorway. Spence grabbed it, held it to his chest.

Weeping, he staggered down the hall, coughing and spitting.

"—fire," Sylva whispered, finishing the spell, though it was far too late.

All the years of waiting, of sacrifice, of deception, wasted now. The years that Ephram had given her back, the ones stolen from Margaret, were fading, retreating into the past. By rights, they should have been hers. *Ephram* should have been hers.

Her wooden lover writhed and twitched on the charred husk of the widow's walk. Behind the wall of flames, he had somehow lost a little of his majesty. But he still had that power, that magnetism that had driven her to sacrifice everything for him. He was dying again, the third and final time, and he needed her. She felt it as keenly as she felt her hair shrinking from the heat, as she felt the moisture of her skin evaporating.

"Sylvaaaaah," he roared, or it might have been the hungry tongues of the flames.

She crawled toward him, into the fire. Unlike the first time with Ephram, this time the fire burned her both body and soul.

As the blaze stole her breath, as her eyes dried in their sockets, as her brain boiled, she realized that possession worked both ways. When you gave somebody your heart, they owed you. And you owed them in return.

Both ways.

Frost and fire.

And pain, a deep freeze of burning agony. The thing called love. A suicidal, murdering thing.

Anna lowered herself, weaving through the branches. Mason was close behind, working his way down with frantic care. The heat from the house flowed over her, bits of wood and ash flying past on the wind of the firestorm. The sensation reminded her that she was alive, that the death she had welcomed was now something she was struggling to avoid. Maybe being alive meant nothing more than fighting to stay that way.

Maybe.

Or maybe Rachel was right. You have to live for

something bigger than yourself, belong to something that matters. Then you earn your rest.

"Hang on, Mason, we're almost there."

"Good. Because I think the house is falling."

They finally reached the ground, Mason stumbling, weak from his wounds. She supported him, leading him across the lawn away from the manor. The heat had melted the frost, and the grass was damp, steam rising. When they reached safety, she and Mason collapsed on the ground, ridding their lungs of smoke, watching Korban's funeral pyre as it stretched its fingers toward the moon.

The giant skeletal framework of the house was outlined in black, and Anna saw Korban's face in the flames, a hundred times life-sized, trapped in his own black tunnel, the one where his dreams died, where his servants abandoned him, where his heart turned to ash. Where he owned nothing and no one and his work went forever unfinished.

The great gables folded, the rails tumbled over the side. The Ionic columns snapped and the portico thundered down. The windows wept fire, the walls tucked themselves into each other, the piano works made a brassy clamor as they tumbled into the basement. Glass shattered and flames sputtered, smoke funneled from the top of the house like the mouth of hell at the end of the world.

"Look," Anna said, pointing across the frost-coated lawn to the edge of the forest. Matchstick figures moved among the shadows.

"Some of them got out," Mason said. "They *are* alive, aren't they?"

"Sure." She realized her Second Sight had been blinded, somehow it had perished along with the ghost of herself she had given to Ephram Korban.

Good riddance.

Horses galloped across the meadow, whinnying in

fright. Then the night was torn apart by a soul-searing shriek that echoed across the mountains. The ground shook, trees bent backward, and the barn collapsed. The fences also fell, gleaming like wet bones in the moonlight.

"He's taking it all with him," Anna said.

"Does that mean he's . . . ?"

"Dead? Do we even know what that means anymore?"

He put his arm around her, and she relaxed against him, grateful for his warmth. "I think it's all a dream. But dreams aren't such a big deal. I like being awake better."

"So do I."

They sat in the grass, watching the fire dwindle, and waited for dawn.

CHAPTER 30

"The bridge is gone," Cris said. "There's nothing left but some timbers braced against the edge of the cliff."

"I'm not surprised," Anna said. "Korban took everything that belonged to him. A control freak to the end."

The morning sun had lifted over the ridges, melting the remainder of the frost, and the mist rose off the ground like lost spirits, joining the last threads of smoke from the smoldering house. Anna and Mason sat on bales of hay, along with Zainab and Paul. Anna had tethered the two Morgans to a nearby locust. The other horses and the cattle had wandered into the orchard, no longer fenced off from the sweet autumn grass. Pigs played at the edge of the little pond at the foot of the slope, and wrens sang like the world was new.

Anna checked on Mason again. He held his hand in the watering barrel, where a pipe supplied cold spring water from the hills. He had a second-degree burn. There would probably be scars, but the wounds would heal eventually.

EVERYTHING heals eventually, Anna thought. *Even*

if you don't have the power of charms and spells and herbs. Or the power over life and death.

Paul tore a strip off the waist of his shirt, dipped it in the water, then wrapped Mason's cut arm. "Used to be a Boy Scout," he said.

"Eagle?" Mason grunted.

"No. One of the lesser birds. Buzzard, maybe."

"Sorry about your friend."

"Yeah. I'll deal with it after I quit lying to myself. After I figure out what happened."

"We all have our guilt to deal with," Mason said. "And we learn from our mistakes."

"I sure as hell wish I had salvaged my videotapes, though. I could have been rich and famous. Who will ever believe it now?"

"You don't want any evidence," Mason said. "And if you look at what you have to pay for success, it's not such a hot deal."

"Is he in shock?" Anna asked Paul.

Paul looked into Mason's eyes, then felt his pulse. "No. Maybe on the edge, but—"

"You're not getting rid of me that easily," Mason said.

"Shock's not a bad way to go," Anna said. "A dying soldier's best friend."

"Where in the world did that come from?"

"I don't know. Just popped into my head."

Paul stood up and rubbed at his eyes. "I guess we're all suffering from disorientation. Or maybe mass hysteria. Because my camera didn't lie."

"All of it had to go," Anna said. "Because it all belonged to Ephram Korban."

"Then how will we ever prove it was real?"

"I don't think we *want* to prove it," Mason said.

"I wonder if they saw the smoke from down in the valley," Cris said.

"Probably not," Anna said. "There would have been sirens or a Forest Service helicopter by now."

It was strange to be reminded that another world existed off this mountaintop, a world of sanity and order, where the dead stayed in the ground for the most part and people drifted through ordinary lives. Anna stood, heading for the wreckage of the barn. "Good thing the fire department didn't get here in time to put it out, huh? I don't think any part of Ephram should remain."

"What are we going to tell them?" Mason said. "I mean, what really happened here?"

"I've got a theory. But a theory's worth about as much as a match in hell. There's supposed to be some old trails that go down the side of the mountain. I'm going to find one and ride down to the river and follow it until it meets a road."

"Need some company?" Mason asked.

"Not the kind that gets woozy from heights. Plus you need time to heal."

"I'll go with you," Zainab said.

Anna shook her head. "No. They need you here. And I've had a lot of experience with horses. It'll be faster if I go alone."

Paul nodded. "The writer's having trouble breathing. Ate a little too much smoke. Good luck, Anna."

Paul, Cris, and Zainab headed up the road, where Spence and Bridget gathered near the house's foundation like ghosts who felt an obligation to haunt. But there were no more ghosts at Korban Manor. They had all moved on, to wherever their destination had been before Miss Mamie copied them as crude little dolls and Korban hijacked their midnight flight to eternity.

Korban Manor was nothing but ash and charcoal and a sprinkle of embers. And Korban was nothing, just a burned memory, a flash in the cosmic pan. A dream that was already half forgotten, one that faded by the minute, and Anna was sure his magnificent marble grave marker was only a handful of dust, those words TOO SOON SUMMONED crumbled like the lie they were.

Just before sunrise, she'd hiked to Beechy Gap and visited the site of the cabin where she'd seen the strange little carved figures. The cabin was gone, a small pile of ash marking its passage. The figures must have exited, too, wended toward the heavens in smoke and fire. Free at last.

Anna sorted through the fallen barn timbers for a saddle and bridle. She lifted a shattered board and saw Ransom's blank face, a trickle of crusted blood at one corner of his mouth. The scrap of cloth from his charm was clenched in one rigid hand. She covered him before Mason noticed.

The dead deserved her respect. Death wasn't romantic or glamorous. She was through worrying about their motives, their hopes, their endless dreams. Her fascination had faded. She had no desire to ever see another ghost, especially her own.

Even Rachel's, though the two of them had shared an intimate bond that ran far deeper than mere mother and child.

Maybe this was how Anna was destined to belong. Those were her people, her connection, kindred spirits, however briefly. In an odd way, maybe they lingered inside her, invisible, in her blood, in the tainted, cancerous cells that corrupted her organs and pushed her inevitably toward the final darkness. She was as much a ghost as she was a mortal. A stranger in two strange lands.

But they all were. Every organic thing that had ever caught the spark of life. The dying begins with the birth.

So what?

Did she really expect that, by becoming a ghost, she would understand what being a ghost meant? She'd been alive for twenty-six years and had come no closer to the meaning of life in all that time. Why should death be any less of a mystery to those experiencing it?

As for today, the air was fresh and the pain inside was somewhere down around six, an arc and trick, or maybe a five, a broken wing. A hell of a long way from zero. She could live for those who had gone before, and those yet to come. Weeks or months, it was all a precious and fleeting gift.

Anna saw a flash of dull silver in the broken lumber, moved some timbers, and found a bridle, then a saddle and blanket. She pulled them from the rubble. Mason watched with interest as she harnessed one of the Morgans.

Some of the smoke that had collected in her lungs had started to rise. She cleared her throat and spat loudly. "Is that how they do it in Sawyer Creek?"

Mason smiled at her. It wasn't such a bad smile, though it was surrounded by a face gray from smoke, ash, and weariness. She carried the blanket to him and covered him up.

"Better keep you warm, just in case," she said.

"Go out frost?"

"That's not funny."

"I know."

Spence grabbed at a piece of black ash as it wafted to the ground.

No. It wasn't the Word.

He grabbed another, then another.

The Word would endure. Mere fire couldn't destroy it. He coughed. The ashes had stuck to his tears, making his cheeks feel thick and clotted. He coughed again, his stomach quivering.

"Why don't you come away from there? That smoke's no good for you."

He turned. The Muse?

No. Bridget, Ms. Georgia Peach, the latest corruption.

"You stupid blowhard," Bridget said. "Be glad that stuff got burned. Maybe someday you can write a real story, something that's not possum vomit."

Real? How dare she criticize—

"And you can leave me out of it." She walked away, then turned and stood with her hands on her hips. "I don't know what I ever saw in you. But I can sure see you now."

"Don't leave."

"I believe you said this was always your favorite part. 'The End.' Well, it sounds good to me, too."

Spence watched her go. She didn't matter. She was just another prop, another character sketch. One of the little people. He stood under the snowfall of gray and black, waiting for the Word to come from on high.

Maybe if he could remember the story, bring it back to life, it would lead him again to the Word.

Something about the night? He touched the crumpled page he'd tucked inside his jacket. Maybe later, after years had passed, he would be able to read it. And maybe it would contain some hint of the night's long spell.

But the night was leaving, retreating over the far steel-blue hills, going on to other writers, other vessels. It would spread its loving cloak on another part of the world, shower its gifts elsewhere, whisper its secret sentences. And Spence was again alone, with nothing but himself and words.

The ashes rained on.

Mason tried to curl the fingers of his scorched right hand. A strip of electric pain jolted up his arm, pausing only briefly at the cut in his shoulder to gather momentum before reaching his brain. He bit his tongue to keep from crying out.

Maybe this was what suffering was all about. The art of sacrifice. It wasn't about enduring starvation, struggling for recognition, fighting the fear of failure. Maybe it was about finishing, letting go. And realizing that the dreams you bring to life sometimes have no place in the world, and are best left as dreams.

The toughest critics weren't in New York or Paris. They weren't in the art schools. They didn't wear berets and sport tiny mustaches and drink espresso. Sometimes they lived in your mirror.

"How are you holding up?" Anna asked, tightening the cinch around the horse's girth. She had strong hands.

"Well, I don't think I'll be doing much sculpting for a while." Mason thought of his tools, buried somewhere under the heap of ashes and bones in the basement. He had no desire to see them again.

Anna nodded at him and adjusted the saddle, then stroked the horse's ears. The Morgan snorted with pleasure.

He had to ask. "What was it like . . . you know?"

"To be dead?" Anna's cyan eyes fixed on a faraway point somewhere beyond the range of sight.

"Uh-huh."

"Somebody who loves me said it's the same as being alive, only worse."

Mason looked up at the thin pillar of smoke. The wind was carrying it away, and he caught the odor of apples. Now that the sun was out, the sky was a shade of winter-born blue.

December would come with its soft snows, then the nights would get shorter and spring would arrive. Grass would grow over the ruins, locust and blackberry vines would spring up from the burned-out spot. The granite would sleep under its skin of dirt. The sun would rise and fall, the seasons would turn, the clock's restless hands would spin in only one direction.

Forward.

"What are you going to do later?" Mason asked.

"I don't know. I think I'm cured of metaphysics, though. Let the dead rest. They've earned it." She put a foot in the stirrup and swung astride the horse. It was a natural fit. "What about you?"

"Depends. As soon as I get to back to Sawyer Creek, I'm going to tell Mama that dreams aren't the only thing we got in this world."

"Really. What else have we got?"

"Pain."

"Dreams and pain. Well, that's a lovely mix. Maybe you can add 'faith' to that list."

The kind of mix that maybe love was made of. Mason wondered if one day he might find out. He looked down at the ground and saw a bit of color amid a pile of loose hay. He kicked at the hay, and then saw the flowers. A bouquet of bluets, flame azalea, daisies, baby's breath, painted trillium. Spring mountain flowers, fresh-cut and sweet, the stems wrapped in clean lace. He carried them to Anna. "Somebody must have left these for you."

She took the bouquet and held it to her nose, eyes moist. "Dead stay dead," she whispered. "And rest in peace."

Anna tucked the bouquet into the bridle, eased back on the reins, and the Morgan raised its head.

"See you soon, Mason. Take care of yourself."

She twitched the reins and the horse started down the dirt road.

"Hey, Anna," he yelled after her. "Did you mean what you said up on the widow's walk?"

She didn't stop, but turned in the saddle and looked back. She shouted over the steady clop of the horse's hooves, "About trusting you? Maybe."

Anna gave him a half smile, then left him to wonder which half of it she meant.